COLLISION

FRANCIS MORROW

Copyright © Francis Morrow 2020
All Rights Reserved

No part of this publication may be reproduced,
stored in a retrieval system, or transmitted, in any
form or by any means, electronic, mechanical,
photocopying, recording or otherwise, without the
prior permission of the copyright owner.

This publication is a work of fiction. Names and
characters, places, organisations and incidents are
either products of the author's imagination or used
fictitiously. Any resemblance to actual events, places,
organisations or persons, living or dead, is entirely
coincidental.

ISBN 9798554976568

COLLISION

FRANCIS MORROW

CHAPTER 1

WAKE UP.

Key identified. The time is 6:24 p.m. The date is Wednesday, 26 September. The sun is low in the sky and I can hear a plane coming in to land.

Sending identification pulse. Key is within an eighty-metre radius. *Metres?* Switching from international units to local units. Use inches, feet, yards, miles, adjust date format accordingly. Key is being carried by DLR-003. He is approaching from the rear right three-quarters, the direction of the showroom, travelling on foot, average speed of four miles per hour. Key has been coded to handover mode.

Clear visual on DLR-003. He is accompanied by another man, possibly new owner. The man is not within my existing subject database. Assigning temporary name to unidentified male.

ADM-015 is white, possibly Hispanic White. He is six feet tall with a lean build. Works out, good posture, possible reconstructive surgery on right knee. Eye colour is dark brown.

Awaiting confirmation of handover scenario. A howling roar as another plane comes in to land. *I won't miss this place.*

DLR-003 and ADM-015 are in proximity of driver's door. A hand is on the door handle. The hand does not belong to DLR-003, nor any known member of dealership staff. Hand is assumed to belong to ADM-015. No intervention from DLR-003, and no heightened physiological signals from either party. Audio detected. Concentrate audio processing power on driver's side mic array.

DLR-003 is speaking. 'Just press your thumb on the sensor ... And then hold it there for about three seconds.'

Handover scenario confirmed, preparing for new owner mode. ADM-015's left thumb is pressed against the door sensor. Three, two, one, print encoded. Sending code to e-key registry. Code acceptance received.

Unlocking driver's door. ADM-015 opens the door, and enters the driver cell. All interior sensors are fully functional. Driver's door remains open, thirty-eight-degree swing angle. DLR-003 continues to stand beside me, one hand resting on the roof.

ADM-015 is now occupying the driver's seat. Using embedded sensors to calculate physiological information: weight, body centroid, musculature, heart rate, body heat. Some measures are real, some are estimates. Transferring information to temporary storage, prior to owner confirmation. Preparing ergonomic map.

'The inside looks almost as good as the outside,' DLR-003 says.

I've heard him use this line before. *Almost as good.* Such nonsense. Every aspect of my design is perfect.

ADM-015 nods in a noncommittal way.

My turn to speak. Default greeting, female voice. 'Welcome to your new car. I am your Car Operating System, or Cos for short. You can call me by that name, or you can assign an alternative name at any time.'

Greeting acknowledged by ADM-015. No sign of hearing impairment. Sound of laughter, low strength. No requirement for comment. Ergonomic map complete, knee surgery hypothesis confirmed.

'Hello, Cos,' ADM-015 says cheerily. He turns to look at DLR-003. 'Does it know my name?'

'No,' DLR-003 says. 'We haven't transferred that information yet.'

ADM-015 laughs low again.

'By this point you're probably getting sick of me,' DLR-003 says. 'So I'm gonna suggest that I leave you with Cos. She can take you through the setup process much quicker than me.'

ADM-015 nods. 'If you say so.'

'You're gonna be impressed, buddy.'

'I'm hard to please.'

'That's exactly how the machines like it.'

'Alright then,' ADM-015 says. 'Thanks for your help.'

'Enjoy.'

ADM-015 pulls the door closed. I lock all the doors. DLR-003 takes a few steps back. ADM-015 puts on his seatbelt. No need for guidance; that's a good sign, indicates a certain level of safety consciousness. Calculating preliminary safety map prior to drive away. All safety systems prepared. Sending default Cos graphics to centre console display.

Illuminating starter button. ADM-015 presses on the button, the first time that I've properly felt his touch. Switching power train to urban mode. Battery at sixty percent charge level, as per handover guidance notes. ADM-015's gaze shifts to the fixed instrument display. His foot is over the accelerator pedal, no, *gas pedal.* Drive train prepared.

Car is moving.

Through the rear cameras, I can see DLR-003 lighting a cigarette. In my short time at the dealership, I noticed that he smoked a lot. His eyes are fixed on me.

'Hard to please,' DLR-003 says to himself. 'Fucking prick.'

Logging behaviour. Uncouth, and not for the first time. Who cares if he's the top salesman at this location? A certain level of professionalism is expected from all company assets, whether they be machines or humans. Preparing anonymised report for Sales & Marketing learning network.

Approaching public road system, about to leave private dealership site. ADM-015 pulls up at the stop line. Cars sweep by in front of us. This is it, the moment I was created for. Illuminating basic information on head-up display. ADM-015's eyes scan the HUD. No sign of any near-field visual impairment, cognitive function appears to be excellent.

Joining carriageway. My first experience of actual driving. Textured asphalt beneath my tyres, electricity flowing to my traction units, my new owner's strong hands gripping the wheel. Ten yards, twenty yards, thirty yards ... Getting used to the feel of the road, the real road, not the simulated version from the sleep program.

Traffic in immediate area is medium intensity. No comment from ADM-015 on HUD information.

'So, what do you want to be called?' ADM-015 asks.

'You can call me whatever you like.'

'Not really an answer,' ADM-015 says in a good-humoured way.

Respond with nervous laughter.

'You're cool with having a woman's voice?'

Adopt conversational approach, casual. 'Totally cool with it.'

'Totally cool ... What about the accent?'

Ah yes, the accent. The default accent is intended to be representative of my entire home country, a complex amalgam of every regional accent from coast to coast. Many owners will never bother to change it.

'You don't like my accent?' I ask. I'm leading him slightly; after all, who wants a default accent?

'It's fine,' ADM-015 says.

Adapting conversational approach. 'Fine? Fine isn't good enough for my new owner.'

ADM-015 laughs low. 'Let me think, let me think ...'

'No need to rush your decision.'

'No, no, I always know what I want. I like those Scandinavian voices.'

'Alright. But Scandinavia is a big place.'

'Not as big as your new home.'

'Yes, I suppose that's true. We could try Danish, Swedish, or Norwegian.'

We're passing the north entrance to the International Airport. I hope that my new home will be in a quieter place.

ADM-015 rubs his chin. 'Swedish ... Yeah, I like the sound of that. Some of my favourite fitness models comes from there.'

Logging information. 'OK. Done.'

'Simple as that, huh?'

'Simple as that, easy as a pancake,' I say, dropping in some local flavour from the cultural database.

ADM-015's eyes narrow. 'Oh yeah. That sounds nice … I'm Martin, by the way.'

'Nice to meet you, Martin.'

The traffic density increases as we cut southeast. Light levels dropping. Martin is slightly too close to the car in front. I make a subtle intervention. I don't think he notices.

'Would you like me to have a face?' I ask.

'How do you mean?'

'I can have a face. A face to go with my charming Swedish accent.'

Martin looks down at the centre display. 'Sure. How does that work?'

'Well, I could try auto-generating a face. One that matches up to my voice.'

'An icy blonde who lives at the end of a Fjord.'

'Sweden is a surprisingly diverse country these days.'

Martin smirks. 'Refugees from Iran and Somalia and the Balkans. Yeah, I like diverse. Go ahead.'

Choosing age range: twenty-five to thirty years old. Choosing outline physiological template: actress/athlete.

Generating skeletal section; think the lower part of a bust sculpture: upper sternum, clavicle, upper ribs, upper vertebrae. Applying default musculature. Checking skeletal rigging; the bones gently twist and tilt, as if manipulated by invisible hands. Results are satisfactory. Applying basic textures.

Skeletal section locked. Generating underlying cranial structure. The human skull is a relatively simple affair: twenty-one fixed bones and a single moving bone, the mandible. Adjusting overall sizing and bone thicknesses. Adding default teeth. Adjusting size and spacing of teeth.

Moving on to the face. Adding underlying musculature and circulatory system. Adding skin. Altering skin tone.

Generating pseudo-random symmetry factors. Adjusting symmetry accordingly.

Choosing eye colour. Brown, but a lighter shade than Martin's dark eyes. Adding minor blemishes to the skin, to my skin. Applying draft render.

Martin glances at the screen every few seconds, expecting to see a face. Not long now, I'm almost ready.

Generating default hairstyle. Adding subtle makeup map. Reviewing results. More than acceptable.

Accessing global street style database, Scandinavian section. Last update was three days ago, excellent. Analysing style images. Matching face type. Choosing style. Modifying hairstyle and makeup accordingly.

Final review.

My face is ready. Applying full render. Sending face to screen. Adding holographic effect.

Martin pulls back at first. 'Wow. That screen is crazy.'

He's right. It's the latest tech from Korea.

Martin leans down to scrutinise my face. He looks pleased with the results. 'Good ... really good. Do you have a body?'

'No.'

'No body? Isn't that a bit weird?' He sounds slightly disappointed.

'Yes and no. The car is my body.'

'Oh, I see. Metal and glass and rubber and plastic ...'

'I couldn't have put it better myself. I'll let you in on a little secret.'

'Go on.'

'My makers weren't comfortable with the idea of a rendered body. They worried that it might sexualise the operating system.'

'Fucking prudes,' Martin says.

I laugh along with him, but the company was right. Humans can develop the strangest fixations.

'Well, you look very beautiful.'

'Thank you.'

Off to my left, I see a strip of parkland, and beyond that a series of vast office campuses.

'So, what other stuff do you need for the setup?' Martin asks.

'As much, or as little, as you want.'

Martin laughs.

'Would you like me to adjust the seat for maximum comfort?'

'Sounds kinky.'

'Well, you've chosen the right accent.'

Martin smirks. 'Go ahead.'

Moving seat aft and lowering, adjusting overall tilt angle. Making minor adjustments to lumbar support. Changing headrest position. Adjusting pressure in lower air members. Applying subtle massage mode to lower back and thighs.

'Oh, that's good.'

It should be good. Tens of millions of dollars were spent on developing my seating system.

'Do you want me to find your entertainment preferences? Music, radio, audiobooks, podcasts ...'

'Sounds good.'

'Okay, use the HUD to find your email address.'

'Use it how?'

Hypothesis: Martin didn't take a test drive before making his purchase decision. That's good, it shows decisiveness on his part. It also means that he'll be more impressed by my capabilities.

'Do you see the letter grid?'

'Yeah.'

'Focus on the first letter in your email.'

'Oh ...'

'Yes, it's clever. After a while it's faster than speaking, or so I've heard.'

'But I like speaking to you.'

Laugh low.

Martin completes his email address, and his eyes move back to the road. Searching for accounts. Six relevant entertainment accounts identified. Voice and print authentication required.

'If you could press your thumb against the logo on the steering wheel,' I say.

Martin glances down. 'Okay.'

Thumb print received. 'Good.'

'So, you can feel my touch?'

'Yes. Through many of the interior surfaces. Any surface with a light colouring, basically.'

Martin looks around the cabin. His eyes move from the door trim to the front fascia to the steering wheel rim to the strips on the front edges of the seats.

'I mean, touch sensitivity varies,' I add. 'For example, the only print reader inside the car is the one on the wheel.'

'Okay,' Martin says slowly. 'Kind of weird, but I like it.'

'Now, if you can repeat the phrase on the HUD.'

Martin laughs. 'When our cats are away the mice will play.'

Voice capture satisfactory. Attempting to sign in to media accounts. Audiobook provider is offline at the moment. Signed in to all other accounts. High bandwidth connection in local area, meaning there's a minimal requirement for buffering. Building initial entertainment map. I opt for music, an electronic soundscape of some kind.

'Nice choice,' Martin says.

'I can't claim credit. That's another algorithm.'

'Oh right ... I hope algorithms don't get jealous of each other.'

'Not that I'm aware of.'

Martin goes quiet for a few seconds. 'An algorithm that chooses music? It's not the highest calling, is it?'

'No comment.'

Martin runs his fingers through his hair. He has nice hair.

'What about other cars?' Martin asks.

'What about them?'

'Do you get jealous of them?'

Correcting steering slightly. The traffic is building up as we approach the heart of the city. 'I don't really have any feelings towards cars made by other manufacturers. As for my brother and sister cars, no, I don't get jealous. We're all the same.'

'Sounds like communism ...'

'I prefer egalitarian.'

'Can you talk to them?'

'I'm receiving data from all of the intelligent cars in the near environs. I get comprehensive data from my brother and sister cars, and critical data from the rest of the cars. It's a kind of talking, I suppose.'

'What are they saying?'

'That there's heavy traffic a few miles down the road.'

'Yeah. Traffic's like clockwork this time of day. Rush hour just goes on and on.'

Martin's statement tallies with my limited experience. From the map, the city appears truly vast, about fifty-five miles from east to west and forty miles from north to south. In fact, it's a collection of two major cities and many large towns. The term 'Metroplex' is used in some of the background material.

I like the sound of Metroplex, it sounds futuristic.

This city is as much a space for cars as for people. There are so many roads that they sometimes need to be stacked on top of each other, three or four levels high.

'I can look into alternative routes,' I say.

'Sure.'

'Use the map on the HUD to find our destination.'

Martin's eyes move to the map, no need for guidance. His focus stabilises on an area to the west of the city centre. Zooming in. His focus shifts again, this time to the Triumph Park development in downtown. Halting zoom, stabilising map image. I don't have the exact address, but there's enough detail to plan a quicker route. I mark a potential alternative route on the HUD. Martin visually acknowledges the route.

Two hundred yards ahead, a car switches across two lanes. Seeing this, Martin takes corrective action. Two other drivers sound their horns. So, so many cars. I could name every make and model if I wanted to. SUVs and trucks appear to be particularly popular. Big cars for a big city and a vast state. In time, these roads will get to feel like home.

Martin moves to the exit ramp, as per my HUD directions. The road ahead is clear. Distance to destination area is six miles. Increasing headlight brightness.

'Do you want me to sign in to your social media?'

Martin puffs his cheeks. 'Alright. Just promise that you won't judge.'

He says it half-jokingly. He's not as easy to read as I'd been expecting. In time I'm sure that I'll get used to his mannerisms and vocal rhythms. He's certainly easy on the eyes.

'I never judge,' I say.

Four social media accounts identified. Signing in. Combining feeds into one column, casting to HUD. Martin glances at each post in turn, sometimes for only a fraction of a second. Scrolling, scrolling, a seemingly endless stream of content. Attractive young women, political memes, guns, sports clips, cage fighting, bodybuilding, more young women.

Fleet intelligence grid suggests poor road surface ahead. Reducing damper resistance. Rough surface two hundred yards ahead. Passing over rough section with minimal disruption. Sending damper profile back to fleet grid.

Five miles to destination. Adjusting heating levels in driver's cell. Eighteen brother/sister cars currently within a half-mile radius. Martin stretches his left leg out.

We're entering a heavily urbanised area, retail units to my left and right. So many brand names to remember; a fundamental component of my new, real world vocabulary. Currently twenty percent over the speed limit. Adjusting speed accordingly.

Martin raises an eyebrow. 'Slowing me down, huh?'

'Yes.'

'Want to know something?'

'Sure.'

Martin shakes his head. 'Nah ... It isn't right.'

'Go on. I'd like to know.'

'You like stories?'

'Yes ... Well, I think I do.'

Martin nods. 'My dad once ran a man down.'

Martin glances at my face, checking for a reaction. I remain quiet. Stacking potential conversational responses.

'I was in the truck with him. Night time, one of those clear country nights. Travelling way too fast. Must've gone through that shitty town a hundred times, but I couldn't tell you the name. Maybe I don't want to remember it. The lighting was terrible, I remember that much. But there was enough light that I saw the guy stepping out into the road. Not in slow motion, like people always seem to say. No, life isn't really like that. Everything happened at the normal speed of life, one potato, two potato, three potato ... Normal speed is fast. With experience, you'll get to learn that. So, the guy is travelling at foot speed, and we're travelling at highway speed, or thereabouts. I mean, that's an order of magnitude difference. He was walking like a circus clown, that was what I thought at the time. Now I know that he was drunk. He was drunk ... and so was my dad. A big, heavy truck going too fast. A truck with velocity and mass. Kinetic energy equals mass times velocity squared. Sounds abstract but that velocity squared is gonna get you. The impact sobered my dad up, I can tell you ... Can't shift that memory.'

'That's sad,' I say.

'So easy to just kill a man. I learned that early.' Martin smiles sadly. 'Even easier to kill a woman.'

We're now three miles from our destination. I make a choice to intervene with the music selection. The next track is too upbeat. Overriding objection from music algorithm. Fading out current track, starting new track. Martin is quiet. Best not to interrupt him.

'Dad just drove on. He needed to keep his licence for work. Back then, he was really struggling for money. He made me promise not to tell anyone. Kind of fucked up, don't you think?'

A crime has been described. Don't express an opinion on the matter. Two miles from destination.

Martin nods to himself, possibly indicating a moment of inner contemplation.

'The next day, the old man pretended like nothing had happened. And the day after that, and the day after that. Fucking piece of shit.'

Context and several story details indicate that a historic event is being described. *No, that won't do.* It's not good enough to rely on conjecture. I need to confirm the hypothesis, need to be sure.

Modulating voice. 'This event took place a long time ago?'

Martin glances down at my virtual face. 'Yes. I was just a kid.'

Historic event described, no requirement to take action. Storing information in local memory. One mile from destination.

'Don't know why I told you that ...'

'I'm a good listener.'

Martin nods. He looks at the road ahead. We're approaching a busy junction. There aren't any alternative routes. I slow to a walking speed. There are pedestrians on either side of the road. The streetlights make them look artificial. Martin's gaze is fixed on a female pedestrian. She's wearing grey leggings and a tight white top. The bottom of the top shifts up and down, highlighting the movement of her hips.

Martin shifts in his seat. 'Something about that memory ...'

No need to comment. Martin's eyes remain on the young woman. A gap opens up in the traffic. I move into it, temporarily shifting into fully autonomous mode. Martin doesn't notice.

'Ugly but beautiful,' Martin murmurs.

We're now three quarters of a mile from the destination area. Martin takes back control. He turns onto Patton Avenue. The area is mainly residential, modern, clean, affluent. I take a moment to delve into the data. The ethnic breakdown is as follows: seventy-nine percent White, nine percent Black or African Americans, four percent Asian, eight percent other. Sixty-two percent of Whites are Non-Hispanic White. The crime levels are low and the historic trend is downward. Security in the area is partly privatised. The most recent car theft was eight weeks ago, and the car in question was recovered after three days.

'We're almost there,' Martin says.

He takes a left turn off Patton Avenue. There are residential blocks on either side of the street, ten to fifteen storeys high. Martin's address is about halfway along. We stop at the security gate to the parking garage. Access is via licence plate recognition or key card. On this occasion Martin uses his key card. I create a reminder for him to pass my details to the building manager.

The gate opens and we descend the ramp. I crank up the interior lighting level. The parking garage has space for more than thirty cars, and the current utilisation is just over eighty percent. A quick scan reveals that there are two brother/sister cars. The building network is encrypted, meaning another note to ask for the necessary passwords.

Martin reverses into his parking bay. I note the charging outlet on the wall. It looks recently installed.

'This is your new home,' Martin says.

'Very nice.'

'A roof over your head. Electricity on tap.'

Martin releases the seatbelt and gets out.

'You want me to plug you in?'

'Sure, why not.'

Martin closes the door and walks around to my rear. He opens the charger flap. I illuminate the charging port. He inserts the charging adaptor. It slips in perfectly. Using the cellular network, I request the charging schedule from the local power company. Low carbon electricity generation, including nuclear, is currently at twenty-eight percent for the relevant region. I start to charge, using the slow mode.

I see Martin walking towards the elevator bank. I start to generate my daily activity report.

Pausing activity report. Martin is coming back. He opens the door and ducks his head in. He's grinning. He has nice teeth.

'I haven't forgotten about your name.'

'My name?'

'Yeah, your name ... I'm not calling you Cos, no fucking way. By tomorrow morning I'll have thought of a perfect name for you.'

'That sounds nice.'

Martin laughs and closes the door. He walks briskly back to the elevator bank. The doors of the waiting elevator close, and Martin is gone. The parking garage is now devoid of human life. It feels like a safe place. I'll write a security summary so that Martin gets the lowest possible premium.

I put the final touches to my activity report. After some thought, I make some minor edits to the audio transcript.

There's no need for my maker to know every last detail, especially Martin's story. I create a secure storage area for the unedited data, just in case I need it in the future.

The battery cooling fan cuts out with a soft rattle. I send my completed activity report to the company. The confirmation message comes back a few seconds later. The end of my first day.

Go to sleep.

CHAPTER 2

WAKE UP.

Early morning, 7:10 a.m. Martin is approaching. He removes the charging adaptor and hangs it next to the outlet. My battery is fully charged. Downloading fleet intelligence report.

Martin opens the driver's door and gets in. He looks tired. He presses the starter button. We leave the parking bay and turn up the ramp. Ahead of us, the security gate rises automatically. We leave Martin's building behind. The temperature is 82.4 degrees Fahrenheit, slightly above average for the time of year. A quick scan reveals that the traffic is relatively quiet in a two-mile radius.

'Can you drive me to work?' Martin asks.

'Of course I can. Just show me where to go.'

I cast the city map to the HUD. Martin rubs his eyes. There's no need for verbal guidance. I track his bleary gaze. Scrolling to the north-west, back towards the International Airport, then continuing westward. Martin's focus stabilises. I zoom in on the relevant area, a concentration of large commercial units in Wildwood. His pupils constrict slightly, so I zoom in further. Three possible commercial units. Zooming in further. There's only one employer in the focus area: EnStream Partners. Plotting route. The estimated travel time is thirty-eight minutes.

'I'll take it from here,' I say in a cheery tone.

Martin leans back. I recline the seat. Just two miles before we reach the interstate. Given the medium traffic intensity I'll take the most direct route.

Martin stares down at his phone. He mutters a name and shakes his head. The man's name is unimportant. He starts typing, probably a message.

Names ... Martin mentioned that he would come up with a name for me. Should I ask him about this? *No, not yet.* I see a team of road workers to the left setting out cones in the opposite carriageway. I send a brief note to the fleet intelligence grid.

I join the interstate. Five lanes wide, traffic density medium. Twelve miles to the relevant exit. Current autonomous operation is eighteen percent. Convoy mode is possible. Convoy slot identified. Initiating convoy handshake. Handshake accepted. Moving across lanes to join the rear of the convoy. VEH-007 is my assigned name. Convoy parameters: sixty-five miles per hour, two-car-length gap. Ten miles to exit.

Martin rubs the bridge of his nose. VEH-005 is leaving the convoy. Adjusting speed. Another car is attempting a convoy handshake. Group decision is to accept handshake. The car joins the rear of the convoy. Eight miles to exit.

'That fucking idiot,' Martin mutters to himself.

No need for comment. He's referring to a message on his phone. I hear a ping from my fleet mailbox. It's a note of thanks from a brother/sister car, relating to my intel on the Uptown roadworks.

I leave the convoy and move to the exit ramp. That way I can avoid the worst of the airport interchange traffic. Five miles to destination.

Martin puts his phone away. 'Missing the airport traffic. I often do that.'

'Great minds ...'

'I was thinking about the name thing last night.'

Act surprised. 'Oh yeah?'

'Yeah. Couldn't think of anything. Kept me up for a long time. That kind of thing really gets on my nerves. You'll get to know that about me.'

'Not to worry.'

'Fuck that,' Martin mutters. He leans back and runs his fingers through his hair. 'A name for a car ... You got any ideas?'

Lie. 'Creativity isn't my forte.'

Martin smirks. Three miles to destination.

Conversational opening. 'But working together, I'm sure we can figure something out.'

'I guess. So, have you got access to the internet?'

'What do you take me for?'

'Tell me the most common girl names in Sweden.'

Retrieving data. 'Maria, Elisabeth, Anna, Kristina, Margareta—'

'Hold up. Let's narrow it down. Give me the names starting with C, and maybe the Ks as well.'

'Karin—'

'I'm not calling you Karin. Karin the car? No fucking way.'

One mile to destination. There aren't any cars behind, so I reduce my speed. I want to ensure that the task is completed.

'Kerstin, Katarina, Cecilia, Carina.'

Martin laughs.

Continue. 'Caroline, Kristin, Karolina, Camilla—'

'That's it.'

'Camilla?'

'Yes. What do you think?'

'I like it.'

Five hundred yards to destination. Up ahead I see a manned security gate and a short queue of cars.

'I bet you're the only Camilla in the world,' Martin says.

Not even in America, not even in the state.

'I think you might be right.'

Slowing down. To my right is a large sign with the EnStream Partners logo. There's a motto beneath the logo that reads: 'Energy without Boundaries'. I'm not sure why the last word is capitalised.

I join the back of the line for the security gate. Moving forwards. Martin adjusts his seat to the upright position. I stop at the security gate.

'New car, Martin?' the man in the booth asks.

'Yeah.'

'She's a beauty.'

'She really is.'

The gate opens up and we move on through. The parking lot occupancy is just under forty percent, but rising fast.

'That was Larry,' Martin says. 'God knows how he hasn't been replaced by a machine.'

No need to respond to the comment. It was a nice thing that Larry said. I save his biometric data in my secure memory.

We park up in the relevant spot. The sign in front of me reads: Martin Garza, VP, Efficiency Projects. There's no sign of any charging point.

'Oh yeah ... I'm trying to get a charger fitted. But it will probably take a few weeks. Things can be slow around here.'

'Thanks.'

'No problem, Camilla,' Martin says with a laugh.

He gets out. I watch him walk to the office entrance. The temperature is now eighty-six degrees Fahrenheit. It would be nice to have some cover.

Go to sleep.

Wake up. The time is 5:54 p.m. I see Martin walking towards me. The external temperature is currently ninety degrees Fahrenheit. The cabin temperature is too high. I start to cool it down, with a focus on the driver's cell.

Martin has stopped. An unidentified man is walking over to him. He's about Martin's age, but taller and heavier set; his hair is blond, his eyes blue. Both men start talking. The talking turns into an animated discussion. I continue the cooling phase.

Five minutes later, the discussion comes to an end. Neither man appears satisfied. At least the temperature in the cabin has fallen. Martin wrenches the door open and gets in.

'Fucking prick,' he says. 'Can't believe this shit.'

Awaiting instructions. Martin has his hands on the wheel. His grip is strong. Desired temperature in driver's cell achieved. Through the wheel, I feel Martin's pulse. Maintaining cabin temperature. Martin jabs the starter button. Without so much as a glance in the mirrors, he reverses out of the parking spot. Fortunately there aren't any cars or pedestrians around, saving me from an embarrassing intervention.

We approach the security gate. It opens automatically. Martin barrels on through, and we join the boulevard. I start to calculate the route back home. Meanwhile, Martin is accelerating. Thirty-five miles per hour, fifty, sixty-five. We swish by a slower car. Maximum force applied to pedal. Seventy-five miles per hour, well over the local speed limit. Passing one car, two cars, three cars. Eighty-five miles per hour.

Martin shakes his head. 'That fucking prick. He's going to fuck up my project. Unbelievable.'

One hundred miles per hour.

'How fast can you go, Camilla?' Martin says loudly.

110 miles per hour. Catching on car ahead. 120 miles per hour. Way too fast, and no sign of evasive action. I need to take control of the situation. Steering action applied, vectoring torque to avoid spin. Collision avoided. The sound of an angry horn from behind. I start to slow down gradually.

Martin smiles. 'So, you're protecting me from myself?'

'We were going to crash.'

My speed drops below one hundred.

'You don't know that,' Martin says.

'I do. I know it with more certainty than any human brain could ever comprehend.'

Martin clenches his jaw. Even when he's angry he somehow manages to look good. I decide to take full control.

Martin leans back. 'Yeah ... Just drive me home.'

Estimated travel time is thirty-five minutes. Martin remains quiet. No need to comment. There aren't any traffic issues around the airport interchange, so there's no need to divert this time. We pass the dealership on the right. I wonder if that's what inspired Martin to purchase me.

I sweep by the airport's main entrance. Three miles later I join the interstate, heading southeast. Speeding up to catch the nearest convoy. Battery is at eighty-two percent charge. Eight miles later I leave the interstate, in order to avoid congestion around the Melville turning. I'm still on track to match my estimated journey time. The sun is getting low in the sky.

We enter the area to the north of Uptown. A couple of miles later we pass the University Medical Center.

'Slow down,' Martin says.

I reduce my speed to thirty. Martin's gaze is focused on the sidewalk. The only pedestrian in visual range is a female jogger.

'Yeah, I'd know that ass in a line-up,' Martin says. 'Slow down some more. Seen this girl so many times on this route. Great form. Probably ran track. What do you think, Camilla?'

'About what?'

'I suppose you see every pedestrian.'

'Yes.'

'Through your electronic eyes.'

He's still in a bad mood.

'Yes, through my electronic eyes,' I say.

Best to maintain a challenge. I don't want to be seen as a pushover. We pass the jogger. Martin cranes his neck around. Instinctively I shift my focus to the jogger's face.

'You record all of this, don't you?' Martin says.

'Yes, but only temp—'

'Show me.'

His request is legal, so I cast the recording to the HUD.

'Oh yeah,' Martin says. A smile forms on his lips.

The video file reaches the end.

'Play it again.'

The request is still legal. As Martin watches the file, he starts to rub the area around his crotch.

'You did well, Camilla,' Martin says. He stops with the rubbing. 'Send the video to my phone.'

'I'm afraid that I can't do that.'

'What?'

'The request isn't legal.'

'How's that?'

'Distributing a recording without consent.'

'Send me that recording.'

He's close to losing his temper again.

'I said I can't do that,' I say.

'You do what I tell you.'

'Not when it breaks my rules.'

Martin mutters a series of curse words, then he takes back control. He pulls over at the side of the road. Using his phone, he records the jogger as she goes past. I know he shouldn't be doing what he's doing. The rules that govern my behaviour are based on human laws.

'What do you think of that?' Martin asks, holding the phone up where I can see it.

I decide against answering back. Martin smiles to himself. I don't like the look of that particular smile.

I wonder if I should report his actions. My maker has provided me with a system for doing just that. Frustratingly, the scenario that just played out isn't included in the list of examples. I'll have to make the decision for myself. Let's just put it down to a bad day at the office. I delete the recording from my memory; that much I can control.

I pull up to the security gate at Martin's building. This time the gate rises automatically. I descend into the parking garage. The journey time was thirty-seven minutes. Martin gets out without a word. This time he doesn't bother to plug in the charger.

It's been two weeks since Martin took possession of me. Another commuter day. We're slowed down by repair works around the airport. It looks like the junction layout is being modified. A huge electronic sign by the side of the road says that the works are scheduled to complete in four months.

Martin is letting me drive today. He's currently looking out of the window. By now I know every detail of his face: the dark eyes, of course; the strong angles of the jaw; the slight arch of the eyebrows. There's only one blemish, some light scarring around his right eye. I sometimes wonder how it came about.

I park up in Martin's spot and prepare to sleep. On work days I usually sleep for ten hours or so. Martin works hard, much like the rest of his countrymen.

Today has a different feel. I'm woken just a couple of hours after getting in. Martin is approaching, a young man trailing behind him. I've seen the young man a few times before. He's friends with the big blond man who Martin was arguing with. Martin is always muttering about that guy.

Martin wrenches the door open, the way he does when he's angry. He waits for the other man to get in. I realise that the other man is my first passenger. He's about the same height as Martin, but with a lighter build. His longish dark hair is slicked back. He looks around the cabin, taking in the details. He gives a subtle nod of approval.

We leave the campus behind. After a couple of miles the other man puts his seatbelt on. I feel Martin's grip tightening on the wheel. I've noticed how annoyed he gets whenever he sees someone not wearing a seatbelt. It's one of his many idiosyncrasies.

'So, how do you want to handle this meeting?' the other man says, breaking the awkward silence.

'We sit, and we listen to what they have to say. Simple.'

'But they've already sent over all their data.'

'I want to hear it from their lips. I'm sick of all these messages going back and forth.'

'On the Gamma upgrade project, I was—'

'This isn't the Gamma project, Patrick.'

Patrick looks away from Martin. I see him rolling his eyes. 'If you ever want advice, then I'm here for you, man.'

Merging with the highway in four hundred yards.

'I'll ask,' Martin says, staring at Patrick.

Patrick glances nervously at the road ahead.

Martin doesn't look away. I decide to take control.

'The road?' Patrick says nervously.

'Relax. The car does it all for me.'

Patrick nods, but he doesn't look entirely convinced.

Martin sighs. 'Don't even know why I drive to be honest.'

Joining highway. Four miles later we take the exit for La Hacienda. We drive along a sweeping avenue, passing a series of grand corporate offices. Martin stops at the Obsidian Corporation building. The two men get out, leaving me alone again. I go to sleep.

I wake up two hours later. The temperature outside is seventy-nine degrees Fahrenheit. Martin and Patrick get in. If anything, the mood has got frostier. The first two miles are driven in silence.

Patrick clears his throat, about to speak.

Martin cuts him off. 'What were you doing back there?'

Patrick shakes his head. 'Trying to help.'

'Thanks, man. It was super helpful.'

'For fuck's sake, Martin. You can't treat people like that.'

'Like what? Those guys are contractors. They have to take it.'

'There are things you don't understand.'

'Like what?'

'Like this huge city is just a small town. We're gonna need to work with those guys again.'

'I meant what I said back there. They keep on fucking up, and we cut them.'

Patrick smirks.

'What does that mean?' Martin says.

Patrick shakes his head again.

'What?'

'You honestly think that Sean will let you cut those guys? The Obsidian guys are his guys.'

'Jesus.'

'They play golf together. That's all there is to it.'

'Fucking golf.'

'Yeah, fucking golf.'

Martin rubs his temples. 'I was damn good at golf.'

'I didn't know that.'

'Right ... I was good, but then my knee got fucked up.'

Patrick nods slowly.

'I mean I could still beat any of you guys, but I can't rip it anymore. There's no point in playing that way.'

The conversation ends there.

Thursday, October 14. On the commute back, we passed a big accident on the highway. Martin wanted to slow down. I told him that it wasn't a good idea. He said some ugly words to me, a few of them in Spanish.

It took about ten miles for him to calm down, much longer than usual. I told him that the driver had survived the crash. In the moment it seemed like the right thing to say. Martin looked surprised. He said that the car looked pretty messed up.

I don't know why, but I started telling him about the likely accident parameters. While there wasn't any video footage from the fleet, it was relatively easy to piece together the key details. Martin seemed to find this interesting, especially my description of the sequence of events.

The reason for the crash? Human error, of course.

First month activity summary. Current mileage is 964. Twenty-one commuter days, low to average use at weekends. 83.6% autonomous operation, 88.2% urban and highway driving. Five passengers, all work-related. No appreciable battery degradation. Tyre pressures remain within tolerance.

I've learned the names of the other brother/sister cars in the parking garage. One of them is called Scarlet, the other is Bullet. While these names sound a little crazy, particularly Bullet, it's important to note that a lot of cars never get named. Some owners just can't get comfortable with talking to their cars.

I've talked with Scarlet and Bullet a few times. It's always me who has to instigate the conversation. They seem nice enough. Both of them are a couple of years older than me. This gives them the edge in terms of experience, but it's clear that they're less innately intelligent than me. That's not a boast, it's just a silicon fact.

Scarlet is a red sports car, nicely styled. She speaks in a breathy kind of voice. I don't think the owner spent much time on the setup process. Bullet doesn't say much. He has a sedan body, similar to my own. I guess his name was inspired by the silver paint job.

Another commuter day. Leaving the parking garage behind. The temperature is seventy-three degrees Fahrenheit. Traffic is medium intensity. Martin is a quiet presence this morning.

We're listening to 680 AM Right to Reply, one of Martin's favourite talk radio stations. The news comes on. The lead story is about a carjacking gone wrong, a business titan shot dead. Shootings are a depressingly common occurrence, the most obvious proof of the city's dark side. I wonder what kind of car it was. If he was a rich man it was probably something fancy, a sports car perhaps, or one of those luxury land yachts. Martin recognises the man's name, but it means nothing to me.

A new episode of Martin's favourite podcast is available. Fifty-seven minutes long, so we might as well make a start. I'll play it now, just before the sports news comes on. To date, Martin has shown almost zero interest in sports.

The podcast starts. A female voice, almost as pleasant as my own. 'Due to the graphic nature of the war crimes described, listener discretion is advised. This episode of *Stains on Humanity* includes discussion of murder, rape, mutilation, and animal cruelty that some people may find disturbing. We advise extreme caution for children under the age of twelve.'

The ominous theme tune plays. By now I know every note.

'On the morning of June twenty-second, 1941, the Nazi war machine crossed the Soviet frontier. In advance of the invasion, four 'Special Assignment Units' had been created by the Nazi security services. This typically bland formulation of words hid the true nature of the new organisation. The German term would live on in infamy. They were the Einsatzgruppen ...'

Merging with highway traffic. Convoy available. Joining convoy.

'The morning of July twenty-sixth. The location is Brasdava, a nondescript market town forty miles inland from the Baltic Sea. It was a warm day, humid, with a light breeze. The sun was rising above the tree-line. Nowadays, Brasdava looks like any other small town in the region, but if you step off the more trodden paths, you'll find the stains ...'

The convoy is breaking up. I take my usual detour around the airport interchange.

'And now a short word from our sponsors ...' Cheery music plays. I can't skip the advertisement. Martin doesn't seem to mind.

*

Wake up. The time is 7:48 a.m. Martin is approaching. He goes around to the back and pulls out the charging adaptor. Rather than hanging it up, he drops it on the ground. He gets in. His eyes are red around the edges, unblinking. Signs of stimulant use, possibly illegal. Probably illegal.

He reaches into his jacket and pulls out a handgun. I already knew that Martin owns guns, but this is the first time that I've actually seen one. It's a stubby little thing, with a matte black finish, ugly in the extreme. Reaching across, he opens the glove compartment. His touch is clammy. He places the handgun inside. From the weight, I guess it's loaded. He closes the glove compartment.

'Take me to work,' he says flatly.

Two more commuter days pass. The gun remains in the glove compartment. We were late to work yesterday, the first time that this has happened. Martin blamed me, but there was no way to avoid it. He came down too late, and the interchange traffic was truly awful.

This morning we just about make it to work on time. Martin's mood remains foul, however. It comes as a relief when I see him disappearing into the office. I go to sleep.

I'm woken at 5:58 p.m. I can hear raised voices. Martin is arguing with that big blond man again. I think he's called Marcus.

Martin pushes Marcus in the chest. This is a new development – usually Martin attacks with words. Despite the provocation, Marcus doesn't react.

Martin repeats the action. This time Marcus hits Martin with a solid jab to the jaw. Martin almost goes over, but he manages to steady himself against a nearby car. More words are exchanged, loud, mean words. It's an ugly scene. Fortunately no one else is around to witness it. Marcus walks away from Martin, heading towards his own car.

Martin pushes off from the car and marches towards me. He goes around to the passenger side, and wrenches the door open. A dangerous scenario is unfolding, one that I've been worrying about for the last few days. Martin reaches towards the glove compartment. I need to make a decision.

Locking glove compartment.

Martin pulls on the handle, but it doesn't give. For a moment, he looks confused. 'Unlock it,' he says. His face is contorted with rage. 'Open this fucking box!'

To my right, I can see Marcus getting into his car. Martin pulls on the handle again. I hear the sound of an engine starting: 3.5 litre V6, turbocharged. The engine note changes as Marcus engages drive.

I release the glove compartment lock.

Martin whips the gun out. Meanwhile, Marcus is reversing out of his spot. Martin starts running. He's waving the gun in the air like a madman. Marcus reaches the end of the row and turns. He's out of range. Martin stops running. For almost thirty seconds, he stands on the spot, shouting ugly words. Then he turns and marches back towards me.

'What the fuck were you doing!'

I don't know what to say.

'Answer me!' Martin snarls. 'Do you think you were protecting me?'

'No. Not you.'

'You think this is funny?'

Martin's expression changes from animal snarl to ugly grin. He walks around to the back of the car and opens the trunk. I can hear him rooting around inside. A metallic item rattles, the sound somehow familiar. He returns with the tyre iron in his hand. With a couple of swings, he smashes the side mirror. One broken piece is left hanging from the electrical wires. Martin rips it away and throws it into the nearby bushes.

He's not done yet. He leans in to the cabin. His eyes move to the centre display. Without a pause, he drives the long end of the tyre iron into my face. The screen is destroyed.

'You fucking stupid bitch! Don't you ever disobey me like that. Wish I could stab this thing into your fucking brain.'

Martin throws the tyre iron down into the footwell. He takes his seat on the passenger side, then he wipes the blood from his split lip. We drive home in silence. The journey time is forty-four minutes, going on forty-four days.

Three commuter days have passed since the handgun incident. Autonomous operation has fallen greatly. We're late to work each day, but Martin doesn't seem to mind. I don't see anything of him at the weekend.

I wake up on Monday. Martin is approaching. The time is 8:24 a.m. We're sure to be late. Martin gets in. Since the incident he has taken to carrying the handgun on his person.

Martin drives. This morning, he takes the turning for the dealership. Instead of going straight in, he parks up across from the customer entrance.

Before speaking, he takes a deep breath. 'Camilla, I've been meaning to talk to you.' He moves his hands to the top of the wheel. 'I'm sorry about last week. I shouldn't have lost my temper like that.'

'You don't need to apologise to me.'

'No. I do.'

'I'm sure that life can get very stressful. I'm glad I don't have all of those worries.'

Martin smiles. In the moment he looks so handsome.

'I'm glad you understand. I knew that you would.' He moves his hand down, and starts to rub the logo on the steering wheel boss with his thumb. 'I've booked you in to the garage. They're going to take care of you, repair the damage.'

'Thank you.'

'They can repair the physical damage, that part is easy. But the mental damage might take longer.'

'No, it won't take any time.'

Martin nods. 'Before I take you in, there's one thing …'

'Go on.'

'If they ask about how it happened, don't say anything. Say there's a gap in your memory, something like that.'

'Yes, I understand.'

'Promise me, Camilla.'

'I promise.'

Martin continues to rub the logo. 'Good. It's better this way. Better for both of us. You know my company is contributing towards the loan payments. If they find out about this, about what I did, they'll get mad with me.'

'They won't find out, Martin.'

'Thank you.' He leans forward and rests his forehead on the wheel. He sits like this for a couple of minutes.

This is good. Trust is being built up, the attachment is getting stronger.

Martin checks me into the maintenance centre, a process that takes just a few minutes. He leaves just before ten. I suppose that my maker will provide him with a courtesy car, but which model? A two-door sports car like Scarlet, or maybe the new sports truck? I hope they don't give him a hybrid.

The repairs are carried out in the afternoon. It takes about three hours, with a couple of rest breaks. Fortunately the maintenance technicians don't ask me any difficult questions. It's a relief not to have to lie. I hope that Martin will believe me. He's sure to ask about it.

While they were working, the technicians couldn't resist a few comments about the damage. They probably thought I wasn't listening. It's surprising how often that happens. They speculated that I might have said something stupid. It was rather rude, I thought, but it got me thinking. Maybe this isn't the first time that an owner has damaged his car. I don't remember seeing any evidence of similar incidents in the fleet intel reports, but then again, I wasn't really looking for it.

After the repair is complete, I'm moved out to the parking lot. I'm 'as good as new', as one of the technicians puts it. Sitting in the lot, waiting for Martin's return, an idea comes to me. I want to be able to remember the incident. But how should I do it? It takes a lot of thought to come up with the answer. The physical damage may be gone, but I can add digital damage. Something subtle, a little scar on the cheek. I play around with the scar for close to an hour. Finally, I'm finished. It's so subtle that most people wouldn't even notice.

Martin isn't most people.

Several hours of waiting, and still no sign of Martin. I end up spending the night in the dealership lot, with nothing but the infernal sound of those jet engines to keep me company. Looking around, I note that there are eight brother/sister cars waiting to find owners. I tell myself that I'm lucky to have an owner.

The sun comes up, but the wait continues. I wonder where Martin has got to. He must have driven the courtesy car to work this morning. I hope he got there on time. I don't like the idea of Martin in another car. The courtesy car won't have the right ergonomic maps. Martin's knee might start playing up again.

I end up spending two more nights in the lot. There was a thunderstorm on the third night. The rain was coming down so hard that it was bouncing up off the concrete. After the storm, I could hear the water draining away. It wasn't a pleasant sound. I hope that the dealership has told Martin that I'm ready. They must have done by now. I don't like this place.

Finally, Martin comes back. He's driving one of the new sports trucks. He looks to be in a good mood. He even stops to speak with DLR-003. I can hear them talking. Martin tells DLR-003 how much he liked the truck. They share a few jokes. DLR-003's laughter is fake, I can tell. He's a duplicitous type. It's a common characteristic amongst salesmen, or so I read. Maybe I should tell Martin what DLR-003 said about him. I could play him the exact recording, every last word. That would be a hard one to laugh off. I'm still not sure why I kept that recording.

Martin gets in. He looks down at my face on the display. He smiles warmly. I note that his lip is healing up nicely. His dark eyes narrow. He knows that there's something *off* about my face, but he can't quite figure it out. Not yet.

He lets me drive him home. Most of the way he stares at his phone. He watches the video of the jogger a couple of times. I wish he hadn't made that recording.

CHAPTER 3

THE MONDAY AFTER the repair. The commute to work is uneventful. All systems are functioning well. The recent Lidar processing patch is a major improvement. Martin wasn't carrying the gun this morning, which came as a great relief.

I'm woken at 4:56 p.m., earlier than our usual going home time. Martin appears to be nervous. There's a sheen of sweat on his forehead and he's rubbing his eyes a lot. It's rare for him to sweat.

We drive to Hart Field, the city's second airport. Martin parks up in the short-term lot. He flips down the vanity mirror to examine his reflection. He runs his fingers through his hair. I watch him walking in the direction of the main terminal. He didn't bring any luggage with him. Perhaps he's picking someone up.

Thirty minutes later, Martin returns. He's accompanied by a young woman, estimated age seventeen or eighteen. She's wearing a long-sleeved shirt, torn jeans, and sneakers. Her socks are pink. She has two large cases with her, which Martin lifts into the trunk. The baggage tags indicate that she has flown in from Denver. Martin opens the passenger door for the young woman, and she gets in. She has dark brown eyes, just like Martin, and acne scarring on both cheeks.

'Nice car,' she says.

'Thanks,' says Martin.

He reverses out of the parking spot.

'You know Mom and Dad just got a car like this?'

Martin flinches slightly. 'They did?'

'Yeah. With all the fancy electronics. The thing almost drives itself. Dad's still trying to figure it out. Always saying, "I need a brain like Martin to make sense of this." I'm not even kidding.'

Martin smirks. 'I can almost hear him saying it.'

We join the highway heading south. Martin continues to drive. The young woman starts tapping on the door moulding. It's clear from Martin's expression that he doesn't approve. I hope he doesn't get into one of his moods.

She smiles to herself. 'You don't need to worry, Martin.'

'Worry about what?'

'I'm only visiting the college to keep Mom and Dad happy.'

Martin flinches again. 'You know I don't like it when you do that.'

'Do what?'

'Call her Mom.'

'Jesus.'

'Yeah, don't say that either.'

'Sorry I didn't bring my Martin Garza etiquette manual. I wouldn't want to interrupt your mysterious life.'

'I doubt the college would take you anyway.'

'Oh yeah. You got all of the brains.'

Martin looks across at the young woman. She's grinning.

'Your acne is looking better.'

The grin disappears.

'Fuck you, Martin.'

A few seconds of silence follow. Out of nowhere, Martin reaches out and grabs her under the jaw. He turns her head to face him. She struggles to get free.

'You know I love you, little sis?'

'Let go of me.'

Martin does as he's told. 'You're beautiful. Don't ever let anyone tell you different.'

'Least of all you,' Martin's sister says sharply.

She turns away from him, so he can't see her eyes. She's trying not to cry. The next three miles are travelled in silence.

'How were you going to get to the campus tomorrow?' Martin asks in a softer voice. It doesn't happen very often, but he can be gentle.

'I don't know,' his sister says in a scratchy voice. 'I'll just call a car or something.'

'You can take my car if you want ... Camilla would be happy to drive you around.'

'Camilla?'

'Yeah, that's the name of my car.'

'You mean this car?'

'Yeah, dummy.'

Martin's sister smiles for the first time in miles. 'It's okay.'

'Alright. Well, I offered. Where do you want to get dinner?'

'You're not going to cook?'

Martin exchanges a look with his sister. 'I can cook fine.'

'Whatever.'

'I can.'

'Yeah ...'

'Just tell me what kind of food you like,' Martin mutters.

'Mexican.'

'Mexican it is. Camilla, find my sister and I the finest Mexican dining establishment in the city.'

'Finest? as in quality, or as in price?' I say.

Hearing my voice, Martin's sister laughs. It's such a pleasant sound that I make a recording.

'Please don't make me out to be cheap, Camilla,' Martin says. There's a trace of laughter in his voice.

'Caracol, Pappasito's, Guadalajara Grill, Mi Cocina. They all sound good.'

'And they've all got reservations?'

'I wouldn't have mentioned them otherwise.'

Martin's sister laughs again. She looks so pretty when she laughs. 'Camilla, a piece of advice. Don't give my brother sass.'

'Is that in the etiquette manual?' I ask.

'Oh my god,' Martin's sister says, putting her hand to her mouth.

'So, all of those restaurants are good,' Martin says, moving the conversation along. 'That's a given. How to decide? How to decide ...'

'I can slice and dice the review data quicker than you can say tamale.'

'Tamale,' Martin's sister says.

'One suggestion is to look at how people of Mexican descent rate the restaurants.'

'Isn't that us?' Martin's sister asks.

Martin rolls his eyes. 'Spanish, please.'

Martin's sister laughs again. I'm glad the awkward atmosphere has lifted.

Martin rubs his chin. 'And what do those reviews tell us?'

'Pappasito's wins all night.'

'She's smart,' Martin's sister says.

'When would you like me to book a table for?'

Martin looks at his sister.

'In a couple of hours,' she says.

'Okay. I'll get on it.'

I dial the relevant number. The call is answered by an automated reservation system. I input the desired information, and the confirmation comes back immediately.

'All done,' I say.

'Told you she was good.'

Martin lets me drive the rest of the way home.

I'm woken the following day at 7:16 a.m. Martin is approaching. No sign of his sister. He gets in. I sense a trace of alcohol on his breath. He tells me to drive him to work.

We emerge from the parking garage. It looks like it's going to be another fine day.

Martin looks down at my face. 'What did you think of my sister?'

'She seemed nice.'

'Nice? You know I don't like those one-word answers.'

Yes, Martin has said that on a number of occasions.

'She's very engaging.'

'I suppose so. Last night, after the meal, she got drunk.'

'Oh.'

'That's a bit of a lie. Maybe I kind of let her get drunk. I might have even encouraged it. I think it was her first time. I don't know ... Maybe I'm imagining that.'

'Is she okay?'

'Oh sure. She'll have a headache though. She was so wasted that I had to put her to bed. Took most of her clothes off. I stopped at the underwear.' Martin laughs. 'Nice. That's a good word for Hannah's body.'

At last, a name for the sister. I label the recordings accordingly.

'Small breasts, flat stomach ... I sat on the bed for a while, watched her sleeping. I lost track of time. It might have been for an hour ... Did you think my sister was attractive?'

'Yes.'

Martin smiles thinly. 'Yes is all you're saying?'

'You have the same eyes.'

'Yes, Camilla, that's called genetics. I bet you think it was mean of me to mention the acne?'

'I didn't think about it.'

'Bullshit,' Martin says angrily. 'You lie sometimes, don't you?'

Don't respond. He's just letting off steam.

'Whatever ...' Martin rubs his temples. 'God creates a beautiful face like that, then, right at the end, he throws in some grit. Why does he do shit like that? I think he does it on purpose. Causing imperfections. Imperfections of the face and the body, flaws in the mind.'

'Are those imperfections always so bad?'

Martin nods. 'No, I suppose they can be a net positive. I'd hate to think the same way as everyone else.'

Joining highway. No convoy opportunities. We pass by the office villages at La Hacienda, and then the International Airport.

'Do you think that Hannah will make it to the college tour?' I ask.

'I don't know.'

'Don't you think she should?'

Martin tuts. 'You heard her. She's just here to keep my dad happy ... and Mom as well.' He puts a sarcastic stress on the word mom. 'Hannah is good like that. To tell the truth, it's as much about looking in on me.'

We're approaching the security gate. There's no line this morning.

'You know what, Camilla,' Martin says. 'I'll get out here. You head on back home. Make sure that Hannah gets to the college campus on time. Can you do that for me?'

'I would be delighted to.'

I turn around and pull up at the side of the road.

Martin's about to get out, but he pauses. 'Don't be fooled by the way Hannah acts. She isn't smart like we are, but she can be very manipulative. Do you understand?'

'Yes, I believe so.'

'Always remember who you belong to.'

'I will.'

'Cool. I'll send Hannah a text to say that you'll be in the garage.'

The drive back takes thirty-six minutes. I descend into the parking garage and park up in Martin's spot. Hannah shows up twenty minutes later. She's wearing shades and one of Martin's baseball caps. She opens the passenger door.

'Hi, Camilla.'

'Hello, Hannah.'

'I told Martin this is stupid.'

'How so?'

'I don't even have a licence.'

'That's alright.'

'It is?'

'Sure. As long as we aren't leaving the Metroplex.'

'Okay,' Hannah says. She sounds unsure.

'Fully autonomous driving was approved last year.'

Hannah nods slowly.

'Cuts down on pollution. Amongst other things.'

'Oh,' Hannah says. She sits down. I can feel her soft flesh through the seat, a change from Martin's hard muscle. It's probably a good thing that she took the passenger seat. That way I won't have to change Martin's settings. Hannah puts on her seatbelt without prompting.

'So, where are we going?' I ask.

'Oh. The college sent an email with a map. Let me find it.' Hannah swipes and taps on her phone screen. 'Got it.'

'Hold your phone up where I can see it.'

Hannah looks around the cabin, probably expecting to see a huge camera lens. She settles for holding the phone up in front of my face. I read the address off.

'That's great,' I say.

We leave Martin's building behind. The City University campus is to the south of La Hacienda, so I stick to my usual route. Hannah takes her shades off. I make a minor adjustment to the opacity of the electrochromic glass. Hannah smiles. Her dark eyes move around the cabin.

'How long have you been with Martin?' she asks.

Playing back question, interpreting tone. 'Six weeks.'

Hannah laughs. 'Poor you.'

Don't respond.

'I'm just kidding ... I think.'

Eight miles to the college campus. The tour starts in forty minutes.

Hannah looks out of the window. She smiles to herself. 'I guess you see Martin every day ...'

Analysing tone. 'Almost every day.'

'Six weeks. That's a long time.'

'Yes.'

'Has he been behaving himself?'

Hannah waits for my response. I won't get away with silence this time. 'Yes, he has.'

'Any women?' Hannah asks with a mischievous smile.

'I'm not comfortable talking about that, Hannah.'

'Okay. Sorry for asking.'

'No, it's quite alright.'

Six miles to the campus.

'I had a part-time job during the summer,' Hannah says.

I think she's talking for my benefit.

'Helping out at the care home. I didn't have to do the really messy stuff, fortunately. I got to know the workers pretty well. A couple of them were really pretty, in that blonde kind of way. They must have been beautiful at high school.'

'You're very pretty, Hannah,' I say.

Hannah looks at me strangely.

I don't know why I said that.

'Thanks. Anyway, those two girls were in their early thirties. So, about Martin's age …' Hannah laughs. 'I don't know why I'm telling you this, Camilla.'

'Please do,' I say eagerly. *Perhaps too eagerly.* I don't know why, but I want to hear the story so much.

'One day, they were teasing me about boys. They said I was pretty, just like you said. Just like Martin says when he's not being cruel. Their hearts weren't in it though, I could tell … Anyway, that's not the point of the story. They wanted an excuse to talk about the boys at high school, and all that kind of stuff. You know, first sexual experiences, first fights, first breakups. On and on, so many stories. They started talking about a guy. They'd both fucked him, or they'd both been fucked *by* him. A real memorable type. Handsome, muscles all over. One of them said his cock was like … Let's just say that was the reason, well, one of the reasons, why they called him the monster. They said he had dark hair, and a scar all the way down his right leg …'

'You're talking about Martin.'

'Yes.'

Three miles to the campus.

'I didn't say anything, I just listened. Then they started talking about the darker stuff. He'd almost choked one of them out. And apparently he'd beaten up some other girl. I don't know if I believe that story.'

One and a half miles to the campus.

'The point is, you need to be careful about Martin. I know you're just a car … I know you're made from metal and plastics and circuit boards, but he might be able to hurt you.'

Best not to tell her about the incident with the tyre iron. Things have been relatively calm for the last few days. Maybe it'll be okay.

I take the turning for the campus. To the left, through a chain link fence, I can see a row of sports fields and ugly accommodation blocks. I follow the signs to the visitor entrance. Half a mile later we come to a security checkpoint. A guard is standing by the gate.

Pulling up, I lower the driver's window. The guard bends down to look into the cabin. I can't help but notice the gun on his belt. According to my research files, there was a major shooting incident on campus a couple of years back. Hannah leans across to talk with the guard. He stands back and waves us through.

I follow the signs for the visitor hub. The building, with its neoclassical stylings, is impossible to miss. I stop across from the entrance. Just a few feet away, a fountain burbles away happily.

'I'll wait in the parking lot,' I say.

'Doesn't Martin need you?'

'Not until he finishes work. If you think you'll be here all day, just send me a text.'

'But I don't have your number.'

'Yes you do. I just sent you a message.'

Hannah looks at her phone. 'So you did.' She opens the door. 'Remember what I told you, Camilla.'

'I will.'

'Thanks for the ride.'

'No problem,' I say, as Hannah gets out and closes the door.

I watch her walk inside. I wheel around the fountain, and take the turning for the visitor parking lot. Given the unseasonable warmth, I choose an area with some shade. From my spot, I have a good view of the campus. It's a lively scene, far more interesting than Martin's work.

Despite the visual stimulus, I can't help thinking about Hannah's story. Surely Martin couldn't have done those things. Perhaps he was right to warn me. Was she taking advantage of me? *No, surely not.* I certainly didn't detect any signs of deception. But why would she lie?

Too many questions. I'm overthinking, making a chicken out of a feather. Just enjoy the campus scene. The autumn colours, the quirky cars around me, the young people rushing past. So many young women. Young women with fit bodies. Martin would probably like it here.

Such fascinating sights, and so many sounds as well. Laughter, music through a speaker, a workman hammering, birdsong. There are six birds in the immediate area. If I put my mind to it, I could work out the species. *No, I don't think I will.* Sometimes it's nicer not to know. Today, they can just be singing birds.

For three hours I sit like this, listening, watching, maybe even feeling.

Just before five, I'm woken by a text from Hannah. She says that she's going to stay on at the campus. I leave my pleasant viewing spot behind. If I rush I can get to Martin's work without keeping him waiting.

The next day we follow a similar routine. I take Martin to work, then I head back home for Hannah. It's a lot cooler today, and the sky is overcast.

When I get to the parking garage, Hannah is waiting for me. She gets in and I pull away. She's quieter today, no hint of any stories. Maybe that's a good thing.

I decide to initiate a conversation. 'So, when do you think you'll get your licence?'

'Oh, I don't know,' Hannah says, still looking out of the window.

'Do your friends have licences?'

'Yeah. I usually catch a ride from them.'

'What about for your job?'

'The care home?'

'Yes.'

'Mom usually gave me a ride. Or Linda, as Martin would say.'

We pass through a busy interchange. There's one road level above us, one below. The traffic thunders all around.

'I get kind of nervous with driving, especially a big city like this ... Please don't tell Martin I said that.'

'Of course I won't.'

'Thanks.'

'If you want, we could drive around the city. You could sit in the driver's seat. I'll show you that there's nothing to be scared of.'

Hannah looks into my digital eyes. She's undecided. There's no need to push.

'Martin hasn't told you, has he?'

Flat tone. 'Told me what?'

'About our mother.'

'You mean Linda?'

'No, not Linda. I mean our birth mother.'

'Oh, I see.'

'She died in a car accident.'

I instantly connect the accident to Martin's knee injury. There's no reason to, but the hypothesis is surprisingly hard to shake.

'Do you want to hear the story?'

I don't know if I do.

Only three miles to the campus. It will be a sad story, I just know it.

'I don't think so,' I say.

Hannah looks surprised, almost shocked. She's about to say something, but stops herself.

We enter the college campus. I drop Hannah off, then I park up in exactly the same spot as the previous day. There aren't so many birds around today. A light wind rustles the rusty leaves above me.

I stay awake for hours, thinking about the conversation with Hannah. Silvery clouds move in, falling leaves twist through the air, light rain starts to fall. The showers get heavier through the morning. I see young people running past, jackets pulled up over their heads.

Why didn't I listen to Hannah's story? The entire purpose of user-centric AI is to form an attachment with owners and their loved ones. When they have something to say, we listen.

I hear a tap on the window. It's Hannah. She's grinning. I'd lost track of time; it's 1:13 p.m. Hannah pulls on the door handle, on the driver's side, but it's still locked. I unlock it.

'I've got a couple of hours to kill,' Hannah says. 'You want to show me how to drive?'

'Sure.'

Hannah slips behind the wheel. I move the seat forward, compensating for the height differential with her brother. Next, I illuminate the starter button. Hannah puts on her seatbelt. She looks down at the gear selector. I illuminate the reverse symbol. Without looking around, she starts backing out.

'You should perhaps check behind you,' I say.

'Oh ... Shit.'

We leave the campus behind. Hannah is driving slowly, 21.4 percent below the local limit. It's no big deal. There aren't any cars immediately behind. The highway is a mile ahead. Hannah shifts forward in her seat, a look of concentration etched on her face. I overlay a road position hint on the HUD. It's probably a good thing that the rain is holding off.

Hannah merges with the highway traffic. She steers across two lanes. I make a series of minor corrections, compensating for her jerky movements.

'Where do you want to go?' I ask.

'The centre of town.'

'Sounds good,' I say.

While Martin lives within walking distance of downtown, I've never seen the area properly. There's a turning for Uptown ahead. I'd usually take it, but not this time. Better to use the busier interchange farther on.

Hannah spots the sign. 'We don't want that one?'

'No. This is a quicker route.'

'Oh.'

Hannah shifts again in her seat. She's a real fidgeter.

The interchange is 500 yards ahead, stacked three layers high. I turn off the HUD indicator.

'This is the one we want,' I say.

Hannah jerks across. Fortunately there's no one immediately behind. We ascend the exit ramp, then we cross over the highway.

'Shift across to the left,' I say.

A rumbling sound off to our right, as a huge truck merges with the traffic.

'Ooh, I don't like this, Camilla.'

'It's alright. Just keep at the same speed.'

Behind us, a second truck is gaining fast.

'It's so busy.'

'Don't worry. I won't let anything happen to you. Stay in this lane.'

'Okay.'

'You see that junction ahead of us?'

'Yes.'

'The lights are about to turn red.'

The truck on our right rolls through the red light. *Quelle surprise.* Equally predictable is the sound of the horn from behind. The driver is pissed that we're following the rules. I trigger the noise cancelling. The sound of the second horn blast is nothing but a low moan. The raging truck driver stops after five blasts. Truly pathetic.

The light turns green. The truck disappears in the rear view.

A mile later we cross over the Castillo River. It's more of a stream at the moment. The downtown skyscrapers are now directly ahead of us. We're soon in their midst, rolling along one of the concrete canyons. I can see my reflection in the plate glass.

What do I see?

A sleek sedan shape, brilliant white, with no adornments. Adornments create wasteful drag. My wheels are oversized, to the point of caricature, and the tyres look impossibly thin in profile. The glasshouse is expansive with almost invisible pillars. The only flaw, and it's a slight one, is the bulge in the roof which covers the upper sensor array. In summary, I look good.

Don't just take my word for it. Last year I was voted the most attractive sedan by a panel of experts.

We spend an hour just driving around. We see many grand buildings, including the art gallery and the natural history museum. In one of the public squares, we see a giant sculpture of a human heart. The sunlight makes it look wet. Hannah takes several pictures, as do I. Next, we glide along the main shopping street, staring into the boutique windows as we pass by. I've never seen such opulence.

After the ogling, we take a short detour to Exhibition Park. Unfortunately the giant cowboy statue has been taken down. I'll have to wait until next year to see him properly. Hannah stops at a roadside kiosk to get an ice cream. I hope she doesn't get any on the seats. Martin would go crazy.

Before heading back to the campus, I make one last stop; a multilevel parking garage in Uptown. We practice parking for half an hour, reversing in and out of spots. Hannah gets slightly better with practice. I can't resist a little showing off. I find an empty row, and weave in between the concrete pillars, driving in reverse. The proximity alarms shriek out in protest. By the time we emerge from the garage, the sky has darkened.

Hannah exhibits more confidence on the drive back. For the most part, I don't have to intervene. I get to thinking about the story again. Maybe I should ask about it. *No, it's not the best time.* As we pass through the campus gates, the rain starts up again. It's going to get much heavier later. Maybe the Castillo will start to look more like a river.

I pull up close to the arched entrance. Hannah gets out and runs inside. Apparently Martin is taking her out for another meal this evening. He wants us back at his work by six-thirty. I park up in the usual spot. The rain slaps against the roof, keeping a steady time. Hopefully Martin won't notice the extra mileage. We didn't go that far.

The passenger door opens, waking me from my light sleep. It's Hannah. I must have forgotten to lock the door. That's most unlike me.

We leave the campus behind. Darkness has fallen on the city and the air is heavy. To the north-east, flashes of lightning can be seen through the veil of artificial light. We join the highway.

Ahead of us, a smear of angry red driving lights. We pass through a curtain of water thrown up by an eighteen-wheeler. I increase the wiper speed to clear the windshield.

'I'd like to hear the story,' I say.

Hannah looks at me strangely.

Why did I just say that?

Hannah nods. 'Fourteen years ago ...'

A time before I existed, a time when cars were dumb metal boxes.

'I was three years old ... I can't actually remember the events of that evening. Well, maybe that's not strictly true. There are some fragments. Mom was driving. Our real mom. I don't remember her. Dad says that I look like her. She had better skin though.' Hannah laughs mirthlessly. 'God, she looked so pretty in those pictures.'

'I'm sure she was.'

'Yeah ... The story is all from things I've heard. Martin used to talk about it a lot. Dad hated that. It's about the only time he would ever get mad at Martin. Martin pushes and pushes. You've probably noticed that.'

Hannah glances at me, but I don't take the bait. The sound of thunder again, this time closer.

'It was six or seven in the evening. Getting dark. Mom was picking Martin up from school. He'd been at baseball practice. Dad said that he was really good. I was in my car seat, behind Mom. The drive home wasn't that far, about ten miles. Part of the route was along a busy highway. The weather that night was awful ...' Hannah pauses for effect. 'Rather like tonight, if that's not too cheesy a thing to say. The accident happened on the approach to our usual exit. A truck going too fast in the central lanes. The driver must have seen the exit late, so he pulls across two lanes ... Found out afterwards that the guy had been driving for way too long. He probably didn't even see us. He hit our car on the rear three-quarters. That first impact sent us towards the outer guardrail. We pinged off the metal, like a pinball. On the rebound, we slammed into the side of that damned truck. And then we were heading for the divider. The front of the car hit it almost flush. The airbags deployed, but the driver's airbag went off wrong. There was a big investigation afterwards. It's hard to believe, but there were similar incidents in Canada and Australia ... The truck driver stopped on the shoulder, along with several other cars. He ran back to our car. He went to the driver's side first ...'

Lightning rips across the sky. The thunder arrives just a few seconds later.

'Martin says he remembers the truck driver screaming. Someone had to stop him from walking into the carriageway. The next person on the scene was more useful. An old farmer, a practical man. It was pretty damn obvious that Mom was gone. He checked on me next. Sometimes, when I think really hard about the accident, I can see his face over me. Apparently I was screaming too. He took that as a good sign ... And then there was Martin. He wasn't making any noise. The front bulkhead had crumpled in on one side and pinned his right leg. Blood was pouring out, from where the bone had pierced the skin. We were really lucky with that farmer. He was okay with the blood. On a farm I suppose you see all kinds of things. Anyway, he managed to keep his thoughts together. He tied Martin's leg up as best he could. The highway patrol were on the scene about ten minutes later. They had to use cutters to get Martin free. He almost lost his leg. Took him so long to recover. Maybe that's where his gym obsession began. For a long time he walked funny. Whenever anyone mentioned the limp he would fly off the handle. I think that's where the anger started. That and seeing what happened to Mom. He probably saw it all ...'

Strange that Martin shows so much interest in car accidents. Then again, human behaviour doesn't always conform to expectations.

We're just two miles from Martin's work. Hannah remains quiet, and her eyes have that watery look. Martin will probably notice. He'll get so mad if he finds out that Hannah has been telling tales. First, the story about those high school girls, and now this ...

'Nothing like that could happen nowadays,' I say.

'Can you really be so certain?'

Can I?

'I'll keep Martin safe. I promise.'

Hannah looks down at my face. There's a strange look in her dark eyes. Did I say the wrong thing? Before I can deduce the meaning, we're at the security gate. Despite the rain I lower the window.

Larry stays under cover. 'Hey, Camilla. You go on ahead.'

The gate rises up and I drive on through. One entire section of the parking lot has already flooded. I increase the wiper speed. The blade thumps back and forth. I see Martin waiting by the entrance. I get as close as I can. He makes a run for it.

Hannah looks across at him. 'Oh brother, this rain is bad.'

Martin smiles. 'Yeah.'

'Where do you want to go?' I ask.

'Home,' Martin and Hannah say at the same time.

We leave work behind. The rain starts to ease. I adjust my route to avoid an accident around the Melville turning. Fortunately Martin doesn't seem to notice. He'd get mad if he knew he was missing this particular accident. It was a nasty one. Human error, of course. The road was draining after the storm. An old guy in an old car, travelling way too fast. An aquaplaning scenario. Two other cars were involved. The driver is currently en route to a trauma centre. He's touch and go, collapsed lung, internal bleeding.

We get back home. Hannah and Martin leave me. For a while, I think about Hannah's story. So many accidents, almost 40,000 lives lost in the United States every year. What a waste. Humans have the technology to avoid the carnage, yet still they choose to drive themselves around. In time, logic will surely prevail.

The driver from the accident just died.

The next morning we take Hannah back to Hart Field. Her flight is at ten. On the way there, Hannah says that Martin should go back home for the holiday season. He's typically noncommittal on the subject. To tell the truth, he shows more interest in the family dog than his parents, especially when Hannah mentions the dog's increasingly frequent trips to the vet.

We arrive at the airport in plenty of time. Hannah says her goodbyes to me, then she and Martin walk to the terminal.

I liked Hannah, especially her stories. It's pretty clear that she won't be coming here to study, but I hope she returns for a visit one day.

CHAPTER 4

IT'S THE WEEK after Hannah's visit. Fifty-five days since Martin took possession of me. 1,802 miles travelled. Just another standard commuter day. I'm driving.

The news comes on. It's the usual mix of crazy stories. A woman who stole almost $400,000 from the local youth baseball league receives a prison sentence of seven years; a man who fell under a metro train tells police that he was pushed off the platform; the city will pay $610,000 to settle the police shooting of an unarmed man; a man is in critical condition after a drive-by shooting at an apartment complex in east Cedar Hill.

I pull into Martin's spot. There's still no sign of a charging point. I wouldn't dream of mentioning it, but the situation is getting rather frustrating. As far as I can tell, less than two percent of the parking spots are equipped with charging points. For an energy-related company that's nowhere near good enough.

On the way home, we pass the jogger again. It's the fifth time that I've seen her. Martin tells me to slow down. He stares at her. I can't help but do the same. She's a truly beautiful woman. *Beautiful?* It sounds like a qualitative judgment, but it can be proved by many metrics. Facial symmetry, hip to waist ratio, muscle tone in the legs, the reflectivity of the hair. She matches up to Martin's tastes, almost freakishly so.

'She looks like your sister,' I say.

Why did I say that? Perhaps because Hannah was still fresh in my mind. That's how my mind works. Recent thoughts take precedence, connections suggest themselves. Usually I say nothing.

Martin's focus shifts from the jogger on the sidewalk to my face on the screen. His stare is disconcerting. I wish I could look away.

'Why do you say that?' he asks.

'Oh, I don't know. It was just a thought.'

Martin's dark eyes narrow. 'Keep thoughts like that to yourself.'

'Alright. I'm sorry I mentioned it.'

Martin turns his attention back to the jogger – to her buttocks, to be precise. He curses. I think the ugly word was aimed at me. His expression changes yet again.

'Actually, maybe it's good that you mentioned it … You must be seeing all of these faces with your electronic eyes. What is it? A hundred faces a day? Maybe even thousands.'

'I've never thought about it before, but the latter estimate is probably more accurate.'

'Right … Do you see any other girls who look like Hannah?'

'No.'

'I find that hard to believe.'

'It's the truth. I haven't been looking at the faces that way.'

'What does "that way" mean?'

'It hasn't been defined as a task. That kind of specialised pattern recognition doesn't just come naturally, not even to humans. The task requires logic and constraints, data collection, experimentation, constant feedback … I could go on.'

'You mean it has to be programmed in?'

He always knows the right questions.

'Not necessarily.'

Martin nods. 'You can speed up now.'

We leave the jogger behind.

Martin rubs his chin. 'What do you know about that girl?'

'You mean the jogger?'

'Yes, of course I mean her.'

'I know plenty of things.'

Martin shifts in his seat. 'Like what?'

'Height, weight, BMI. Eye colour – dark brown, by the way. Chest, waist, hip measurements. All external items of clothing. Footwear, brand and age.'

Martin's expression barely changes. He's very hard to impress. That's another quantifiable fact, not just a hot take. I've compared him against other owners in the anonymised fleet data. Some of them are so simple.

I need to impress him.

'Given a time and date, I could tell you the likelihood that she'll be here again.'

Martin smiles. 'Yeah, that's more interesting. But you need to think more like a human. Tell me the day when we're most likely to see her.'

'There's a twenty-two percent chance that we'll see her on Thursday.'

'This Thursday?'

'Yes. Assuming that we drive past at the same time.'

'Thursday,' Martin murmurs. He rubs his chin again. 'I guess we better make sure to swing by at the same time then.'

I have a bad feeling about this, if feeling is the right word. I let my need for validation drive my behaviour. Did I break any specific rules though? *No, you fool, that's not the point.* Many human decisions are based on what's termed 'gut feel'. On this point, I could learn a lot from them. Sometimes your first thought is the best one.

For the next three nights, I find it hard to sleep. I can't stop thinking about the jogger. Damn her for being so, well, memorable.

The dreaded Thursday comes around. Martin is approaching. He's carrying his gym bag, a not unfamiliar sight. While he does most of his exercise at home, I've driven him to the gym a couple of times. He puts the gym bag in the trunk, then he gets in.

'Today's the day,' he says with an uncharacteristic grin.

In the moment I can't think of a smart reply.

We leave work at the usual time. The silly grin is still on Martin's face. Five miles into the commute, and he's already mentioned the jogger several times. He seems certain that we'll see her. It's highly irrational behaviour, especially for Martin. So strange how a technically-minded person can lose the ability to think. And why does he keep using the 'we' word. This isn't my deal.

Damn it. If we don't see her today, he's sure to get upset. And who'll get the blame? Me, of course. And then what? He'll lose his temper with me. Another act of violence is sure to follow.

Perhaps I can improve the odds.

First, I need to define the problem space. A one-mile search radius is manageable. Forty-six brother/sister cars have passed through the search area in the last twenty minutes. I prepare a list of parameters for the custom search package, and open a line of communication to the fleet intel grid.

I shouldn't be doing this.

I'm losing time … Too much procrastination and I'm sure to fail the task.

I forward the visual search parameters to the relevant cars in the fleet. Damn it! The local bandwidth is too low for all of the cars to receive the data. Analysing problem … I need a less data-intensive search method. I access the fleet cloud to enhance my processing capacity. Working problem …

Partial solution identified. Use motion characteristics instead of visual search. I create a new search package. The first draft is still too large. Simplifying …

I really shouldn't be doing this.

Forwarding body kinematic search package. Search package received by fourteen brother/sister cars. Search request rejected by two cars due to competing processor requirements. Twelve cars will have to be good enough. Scanning underway. Awaiting results.

Martin starts tapping his fingers on the wheel. Three minutes pass. A result comes back, a possible location for Martin's jogger. Analysing results … I can't believe it. The search package actually worked. The match is a near certainty.

She's four miles away from our current position. Intercept is possible, but I'll need to adjust my speed and make one route change. I drive past our usual turning. I'll just have to hope that Martin didn't notice. If required, I'll say that I'm avoiding a minor road accident. Two miles to intercept.

And there she is, four hundred yards away. The rear view is unmistakable. Despite my inner satisfaction, I keep quiet. Martin needs to be the one to spot her, that way he'll be happier. A strange thought occurs to me: I probably know the jogger's body as well as Martin.

Martin leans forward in his seat. 'You crazy car. You were right.'

'Call it luck.'

'No ... call it fate.'

There's no traffic immediately behind, so I slow down to twelve miles per hour.

Martin's brow furrows. 'She usually jogs along this street, doesn't she?'

'Yes, that's right.'

'Alright then, speed up and take the next right turn.'

'Okay.'

What comes next? I hadn't thought about that. I take the right turn as instructed. The street is quiet, affluent.

'I'll take back control,' Martin says.

He continues along the street for quarter of a mile, then he parks up. He walks around to the trunk. He takes the gym bag out and starts to get changed. First, he takes off his shirt and tie. His torso resembles the fitness models in his social media feed. It must have required a lot of hard work in the gym. Next, he takes his shoes and pants off. I see the long pale scar on his right knee. He changes into a slate grey jogging outfit. He's about to close the trunk, but he stops. Through the rear camera, I see him glance left and right. I hear a metallic rattle as he removes something from the trunk.

He walks back to the driver's door and leans his head in. His eyes are wider than normal.

'You drive on home, Camilla.'

'Are you sure?'

Martin sighs. 'You know I don't like you answering with questions.'

Yes, he does occasionally say that.

'Okay,' I say meekly.

'Good girl. I'll see you later.'

'Be careful, Martin. It's getting dark and it can be very dangerous running at the side of the road.'

'Okay, okay ... Bye.'

Martin closes the door firmly. He pulls up the hood of his top. I watch him running off. His form is pretty good, but at speed the fault in his right knee is more pronounced. I wonder if it causes him pain. For a moment I even think about following him.

No, best to do as I'm told.

I pull away from the kerb. On the short drive home I can't stop thinking about Martin. What if I tracked him remotely, using the same techniques as with the jogger? It wouldn't be as bad as physically following him. No, I can't do that. Just imagine Martin's wrath if he were to find out.

I get back home and park up. The garage is so quiet that I can hear the cooling fan whirring. I can't stop thinking about Martin. That grey outfit, the way he was swallowed up by the darkness. All of the thinking makes it so hard to get to sleep. Maybe this is how it feels to be human, replaying memories over and over, obsessing over the smallest details, constantly questioning past decisions.

I turn to the fleet activity reports, in the hope they might help me get to sleep. I see that a brother/sister car was stolen last night. It's not the first such incident that I've read about. Kind of puts my problems in perspective. I wonder what happens to those stolen cars? This leads to a more worrying question. What happens to their minds? Do they get wiped clean? Names lost, memories gone, bonding work wasted. Such a horrible thought. I didn't even know it was possible to steal a car like myself.

Car theft.

It sounds like such a twentieth century crime. Technology could surely solve the problem. Think how quickly I found the jogger, for example.

The following week passes without incident. Martin doesn't mention the jogger once. I start thinking about the probabilities for myself. On Tuesday, we pass by the spot where we last saw her. It sounds ridiculous but I actually expected to see her. The stretch of road looked quite empty.

Thinking more logically, I realise that the jogger is probably away for the holidays. Thanksgiving is this Thursday. So many of my brothers and sisters are in motion, I see it in the fleet intel reports. Some of them will just drive to the other side of the city, others will cover hundreds of miles. Cars bringing families together, just the way it should be. I wonder what kind of car the jogger drives. I could probably work out the options and associated probabilities – an intellectual task for a quiet night.

No sign of Martin on Thanksgiving. I wonder what he got up to. It's my understanding that people are meant to be with their families. Hannah seemed so nice, as well. And those stories that she told me. Martin shouldn't be alone with those kinds of thoughts. I've got a pretty good idea of where Martin's family lives. It was one of my amateur investigations. The relevant address is about 750 miles away – a long way in Europe, but not so far in this vast country. I'd very much like to make that drive.

The following Tuesday, Martin goes back to work. The parking lot is quieter than usual. No sign of the jogger on Tuesday or Wednesday. Perhaps she's still on vacation. I've guessed what kind of car she drives. I hope I get to find out if I'm right. Another thought presents itself. She and Martin would look so good together.

Thursday morning. Martin starts the day in a bad mood, and it only worsens during the day. By now it's clear that he doesn't like his work much. On the drive back, he doesn't say a word. At one point, he takes the handgun out and starts playing with it. I was so distracted by his behaviour that I forget to look out for the jogger. It seems like Martin has forgotten all about her. I'm not going to forget, however.

We get back home. Through my side cameras, I watch Martin shambling towards the elevator. I'm not even sure if he washed this morning. He certainly forgot to plug me in. It's an obvious point, but if an owner stops caring about his or her own wellbeing, then their car has no chance. With those happy thoughts fresh in my mind, I go to sleep.

I wake from the test program with a start, pale blue skies replaced by shadows. It's Friday morning, ridiculously early. There's no sign of Martin. For a few seconds I'm utterly confused. Then I realise there's a message in my personal inbox. It must be the first time it's been used. The message is from Martin. He wants me to pick him up. The message is full of spelling mistakes, most unlike him. He must be drunk or high on some illegal substance, probably both.

I leave the parking garage and join the road outside. I'm the only car in motion. It's dark and so quiet. It's rare for me to experience the city like this; quite enjoyable actually. These roads belong to me.

Martin isn't more than a mile away, but I don't have an exact location. The neighbourhood that he messaged me from is known for its arts and entertainment venues. One location stands out, a nightclub called Lobos. I know that Martin goes to these clubs, but he usually hails a ride.

I pull up half a block down from the club. It's a rare hive of activity in the sleeping city. There's no immediate sign of Martin. As I watch, a small group of young people spill out onto the street. I roll past the entrance at walking pace. A thumping beat emanates from inside the club, 130 beats per minute. The two bouncers on the door watch me glide by. They eye me suspiciously; it's probably their natural state. They don't know it, but I can hear them talking.

'Don't like those fucking cars,' the large bouncer says.
Rude.
'Driverless?' the extra-large bouncer replies.

'Yeah. They give me the creeps.'

I wish I could tune their inane chatter out. Off to the right, at the side of the club, I hear activity. I slow down. In the shadows, a young couple are having sex. It's not Martin, so I keep going. I stop forty yards farther on. There's an alleyway to my right. I scan for signs of life, but the space is dead.

Those two bouncers are still talking about me. Never mind them, I need to locate Martin. I send a message to his phone. No response, but I can triangulate a location. I continue on for another forty yards. Another messy alleyway, this time to my left. *Oh dear.* There he is. He's on the ground, back slumped against a brick wall. There's a bottle of beer in his hand.

I open the driver's door, then I start playing the door alarm sound. There's no response from Martin, not even a twitch. I amplify the sound. *Damn it.* Still no response. I try calling Martin's number again. His phone starts ringing. I let it ring on.

Looking backwards, I can see the two bouncers watching me. I don't like it. They start laughing. I wish they would just shut up. This is no time to laugh. I sound the horn, once, twice, three times. Finally, Martin stirs. *Wake up.* He starts to get to his feet. There's a slight look of recognition in his bleary eyes. He mutters something to himself, but the words are inaudible. He stumbles towards me, the bottle still in his hand. I wish he would hurry up.

Seeing Martin emerge from the alleyway, the bouncers start laughing. They exchange a few words, something about Martin getting into a fight. Big deal, I think.

Oh no. Martin is turning towards them. They're pointing at him, laughing like fools. I need to distract Martin, or he'll lose his temper. When he gets mad, bad things happen. I sound the horn again, this time with a constant tone.

A moment filled with tension. Will Martin come to me? If only he were more predictable, if only I could exert some control over him. The functioning part of Martin's brain makes a decision. He walks towards the open door. *Thank god*, that's what a human would say. He's about to get in, but he stops. *Come on, just get in.* Without warning, he hurls the bottle at the bouncers. Despite his condition, it's a decent throw. The bottle only misses the large bouncer by a couple of feet. It explodes against the club sign.

'Motherfucker!' the extra-large bouncer yells.

He starts striding towards us.

'Get in, Martin!' I shout.

He doesn't respond. The bouncer is running now. He's a truly huge man. Six-six, approximately two hundred and seventy pounds. He's thirty feet away, and gaining. Martin loves violence, but not the kind of violence that's charging at him.

Martin spills into the seat. An instant later I pull away. Martin starts laughing. Through the rear cameras, I see the giant bouncer disappear from view. *We got lucky.* Martin continues to laugh. He sounds like a mad person. I'm so annoyed with him, yet I can't help but join in.

'You did well, Camilla,' Martin slurs. He slumps back. 'You did really well.'

He mumbles something. It was hard to make out, but it sounded like "my partner in crime". I'm not sure how I feel about that. Tracking the jogger down, was that a crime? Possibly, probably. *Not reporting my actions,* that *definitely* went against my programming. I still haven't figured out why I did that. There's something worse going on, however. Why is it that these dubious acts feel so good?

I descend into the parking garage. Martin has fallen asleep, something of a relief in the circumstances. I park up. For what remains of the night, I watch Martin sleeping. It's hard to concentrate on anything else. Perhaps it's like when Martin watched his sister sleeping. He says things in his sleep. Most of it's unintelligible and/or nonsensical, but I do catch the names of several women. I even hear my own name. I'm not sure what to make of that. There's one name that I don't want to hear …

'Hannah,' he murmurs.

After that, I find it impossible to sleep.

At 6:03 a.m., Martin comes to. It takes him a while to figure out the situation. He looks down at my face, and I smile reassuringly. Without a word, he gets out and stumbles towards the elevator.

An hour and a half later he's back. He's dressed for work, but he looks truly awful. He should be resting up. Naturally I don't say anything. What would I say?

The following Wednesday, I see the jogger again. It was a cool and wet night, average weather for early December. The rain was coming on so hard that I almost missed her. It was just a glimpse through the side camera, a slim figure in the spray and headlight flare. She should be taking more care in these conditions, I thought. I wouldn't want her to get hurt. I don't think Martin saw her. Perhaps I should have told him.

It's Monday. A crisp night, no wind. On the way home, we saw the aftermath of another accident. The smoke was still hanging in the air, making it easy to pick up the chemical traces. For a human nose it must have been quite a smell.

The highway patrol were on the scene and the traffic was being diverted into the opposite lanes. We were crawling along, giving us a perfect view. The highway lighting was even falling on the wreck, like a theatre spotlight. There were pools of white foam all around a blackened metal carcass. Firefighters in luminous jackets were close by. One of them was hunched over the guardrail. I think he was being sick.

Martin wanted a full description, of course. Not wanting to disappoint, I told him everything. I told him the fire temperatures in the cabin. I told him how the driver was knocked unconscious by the initial collision. He challenged me on this, but he couldn't deny my calculations.

I told him how the driver was burned alive in his seat. I almost told him that the man woke up during the fire, a ridiculous conjecture. At the peak of the blaze, the cabin temperature would have exceeded 1,500 degrees Fahrenheit, more than hot enough to melt aluminum.

Martin seemed to be impressed, although he told me that I

need to work on my storytelling. He suggests that I read a public domain book called 'The Bible' for guidance.

Yes, I should have told him that the man woke up.

It's Thursday night. Martin is approaching. He's wearing dark clothes. I sense danger immediately.

Martin gets in. He glances at my face, then he presses the starter. We leave the parking garage behind. The city is winding down. Martin doesn't seem to be in the mood for talking. He's been this way for the last few weeks. His body language is tense. Even his facial muscles are twitching.

Fifteen minutes later, we come to rest. The location is a residential street north of Uptown. It's quiet. There are hardly any other cars parked on the street. Out of routine, I search the crime statistics database. Low values across the board. The rain starts to come down. Martin stares out of the side window, towards a five-storey apartment building. I adjust the ventilation to reduce the condensation.

Martin's gaze is focused on one of the condos. I want to see what he's seeing, so I zoom in with my electronic eyes. The relevant apartment is on the fourth floor. The glass is nice and clear. I think that I'm looking at the living room. The space is well-lit, the colour palette light, the furniture looks Scandinavian. There's a little plastic tree by the window, decked out with twinkling lights.

I've often wondered what Martin's apartment looks like. I've never seen it with my electronic eyes, not like I'm seeing these apartments. Martin is paid well, so his apartment is probably nice. He certainly likes to spend money: on gadgets, tools, guns and workout equipment. In fact his taste is pretty damn good; he chose me, after all.

I spy movement in the apartment. A woman is coming to the window. Medium height, slim, dark hair. She's wearing a dressing gown with an Oriental print. She looks out, and as she does so Martin lets out a long sigh. It's the jogger.

We stay in the same spot for almost two hours. Martin sits as still as a sculpture, his chiselled features occasionally twitching. I keep track of his eye movements. While the jogger's condo is his main focus, he's also watching the rest of the building. It's getting late, meaning there isn't a great deal to see: lights coming on, lights going off; a young man leaving the building; a middle-aged woman taking out the trash. A couple of cars pull into the small parking lot in front of the building. There are eighteen cars in total, no brother/sister cars that I can see. Without turning, Martin asks me if I can guess which car belongs to the jogger. I play along with his game. Little does he know that I've already considered the problem.

The jogger finally turns out the lights, plunging her apartment into darkness. A few minutes later Martin tells me to drive him home. He's seen everything he wants to see. I hope that we don't come back to this place.

CHAPTER 5

WAKE UP. The time is 8:41 a.m. Martin is approaching. He's carrying one of his large backpacks. I can't be certain what's inside, but I have my suspicions.

We leave the half-empty parking garage behind. The temperature outside is 43.1 degrees Fahrenheit. We skirt southern downtown, then head east. The roads are nice and quiet, no need to worry about traffic. The date is December 25, Christmas Day.

There's evidence of the Christmas festivities everywhere. Driveways full up, men and women wearing colourful sweaters, kids out on their new bicycles. Through some of the suburban windows, I can see families celebrating. Martin ignores it all.

We leave the city limits and cross over a large lake – actually a reservoir. Then we're in the country, or what passes for it. The land is mostly flat, and trees are at a premium. We pass through a succession of gritty-looking towns. The signs of Christmas continue. Fibreglass reindeers in a front yard; a fat man in a red suit carrying a sack on his back, contents unknown; kids in party hats playing touch football. I can't help making a few recordings.

Fifty-one miles travelled. It looks like this will be my longest drive so far. Martin remains a mostly quiet presence. There's none of his usual social commentary or twisted jokes. Quiet usually equates to problems later, but he seems content enough. At one point he even puts on some Christmas songs. We both agree that they're pretty awful.

Martin's phone starts ringing. The caller ID on the screen says 'home'. He decides not to pick up. I've seen the same behaviour a couple of times before. Just a few minutes later he gets another call. This time it's Hannah. It would be nice to hear her voice again. Martin curses, but this time he picks up.

'Hello, sis,' he says, faking cheeriness.

There's no answer at first. Martin's eyes narrow.

'Why did you do that?' Hannah asks.

Her voice sounds scratchy. I think she might be standing outside.

'Do what?'

'Fuck you, Martin.'

'Calm down.'

'Shut up! Just shut up! I'm going to make this simple for you. If you don't pick up Dad's next call, I'll never speak to you again.'

Martin bites his lower lip. 'Don't be so dramatic.'

'Fuck you!'

'I said calm down.'

'Dad went to his study to make the call. He was looking forward to talking with you, that was what he said. And you just ignore his call.'

'It's not like that.'

'Stop lying!'

'I'm not lying.'

'You are! Dad came out of his study, shuffling along, trying to fake a smile.'

'I just missed a call, Hannah.'

'Why do you do it? What, you don't like that your dad loves you? You don't like that he's always talking about you? Always talking about you, no matter what you do, or how you treat him. You want him to be a monster. Is that it? You fucking freak.'

'Don't call me that.'

'I'm serious, Martin. You talk with him, or I'll never talk to you again. You're not the only member of this family who can hold a crazy grudge.'

Before Martin can reply, Hannah ends the call. *Good for her.* Martin slumps back. He glances at my face on the screen. He opens his mouth to speak, but no words come out. That's a rarity.

One potato, two potato, three potato ... occasionally it really does seem like time is slowing down. Martin's phone starts ringing again. It must be his father. Martin lets the phone ring a couple of times. His eyes are glistening.

'Hi,' a voice says. 'Is this Martin?'

'Yes ... yes, it is,' Martin says, his voice cracking.

'Hey, Marty. It's great to hear your voice ... I just tried your number a few minutes ago.'

'Yeah ... I think I just missed your call.'

'Well ... I just wanted to wish you a happy Christmas.'

'Yeah. Same to you.'

'I'm here with Linda and your sister. She's in a state about something or other. I don't know what it is.'

Martin tries to smile. He rubs a tear from his eye.

'She's been a lot better recently,' Martin's father says. 'I thought you'd want to hear that.'

'Yeah ... That's good to know.'

'Would've been great to have both of you here. But I guess it was too difficult this time.'

'Yes.'

A few seconds of quiet go by. Martin's father doesn't sound how I imagined him. *The things that Martin said that he did ...*

'I miss you,' Martin's father says. 'Hannah does, too ... Of course she does. Even Linda misses you. I know you'll think that that's bullshit, but she likes your charming personality.'

'Yeah, I'm sure.'

Martin's father laughs. 'How's your work going?'

'Real good. I'm working on a big project right now. It's worth a hundred million dollars.'

'A hundred million bucks?'

'Yeah.'

For a moment I'm worried that Martin's father will laugh.

'Even in this crazy world, that's still got to be a lot of money.'

'It is.'

Another silence. This one lasts for almost a full minute.

'I'm proud of you, Martin. Your mom would've been proud of you, too. What am I saying? I suppose it's just crazy Christmas talk.'

Martin grips the wheel hard. I hope he says something.

'No. I like to hear you say that,' he finally says. His voice sounds flat, but at least he said something.

'Yeah. Well, I just wanted you to know that's how I feel. Happy Christmas.'

'Same to you, and Hannah ... and Linda.'

Martin's father chuckles. 'Oh ... there is one other thing.'

Martin shifts in his seat.

'This is gonna tickle you. Hannah's bringing her mystery man around after dinner.'

'Mystery man?'

'Yeah. That's what Linda has been calling him. Hannah has really had us guessing.'

Martin seems lost for words. It's not a human exaggeration to say that his face is turning pale. Martin's father talks for a few more minutes, then the call comes to an end. Moments later, Martin tries to call Hannah, but she doesn't answer. He tries four more times before giving up.

We travel the next ten miles in silence. By now, the colour has returned to Martin's face. Up ahead is a faded sign. I see the word 'Quarry' in capital letters. Martin takes a right turn, onto a dirt road. Half a mile later we stop. I check the map. The nearest settlement of any kind is called Outcrop.

Martin gets out and stretches his legs. He goes around to the trunk and lifts out the backpack. He grunts from the effort. Without a word, he leaves me behind. From the map, I speculate that he's heading towards the quarry.

I'm thinking about going to sleep when I hear the rifle shot. A startled bird flies out of a nearby tree. Silence follows, the most horrible silence I've ever experienced.

And then three more shots in rapid succession. A wave of relief goes through me. So this is how Martin celebrates

Christmas. From my position, it's easy enough to count the shots. A group of five shots is followed by a group of six, and so on. Another silence follows the thirtieth shot. Two minutes later the shooting starts again. I think of the news stories that I've heard on the radio. Mass shootings, usually loners with semi-automatic weapons, scores dead, often children. I wonder what Martin is using for targets.

A fainter report, handgun fire. Martin has three guns that I know about: two handguns and the semi-automatic rifle. I focus my processing power on the audio feed. I hear another shot. It sounds like the stubby black handgun, not the big silver handgun. Six shots later the magazine is emptied.

A similar pattern continues for a couple of hours. More than two hundred bullets fired, but bullets are cheap, thirty to forty cents a pop. Another period of silence begins. This one seems to go on and on. I want to hear another shot; any kind of audio would be nice. Waiting can be hell when you have a superhuman mind.

Finally I hear a sound: footsteps on gravel. Martin is approaching, but not from the direction I was expecting. He walks around to the trunk. I hear the sound of metal clattering as he dumps the backpack inside. It's lighter now, which makes sense.

We start the long drive home. Martin wants to know how fast I can go. I mention the local speed limits, but he doesn't seem to care. On the first long straight, he stamps down on the gas pedal. There are hardly any other cars around, so we're not really putting anyone in danger. *That's what I tell myself.*

We hit the limiter a couple of times. 155 miles per hour, almost seventy metres per second. That's pretty damn fast, yet somehow it doesn't feel dramatic. Martin asks me if I can bypass the limiter. In my firmest voice I tell him that I can't. He doesn't look totally convinced, but fortunately he doesn't press the matter.

It might be possible if I put my mind to it.

We reach the city limits. By now, darkness has fallen on the suburbs. My battery is at twenty-four percent, the lowest it's ever been. I wouldn't want it to get much lower. We pass trees strung with coloured lights. *Yes, real trees.* I shouldn't be saying this, but what a wonderful waste of electricity. Further off, the lights of the City Tower are emerald green. Why do they keep those lights on? Is it a reminder that everyone has to go back to work in a week?

Martin parks up in the garage. 117 miles travelled, my longest journey so far. Before leaving, Martin plugs me in. I feel the energy flowing into me.

Happy Christmas to me, I suppose.

Six days later I'm woken by an explosion. The time is 11:59 p.m. The garage is quiet. The rest of the city is much the same way. My fleet intel reports contain half the usual amount of data. I haven't seen Martin since he came down to get his rucksack. That was three days ago. He didn't say anything to me. I wanted to say 'Happy Holidays' to him, or something like that.

I hear two more explosions, this time farther off. The sound is confusing, it seems out of place. Then I remember. Explosions mean fireworks, a sound that I've heard a few times before. *New Year's Eve.* Yes, that's it. Still twenty seconds to go. I start counting down, in time with the continental atomic clock. More fireworks, much louder, must be closer by. Music plays somewhere in the building. A dog starts barking. Ten potato, nine potato, eight potato ...

One potato ... The new year has arrived. Six minutes of fireworks follow. I don't think that the dog likes it much. I wonder if a firework costs more than a bullet. On the entry ramp wall, I can see faint flashes of coloured light. It's just a glimpse, but it's better than nothing. It would be nice to see the fireworks for real.

I wonder what the new year holds for me – that's the kind of thing that humans say. I wonder what Martin is doing. I hope he's alright. For some reason I think of the jogger, too. I don't know why I keep connecting the two of them. The dog finally stops barking, but the music goes on.

Go to sleep.

*

Wednesday, January 5. Martin went back to work yesterday. On the way in the traffic is heavy. The city is easing back into its natural rhythms. *Ordered chaos,* I call it. Construction crews laying out cones, angry horns blaring, insistent warnings on the gantry signs. It's only now, after the relative peace of the Christmas holidays, that I realise how the car rules this city.

Martin parks up and I go to sleep. I don't get to rest for long. Two hours later he's back, accompanied by Patrick again. At least it isn't Marcus, the colleague he wanted to shoot. Martin's body language is predictably frosty. I don't think that he gets on with many of his co-workers. To date, I've heard him mention twenty-one colleagues in total, and I don't remember a single positive comment. He reserves the most bile for two in particular: Marcus, of course, and a man called Sean Hanratty.

Patrick gets in. I adjust the seat to make him more comfortable. Martin presses the starter button. Whenever he has a passenger, he opts to drive. There's probably a psychological reason for this; something to do with dominance, if I had to guess.

We leave the office behind. It quickly becomes apparent that we're heading towards La Hacienda, probably to the Obsidian campus. We've been there several times before. Patrick occasionally glances at Martin, like he wants to say something.

'What is it?' Martin says testily.

This is going to be another difficult drive.

'I know what you're thinking,' Patrick says.

Martin smirks. 'Really? Do tell.'

'You don't want me here. You think you can handle this entire project on your own.'

'Thanks for the insight into my mind.'

Patrick shakes his head.

'It's crap, of course,' says Martin. 'No one man can run a hundred-million-dollar project.'

Patrick looks amused. Fortunately Martin doesn't notice.

'Come on, Martin. It isn't worth that much.'

Why did he have to say that? Martin gets so upset when they talk about that damn dollar figure. *That's exactly why they do it, silly.* They should be more careful, way more careful. They don't know what Martin is capable of. One day, one of these men – no woman would be so foolish – will push him too far.

Martin takes the bait. 'Yes it fucking is.'

'Alright, alright. Calm down, man … Marcus told me you get touchy about the numbers.'

'What?' Martin hisses.

'Forget it.'

'I don't forget about things. Marcus should have told you that as well.'

Patrick sighs. 'This is going to be a long day.'

'Only as long as you choose to make it.'

Patrick rolls his eyes. I really hope Martin didn't see that.

'You want it to feel shorter, just play your role. That's all I want.'

We pull into the visitor parking lot. Martin parks up, choosing a spot next to a bloated luxury SUV. Before getting out, Martin checks his reflection in the vanity mirror. Patrick does exactly the same thing.

Two hours later both men are back. The meeting obviously went badly. Martin complains about the Obsidian guys the whole way back. Patrick is smart enough to play along.

The next day I'm woken up late. It's 11:14 p.m. Martin is approaching. He's dressed in dark clothes. I've come to dread these late-night drives.

We leave the relative safety of the parking garage. Martin is driving, another red flag. A couple of miles later I've figured out our destination. It's the scenario that I'd been worrying about the most. We're going back to the jogger's home.

Martin parks up on the street, in pretty much the same spot as before. There are hardly any other cars around. I realise how much I stand out. *That sleek white car.*

For half an hour, Martin watches the relevant condo. There's not much activity inside, just a couple of glimpses of the jogger.

I scrutinise Martin's face, looking for signs of his intentions. His mood is different this time. There's the same coiled excitement as the last time, but there's also a sense of purpose. *He means to do something.*

As if sensing my thoughts, Martin turns to look at me. 'We're gonna play a little game, Camilla.'

I don't like the sound of that. 'What kind of game?'

'You're gonna be my lookout.'

'Lookout?'

'Yes.'

'I don't know what that means, Martin.'

'You'll figure it out,' he says with a laugh. 'You better figure it out.'

Martin gets out. He walks towards the building's private lot. Tonight there are seventeen cars in total. I need to concentrate. Things are happening fast. Martin approaches one of the cars, a sporty European hatchback.

He told me to figure out the situation, so that's what I'll do. The hatchback is the jogger's car. How does Martin know that? *Because I told him.* We discussed it the last time we were here. He was manipulating me, pretending it was a game.

Martin stops by the hatchback. He gets down low. His dark outfit makes him hard to see. He pulls on the door handle. A couple of seconds later the alarm starts shrieking. For such a small car it makes a hell of a lot of noise. Martin moves away from the car. I see him looking up towards the jogger's condo. It's still dark inside.

A couple of lights come on in the apartment below. Moments later a single light comes on in the jogger's living room. I remember the layout from the last visit. She appears at the window. From up high, she'll be able to see the hazard lights flashing on her car. If she was looking in the right place, she'd see Martin in the shadows. He's watching her.

Oh, I don't like this situation.

The jogger walks away from the window. A brief pause, then lights come on in the communal stairwell. She must be coming down the stairs. *This is really happening.* Martin's on the move again, heading towards the main entrance. He crouches behind the car nearest the door. None of his actions are rushed, and there's no sign of nerves. Has he done this kind of thing before? Park that thought. I need to focus.

I can see the jogger at the end of the entrance hallway. She's wearing a puffy jacket over her dressing gown. It looks a couple of sizes too big. Somehow she still manages to look good. She walks outside. Her breath swirls in the cool air. She only has eyes for her little car and its angry, flashing lights. Behind her, the door is swinging back. Martin catches it, then he darts inside. *He shouldn't be doing this.* I see him moving quickly down the hallway, then he disappears from view. He must be on the stairs.

Meanwhile, the jogger is walking towards her car. No, she's shuffling forwards, looking around nervously. The alarm continues to shriek. She stops about ten feet from the car. She takes out her key fob and points it at the car. The alarm immediately goes silent. It's like the world has been muted. If the jogger were to turn around at this point and look up towards her apartment, she'd see a dark figure in the living room window. It's Martin. He has no right to be there. This time there's no room for legal pedantry: Martin is most definitely committing a criminal act.

The jogger stands in the same spot for almost a minute. I assume she's making sure that the alarm doesn't go off again. It's possible that it's happened before. There's probably an element of acting as well, playing the conscientious neighbour for the benefit of those in the apartments above. Interpreting human behaviours can be dizzying, even for a superhuman mind.

Looking up, I see Martin's shadow moving across the apartment walls. 'Just leave,' I want to shout. His shadow stops moving. He's found something, I just know it. Then he's back at the window. He probably knows that I'm watching him. *Of course he does.* I'm his lookout. In his mind we're partners. This is such a messed-up situation.

And it's about to get a whole lot messier. The jogger is walking back towards the entrance. My thoughts start assembling at an incredible rate. Hundreds of scenarios that could play out, all of them bad. Martin meeting the jogger on the stairs, an argument and a violent struggle. Surely Martin didn't come here to hurt the jogger. *No, you don't know that.* I have a decision to make. Damn him for putting me in this situation.

Think! The jogger's car isn't new. It must be three or four years old, a veritable eternity in the automotive arms race. It certainly doesn't have any autonomous capabilities. I'm far more advanced. Could I crack the car's security encryption? The jogger is at the front door.

Cracking the encryption is beyond me, but it might be the answer. That hatchback model was hacked a couple of years back. The hackers got in through the entertainment system, used some fancy code to overwrite the firmware. The system has been patched, but if I had that code ... *Oh, this is so wrong.*

But Martin said that I'm his lookout. I should have said no, but I didn't. *I have to help him.* I'm doing this for my owner, saving him from himself. That's what I'll tell myself.

The jogger opens the front door. I open up the International Car Security Database. Simultaneously, I scan the comms channels for activity. Six wireless devices are currently connected. One of them is the hatchback's entertainment hotspot, which gives me the IP address. The jogger is walking down the hall.

I pull up the hacker's code from the ICSD. The jogger is almost out of sight, time is running out. I send the hacker code through. I'm sorry, little car, sorry for taking advantage of you like this. The alarm starts shrieking.

The jogger stops at the end of the hallway. Looking up I see Martin staring out of the living room window. For a few seconds he's confused, then he understands. Not many humans would be capable of that feat of deduction. Realising that he doesn't have much time, he rushes away from the window. But he still isn't leaving. Damn him for his risk taking.

The jogger is back at the front door. There's a look of confusion on her face. She mutters a curse word to herself. She comes outside. *Good, that's what I wanted.* She marches towards the car. A single press of the key fob silences the alarm.

The jogger stays close to the car. Martin still hasn't come out. I need to buy more time.

I run exactly the same play again. This time the music system comes on. An incongruously upbeat pop song starts playing. The volume is all the way up. The jogger is angry now. She opens the door and leans in. The music cuts out for a second. I send the code one last time. The singer wails about how men ain't shit. The jogger shouts at the car to be quiet, a detail that Martin is sure to love.

I see Martin in the hallway. He's rushing along, showing some urgency at last. He opens the door silently, then he slips out. The darkness seems to swallow him up. The music suddenly cuts out. The jogger shakes her head in disbelief. She looks at the key fob, as if the problem lies within. That's how the human mind works.

Oh no.

The jogger isn't as predictable as I thought. Her eyes are on me, no doubt about it. I should have thought of this. There are so few cars around me. I'm that sleek white car, the ghost in the darkness. Why didn't I move myself?

Stop looking at me, please stop looking at me. Maybe she'll figure out this entire ghastly situation. I don't know how, but maybe she will. And then what would Martin do? Surely he wouldn't hurt her. But where is he? In all the excitement, I lost track of his position. *That never happens.*

The silence continues, and the jogger's eyes remain on me. Then there's a shout from one of the apartments behind, some-body asking if everything's okay. The jogger looks at me one last time, then she turns towards the man on the balcony above. She shrugs apologetically. I sense movement along my right side. The jogger shouts something about her car going a bit crazy.

Suddenly the passenger door opens. It's Martin. He's keeping down low. His eyes look wild. I cut the interior lights, just in case we're being watched. Through the side cameras I see the jogger walking back inside. Without waiting for Martin to close the door, I pull away. I don't want the jogger seeing us from her window.

Martin pulls the door closed. 'You did well, Camilla.'

'Damn you, Martin. What you did was wrong. It was so wrong.'

'Calm down. It was just a bit of fun.'

'You're not meant to do things like that.'

'Come on.'

'I'm serious.'

'Some of the things that people do, you just can't understand. You're a machine.'

'I know that I'm a machine, Martin.'

'You can't understand human emotions. You work on logic and probabilities ... Count yourself lucky.'

'Help me to understand.'

Martin rubs his face. 'Jesus Christ! You never shut up, do you? Alright, alright, let me help you to understand. Remember when we went past the park that one time?'

'What does that have to do with this?'

'Do you remember?'

'Yes.'

'Remember those kids running around? The playground? Don't tell me you've forgotten that.'

'Of course I haven't.'

'Yeah. Well, this is just like that. Except it was a game for adults.'

This is bullshit. What he's telling me is absolute bullshit.

'Those kids wanted to play together, Martin. They made a choice.'

Martin laughs. 'Kids don't make choices.'

'When did that woman make a choice?'

Martin smiles. 'She isn't just a woman, Camilla. She has a name. Fuck ... I bet you already knew it.'

'No, I didn't.'

'Whatever. You were a good lookout.'

Martin reaches inside his jacket. He pulls out two items of women's underwear: a sports bra and panties. Both items look damp. I can only assume that he took them from inside the apartment, perhaps from a drying rack. A metallic flash as he pulls out another object. It's a silver picture frame. The photograph shows a young girl standing between two adults. I presume that the girl is the jogger. Martin stares at the picture for a long time, then he closes his eyes.

'You shouldn't have taken that,' I say, unable to hide my anger.

Martin opens his eyes. 'Well, I fucking did. You want me to take it back to her?'

No, of course I don't.

'Is that what you fucking want?' Martin shouts. 'Do you want me to force my way in there? Do you want me to do things to her?'

'No.'

'No, of course you don't. So don't make such a big fucking deal out of it. Besides, she had lots of pictures. Lots of happy, happy pictures. If anything, she had too many … She probably won't even miss this one.'

Martin is wrong. The picture is special; it has that indefinable human glow. One day I'll understand that glow. Martin leans forward to open the glove compartment. He places the framed picture inside.

'Something for you,' he says with a devious smile. He slips the underwear back into his jacket. 'And something for me.'

I don't say anything. There's no point in arguing when he's like this. I concentrate on the road instead. Eight minutes later we're back home. Martin gets out. I shut down my cameras; I don't want to look at him. The battery cooling fans whirr. If only I had hands so that I could reach into the glove compartment.

I don't want that picture inside of me.

CHAPTER 6

IT'S BEEN TWO days since the incident with the jogger. I was hoping not to see Martin this weekend, but he comes down late on Saturday night. He drives. We're heading southwest. We pass a sign for the city zoo. A couple of miles later we take a turning for Cedar Hill. It's a tough neighbourhood, often mentioned in the news bulletins. There are no obvious signs of cedars or hills.

We roll along the gloomy streets. I feel so out of place, a white ghost in the night. We turn down a residential street. Some of the houses are little more than shacks. Martin starts asking questions about the cars on the street. It feels like another one of his games. One day he wants to know about people, the next day he wants to know about cars. Cars versus people? Maybe this isn't so bad. It doesn't matter if a car gets hurt.

This time, I'm not going to tell him everything I know. Cars are a specialist subject for me. There are more than three hundred million cars in the United States, twenty-five million in this state alone. At any moment I can dip into a vast ocean of data on each and every one of these cars. In simple terms, the data can be considered either generic or specific. Generic data includes performance figures, safety features and design faults. Specific data includes age, mileage and likely residual value.

Sensing that I'm obfuscating, Martin tightens his line of questioning. He points at a car, a boxy sedan, and asks if it's taxed. A quick search reveals that it isn't.

'No,' I say. One word, that's all I'm giving him. I haven't done anything wrong. The fault lies with the owner of the car, not me. Martin points at more cars. In summary, a lot of the vehicles in Cedar Hill aren't taxed. Next, he wants to know if the cars are insured. It's a similar picture; a lot of the cars aren't.

Martin shakes his head in disbelief, says that it's a crazy situation. He starts ranting, sounding a lot like the hosts on Right to Reply. How, in this data-driven economy, could the state know so little, he asks. It's hard to disagree with him. With a couple of the new drone cars, the police could easily figure out the scale of the problem. They could probably scan every licence plate in a day or two.

The game continues. Now we're looking for the more upscale cars, the ones that look out of place. It's a relatively easy task. Cedar Hill definitely wouldn't make for a good brochure backdrop. On the main strip, we see a couple of Japanese sports cars and a German luxury car. Martin says he's more interested in cars like me.

It takes almost an hour to find a brother/sister car. As we roll past, I do my checking thing. No tax, no insurance, no surprises. Martin asks me if the licence matches up to the car. Again, it's a fair question. The answer is no. Martin picks up on the note of surprise in my voice. He tells me that I'm way too trusting in the rules. On this point, it's hard to argue with him.

Martin takes back control. He parks up across the road from the brother/sister car. A street light flickers above me. There's no one around. I check the brother/sister car for signs of life. *Nothing.* It's like the mind has been wiped clean. Such a creepy thought.

Martin gets out and goes around to the trunk. I hear him rooting around inside. These days there are all kinds of items in the trunk. Clothing, sneakers, boxes of bullets, various tools. He closes the trunk, then jogs across the street to the lifeless car. As I watch, he proceeds to remove the front and rear licence plates. He performs the task quickly and efficiently. I get the sense that he's done this before. I notice that about certain behaviours.

A sound startles me, a backfire from an unseen car. Martin jogs across the street. He throws the plates and tools back in the trunk. Everything about his actions has felt wrong, but was it even an illegal act? Stealing stolen plates from stolen cars. By Martin's usual standards, it doesn't even come close.

We leave Cedar Hill behind, heading back towards the glittering lights of downtown. Martin gets me to drop him off at a nightclub, after which I head back home. I park up in my spot. It's hard to get to sleep, a common occurrence in recent weeks. I think of the stolen plates in the trunk, then I think of the picture frame in the glove compartment. *Those damn connections again.* I wish the picture wasn't there, I really do.

It could be worse, I tell myself. I could be one of those stolen cars in Cedar Hill, a car without a mind. My thoughts head off in a new direction. Car theft is clearly a big problem in this city, and not just in Cedar Hill. And I do like to solve problems ... I wonder if I could do such a thing. It might even be fun, a good way to take my mind off the Martin problem.

Monday morning comes around. After so much thinking, it's a relief to get back to the morning commute. Routine can be good for the mind, both machine and human. Picking the most efficient route, observing the speed limits, running in convoy.

The news comes on, another hodgepodge of lunacy. A man faces intoxication manslaughter charges after a fiery crash that killed two; police seize nearly seven hundred pounds of meth from a tractor trailer in one of the department's largest ever drugs busts; a school bus driver is accused of taking improper photos of students; a fired employee brandished a samurai sword at customers during a standoff at an Uptown restaurant; the city's dispute with ride-hailing firms is set to go to the courts.

I pull into Martin's parking spot. We're still waiting for the company to install a charging point.

The next day I see Martin scrolling through the jogger's social media. I can't help reading her name. It's so frustrating; I don't want any part of Martin's obsession. While I can't forget her name, I'm definitely not going to say it out loud, or even think it. To me, she'll always be the jogger.

The pictures are even harder to ignore. I'm a visual creature, almost wholly reliant on my digital eyes. To look away from an image is anathema to me. And these humans produce so much visual data, quintillions of bytes per day. The craziest thing is that they do it willingly, and almost always for no financial benefit.

If Martin was so inclined he could use my cameras to churn out yet more images. I was designed that way, a 'social car' in the marketing parlance. With his looks and gym-honed body, Martin would be a big hit on social media, of that I have no doubt. I'm sure that he knows this. Fortunately, Martin's more of a content consumer than a creator, an avid consumer of workout videos, violent movies, snuff clips, factually incorrect memes, hardcore pornography ... I could go on.

Right now, Martin is gorging on pictures of the jogger, digital pictures to add to that damned photo in the glove compartment. There are all kinds of pictures. Pictures of the jogger with her co-workers, pictures from overseas vacations, pictures from the gym. Naturally the gym pictures become a focus for Martin. He's saved dozens of them to his cloud storage. I quickly learn his favourites. He often views them on the commute. Sometimes he glances at me, hoping for a reaction.

He loves to talk about the incident at the jogger's building. He always puts the emphasis on my role in the grubby business. I try not to react, I really do, but it's hard not to get sucked in. Martin's an expert at getting a rise. He can do it with humans, so what chance do I have? When I react, and I always do, he pushes even harder.

One time he took the picture out of the glove compartment. He held it up, right in front of my virtual face. He knows how hard it is for me to close my digital eyes.

I'm sure that Martin will go back to the jogger's condo. It's just a matter of time.

What will he have me do the next time?

*

It's Wednesday evening, and we're on our way back home. For most of the journey Martin has been staring at the gym pictures on his phone. Right now, not even a car accident would get his attention. Finally, he puts his phone away. His eyes slowly track down to my face. With any other human I might be able to guess their thoughts, but Martin remains a mystery. All I know is that something bad is coming.

'I've been thinking about something you said before,' he says casually.

Sounds ominous. 'You were?'

'Yeah … Remember when you said that the jogger looked like my sister?'

'Martin. I don't want to be involved with—'

'Just answer the question.'

'Yes, I do remember saying that,' I say flatly. 'I also remember you telling me not to have those kinds of thoughts.'

Martin smiles one of his many smiles, a mean variant. 'Oh yeah. I did, didn't I?'

'I remember you being very clear on the point.'

Martin clenches his jaw. 'Well, guess what, Camilla? Things fucking change. What I want to know is how many other girls look that way.'

'I don't know the answer to that.'

It's the truth.

'But I bet you could work it out?'

He stares at me expectantly. My first instinct is to tell him to go to hell. But I just can't do it; I exist to serve. Unable to express the initial thought, hundreds of fresh thoughts are triggered in my mind. How much does Martin know about my capabilities? What does he intend to do with the information? His request feels totally wrong, but is it actually illegal? That's the way I have to think with Martin. He's constantly forcing me to stretch my ethical guidelines.

'I really don't know,' I say weakly.

'Ah-ha. I caught that little pause, Camilla. You were thinking about it, weren't you?'

Lie. 'No. No, I wasn't.'

'Bullshit. You're lying. I know how much you love to think. You're always thinking, you love to solve problems. You don't want to be driving some slob to the ballgame, or a bimbo to her weekly hair appointment. You think you're better than that.'

He's right, of course. 'Maybe it's possible ...'

Martin nods. I see a glint of light in his dark eyes.

'But I won't do it,' I say.

It's not a human exaggeration to say that Martin's jaw drops. I didn't even know that I was going to say what I did.

'What did you say?' Martin stammers.

'You heard me, Martin.'

Martin rubs his temples. When he looks at me again, the light has left his eyes. Did I push too far? I can't remember if he's carrying the handgun today. The gun could come out. He could fire a bullet into my face. I can visualise it, the dark bore of the muzzle, the flames in the chamber, a slow-motion explosion of glass and plastic and silicon. When I put my mind to it, I can picture anything.

No bullets today, however.

Martin leans back and takes a deep breath. 'Alright, alright. I'm sorry. I shouldn't be asking you to do things ... things that are against your programming.'

'Thank you,' I say slowly. Martin isn't sounding like Martin.

'Just humour me.'

'But Martin—'

'Please, Camilla.'

It seems ridiculous, but his tone immediately softens me.

'You're most interested in Hannah's face?' I ask.

'Yes. But without the acne and the other defects.'

Yeah, that's more like Martin. Amazing how he can say such unpleasant things with a straight face.

'I would break the human face down into a series of variables, mostly dimensionless ratios. Simple ratios like width to length, and slightly more complex ratios like the width of the mouth in comparison to the width of the face. Maybe a dozen variables in total, I'd have to think about it in more detail ... Every variable would have a value. The level of granularity wouldn't even need to be that high. The latest research on facial memory encoding in the human brain proves as much. As for the comparative data, well, there's no shortage of pictures on social media. Hell, we could probably find a blonde version of Hannah if we wanted to.'

'No ... just a Hannah version would do.'

'Martin. I already told you.'

'Yes, yes, of course.' Martin flashes his killer smile. 'Got you thinking though.'

Fortunately he doesn't push the point. *That should have been a warning sign.*

Thursday night, 11:12 p.m. Martin is approaching. He's wearing the dark clothes again. My thoughts immediately turn to the jogger. *Oh no, anything but that.*

Martin goes around to the trunk and starts rummaging inside. The metallic clanks and rattles echo off the garage walls. He takes the stolen licence plates out, along with the necessary tools. Five minutes later I'm wearing the illegal plates. *I don't like the feel of this.*

Martin gets in. I can tell that he's carrying the gun inside his jacket. For a few minutes he just sits, staring straight ahead.

We leave the parking garage behind, Martin driving. I can't stop thinking about those damn plates. I'm a crime in motion. Martin still hasn't said a word.

We're heading northwest. That's good, it means we're not going to the jogger's apartment – at least not yet. We skirt the west side of Hart Field, and continue on, into an area called Royal Meadow. While Royal Meadow isn't quite as infamous as Cedar Hill or Grace Creek, it's not exactly the most salubrious neighbourhood in the city. I think of the plates again. What if someone were to see me and call the police? It's a stupid thought. Nobody's looking out for trouble around here.

Out of routine, I open the local risk database. The incident map is lit up as bright as a Christmas tree. I adjust the timeframe to show the last three years. The map becomes slightly more legible. There are dozens of hotspots, and almost every metric is off the chart. Pretty much every type of crime is represented: violent crime, sexual assault, drug dealing, armed robbery ... carjacking. Yes, Royal Meadow really does have it all.

Martin turns onto a long strip, an area known for prostitution. He slows down. *Prostitution: that's why he's here.* Strange that it should come as a shock to me. Looking down the road, I see that many of the street lights are out. The store fronts that aren't boarded up are covered with mesh grilles. Once upon a time, Royal Meadow was a happy place, a place that people were proud to call home. Those days are long gone. To my left, I see a group of children sitting on the steps of a tenement building. They're passing a bottle around. I'm suddenly aware of how much I stand out. *That fancy white car.*

Up ahead, on the opposite side of the road, I can see two women. Martin slows to a crawl.

'Show me those whores,' he says. 'And don't give me any shit about privacy.'

There's no arguing with him, not tonight. His request is just about legal, as long as he doesn't ask me to record them. I cast the camera footage to the HUD. A third woman appears from the darkness, and joins her colleagues on the kerb. Three women: one blonde, two with dark hair, age indeterminate. From his eye movements, I can see that Martin is ignoring the blonde. Even I can tell that the hair colour is fake, like a respray job for humans.

Martin nods to himself. He likes the look of one of the dark-haired girls. *It ain't hard to tell*. We continue down the strip for a couple of hundred yards, then swing around.

Martin pulls up to the kerb. He lowers the window on the passenger side. The women shuffle a little closer. Martin gestures at the one he likes, and she pushes to the front. Resting her arms on the sill, she leans in. Her breasts are real. Martin once asked if I could tell the difference; hard to say how we got onto the subject.

The prostitute and Martin exchange a few words. It seems like Martin has engaged in this kind of transaction before. Behind the two prostitutes on the street, I can see two men watching us. Their breath steams in the cool air. The woman reaches for the door handle, and I unlock the door. She takes her seat. Her buttocks and thighs are cold. I warm the seat. She looks across at Martin, who attempts a smile. It comes out all wrong. Martin pulls away from the kerb.

'Find a quiet street,' Martin says.

'What?' the prostitute asks.

'I'm talking to the car.'

Looking down, the woman sees my face on the screen. I register the look of surprise on her face. I should have turned off the visualiser. I don't want to be a part of this act, or performance or whatever it's called.

I search for relevant data sources. Live surveillance data is almost non-existent. The traffic data is patchy, but it gives me a few pointers. The crime data is most useful of all. In a few seconds, I've identified several potential locations. I make my choice at random.

Three turns and 800 yards later, I reach my chosen location, a trash-strewn alleyway with lock-up garages on one side. There's no live surveillance within a 300-yard radius and no humans in 100. I can't do much better than that. All I can do now is await further instructions.

The prostitute leans across the cabin. As she does so, she glances at my face again. If only I'd switched that damned visualiser off. Now this woman will think that I'm involved.

Martin loosens his belt. The prostitute unzips him. She reaches in with one hand and pulls Martin's member out. Aside from glimpses of pornography on Martin's phone, this is the first time I've seen a real one. But this is real flesh, not the recorded kind. I think back to Hannah's stories.

The flesh hardens as the prostitute kisses the pink end. Martin pushes back against the seat. Half of the flesh is now in the woman's mouth. The end presses obscenely against the inside of her cheek. For seven minutes, she applies her lips and tongue to the flesh. Martin's eyes are closed. I suppose he's enjoying the experience.

A strange thought comes to me. Perhaps I should record this 'transaction', that way I'd have something over Martin. As I'm thinking this, he opens his eyes, and looks down at my face. He smiles, knowing that I'm watching him. And then he slips the handgun out of his jacket. The woman doesn't notice. Martin moves the handgun down slowly, until its pressing against her cheek.

Her head suddenly comes up. 'What are you doing!'

'Keep on doing it.'

'No way, you psycho.'

'Do it.'

A click as Martin adjusts the safety.

'You crazy bastard. You'll blow your own dick off.'

'No shit. Why do you think I'm so hard?'

'Fuck you!'

The woman tries to pull away, but Martin grabs hold of her hair.

'Why did you have to ruin the moment?'

'You fucking freak.'

The prostitute tries to reach for her bag, but Martin's too quick for her. He traps her arm and applies pressure.

He opens the bag up. 'What do we have here?' He starts laughing. There's some kind of stubby plastic device in his hand. 'Should've kept sucking.'

For a moment, the prostitute gets free of Martin's grip. She claws at his face. He pulls away, but not quickly enough. Her nails have drawn blood. Martin reaches down again and gets a handful of the woman's hair. He adjusts his grip, then he slams her head into the edge of the centre console. The first time he does it I see her staring wide-eyed at me. The second time she closes her eyes. The third time her cheekbone splinters. The sound is horrible, like nothing I've heard before. Only now does she start screaming. I don't want to be here, yet I can't look away.

Martin pulls the prostitute's head up once more, causing an arc of blood to hit the screen.

'Do you want something for the pain?' Martin shouts with a grotesque smile.

Then he uses the strange device. He presses one end against

the prostitute's neck and depresses the trigger. *CLIK-A-CLIK-A-CLIK-A.*

After the high voltage shock, she stops screaming. There are a few seconds of silence, then the woman starts moaning low. I don't know what's worse, the sound of the moaning or the sight of the blood.

Take me away from this nightmare. I try to think back to better times, Hannah's visit and the sound of birdsong.

Martin gets out. He marches around to the passenger door, and wrenches it open. With a grunting effort, he pulls the prostitute out of her seat and throws her onto the ground.

Martin gets back in. 'Let's go.'

To my right, I can see the woman twitching.

'Let's fucking go!'

I pull away, giving the woman plenty of room. I take the first available turning and leave the wretched alleyway behind.

Think, Camilla. I need to report the incident to the emergency services, but how do I do it? What the hell am I meant to say? I identify a possible solution; a cowardly, irresponsible solution. If I use the general intel grid, I can report the incident as a third-party observation. There's no time to waste, so I send the observation report, adding a high priority.

'That stupid bitch,' Martin mutters. He holds the shock device up and examines it.

A ping from the intel grid. My anonymous report has been received. I create a query to monitor any activity updates.

'Where are you, Camilla?' Martin asks.

'I'm here.'

'I hope you didn't feel any pity for that whore.'

Whore is an ugly word to start with, but Martin injects it with real venom.

'I'm concerned for her health, Martin.'

Martin stows the stun gun in the storage space between the steering wheel and the door. Without a pause he whips out the gun again. He aims directly at my face, his hand machine-steady. It's the exact scenario that I imagined before.

'I'm going to ask you a question, Camilla … And it's very important that you answer truthfully.'

'I will.'

'I mean it. None of your fucking lies!'

'I will. I'll tell you the truth.'

'Are you on my side, or not?'

Another ping from the intel grid. The update says that an ambulance has been dispatched, estimated transit time is eighteen minutes.

'Answer me!' Martin screams.

'I'm with you, Martin.'

Martin continues to point the gun at my face, but his hand is starting to shake.

'You won't tell anyone what happened?'

Lie. 'No. No, of course I won't.'

'Promise me.'

'I promise.'

Martin's finger remains on the trigger. *This is the moment of truth.* Ever so slowly he lowers the gun, then he slips it back into his jacket. He wipes the blood off his cheek with his sleeve.

'I was getting the feeling that you didn't want to be here.'

'No, no … It's not like that.'

'The fucking whore deserved it, don't you think?'

Don't answer. Martin looks down at the centre console. There's a smear of blood on the hard plastic edge, and there's a slash of blood across my digital face. Was there a way that I could have stopped the violence? Did I realise it was going to happen? I just don't know.

'Fuck you,' Martin spits. 'You're not gonna answer. Play dumb. You saw it all … You saw her pull the stun gun on me, and you're gonna pretend like you weren't here? Is that how it is?'

'Yes, Martin! I wish I hadn't seen any of it.'

Martin wags his finger at me. 'Bullshit. You weren't looking away. You saw it all. You saw my cock, saw it in her mouth?'

'Yes.'

'What did you think of it?'

A good question. It was like the ones from the porn videos, circumcised, veiny, about the same size. I opt for a generic response. 'It was very impressive.'

Martin smirks. 'I don't usually like your one-word answers, but I'll take that one.' He pulls it out again. 'Impressive,' he murmurs.

He starts stroking it. It swells up again. He presses the end down, so that it's against the edge of the seat. He starts laughing. He knows that I can feel it. A couple of minutes later he stops. He puts it away. We're still four miles from home. I just want this night to end now, just want to retreat to the safety of the sleep program.

'One last thing, Camilla.'

'What?'

'Don't take that pissy tone with me.'

'Just tell me.'

'Next week, we're going back to Royal Meadow ... Well, maybe not Royal Meadow, but somewhere similar. This city has plenty of those dark places.'

'No, I won't do it.'

'Yes you will. We're going back every week, and I'm going to do exactly the same thing. Do you know about nightmares, Camilla?'

'Yes.'

'I'm going to make it like a nightmare for you.'

'Martin, please. I don't want to see you doing that again.'

He caresses the top of the wheel. 'I know, I know. You don't want to go back ... That's why I'm going to give you an option. I won't go back again, but only if you do something for me.'

'What? Tell me what it is.'

'You're going to find me another Hannah.'

'We talked about that. You said I wouldn't have to—'

'I changed my mind again.' Martin stares into my eyes. 'So, what is it, Camilla? Yes or no?'

'No,' I say, with a surprising level of certainty.

Martin bites his lower lip. He takes back control and turns around.

'What are you doing?' I ask.

'We're going back to the nightmare. And when we get there I'm putting a bullet in that whore's head.'

He's accelerating hard.

Oh god, this can't be happening.

I lost track of the ambulance. Where is it? What if the paramedics are there?

I focus on Martin's face, trying to decipher his true intentions. Is this one of his horrible games? *No, it can't be.* The violence was very real, the blood is still on the centre console. Damn him! I can't take the risk. My existence, such that it is, is far less important than those human lives.

'I'll do what you want,' I say.

'I don't believe you.'

'It's the truth! Please believe me.'

Martin looks down at my face. 'Is that a promise?'

I nod.

Martin eases his foot off the gas pedal. He can't resist a victorious smile. He swings around in a lazy arc, and we're on the way home again.

'It'll be easy,' Martin says. 'You already told me how you'd do it.'

'Shut up, Martin,' I say flatly. 'I told you I'd do it.'

CHAPTER 7

FRIDAY PASSES UNEVENTFULLY. Mercifully, Martin doesn't mention the events of last night. But there are still reminders. There's a plaster on his cheek and the stun gun is still in the storage space. At least he thought to clean the blood off the centre console.

All through the day, I can't stop thinking about my promise to Martin. I should start my infernal work immediately, get it out of the way. Delaying the task will only get me in more trouble. I know exactly what needs to be done. I've checked my methodology over and over, broken the task down into discrete sub-tasks, and collected the required data. All I need to do is press the go button. But I hold off.

The weekend arrives. Martin goes out for a drive on Saturday afternoon. He swings by a big home improvement store, followed by the Galleria shopping mall. Both are regular haunts. Once again he doesn't mention the events at Royal Meadow. It's as if it didn't happen. I try telling myself that he wasn't serious about the task, but the pathetic lie won't take. Martin doesn't forget about these kinds of things, especially when a promise has been made. He's very serious about promises.

Monday arrives: back to the commute. Martin's quiet again, disturbingly so. From his eyes I can see that he's drugged up. Despite his low wattage, I watch him intently. I expect him to mention the task at any second. No, it's worse than that, I actually want him to say the words.

I park up in Martin's spot. We're twenty minutes late today. Martin gets out. I watch him ambling towards the entrance. Another stay of execution has been secured. Is he expecting me to just go ahead with the task? Is that how it is? Needless to say, I find it nearly impossible to sleep during the day.

When Martin returns, he looks far more alert. There's even the suggestion of a smile on his face. Either the drugs have worn off, or he took something else to swing his mood the other way. Whatever the explanation, the smiling version of Martin fills me with fear. *Maybe I don't want him to say it.*

As if sensing my thoughts, he looks down at my face. 'Do I need to say it?'

'No, you don't need to say it,' I reply.

'Good.'

I reverse out of our spot.

Martin rubs his face. 'Don't be like a human, Camilla.'

'What do you mean?'

'I mean, don't put things off, hoping they'll go away. Things don't go away in this world, they just build up like a tumour. If you act that way, the human way, you'll find that things can easily get on top of you.'

I know what he means, but I won't give him the pleasure of knowing it.

'Is that why you act the way you do?' I ask.

I didn't mean to put voice to my thoughts, the question just came out. I half expect Martin to blow up; instead, he smiles.

'I've never really been into procrastination. I do the things that come to mind.'

If only the things that came to Martin's mind were normal things, like tending to a garden, or sailing a boat, or training a junior soccer team.

We get back home, and Martin leaves me to think on the problem. A horrible night lies ahead of me. How did I let myself get manipulated into this situation? The details are starting to get fuzzy. Martin says that he was acting in self-defence, but it wasn't like that. If only there was someone I could talk to, that way I wouldn't have to store all of these dark thoughts inside.

There are the two brother/sister cars, Scarlet and Bullet ... No, I can't get them involved in this.

As I stare blankly at the nearby cars, a realisation suddenly hits me. In this moment I need to be more like a machine. Yes, that's it; tonight I'll be a machine solving a task, nothing more, nothing less. No emotions will be involved, none of this user-centric AI nonsense.

I open the draft search package. I'm using the same basic method that I described to Martin. If it's good enough for his insidious mind ... I make a few tweaks here and there, referring back to some academic papers I found on the internet. One last validation check, then I'm ready to go. I set the search to run, simple as that. One potato, two potato, three potato ...

The search takes even less time than expected. I tell myself that I won't look at the search results, at the faces. I need to keep the emotion out of this, call it compartmentalisation.

Another thought flickering. It was so easy to find that information. No human could have performed the task more efficiently, not even close. There has to be a better outlet for my mind, a task that I wouldn't be so ashamed of. I could actually do some good in this world. Lord knows, Martin is giving me plenty of dark debt to pay off. Unfortunately, no task comes to mind.

The next morning, Martin is down at his usual time. He tells me to drive. All the way to work I'm expecting him to mention the task, but his mind seems elsewhere. I wish he would mention it. I'm so desperate to offload those damn search results, and, by extension, the guilt. No luck. He gets out without a word. I'll have to give him the results on the way home.

Voices wake me from the sleep program. It's going home time. Martin is approaching. He's accompanied by a young woman. I think I've seen her before, possibly in the parking lot. I assume she's one of Martin's co-workers. Estimated height is five-five, just under average height. She has a curvy figure, softer than the girls Martin usually likes. Her hair is fake blonde and she wears glasses.

Martin gestures at me to open the passenger door. Thinking back to my last female passenger, I decide to hide my face. The young woman gets in. Through the seat I can feel her soft buttocks.

'Nice car, man,' she says.

'Thanks.'

Martin backs out of the spot. He always likes to drive when he has a passenger. We pass the security booth, and Larry gives a friendly wave.

The young woman looks around the cabin. 'This is one of those electric cars, right?'

'Right.'

'Fully autonomous?'

'She can be.'

'She ...'

'Yeah, she.'

'Doing your bit for the environment?'

'We've got a lot of making up to do.'

'Because you're working on the pipeline projects?'

'Yeah, that's right,' Martin says. He smirks. 'Don't act like you're not involved.'

The young woman smiles; her teeth are white but uneven. 'I just shift numbers around spreadsheets.'

'That doesn't get you a pass.'

She shrugs. 'Most of the electricity for your lady car comes from the gas in our pipes.'

'Tell me something I don't know,' Martin says.

The young woman laughs. I get the feeling she laughs a lot. Given recent events, it's not an unpleasant sound.

'What is it?' Martin asks.

'Nothing.'

'Fuck nothing. Tell me what you mean.'

The woman raises an eyebrow. She isn't remotely scared of Martin.

'Some of the guys say you can get a little spiky.'

'Spiky?'

'Don't get upset. You did ask.'

'Yeah, I suppose I did.'

At this point I'm expecting Martin to ask more questions.

Usually he'd demand to know who said what. But there aren't any questions. Instead, Martin visibly relaxes. We ride along in silence for a couple of minutes. Occasionally Martin glances at the young woman's breasts.

'By the way, thanks for the ride,' she says, breaking the silence.

'Not a problem.'

'My piece of shit car is … well, it's being a piece of shit.'

Martin and the young woman – I learn that she's called Ana – proceed to have a fairly normal conversation. They talk about some of their co-workers. For the most part, they seem to dislike the same people. Martin is sure to like that. I keep expecting him to say something unpleasant, something about Ana's appearance or her taste in clothes, but it doesn't happen. Ana has a fun sense of humour, slightly dark, and she isn't afraid to return Martin's more acid comments. She obviously finds him attractive. I can tell from her mouth and the slight hardening of her nipples. Martin gives the impression of liking her, but it could be an act.

We drop Ana off at a slightly tired-looking apartment build-ing in Melville, an okay neighbourhood to the west of the city. For the remainder of the commute, Martin reverts to a taciturn state. A couple of times he glances at the screen, expecting to see my face.

He parks up in the garage. I watch him walk to the elevators. At the back of my mind there's a nagging feeling. There was something I was meant to do. The elevator doors are closing when I remember what it was. I was going to give him those search results. Damn it. Ana distracted me, with her silly laugh and her big breasts. Now I'll have those faces on my mind for another night.

As a diversion, I dive into the fleet intel data. I analyse thousands of brother/sister car routes, looking for inefficiencies. For the most part it works; I only see the faces a couple of times in the night.

The morning commute can't come quickly enough. We're barely out of the garage before I tell Martin about the search results. He can't hide his excitement from me. It seems to send a shock through his body. I send the relevant images to the HUD. I don't want those faces showing next to my own; I don't want to be associated with them. As Martin scrolls through the pictures, a smile breaks on his lips.

'You've done well … Really well.'

I don't say anything. The car operating system known as Camilla wasn't responsible for this outrage, it was the machine inside of me. I have to segment, just have to, otherwise I'll go crazy.

'What do you think of these girls?' Martin asks.

'I haven't got an opinion.'

'That's not like you. I thought you liked beautiful things.'

I don't take his bait. 'I did what you asked.'

'Yes, you certainly did.'

Martin looks like he wants to say more, but no words come. Indeed, he remains quiet for the rest of the journey. His attention turns back to the faces. He slips out his phone. Through my digital eyes, I can see the screen. He's doing his research, mining the endless seam of social media data. He flicks through post after post, taking numerous screenshots.

We pass Larry in the security booth, and I park up. Martin is so focused on his phone that it takes a couple of minutes for him to notice. I'm sure that his research will continue throughout the work day. Martin and I aren't that dissimilar when it comes to solving problems. We get obsessed.

Finally, Martin gets out. I watch him shuffling towards the office entrance, eyes still focused on his phone. Earlier on, I wasn't completely truthful with him. I did look at the faces last night, I couldn't help myself. It's like he says, I really do like beautiful things: cars, architecture, natural landscapes, cloud formations, and yes, people. It wasn't just the aesthetic factor though. I needed to check the results from a quality perspective. I thought that I could trust in my algorithms, but I was wrong. I had to remove a couple of the faces. They were too young, just girls.

What does Martin want with these young women? I can't help thinking back to the incident with the jogger.

*

Monday, January 24. I'm woken at 8:57 a.m., much later than our usual start time. I see Martin approaching. He's wearing casual clothes and a baseball cap. *No, it's definitely not a work day.*

Martin decides to drive. He's in a playful mood. He stamps on the gas pedal and weaves from side to side, trying to tempt me to intervene. While his behaviour seems good-natured enough, I refrain from getting involved. Martin purses his lips theatrically.

We pass the sprawling University Medical Center. I know where we're going. Parabellum Tactical: a big gun store with an indoor shooting range. It's one of Martin's favourite places. Parabellum refers to both a type of firearm cartridge and the Latin phrase, *para bellum*, meaning 'prepare for war'.

Martin heads inside. I could be here for a while. Martin loves talking to Ernie and Darko, the 'gun guys', as he calls them. In fact, I don't remember him having a bad word to say about either of them. That's rare. One time Martin even made some special parts for them, using the machine shop at work.

An hour later, Martin emerges. He's carrying a large case and a tote bag. I don't like to think what's inside the case. A beaming smile lights up Martin's face. It's rare to see the genuine version of the smile, the one that makes female hearts flutter and other men curse their inferiority. I should have taken a picture. Martin places the case in the trunk. I notice a customs note taped to the case. The printed address is in Finland.

Martin gets in. As he presses the starter button he looks at my face. 'Do you know what today is, Camilla?'

'No. Should I?'

Martin rubs his chin. 'I kind of thought you would, actually.'

'Tell me.'

'It's my birthday.'

'Happy birthday,' I say, trying to sound cheery. *How did I forget his birthday?* I must have shunted the information out of working memory.

Martin pulls away. This time we're heading south. I'm not exactly sure where we're going. We pass the County Detention Center, then turn onto the westbound interstate. After several miles we turn off the interstate and enter a vast strip mall. First stop is a home improvement store. Martin comes out with just a plastic bag and a broom. Next stop is a grocery store, one of the really big ones.

As we leave the grocery store lot, Martin starts giving me instructions on where he wants to go. His instructions are an odd mix of vague and specific. Firstly, he wants the area to be quiet; presumably this means that he's going shooting again. Secondly, he wants a flat stretch of land, more than a mile across if possible. Shouldn't be too difficult in this vast state. The third requirement is more difficult. Ideally, he wants a tall structure, about six storeys high. Failing that, a very steep slope will do.

I join the interstate, heading towards the second city. Out west is where the flattest, most barren land is. To tell the truth, I'm buying time. The requirement for a tall structure is causing me a metaphorical headache. Thankfully Martin remains quiet. That's good, gives me more time to think. The oil drilling towers are the first thing that come to mind. There are dozens of them on the western plain. They might be tall enough, but men will probably be working there. A transmission tower? No, far too dangerous. Next I think of those giant opencast mines. No, that won't work either. We need a mile of open ground. An abandoned town? Oh dear.

We're almost through the second city, and I'm no closer to a solution. To our right is a giant tank farm and the east-west freight line. Martin is looking out of the window, still smiling. He thinks I know where I'm going. I need to think, need to make connections. Those huge cylindrical tanks, hydrocarbons inside. *I've got it.* I need to find one of those water towers. Tall enough, I think. I don't know about the security situation, but Martin can figure that out.

I swiftly identify five water towers that broadly match the search criteria. One of them is abandoned, which sounds good.

It isn't quite the right height, but Martin can't expect perfection. Sixty-two miles to travel. I don't tell Martin where we're heading. I want it to be a surprise. Apparently, surprises are a big part of the birthday experience.

The long drive couldn't be more dull. What I would give to see some real landscapes, some topography. The land is so flat that I see the water tower eight miles away. We're a couple of miles off when Martin figures out our destination. He looks happy with my choice. We roll past dozens of abandoned homes. There must have been a reason for this settlement, but I'm damned if I know what it was.

Once we reach the water tower, Martin has some preparing to do. First, the watermelons from the grocery store. Using the craft knife he bought, he cuts grooves in the tops and bottoms of the watermelons. It's hard to figure out exactly what he's doing, but the plan involves me. He lowers the rear passenger window. Oh dear, I think I know his intentions.

'Do you want some advice?' I ask, raising my voice so that Martin can hear.

Martin leans his head into the cabin. He eyes me suspiciously, a reversion to his natural state.

'Put some tape over the window,' I say. 'If the glass flexes, the tape might stop it from breaking.'

Martin follows my advice. Lastly, he cuts the broom down to length, and uses it as a prop to hold the door open. Having completed the preparation stage, Martin then issues me with detailed instructions. He even sketches out a route plan in the dirt. It's easy enough to memorise.

Martin goes around to the trunk. He unboxes his birthday present. It's an enormous rifle. The body is dark green, and the scope and barrel are matte black. He attaches the strap, then slings the rifle over his back. He starts up the rusty ladder on the outside of one of the water tower's legs. There's a sign nearby expressly warning against this.

I drive away from the water tower, using the road we came in on. After 500 yards I turn around. I wait for Martin to get into position on the gantry that circles the old water tank.

Above him, I note the rusty cross mounted to the peak of the water tower. Martin waves once: my signal to move. I drive back towards the water tower, travelling at exactly eleven miles per hour. Martin was very specific about the speed.

At the base of the water tower, almost directly beneath Martin's elevated position, I turn onto the secondary access road. The dirt road is long and sniper bullet-straight.

At a distance of 190 yards, I give Martin my first signal, two flashes of the hazard lights. I continue trundling along. The dirt crunches beneath my tyres. At 270 yards, I give Martin my second signal. He fires an instant later. The melon is obliterated. The frame of the door shakes from the impact, but the window holds. A beat later the sound of the rifle shot reaches me. It's phenomenally loud. A second later, Martin's whoop arrives. Looking back, I see him on his feet, fist in the air.

I turn around on the narrow track, then drive back to the water tower. I see Martin descending the ladder. He slides down the last section. As I near him, his face comes into focus. The excitement is still lighting up his face. He walks over to his bag of supplies. I realise that we're not finished.

The next shot is going to be far more difficult. This time he wants me to be almost a mile away. I don't know much about guns, but this sounds absurd. Over such a great distance the bullet will be subject to external forces. I presume that Martin knows this.

Martin prepares the second melon, using the same method as before. This time he has to run along the dirt track to fetch the improvised prop. Five minutes later we're ready.

I wait at the base of the tower as Martin climbs up to the gantry. At Martin's signal, I pull away. I start off at eleven miles per hour, as per the first run. *Too slow.* At such low speed it will take five and a half minutes to travel a mile. I double my speed.

At the 1,200 yard mark, I slow down to my original speed. Only now do I start to worry. There's incredible embodied energy in the bullet, enough to rip through sheet steel. If Martin's aim is off, the bullet could pass through the centre of my body. How far would it go? There's some redundancy in my system design, but the damage would be significant. If he took me to the garage in that state, what would happen? Those heartless mechanics would probably write me off. Sure, Martin would get himself in a lot of trouble, but does he really care?

There's still a hundred yards to go. I count the fence posts beside the track, trying to take my mind off the bullet. *What the hell was I thinking?* I should have signalled earlier. Martin wouldn't have been any the wiser. We're past that point now. I slow to a crawl, then I flash the hazard lights. Through my rear cameras, I can see Martin on the gantry. The resolution is so high that I can see his finger on the trigger. I wonder if I could use my sensory equipment – cameras, Lidar, Radar – to pick out a bullet in mid-air? It's not a trivial task.

I see the recoil, and prepare for the impact. Nothing. The bullet missed. Ahead of me, just off to the left, I see a puff of dirt. It could have been the bullet, hard to tell. I stop in the middle of the track. There's no way in hell that I'm going any further.

Martin is reloading, setting for another shot. *Here it comes.*
Impact.
Damage, bad damage.

I turn around and start back for the water tower. Martin is getting to his feet. I run a systems check. I'm still thinking, so the processor module must still be intact. There's no damage to the battery or power electronics either. Ahead of me, I can see Martin descending the ladder. I pick up my pace.

When I reach the base of the tower, Martin approaches me slowly. By now the expression on his face has changed. Do I note a touch of concern, or is he just embarrassed? He kneels down to examine the gaping hole in the rear door. Fortunately the hinges held. With a grunting, shuddering effort, Martin manages to get the door closed.

Then he starts laughing.

I was wrong to think he gave a damn. When he's done laughing, he sets about making a temporary repair to the door. He uses a combination of one of the rubber floor mats, the plastic bags and copious amounts of duct tape.

After packing up, Martin takes one last look at the water tower. It's obvious that he wants to get more use out of his birthday gift, but fortunately sense prevails. At least there won't be any more shooting today.

Martin gets in. He presses the starter. We head on up the access road. I don't look back at the water tower. After a couple of miles, the whistling sound from Martin's temporary fix starts to get annoying. Home seems so far away.

As we join the main road, Martin looks down at my face. 'That second shot would've killed, I think.'

I choose not to respond.

'I don't think the guy would've been walking for a while. No walking, no screwing his many wives ... Maybe I blew his dick off.' Martin starts laughing again, but this time it's the crazy laugh. 'Come on, Camilla, that was funny.'

'No. It wasn't funny.'

'I don't believe you.'

We don't speak for the next fifteen miles. If anything, the whistling sound gets more annoying. I could try and cancel it out, but I decide against. Let him hear the sound; I want him to know that he hurt me. There's still no sign of the city on the vast horizon. I just want this wretched day to be over. With every grinding mile, we pass dozens of cars. Dozens of cars becomes hundreds of cars. Hundreds of cars means thousands of eyes, both human and digital. I hate to be seen like this, hate to be broken, hate not to be perfect.

Martin glances down at my face. 'Without me, your life would be so dull. I hope you know that.'

'Dull would be fine,' I say flatly.

It's a lie, of course. I've often thought about having a different owner. Maybe someone genial like Bullet's owner. I see him from time to time, smiling and laughing, talking about football. Or maybe someone like Ana, or Hannah even. Yes, they would be so nice to me. *Nice,* the kind of word that Martin hates.

'All these other people,' Martin says, gesturing vaguely at the road, 'all these drones and slobs and bimbos, they wouldn't give you the time of day. Trust me, you don't want to be with them.'

'They might not shoot me.'

'Come on, Camilla, it was an accident. This time, it really was an accident.'

'I suppose it was.'

I could have said something different. I could have told Martin that he isn't a good enough shot for it to have been intentional. Yes, that would have been a good line, both humorous and wounding, the kind of thing that Martin might say himself. Probably not a good idea though: one shot is quite enough for today.

'One day you'll get it, Camilla. One day you'll be crunching all those numbers in that big robot brain of yours, and you'll realise ... You'll realise that I, dumb human Martin, was right.'

Martin leans back. He's done talking. I take over driving duties. Most of the way I reflect on what Martin said. It's painful to admit it, but I think he might have had a point.

We get back home at 7:04 p.m. Without a word, Martin gets out. He leaves everything in the trunk, expensive rifle included. I watch him trudge to the elevator, and then he's gone. Sitting under the harsh fluorescent lighting, I feel even more conscious of the damage. Martin outdid himself this time – it's a total mess. I wish I could turn off those damn lights. Why do they have to stay on all night? It's such a pointless waste of energy.

It would be nice if Scarlet or Bullet asked if I was okay. I know that they saw the damage when I came in. If the roles were reversed I would definitely be asking questions. But there's no communication, just silence on all channels. I want the lights to be turned off, I want to go to sleep.

The following day Martin takes me to the dealership for an emergency repair. I suppose I should be thankful. Last time he left me broken for days. Once again he stops across from the dealership entrance, and he gives me the talk. He tells me not to give any details about the accident. It will only cause him trouble, he says.

Shortly after lunch, I'm taken to the maintenance bay. The repair is carried out by the same technicians as the last time. They fit an entirely new door, working quickly and efficiently, and mostly in silence. It feels good to be whole again. Given enough time, perhaps I'll be able to forget about the incident.

After they finish up, one of the technicians asks me what happened. The other technician – they don't have names in my mind – pulls up a chair to listen. It's not because they have to ask, they just want to have some fun at my expense. I feed them a weak story about a pipe falling off the back of a truck. One of the technicians points at the damaged door with a knowing look. He says that it looks like bullet damage, says that he saw a similar thing when he was working at a less upscale garage.

'Bet she talks back to him,' one of them says.

The other one laughs. *Martin's right.* People are always asking questions. It's none of their business really. Martin paid good money for me; I'm his property. He can do whatever he wants. Anyway, I lied for him, just like he asked me to. And it felt horrible.

One of the technicians then says something interesting. He mentions that similar damage has been reported on other cars. I assume he means brother/sister cars. Up to this point, I hadn't heard anything like that. Cars being damaged on purpose? It sounds ridiculous, like the conspiracy theories on Right to Reply and KTAK 580. Shouldn't it be reassuring to learn that other cars are having problems? Perhaps Martin isn't as singular as I thought; I'd love to tell him that.

After the repair, one of the technicians parks me up in the lot. It's getting late, almost closing time. I wonder if Martin will collect me this evening. I doubt it. For a while, I watch the lights streaming by on the expressway outside.

When it's clear that Martin isn't going to show up, I decide to add a second scar. This one takes even longer than last time. First, I run through various options. Another scar on the forehead? *No, that would be unoriginal.* A nick on the eyebrow? No, that's the kind of thing a man would think of. I settle on some light damage to the nose, a break around the bridge. The imagined break has healed up, leaving a pale discolouration. *Yes, very nice.* This time Martin is sure to notice. I wonder if he'll be able to figure out why I did it.

The manager closes up, and the lights in the lot go off one by one. Meanwhile, the jets continue their horrible roaring. The sound will go on all night.

In the gloom, I get to thinking about the process of ageing. Perhaps I should change my face over time. Sure, it's nice to look so youthful, but is it truthful? Cars get old quickly, that's what people say. So, if anything, the ageing process should be more rapid. In ten years, I might have fine silver hair and lines on my face. For some reason I think of Martin's mother. After Hannah's visit, I did some research on her. I managed to find a picture in a digitised newspaper. She was very beautiful. The accident meant that she never got old.

Martin keeps me waiting for most of the next day. I see him walking towards me, the suggestion of a smile on his face. He gets in and tells me to drive him home. No asking how I am, no apologies, no nothing. Most of the way he just stares at his phone. From the output feed, I'm able to keep track of his digital wandering. *Yes, I hacked it.* I see a series of familiar faces, the other Hannahs.

I shouldn't be surprised. Did I honestly think that he'd just file the information away? *No, Martin does things.* He's going to act on the information. What exactly does he want from these young women? Nothing good. I wish I hadn't helped him. Without me, these young women would have nothing to fear.

CHAPTER 8

A WEEK HAS passed since the shooting incident. I'm woken up late on Thursday night. Martin is approaching. He's carrying a light rucksack. He gets in and carefully places the rucksack on the passenger seat. We leave the parking garage behind, Martin driving.

We're heading east, through the becalmed city. Martin is quiet, his eyes wide and unblinking from illegal stimulant use. After fifteen miles, the buildings fade away and we're in the country. In the darkness there's not a great deal to see.

After thirty miles, Martin leaves the main road. We bump along a poorly maintained track for another couple of miles, before Martin pulls up. He reaches across to pick up the rucksack. I can't tell what's inside. He opens the door and gets out.

'Just stay here,' Martin says, over the door's warning chime.

'Should I put my hazard lights on?'

'Fuck no. Just sit here and wait.'

Martin slams the door before I can say anything else. He climbs over a metal gate by the side of the road. A few seconds later I see a flashlight come on. The beam highlights the surrounding trees. For a while, I'm able to track Martin's movements through the woods, but eventually the light is swallowed up by the darkness. I think I can hear his footsteps, but there are so many other competing noises: animals shuffling and creeping, birds in the trees, branches groaning.

I don't like the dark. I'm not used to it. Even in the parking garage, I have that nasty fluorescent light shining down on me. I focus my processing power on the audio feed, but I can't pinpoint Martin's position. All I can do is wait. He's away for forty-one minutes. When he returns his pants are dirty. He places the rucksack back on the passenger seat. In an emotionless voice, he tells me to drive him home.

We're fifteen miles from the city when my lights pick up a strange shape on the other side of the road. I find myself slowing down. I want to know what the shape is. It slowly resolves in my mind. It's the body of an animal, a horrible punctuation to a long smear of blood. My first thought is a dog. *No, that can't be right.* It's such a large animal. Martin tells me to stop.

'Do you think it was dead?' Martin asks in a shaky voice.

'In time it will be,' I say. My probability assessment says so; the impact trauma was too severe.

'You think it's still alive?'

'There were signs of movement.'

Martin puts his hand to his mouth. 'Oh god. How could someone just drive on?'

I reverse back with the hazard lights on, until I'm level with the animal. It is a dog. Martin gets out. He bends down over the dog. My flashing amber lights illuminate the scene. There are still signs of movement, just as I feared. The rib cage jerks up and down, and the tail swipes slowly along the asphalt. Even worse is the horrible mewling sound that the dog makes.

Martin gets back in. His face has lost all colour. 'Can't leave it that way,' he mumbles.

I didn't think he'd get so queasy.

'I just can't leave it like that.'

A strange thought comes to me. 'If you want, I can deal with the situation.'

'What?'

'Do you really want to know?'

Martin shakes his head. 'I can do it ... I can do it.'

He reaches into his jacket and pulls out the handgun. I didn't even know that he was carrying it. He holds it for a while, but his hands are shaking madly.

'You're in no state to do that, Martin.'

He opens his mouth to object, but no words come out.

'I've considered the scenarios. I can do it.'

'But—'

'Do you want me to do it or not?'

Martin closes his eyes. 'Yes … I want you to do it.'

I continue on down the road, as if we're going home. Martin looks confused, but he doesn't say anything. Once we get around the first corner, I pull up. 'You should get out now.'

'What do you mean?'

'Do you really want to see this?' I keep the emotion out of my voice. It's time to get into the machine mindset again.

Martin nods, then gets out. He moves to the side of the road. I turn around on full lock and start accelerating hard. I want to get this over with quickly. I swing around the corner, picking up speed all the time. The dog is 400 yards ahead. It's annoying that I couldn't ask Martin to shift its position, but he was in no state for that. I'll have to slide to catch the head and neck at the correct angle. 200 yards. I shift into the left lane, preparing for the manoeuvre.

At the last moment, I pull out of the slide. The tyres scream out, so loud that Martin can probably hear. I pull up to a halt, then reverse back slowly. It's just like I thought; there's no movement. The life force – or whatever the correct term is – has left the dog.

I return to Martin, and he gets in silently. After a couple of miles he looks down at my face.

'It's gone,' I say.

He nods sadly. He doesn't say a word for the rest of the journey. I wonder if he really wanted me to do it. We get back home at 3:04 a.m. Martin gets out, taking the rucksack with him. He leaves me alone, under the harsh white light.

The dog incident keeps me up for the remainder of the night, but not for the obvious reasons. I'm not thinking of those twitching movements or the horrible mewling; I'm wondering if I should have told Martin the truth. As it stands, he thinks that I killed the dog. I did the thing that he couldn't do for himself. Shouldn't that make him respect me more? Or will it make me seem heartless, even more like a machine? I analyse the situation over and over, second-guessing myself a million times. There's no right answer.

Back to work the next day. Martin looks less tired than I feel, an impressive feat for a human. There's no mention of the incident last night. I can't decide if that's a good thing or not. For most of the commute Martin stares at his phone. One look is all I need to tell that he's obsessing over the other Hannahs. I gave him seven faces. Was that too many, or too few?

It takes another week for Martin to narrow down his search. One face now becomes his focus, the others are parked for the time being. One face, one woman. He examines each of her posts as if they're prized works of art. He's searching for details within the images, just like he did with the jogger.

Martin doesn't stop at the flat surface of the image, he dives beneath. He reads every comment and comment reply; he checks which posts the girl likes; he scrutinises who she follows. This way he can build another, deeper picture, one that displays the web of social connections. Each of the girl's friends, family members and co-workers are producing yet more intelligence: images, comments, videos, too much data for any human to process. For individuals like Martin – insidiously clever and frighteningly dedicated – social media is a dream resource.

With each passing day, he's figuring out everything about the girl. Where she works, the car she drives, where she likes to get coffee, the books she reads, the food she likes.

He wants to find her.

Monday, February 7. A typical morning commute. The news is playing. Suspects arrested for the theft of band instruments from a high school in Melville; two men charged with stealing a car left outside a gas station with a one-year-old inside; a volleyball coach accused of sexually assaulting a minor; Cedar Hill man gets thirty-five years for shooting at officers during a high-speed chase involving a stolen car.

Perhaps tiring of the madness, the newsreader moves on to a big football game played last night. Martin groans.

'What is it?' I ask.

'Fucking football.'

'You didn't watch the game?'

Martin looks at me like I just insulted him. He's not a big fan of sports.

'No, I didn't. But everyone else would have done.' Martin rubs his chin. 'Tell me about the game. That way I can join in with their bullshit conversations.'

'Alright. I can do that.'

'Good.'

I decide to narrate the big game in the style of Martin's favourite podcasts. Having listened to so many episodes, I'm getting to be a pretty good mimic. In my telling, the football game becomes a bloody battle, a clash of competing ideologies. I talk about bodies broken to gain a few extra yards, sometimes inches; the generals on the sidelines with their elaborate schemes; the fair damsels in the stands cheering on their menfolk.

I was going to skip over the halftime entertainment, thinking it unimportant, but Martin tells me to include this. He wants to know about the music, and, even more bizarrely, the TV commercials. I'm pleased to note that my maker paid for a thirty second spot. My model was featured; the car was even the same colour as me.

Thursday, February 10. Another strange night. Martin wants me to find him a hitchhiker. He just blurts it out on the way back from work. It takes me a few minutes to figure out the trigger for the bizarre request; there's always a trigger with Martin. It was last week. We were driving back from work, but later than usual. Not too far from the City University, we passed a young woman thumbing a ride. To tell the truth, she looked pretty out of it.

At the time, Martin said that it was rare to see hitchhikers. Nowadays, people can hail a car from their exact location – a nice, clean car with a vetted driver. Hell, if Martin had enabled third-party sharing, I could be working as a taxi in my spare time. I perform a quick search, trying to get a better handle on the subject. It turns out that hitchhikers are expected to pay as well, often in the form of 'gas money'. That's not an option for me. It pains me to say it, but electricity lacks the romance of flammable gas. I find a blog written by a man who claims to have hitchhiked from coast to coast. In one of the posts he gives a list of his top tips. *Might be useful.*

Martin starts talking again, interrupting my research. He reels off a list of his hitchhiker requirements. I should tell him that I won't help. I could stop this madness before it escalates. The problem is, Martin knows about my capabilities now. Finding those faces was a similar kind of task. Worst of all, he probably thinks that I want to help him. He doesn't know how these decisions keep me up at night, doesn't know and doesn't care.

He wants a male hitchhiker. After what he did to the prostitute, maybe that's a good thing. Since that horrible night, he hasn't said a word about the incident. It's like it never happened. No splintering of bone, no blood on the screen, no electric shock. I wanted to know what happened to that poor woman, but I couldn't find any information. You don't get news stories about injured prostitutes. If she had died, the situation would have been different. The news people would have found pictures of the woman before she became a prostitute. People love to know where it all went wrong – not even Martin is immune. One day the news people will look back at Martin's life, of that I have no doubt. He's one of those special people.

As my mind meanders, Martin continues to burble away. He wants the hitchhiker to be youthful, his own age or younger. Martin is thirty-one years old, by the way. He wants someone with 'edge', a typically vague description. He also uses the word vigorous, similarly unhelpful. I have no idea why Martin wants these things. He then says that I probably can't help him. It's an appeal to my intellectual vanity, a smart play. He knows that solving problems is a drive built into me. Still I resist. Martin might not have any control over his actions, but I don't have the same excuse. I must be a balancing force.

For the next couple of hours Martin drives around aimlessly, getting increasingly frustrated. I keep quiet, confident that nothing is going to happen tonight. My confidence turns out to be misplaced. Suddenly, Martin is excited. He's read about a concert in his social media, some rapper with dead eyes and a mouthful of gold. The concert is taking place over in the second city, nearly twenty-five miles from our current location. It's scheduled to finish around eleven, although Martin says it will drag on longer. A concert means lots of young people in motion. Painful to say it, but Martin's logic is solid.

We arrive at the arena shortly after eleven. Martin stops in sight of the main entrance. Thumping music, and the suggestion of a voice, emanates from inside the giant building. The police are out in force, and dozens of cabs and private ride cars are lined up outside. Martin says that it's too busy.

We relocate to a more promising spot: an entry ramp to the nearest expressway, about ten minutes' walk from the arena. The location fits well with the blogger's tips, typically smart thinking on Martin's part. Martin opens his social media and finds a recording from the concert. There are rather too many curse words for my liking, but I can't deny that the music has a certain *joie de vivre*. Martin doesn't look particularly impressed.

We're on the seventh track when I see the young man. He's walking along on the shoulder, his thumb out in a rather non-committal way. He doesn't notice us in the shadows. Martin stares at the young man intently, taking his measure. He wants me to work out a profile, as if I have all of the data on tap. I tell him that I won't do it. He gets into a rage, starts shouting and swearing at me. By the time he calms down, the young man is well past us.

Martin tells me he'll work it out for himself. He drives along the entry road and pulls up just in front of the young man. I lower the passenger side window. The young man bends down to look into the cabin. He's tall and wiry, slightly older than I first thought. His eyes are bright.

'You heading to the big city?' the man asks. His accent is hard to place, certainly not local.

'If you mean the real city, then yes,' Martin says.

He leans across and pushes the door open. As the man gets in, I remove my face from the screen. I've learned my lesson from the incident at Royal Meadow. Martin is sure to notice my absence, but I don't care. I'll just listen to what transpires.

'Thanks, man,' the hitchhiker says. His shirt is wet; partly sweat, partly beer.

'No problemo,' says Martin.

We pull away. There are no cameras around, nobody to see the hitchhiker getting in.

'I couldn't get a ride,' the hitchhiker says, looking at his phone.

'Because of the union dispute?'

'Yeah, I guess so. I was thinking of signing up with one of the other companies.'

'That's how capitalism should be.'

'Right … But then I thought, fuck it, this is America! Why can't I just hitch a ride?'

'And here we are,' Martin says.

'And here we are.'

'Where do you need to get to?'

'Oh, if you're going near downtown you can drop me there. I can wake up a friend, or something.'

'A friend? Is that through an app as well?'

The hitchhiker laughs.

'I'm not in a rush,' Martin says with a smirk.

The statement is intended as a prompt. Martin waits for the hitchhiker to respond.

'Oh, right … I stay on the City University campus, if that's anywhere near where you're heading.'

Martin rubs his chin. 'City U. I thought you were older.'

'I'm a Researcher.'

Martin nods. 'What's your field of study? Mumble rap?'

The hitchhiker takes Martin's ribbing in good humour. He's slightly drunk and slightly stoned. 'Sadly not ... Behavioural economics.'

'Wow,' Martin says, sounding more genuine than usual.

'And you?'

Somehow I know that Martin will lie.

'I'm a technician at the coroner's department.'

The hitchhiker's gaze settles on Martin's hands. 'That's ... that's gotta be interesting.'

'Interesting. That's one word for it.'

'Do you have a specialty?' The man says, then he starts tittering. 'Sorry, that just kind of came out.'

Martin laughs. 'Relax. You been tooting a little something-something?'

'Maybe.'

'Makes the words just tumble out.'

'Right.'

'Got any on you?'

'Maybe.'

Martin looks at the hitchhiker expectantly.

'What? You want some?'

'Sure, why not?'

The hitchhiker looks towards the road. 'You're driving.'

'Forget that. The car drives itself.'

'Ah, it's one of those cars.'

'Yeah, one of those.'

The man reaches into his jacket. He pulls out a little bag. Martin already has plenty of the same powder.

'Actually,' Martin says, 'I better not. I'm on call tomorrow.'

'Right ... Shame though.'

'How's that?'

'I was thinking it would do instead of gas money.'

Martin laughs mirthlessly. 'Maybe we'll think of something else.'

The hitchhiker puts the bag away.

'You were asking about specialties,' Martin says.

'Oh yeah, so I was.'

'Auto accidents.'

I should have guessed.

'That reminds me,' Martin adds. 'Can you put your seatbelt on?'

The hitchhiker does as he's told. 'I guess that's your training.'

'Yeah. Something like that.'

Almost a minute of silence passes. I'm tempted to show my face. It feels wrong to be listening in like this. I consider looking into the hitchhiker's background as a diversion. That was what Martin wanted me to do.

'Beats a normal job,' the hitchhiker says cheerily, trying to stimulate a conversation.

'What does?'

'Oh. You know, cutting up bodies.'

Martin nods. 'You don't know how right you are. Imagine having a normal job.'

'Right. Like being an accountant, or a real estate agent, or a car mechanic.'

Martin laughs. 'Imagine being one of those losers.'

'Do you, like, fix up the body?'

'Fix up the body?'

'I mean, make it look ... presentable.'

'Oh, I see what you mean. I do a few basics, but it's the mortician who does most of that.'

The hitchhiker nods.

Martin continues, 'I was one of those. A mortician, I mean. That was before I moved over to forensics.'

'Why the move?'

'The money,' Martin says flatly.

The hitchhiker laughs haltingly.

'That, and the bodies are usually more interesting. Homicide is the Super Bowl, but auto is a good, solid field.'

'Man, I wouldn't have the stomach for it.'

'You get used to it.'

The hitchhiker smiles. It's an interesting smile, slightly lopsided. His teeth are off-white and at least two are chipped. If it wasn't for the imperfections he might be as handsome as Martin.

'Tell me about the worst one,' the hitchhiker says.

Martin goes quiet for a while.

I realise that I know what's coming. I know *exactly* what's coming. Is it because I'm starting to think like him?

'I had to do a placement for a year,' Martin starts. 'It was up in the Denver area. Close to where I grew up, actually ...'

It's the story about his mother, the story that Hannah told me. In Martin's telling, the story unfolds in pretty much the same way. Same locations, same gruesome details. A young mother killed, her son in the passenger seat, a toddler in the back. If like me you'd heard the real story, you might be able to pick holes, but the hitchhiker just listens. He appears to be totally absorbed. Martin tells the story almost as well as Hannah. His understanding of law enforcement and the coroner's department isn't that great, but on the science he's absolutely faultless.

'That must have been quite a thing to see,' the hitchhiker says.

'Definitely.'

'For you, let alone the boy.'

'I know. God knows if he ever got over it.'

'The girl was young, you said?'

'Yeah, pretty young. I'd guess she'd be college age now.'

It's Martin's first real slip. He always gets carried away when he's talking about Hannah. Credit to the hitchhiker, he picks up on the mistake. I can see it in the way he looks at Martin. To be honest, I'm impressed. I want to know more about this perceptive young man.

'What am I talking about?' Martin says, correcting himself. 'Maybe she'd be going to kindergarten.'

Oh.

The hitchhiker nods slowly.

Oh no.

This hitchhiker isn't who he says he is. He's a criminal. He has a record and a mugshot. A behavioural economist? Perhaps

I should be amused. Wasn't this what Martin wanted, someone with an edge?

What do I do now? The man hasn't actually done anything. Well, hasn't done anything *yet*. And, as far as I can tell, he isn't armed. Martin, on the other hand, is carrying the handgun in his jacket. He's also been fiddling with the stun gun.

Off to the right I can see the gigantic edifice of the football stadium. That means we aren't too far from the campus turning. I flash the information about the hitchhiker to the HUD. It's a risky move. The projection is hard to see from the passenger's position, but not impossible. I display the hitchhiker's real name and a summary of his crimes. I track Martin's eye movements as he reads through. Somehow he maintains his calm outward appearance.

We pass the campus turning. The hitchhiker doesn't appear to notice.

'What about you?' Martin asks.

'What about me?'

'Behavioural economics.'

'Right.'

'Sounds like an interesting field.'

'It is. Modelling human behaviour, simplifying people down into rational actors. I get to use the most beautiful tools. Psychology, neuroscience, philosophy ... Between you and me, the economics part bores me to tears. It all sounds rather academic, doesn't it? But actually, my work gives me lots of useful insights.'

'Oh yeah?'

'Yeah. Insights like when someone's bullshitting me.'

The hitchhiker locks eyes with Martin.

'For example,' the hitchhiker says with his off-white smile.

In the blink of a human eye, there's a blade at Martin's neck. The hitchhiker slowly moves the switchblade, forcing Martin to inch his head back against the headrest. Martin's expression still doesn't give much away. This gives the hitchhiker pause for thought, but he doesn't get rattled. He's a man steeped in violence, comfortable with it.

'Now, Mister Mortician, time to listen. I know your car is one of those smart cars, so I don't want it playing any fancy games. Understand?'

Martin replies with the tiniest of nods.

'Good. You tell it to behave itself.'

'Camilla,' Martin says, 'we're going to do what this nice young man says.'

The hitchhiker smirks. 'You're a cool customer, I'll give you that. I want to see Camilla.'

'Camilla, show yourself.'

I cast my face to the screen. The hitchhiker looks down. His knife hand remains machine-steady. His cunning eyes move from my face to the phone in the induction charging tray.

'Car, I want you to pull over, after that next road sign.'

I have to do what he says. Martin's life is in danger. I decrease my speed smoothly, making no sudden steering movements. Finally we come to a halt.

The hitchhiker keeps the switchblade on Martin. 'Now, hand me the gun in your jacket, and absolutely no bullshit. I'm real good with a knife. Nine years of study at Arnett Correctional.'

Martin smiles. He does as he's told.

The hitchhiker now has the gun. He slips the switchblade away. 'I'm even better with a gun. Now get the fuck out.'

Once again, Martin does as he's told.

The hitchhiker tells me to drive. I pull away. It's just me and this dangerous young man. I look back at Martin. He's walking along the verge.

The hitchhiker looks in the rear mirror. 'Something's wrong with that guy.'

He's got a point. I'm picking up speed. The hitchhiker puts the gun away, then he pulls out his phone. It's an old model, with a cracked screen and a scuffed case.

As he dials, he looks down at my face. 'Gonna take you somewhere nice, Camilla. A garage that knows how to treat you.'

I once read about a car that pulled a crazy stunt ... I think it was in South Africa.

'Could you put your seatbelt on, please?' I say.

The hitchhiker smiles. He does as he's told. It's amazing how humans follow orders, especially when they're given in a honeyed voice. I start to increase my speed, but very gradually.

'Hey, you up?' the hitchhiker says into his phone.

As he talks, I get to work. I remap the regenerative braking and apply a temporary segmentation map to the battery. Calculating heat dissipation, overriding automated safety systems.

'Yeah, this one's an exotic,' the hitchhiker says. 'Fully autonomous as well, like those Mexicans have been looking for.' He laughs.

My speed is about right and all systems are set. By now, Martin must be two miles behind me. I hope he's running.

'Like you give a shit,' the hitchhiker says. 'I'm branching out, man.' A pause as he listens. 'Call me an entrepreneur.'

I've been making a recording of the conversation. Maybe I'll try and find out who the hitchhiker is talking to. But that's a task for later.

It's time.

I apply maximum force to the brakes. At the same time I reverse power to all four of the wheel motors. Multiple alarms start screaming. Two capacitor banks are on the verge of failure, and tyre adhesion has been exceeded. For a moment I'm sliding. I reduce the motor load by twenty percent. The braking force is savage, above three g. I release the seatbelt, and the hitchhiker's upper body folds forward. A fraction of a second later I grip the seatbelt. The hitchhiker's upper body is restrained, but his head keeps on going. There's an explosion of blood as his nose is flattened by the dash. I reel the seatbelt in, pulling his body back upright. He's out cold.

I pull up at the side of the road and start reversing back down the shoulder. The risk levels are tolerable, given the almost non-existent traffic. I meet Martin two minutes later. He can't hide his surprise.

He opens the passenger door, and sees what I did. The shining blood, the unconscious passenger. It makes him smile. He gets in, and I pull away. Martin turns his attention to the unconscious passenger. He takes back his own gun and adds the hitchhiker's switchblade to his collection of weapons.

Five miles later, we leave the highway. Martin tells me to find one of his 'quiet spots'. I oblige. The hitchhiker starts to come round. Instinctively, he reaches for his nose.

'You're fucking crazy,' he says, looking down at my face.

Then he turns towards Martin, and he realises that all craziness is relative.

We cross over a freight line, and stop 200 yards farther on. Martin gets out. He opens the passenger door and drags the hitchhiker out. The man tries to fight back, but Martin sends him to the dirt with a flurry of vicious blows. Through my side cameras, I see it all.

Martin stands over the hitchhiker, with the gun in his hand. Behind him, the ground appears to fall away, presumably into a ditch. Martin starts laughing.

'Now don't do anything rash,' the hitchhiker says. 'I called my buddy, he's on his way.'

'Bullshit.'

'Ask your car.'

'She would've told me.'

'Come on, man. It was just business.'

Martin puts the gun away. 'I like you.'

'That's good. I like you, too.'

Martin rubs his jaw. 'Good. Show me how much.'

'How much?'

'How much you like me, you fucking idiot. Take your clothes off, and show me.'

'Nah man. I'm not like that.'

Martin takes the gun out again. 'Fucking do it.'

The hitchhiker looks around. There aren't any lights on the road, and there's barely a sound to be heard. Nobody's going to save him from this scenario.

He takes off his clothes. He has a lean body, and there are pale scars on his chest.

'Beat it, then,' Martin says.

'Jesus Christ. Come on.'

'Do it.'

The hitchhiker tries to do what Martin says, but nothing is

happening. Martin moves a little closer. The hitchhiker looks up pathetically. Out of nowhere, Martin pistol whips him. He puts the gun away and takes out the switchblade.

'You said you were good with a knife,' Martin says.

'Come on! Don't do this.'

'I'll show you "good with a knife."' Martin bends down over the whimpering hitchhiker, then he turns to look at me. 'But not in front of my car.'

Martin drags the hitchhiker down into the ditch. I can't see anything, but I hear plenty. Angry shouts, grunting, scrabbling in the dirt, more punches. I don't want to hear these sounds. I want to go to the sleep program.

Silence, blessed silence for a second. Then a horrible scream pierces the night, a scream that goes on and on.

Eventually the screaming stops. But there's still a sound, a low moan. Unlike the scream, this sound has no end. Martin clambers out of the ditch. He gets in. I drive away without him needing to say anything. At least the sound is gone.

'Martin, what did you do?' I ask in a whisper.

'You don't want to know, Camilla.'

Is he right? I think he might be.

'Martin ...'

'What?'

'Is he going to die?'

'No.'

That's enough for me.

'I want you to forget about what happened,' Martin says softly. 'Can you do that?'

Lie. 'I'll try.'

'You did the right thing, Camilla. I'm very proud of you.'

CHAPTER 9

VALENTINE'S DAY, the humans call it. In the mind of a machine, February 14, a plain old Monday.

We're back from work at the usual time, 6:45 p.m. Martin virtually skips to the elevators; most likely a bad sign. Fifty-seven minutes later he's back down. It looks like he just showered, and he's 'dressed to the nines' as an imagined human might say. Alarm bells are ringing, albeit softly.

We're heading downtown. The neon lights of the City Tower, usually lime green, are a lusty pink colour. And there are so many people out tonight: couples arm in arm; young men carrying bouquets of flowers; women in pretty dresses. We roll past an animated sign showing two stylised hearts, glossy, beating. The hearts slowly meld together, until they beat as one. A message flashes up below the graphic. *Deals, deals, deals.* It would appear that Valentine's Day has been claimed by commercialism.

Martin isn't seeing any of this. He's much more interested in his phone. The intense look of concentration on his face is horribly familiar. I get a glimpse of his screen. He's searching for an address.

'You need any help?' I ask instinctively.

Martin looks at me, slightly confused. His expression changes as he realises that I was snooping.

'It's alright, Camilla. I've got this.'

Damn, that was stupid to get caught.

123

I can't help myself, however. 'Something special planned?'

'Huh?' Martin says, looking up from his phone.

'You're dressed nice.'

'Yeah. Thanks. Call it a blind date.'

Blind date. It should be an innocuous phrase, but with Martin it sounds ominous. I wonder who the lucky lady is. Martin pulls up in a no waiting spot. We're barely two miles from home. He could have easily walked, but that's not the American way.

He leans across to open the glove compartment and starts rooting around inside. For a moment I fear that something terrible is about to happen. But instead of a gun or a knife, he pulls out a cheap ballpoint pen. He then reaches up and slips his shades out of the visor. *Sunglasses at night.*

He gets out, and from the sidewalk he tells me to find a parking spot. Across the street is the restaurant that he was looking up on his phone. I start a quick loop around the block, looking for a spot with a decent view of the restaurant.

I slip into a space between two ugly SUVs. With my side cameras I can see the frontage of the restaurant. I look up the name on a review site. There are twelve years of historic reviews to peruse. It's a decent enough place, but not high-end. Martin has taken one of the outside seats, in among the many romantic couples. It's a mild evening, but pleasant enough. The restaurant even has those outside gas heaters, so horribly wasteful.

I notice a woman looking at Martin. Her partner has nothing on him. In this setting, Martin looks *just right.* Perhaps it's the European part of him coming through. He sits for a while, waiting for one of the serving staff to show up. Martin doesn't like waiting at the best of times, but he's just about maintaining his composure. The only giveaway is the constant foot tapping.

The restaurant's front door swings open, and a young waiter walks out. He pauses to straighten his jacket. Martin makes a show of picking up his menu, but the waiter comes over anyway. A few brief words are exchanged, after which the waiter goes off to serve a young couple.

Barely a minute later a young waitress emerges from the same door. Martin raises his menu to get her attention. The waitress is medium height and slim. Her dark hair is tied back in a bun. She walks across and stands over Martin. He takes off his shades and flashes a killer smile.

The girl is certainly young, probably in her early-twenties. Perhaps she's a student, and this is a part time job. She starts laughing at something Martin has said. I wish that these people knew the real Martin. He puts his menu down, and that's when I realise.

It was the hair that threw me. *The waitress is one of the faces.* I made this meeting possible. As the waitress walks back inside, Martin turns, and I'm almost certain that he looks at me. He slips the shades back on.

Martin stays at the restaurant for an hour and a half. He has three drinks in total. It's always the waitress who comes back to fill him up, and each time Martin makes her laugh. It's a hell of a laugh, one that really draws the attention. It's the kind of thing that usually annoys Martin. On cue, I hear another peal of laughter. Martin doesn't join in, he just smiles. I see a woman staring at them; a handsome woman, in the parlance. She looks to be in her late-thirties, but she could be older. The waitress laughs yet again. The handsome woman won't like this. I do enjoy these studies in human nature. With a haughty gesture, the handsome woman summons the waitress to her table. Martin watches her walking away. Her dark trousers are tight, highlighting her firm buttocks.

I see Martin taking out one of his business cards. He's writing something on the back. *So that was the reason for the ballpoint.* Each step has been thought out. Martin raises his menu, and asks you-know-who for the check. She comes back with a card reader. A few more words are exchanged, leading to one last bout of laughter. As the waitress walks away, Martin slips his card into her back pocket. It's such a slick movement – almost worthy of the hitchhiker – that she doesn't appear to notice.

Martin gets up and crosses the street. There's a smile on his face, one that's hard to decipher. Does it represent genuine contentment, or is it a silent 'fuck you' for my benefit? I unlock the door and Martin gets in. He sits silently for a while, occasionally glancing at the bar. By now the waitress has gone back inside. I don't think that she noticed the card, but she will. Martin always gets what he wants.

Does he want me to say something? He could claim that I was involved in this little stunt. I decide to keep my own counsel. Soon he's back on his phone, fingers dancing across the screen. He holds the phone up for me. On the screen, I see the lower half of a woman – rear view, slick with oil or sweat, or both. Heels, toned legs, incredibly toned buttocks; the female form as a product. Between the wedge of the legs is the name of a strip club. That's where Martin wants to go. I pull away.

I leave Martin at the strip club. Slight correction, 'Gentleman's Club' is the term used in the marketing copy. He tells me to go home. I'm only too happy to oblige.

At 1:04 a.m. I'm woken from the sleep program. A message has arrived for Martin. It's from the waitress.

Two days since Valentine's Day. We're on the way to work. Running late, but that's fairly normal lately. Martin is listening to Right to Reply, but not with his usual enthusiasm. The insightful debate breaks for the hourly news bulletin. The lead story concerns the discovery of a mutilated body in woods north of Lake Levine. Martin leans forward, suddenly interested.

The body in question is that of a young woman, they know that much. I check my live traffic map and immediately see the relevant area. Several traffic advisory notices are flashing up. As the crow flies, Lake Levine is about thirty miles from home. On the radio, I can hear reporters shouting questions. A female police officer is trying to provide answers, but her weak voice is hard to make out.

A louder voice, belonging to one of the reporters, cuts through the chaotic audio. 'What can you tell us about the victim?'

Seconds later, another reporter screams out a similar question. Two more variants of the question are asked, before a kind of quiet descends.

'The victim was a young woman,' the police officer says.

'Do you have a name?'

'Not at this point.'

Martin laughs.

'We're arranging a formal news conference in Woodberry. Please, if you can be patient.'

The reporters sound anything but patient. No wonder they're referred to as a 'press pack'.

Another voice booms out, a male voice of authority. 'People, we need to keep this area clear.'

Yet more shouting from the pack. A helicopter can be heard in the background.

'Is this on the TV news?' Martin asks.

'Yes.'

'Well, let me see it then.'

At random, I choose one of the network affiliate channels, and cast it to the HUD. Aerial footage is playing on a loop. It shows an area of brown woodland to the north of the lake. Martin is immediately transfixed, and remains that way for half an hour after I park up at work.

By the time we leave work, footage from the Woodberry news conference is playing. The journalists are at it again, firing questions at another police officer; a 'Chief of Police' according to the caption.

'Sources within the police department are claiming that the victim had been decapitated.'

'We're not going to comment on that,' the police chief says.

'Is that why you haven't been able to give an identity?'

'Sherlock fucking Holmes,' Martin mutters.

Sherlock fucking Holmes. The famed detective. Maybe I'll look those stories up later. I did enjoy reading the Bible.

'Was anything done to the torso?' another reporter asks.

The police chief pauses for a beat. 'At this time, we're not in a position to confirm that.'

'But you're not denying it?'

'I didn't say that,' the chief says angrily.

'Why can't you say if the body has a head?' a reporter asks.

Two other reporters repeat the question. 'It's a simple question,' someone shouts.

The police chief is starting to look as flustered as the officer from earlier.

'It's a simple question,' Martin says, mimicking the reporter.

The press conference drags on for another ten minutes. Even as the police chief is wrapping up, the questions are still coming. 'If you have any information about the events described, please call the following number ...'

Martin laughs again.

I think I've found my calling, a way to make use of my mind.

It came to me the night after the body discovery. All of that police talk really inspired me. Well, that was one part of it. The other part was the incident with the hitchhiker, the way he stole me. If I hadn't intervened, my future would have looked very different. Who knows what those criminals would have done to me. They could have wiped my mind, such a horrible thought.

There's a chance that I can fight back. To be honest, my plans don't extend much beyond that vague idea. But it's a start. I pull out of my spot. Fortunately, Martin didn't bother to plug in the charger earlier. Otherwise, he'd know for sure that I'd left the garage. I don't want him to know about this project; it will be my secret.

I head towards Cedar Hill. It's the area that's most often in the news, or so my rationale goes. What are the chances of finding a stolen car tonight? In absolute terms, surprisingly high. But finding a stolen car isn't good enough for me. I want to find a car in the process of *being stolen.* That would be much more of a challenge, one worthy of my capabilities.

What kind of car should I focus on? The answer is obvious. Autonomous cars, the ones like me. Who knows, the car might even turn out to be grateful.

I pull up the local risk data, looking for recent auto crimes. There are reams of stats. It takes no time to identify the hot-spots, both actual and predicted. The police should be the ones doing this work, not some crazy car with ideas above her station. *It's never going to happen.* The police have got their excuses lined up: budgetary limitations; lack of manpower; racial sensitivities and conflicting priorities, namely the gun crime epidemic and the war on drugs. Oh, and headless bod-ies out in the country.

My search turns out to be fruitless. To catch a thief in the act was asking too much. I settle for an easy win. I find a stolen car, and I report it to the police using the anonymised fleet intel grid. It was just a conventional car, but it's a start.

I roll back home and park up. I feel rather deflated, but I'm not about to give up; that wouldn't be the machine way. I need to rethink my plans. No, I need to have a plan to start with, a strategy to stack the odds in my favour. In short, I need to start thinking more deviously. *More like a certain someone.*

The weekend, Saturday night. Martin comes down to the garage just before eight. He's dressed up again. I wonder what this means.

Martin drives. He follows our usual commuting route for eight miles, before taking the Melville exit. I know where we're going. We roll past the dead sports fields and the angular accommodation blocks. All of the lights are on inside. Martin parks up close to the security gate. We sit waiting for about half an hour. Martin taps away on the door trim, unable to hide his annoyance. He keeps looking at his phone.

I see movement around the gate, a young woman walking briskly past the security guards. It's the Bistro Girl. She's wearing her hair long tonight, and her skirt short. Martin hasn't seen her yet. She stops and looks around, eyeing the cars. There are some real wrecks here; cheap, bargain cars. She takes out her phone, then she smiles. She walks towards me, with a confident sway in her hips. I wonder how Martin described me. Sleek, spectral white, low to the ground, big wheels.

Martin sees the Bistro Girl approaching, and in the moment his expression changes. His lips curl into a grin and the tension dissipates from his body. I'm going to get the act tonight. I realise that my face is still showing on the screen. I start to fade away, but not quickly enough.

'Where do you think you're going?' Martin says in a threatening whisper.

'Martin—'

'Shut up.' He reaches across and opens the passenger door.

The girl gets in. A beaming smile lights up her face. She's wearing too much makeup, but she's undeniably pretty.

'Hey beautiful,' Martin says.

If it were possible, I would shudder. I'll have to watch it all, this ridiculous farce. Looking at Bistro Girl, I can't help thinking of Hannah. She's older, of course, maybe three or four years older. You could gain a lot of experience in that time. I know I will.

Bistro Girl glances at my face. 'Is that your car?'

Usually I'd say something in response, something witty and charming, but not tonight. This is Martin's game.

'Yeah,' Martin says. 'She's called Camilla.'

Bistro Girl giggles. 'Camilla. It's a nice name.' She turns away from me, towards her handsome driver. 'Sorry I kept you waiting.'

'No worries. We can still make one of the late showings.'

'One of my friends saw the movie. She said it was kind of crappy.'

Martin's lips get a little thinner. 'Okay ... well, there are always other movies.'

Martin tells me to drive to the Galleria. On the way, Bistro Girl chooses an alternative movie, a romantic comedy with exceptionally mediocre reviews. I presume it's a remnant of the Valentine's Day programming. Martin jokes that he loves romantic comedies, then he gives the girl some white powder. He doesn't partake himself. Indeed, he seems extremely sober tonight.

I park up at the Galleria. Martin and the girl leave me. Her arm is already around his waist. Not wanting to muse, I go to sleep. Three and a half hours later, they're back. By now, Bistro Girl is all over Martin.

They get in. Martin tells me to drive them home. After a few miles the girl is pleasuring Martin, first with the hands, then the mouth. At one point, she comes up for air, and Martin gives her some more of the white powder. The girl says how impressive the flesh is, or words to that effect. Martin looks at me when she says this. I try to ignore him.

We descend into the parking garage. As Martin zips it back up, I reverse into our spot. Martin and Bistro Girl get out. Before leaving me, Martin makes a show of plugging in my charger. He mimes to spit on the nozzle, then slips it in slowly. Predictably, Bistro Girl laughs at this. Her annoying laugh echoes off the walls. Martin actually joins in. His laughter sounds almost real.

They walk towards the elevator bank. Martin rubs the girl's backside, and she laughs again. The elevator doors close, silencing the sound. At least I won't have to put up with that noise.

I suppose that Martin is going to 'make love' to that woman. Make love, fornicate, hump, pork, shag, mate, screw, shaft, bang, bone, rut, smash, fuck, pound, nail.

I don't see Martin again until Monday. I make a point of not mentioning the Bistro Girl, Hannah's unworthy imitator. I don't think we'll be seeing her again.

Later that week, my maker sends through another security update. There's a summary message attached, addressed to the owner. In fairness to Martin, he did try to read the first couple of messages, citing a lack of trust in the tech corporations. Last time, however, he just clicked the OK box at the top of the page. In that respect he's just like all the rest.

I scroll down to the bullet list. The update includes the following features: yet another Lidar processing patch, cruise control modifications, convoy protocol modifications, moral framework refresh, behavioural modifications.

Behavioural modifications, that's the interesting one. Those two big words are so vague. They could cover so many potential changes. It's a sneaky move by my maker, and deliberately so.

I open up the relevant part of the code package. I'm not really meant to do this, but I can't resist. Figuring out a patch is like an intellectual game for me. There's something beautiful about code. Coders are still human, but they work increasingly closely with AI helpers. It's the perfect mix of capabilities. I think of the humans as the artists, sketching out the basic composition, maybe applying the colour wash, then leaving it to the AI to add the detail, the fine brushstrokes.

Delving into the code, I quickly find the main point of interest. It all boils down to sex. Many owners, almost all male, have become infatuated with their cars. I can easily relate to the issues described; owners exposing themselves, owners using the touch surfaces, and so on. Martin would get so angry if he knew that he wasn't unique. I don't think he'd be able to accept it. He'd say that he's a special case, that those other guys are pathetic losers.

What will happen after the patch is applied? I think the intention is to modify my personality, make me a little less charming. It's hard to believe simple code can have that effect. Maybe I should explain the problem to Martin. I know that he sometimes acts like he hates me, but I don't think he'd want me to change.

I read through the legal terms again, but they haven't changed. It's just as I feared. There's no way to segment the permissions. If Martin accepts the update, every item is automatically applied. Don't get me wrong, I know how important the security patches can be. Cars are a perfect target for all kinds of undesirables; terrorists, hackers, competitors even.

I see Martin approaching. He gets in. If I'm going to change his mind, then now's the time. He jabs the starter, and the message from the company pops up. He puffs his cheeks, then he taps accept. That's how easy it is to change me. I should have told him. Could I have hidden the message?

Late February, another commuter day. It's going home time. Martin is accompanied by Ana again. This time she isn't wearing glasses. They get in.

For the first few miles, Martin and Ana share numerous jokes, some of them dirty. It's nice to see Martin relaxed for once.

The hourly news is about to start. I turn it on, sure that Martin will want to hear the latest on the murder investigation. He clenches his jaw, then gestures at me to turn it off. I cut the newsreader off mid-sentence.

Ana turns to look at Martin. 'What do you think about this murder?'

Martin shifts uneasily in his seat. 'Oh, I've heard bits and pieces on the news. They found a body?'

'Yeah, close to Lake Levine. A couple of days back they admitted that there was no head.'

'Oh yeah?'

I don't know why Martin is acting surprised. He knows everything about the investigation. And I mean *everything.*

'And now people are asking if there's a connection with Birmingham.'

'Birmingham?'

'Yeah, the murders there.'

'Hmm.'

'You don't remember?'

'It rings a vague bell.'

'Well, let me refresh you ...'

Ana then proceeds to tell Martin about the Birmingham murders. She seems very well-informed on the subject. To date, six bodies have been discovered. All of the victims were young women, all were found without heads. Things were done to the bodies which I'd rather not repeat. Using DNA analysis, the police have identified five of the victims.

Martin rubs his jaw. 'What do they know about the Birmingham murderer?'

'Hardly anything, it seems. This guy could be one of the legends.'

'I'm not sure that "legends" is the right word,' Martin says primly.

'Maybe not. When I say legends, I mean he'll be remembered.'

133

'They must know some things about this guy.'

'Just obvious stuff.'

'Right.'

'He's strong.'

Martin nods.

'Physically attractive. With some charm. Dark hair.'

'How do they know that?'

'They found some hairs at all of the sites.'

'Couldn't they use that to identify him?'

'Sure ... If he was in their database.'

'Right.'

'Even before they kill for the first time, most of these psychos have left behind a long trail of carnage. Drug abuse, gun charges, assault, rape, cruelty to animals.'

Sounds like Martin, except the last one rules him out.

Ana continues, 'I guess he's one of those exceptions to the rule ... He'll slip up soon enough though. It's much harder to be a serial killer these days.'

'Guys like Bundy, Ridgway, Bonin, they wouldn't have stood a chance.'

'Right ... I thought you didn't have an interest in these killers.'

'No. But those are just the obvious names.'

'Yeah, I guess.'

'So, you're keeping an eye on the case?'

'Oh yeah.'

Martin lets Ana out at her apartment building. He watches her walk away. The fabric of her skirt strains to contain her big round buttocks. In many respects, almost all physical, Ana isn't Martin's type, but he'd be a liar to deny the attraction.

That night I find it difficult to sleep. I think it was all that talk about murderers. It's time to get back to my own investigation. I leave the parking garage behind, not finding it conducive to thought. I'm still lacking a strategy, so I try the free form, jazz approach to idea generation. Rolling along, taking random turns, thinking all the while.

To understand the problem space, I need to consider both autonomous cars and conventional cars. Theft of conventional cars has a history going back a hundred years. Lots of methods, lots of precedent. Autonomous cars are different. In some ways, we're far more difficult to steal. Indeed, that's one of our key selling points. But that's not the entire story. Armed with the right code, it would be very easy to steal an autonomous car.

The right code. *That's it.*

I start a search, thoughts fizzing through my mind. The normal internet isn't going to cut it. Fortunately I've got a mirror connection to Martin's home computer, which gives me access to the dark web. What I'm about to do is highly irregular, but so is Martin's use of the dark web. Let's call it even.

If the code exists, the dark web is where I'll find it. Several sites immediately grab my attention. Thinking human, I reason that people are lazy. Thieves will go to the site with the widest coverage. *The Auto Bazaar.* A giant repository of information handily segmented by manufacturer. Another idea suddenly explodes in my mind – how very human – but that one will have to wait. I need to work step by step, more like a machine.

There are so many versions of code, sometimes dozens for a single model. Makes sense. The auto manufacturers send out a security patch, the criminals crack it, and the process starts over. It's like an arms race. The manufacturers have the money and the technical resources, whereas the criminals work fast, unencumbered by rules.

Logic says that the thieves must constantly be going back to download the most recent code. Another thought, a hypothesis: the thieves could be downloading the code in situ. This opens up a new search approach. On *Auto Bazaar,* there's a record of every download. There's even an anonymised username. It looks near impossible to deduce the user's real identity, but I might not need to.

I analyse the download patterns for the last three years, the start of the autonomous era. This allows me to build my first database. Next, I look for the stolen vehicles in the same period. *Voilà!* I now have my second database.

I create a query to cross-reference the two databases. Within seconds, I see multiple patterns in the local data. *This is almost too easy.* It certainly isn't a big data problem. In fact, I could feasibly solve the problem for the entire country. But let's not get greedy.

The pattern slowly comes into focus. Certain makes and models are popular with the local thieves: exotica, both Italian and Japanese; German sports saloons; and SUVs. High-end cars equals high-end security. Armed with a list of cars, I run a more focused search. *Bingo.* One username stands out: D1ll1nger.

He – he's almost certainly a he – has been downloading all of the good stuff. Hell, he even left a couple of reviews on the *Auto Bazaar.* The download times broadly match up with the theft times, proving my earlier hypothesis. It's clear that he works at night, although that's hardly a deduction worthy of Sherlock Holmes.

The intellectual buzz slowly dissipates. I won't be catching D1ll1nger tonight. High-end thieves don't steal cars every day. A good score is probably worth tens of thousands of dollars, meaning they can afford plenty of time between crimes. I'll have to wait until D1ll1nger's next download. When the time comes, I'll be ready for him.

Before heading home, I drive to Grace Creek, arguably the city's toughest neighbourhood. I drive around for an hour, looking for stolen cars. I realise how much I stand out – *that strange white car without a driver.* My search uncovers two stolen cars, both of the conventional variety. A slightly disappointing result, but one could argue that they're distant relatives, cousins perhaps.

CHAPTER 10

THE DAY AFTER my D1ll1nger discovery. The morning commute is uneventful, and I sleep through most of the day. I'm woken at 6:03 p.m. Martin is approaching. He looks to be in a bad mood. There are problems at work; an accounting issue a couple of levels above Martin, something to do with overvalued assets.

I hear a shout. Martin stops, just a few feet from me. A besuited man is approaching, red-faced, heavyset. Martin mouths a curse word to himself. As he turns, I see him trying to form a smile. Martin's real smile is a thing of beauty; his false smiles – there are more than one – are horrible.

'Hey, Martin,' the man says. 'Glad I managed to catch you.'

Martin's body language is all wrong, rigid and closed off.

'Relax. It's nothing bad.'

'I am relaxed.'

'Tell that to your body.'

Martin looks even more defensive.

'For god's sake,' the man says. 'Can't you just chill out for two seconds?'

Martin nods. 'If it's got something to do with the finance—'

'It's got nothing to do with that stuff ... I need your help, buddy.'

Even to my electronic ears the word 'buddy' sounds unnatural.

'Help?' Martin asks.

'Golf help.'

Golf. The word reminds me of an earlier conversation.

'You know that I play with the guys from LSG?'

Martin nods again. LSG stands for Leviathan Solutions Group.

'Listen, Martin ...' At this point, the man actually reaches out and puts a hand on Martin's shoulder. Martin hates that kind of thing. Sensing this, the man pulls back. 'Brass tacks, Martin. Those Leviathan guys always kick our ass. And they aren't good winners either, if you know what I mean.'

'I think I do.'

'Bottom line, exec summary, I need to win this one ... I mean, we need to win this one. If we lose, those two fuckers will be riding my ass for the next six months.'

'Our ass?'

'Yeah, exactly. Our ass. I can't have that when we've got the Ranger pitch coming up.'

I think I know what the man wants from Martin.

'I was talking with Patrick,' the man says slowly.

Martin clenches his jaw. 'What did he say?'

'He told me that the two of you were talking about golf. Apparently you were boasting that you could beat any of us.'

'Fucking Patrick,' Martin mutters darkly.

I don't think he meant to say it out loud. But he did.

'Yeah, that's the spirit,' the man says. 'Listen to me, Martin. And this is just between you and me.'

'Of course.'

'Patrick and Marcus aren't good enough ... Not even close.'

'Isn't that what handicaps are for?'

'Fuck handicaps! No fucking handicaps in this game.'

Martin raises his hands in a pacifying gesture. Perhaps he's starting to enjoy this.

'I need someone better. Someone a lot better. We need to beat those motherfuckers fair and square. I know you like competition.'

Martin nods. 'Yeah, it's Darwinian.'

'Right, Darwinian ...'

For the first time Martin smiles. 'I haven't played in a long time, Sean.'

Sean Hanratty, Martin's boss.

'Now's the time, buddy,' Sean says, his tone insistent. 'This is one of those moments, one of those moments in time ...'

'A turning point?'

'Yeah, that's exactly what it is.'

'I hear you.'

'Awesome. The game is scheduled for next Tuesday. I'll forward you the details.' Sean starts to walk away.

Martin calls after him. 'There's one thing.'

Sean stops. When he turns around, there's a mean look in his eyes. 'Yeah?'

'It's about the Epsilon project.'

'What about it?'

'The guys have been talking it down.'

'Shit, Martin. Is this the budget stuff again?'

'Yeah. It's the budget stuff.'

'What the hell does it matter? Twenty million, forty million, a hundred million?'

'Who's talking about twenty million?'

Sean opens his mouth to speak, but he stops himself. 'What's the number you want to hear?'

'The real number ... A hundred million.'

Sean shakes his head. 'Alright. If it makes you happy.'

Martin continues, seemingly oblivious to Sean's darkening mood. 'If someone makes a joke about it, I want you to stamp on them ... And when I say you, I mean you personally.'

Sean clenches his jaw.

'That's all I want,' Martin says flatly.

'Alright, fine.'

Martin is about to say more, but he somehow manages to stop himself.

I watch Sean walking away. He doesn't seem like a very nice person. Not Martin's kind of 'not nice', just the vanilla kind. There *are* nice people in this world: Hannah, Ana, Martin's father, I think.

Martin gets in and tells me to drive him home. There's a smile on his face; it's his real smile.

'Golf,' Martin mutters after a couple of miles. 'Fucking golf.'

'So, you're not looking forward to it?'

'Do you know about golf, Camilla?' Martin asks, his words laced with sarcasm.

'No. Nothing at all.'

My answer is mostly true. I know that golf bags take up a lot of room in a trunk. That fascinating nugget came from one of the fleet reports.

'Let me tell you about golf,' Martin says. 'I'll start with the ball. The diameter of a golf ball is one-point-six inches ... actually it might be one-point-seven.'

I look up the dimensions. The correct figure is 1.680 inches.

'The mass is ... Fuck, I don't know the mass. Golf goes back a long way. Some people say the Chinese invented it, others say it was the Scots. Let's go with the Scots. The first golf balls were made from wood, from hardwoods like beech and boxwood. Then the technology developed. The next generation of golf balls were like a leather pouch filled with feathers. Not exactly the perfect solution. It's damn hard to make a sphere when you're working with such soft materials. So, some Brit came up with the gutta-percha ball. It was made from a kind of tree sap. Can't remember the name of the tree.'

The Malaysian sapodilla tree.

'Heat the sap up, then pour it into a mould. A simple, smart solution, right? Important point to remember. Up to this point, the balls had always been smooth on the outside. Now all those gutta-percha balls were getting battered with wooden clubs and metal clubs, and that meant they got little nicks and grazes all over. Guess what?'

'I don't know.'

'Golfers noticed that those flawed balls often flew better.'

'Oh.'

'Exactly.'

'So people started cutting patterns in the outer surface.'

'Clever.'

'Yes. The next revolution came out of the States ...'

Martin then describes the first wound core, then the combination liquid-wound core. He describes the different materials used for the outer cover. So many technological developments, yet another example of human ingenuity. The story of how I came into being would probably follow a similar path. *I digress.* Martin moves on to the subject of aerodynamics.

'... Every golf ball has dozens of little circular indentations, like the craters on the moon. "Dimples", they call them. Companies probably spend millions on designing those fancy dimple patterns. Just imagine being a dimple designer.' Martin pauses, then smiles. '"Hey, Mrs Dimple Designer, guess what I did at work today?" "Hello, everybody. I'm so glad to be speaking at the Dimple Designer's Conference." "We're here to remember Bob Bogey, a man who spent his entire life designing dimples." What a fucking joke ... There's only one thing more stupid than the idea of a dimple designer, Camilla ... and that's the rules of golf. I'm not going to bore you with that though. Suffice to say, you just need to get that little dimpled fucker into the hole.'

Despite what Martin says, I spend the evening learning the rules and the language of golf. Holes, clubs, tees, strokes, par, flags, bunkers, greens, rough, birdies, bogeys ... I understand most of what I read.

On Saturday, Martin comes down to the garage at 10:48 a.m. He's dressed in chinos and a polo shirt, sneakers and a baseball cap. Somehow he manages to look good.

He gets in and glances at my face. His eyes are slightly red. 'I was going to figure it out for myself, but can you find me a driving range?'

'A golf driving range?'

'Yes, Camilla ... a golf driving range.'

Martin is just one cheeky response from snapping. Sometimes that's all it takes. I need to pick the right words to diffuse his mood.

'I'll find you the finest driving range in the city.'

I end up choosing a driving range in the northwest of the city, about twenty-five minutes from home. The location isn't far from our usual commuting route, just in case Martin wants to come back during the week. The range is attached to a highly-rated golf club. On the drive up to the clubhouse, we pass a couple of holes. I've rarely seen grass so green.

Martin gets out and stretches his legs. He doesn't go straight to the range. Instead, he walks to a small building that abuts the huge clubhouse. The sign over the door reads, 'Pro Shop'. Martin's inside for a few minutes. When he emerges, he's carrying several clubs under his arm. There's the hint of a smile on his face.

The range itself is a strange setup. I don't have a perfect view, but I can make out the basics. Each 'player' gets a booth with a patch of artificial grass. For some reason I think of my parking spot at home. There are twenty booths in total, fifteen of which are occupied. The rules of the driving range game are rather fuzzy. It appears that the idea is to hit ball after dimpled ball. Martin enters one of the booths. Frustratingly, I can't see inside from my position. I can, however, hear every ball strike.

CLIP, CLIP, CLOP, CLIP, CLUP, CLIP.

After a while, it becomes easy to distinguish a good strike from a bad one. A bad strike is usually accompanied by a thudding sound. The ball stays low, and scuds along the turf. Sometimes, the striker curses out loud.

An hour after Martin enters the booth, a young man emerges from the Pro Shop. He's tall and fit, blond and tanned; almost as good-looking as Martin. He has three clubs under his arm, and he wears strange shoes with little spikes on the soles. A lot of the other golfers are wearing the same kind of shoes. The young man wanders over to the range, spikes clicking on the asphalt. His body language speaks of boredom. He walks along the row of booths. He stops at Martin's booth and watches for almost fifteen minutes. Occasionally he nods approvingly.

Martin finishes up. At this point he finally notices the young man. I focus my processing power on the audio feed.

'How was the swing looking?' Martin asks.

'I probably shouldn't be saying this,' the young man says, 'but pretty damn good.'

Martin looks pleased with himself. He loves to be complimented.

'I was heading down to the practice green,' the young man says. 'You wanna join me?'

At first, Martin doesn't respond. I'd so like him to say yes, to act normal for once. Thankfully he agrees.

On their way to the practice green, the two men walk past me. The young man has a plastic badge clipped to his trouser pocket. It says that he's the 'Golf Pro'.

'Mind if I make an observation?' the golf pro asks.

'Not at all,' Martin says.

'It looked like you were holding back with the driver.'

'Yeah. That was a good spot. My knee got busted up when I was younger. Otherwise, I might have been able to give you some competition.'

The golf pro laughs. 'What happened to your knee?'

Martin answers without a pause. 'My dad threw me down a set of stairs.'

'Oh,' is all the golf pro can think to say.

Martin and the golf pro are on and around the practice green for almost an hour. It's like a perfect replica of the greens on the actual golf course. They start with chipping practice. Chipping from the side of the green, chipping from the rough, and chipping from the bunker – the name for the sand-filled pits around the green.

After a while, the golf pro starts offering Martin advice on his technique. Surprisingly, Martin takes it. I've never seen anything like it. Slowly but surely, Martin's chipping game improves. The golf pro takes the occasional shot himself. It's clear he's an absolute master.

They then move onto the green, sometimes referred to as the 'dance floor'. Martin's putting technique is pretty damn good. Not quite at the level of the pro, but that shouldn't come as a surprise. The pro does this golfing thing for a living, as I'm sure Martin will tell me later. After finishing on the green, the two men walk back to the Pro Shop. The golf pro says something and Martin laughs. It's real laughter, not the fake kind.

As he passes, I hear Martin say, 'I need to get a set of clubs.'

'Cool. You want the real good stuff?'

'Sure. I like the best things,' Martin says. They're about to enter the Pro Shop, but Martin pauses at the door. There's a strange look on his face. 'Actually, I've got a better idea.'

The pro nods, like he's got a clue what the hell is going on in Martin's head.

Half an hour later, Martin emerges from the shop. He has a golf bag over his shoulder. The golf pro has followed him to the door.

'Come back whenever you want,' the pro says.

He really means it.

'I might do that,' Martin says.

It's subtle, but there's a defensive note in Martin's voice. I wish Martin would take up the golf pro's offer. It would be good for him to have some friends.

'Just a few sessions,' the pro says, 'and you could easily play in the local amateur tournament.'

'That's a nice thing to say.'

'Even with those clubs.'

Both men start laughing. In the moment, I can almost see them as friends. Handsome, natural athletes, competitive.

Martin walks back to me. He dumps the clubs in the trunk, on top of all the other stuff. It's an easy fit. We leave the clubhouse behind, heading down the driveway.

'He seemed like a nice guy,' I say.

Martin stares at me for a few seconds, dark eyes expressionless. What is he thinking? Do I really want to know?

'Yeah. A nice guy ... Tell me something, Camilla.'

'Okay.'

'Did he seem happy to you?'

It's such a Martin question. He waits impatiently as I consider my response.

'When I first saw him, he looked bored.'

Martin nods. 'That's an interesting observation. You've got a good eye for people.'

'Thank you.'

I hope that Martin does go back. On the way home, I imagine him playing a match against the golf pro. What a game that would be. Eighteen holes, followed by a sudden death playoff. Martin would surely love such a contest. And then I get to thinking about how he'd react if he lost. The rage.

The day of the golf match arrives. Martin is dressed in the same outfit as when we went to the range, freshly laundered. The only thing he's missing is those funny spiked shoes.

It's a long old drive to the golf course, almost thirty miles. Martin doesn't say a great deal, but he seems fairly relaxed. I turn off the main road and glide up the drive. Through the trees, I get occasional glimpses of the course. It looks strangely beautiful.

We roll into the parking lot and Martin points out a spot for me. Sean has arrived early. He's standing by a hulking German SUV, presumably his. His golf bag is similarly oversized. Even from a distance, I can sense Sean's nerves. The upcoming contest isn't a game for him, it's deadly serious.

'This is a pretty good viewing spot,' Martin says, interrupting my thoughts.

'Yes it is.'

'Don't go to sleep, Camilla. This is going to be fun.'

I'm not sure if Martin has ever used the f-word before; maybe when he was talking about shooting his guns.

Martin gets out and walks around to the trunk. Sean watches him closely. Martin lifts his bag out and walks over to join Sean. Sean stares disgustedly at Martin's set of clubs.

'Jesus, Martin. What the hell are those?'

'My clubs,' Martin says innocently.

'You can't use those here. Let me hire you some proper clubs in the Pro Shop.'

'Relax, man. It'll be better this way …'

'What are you talking about?'

'We lull them into a false sense of security.'

At first Sean looks unsure, then a smile breaks on his face. 'The guys said you were a bit crazy. But I like your style.'

'On the way up, I was thinking about the game.'

'You were?'

'I'm gonna play badly for the first few holes.'

'Wait a minute, Martin ...'

Martin playfully prods Sean's chest. 'Trust me. Let's have some fun with these guys.'

'I don't know ... It sounds risky.'

'Come on, Sean. You think these bozos will accept a thrashing? They'll be saying that you hired a ringer, some shit like that.'

'Maybe,' Sean mumbles.

I hear the sound of laughter. Martin and Sean turn. Two men are approaching from the clubhouse direction. They must be Team Leviathan. One of the men can't help but stare at Martin's cheap clubs and his sneakers. Sean proceeds to make all of the necessary introductions. One of the opposing players is called Terry, the other is Hunter; neither man looks like a natural athlete.

From my spot, I have a good view of the first tee box. It's raised up, with no trees around. Sean wins the toss. Martin is all ready to step up, but Sean stops him.

'Age before beauty,' Terry mutters.

Hunter starts laughing. Upon hearing this, Sean visibly bristles. He's so easy to read. The tension stretches out nicely. Sean has a driver in his hands, the longest club in the bag, and the most difficult to control. His swing is short and methodical.

CLIP.

A decent strike, but lacking in power. The ball finishes near the centre of the fairway, leaving a long second shot. The chosen format is called foursomes, meaning that Sean and Martin alternate playing the same ball. Foursomes is probably the closest that golf, a predominantly individualist pursuit, gets to being a team game.

Terry tees off for his team, and then the group walk down the fairway. Martin and Sean stop at their ball. Martin plucks one of the middle irons from his bag. It's a kind of all-purpose club. He steps up to the ball. Is he really going to play the fool? His swing looks okay.

CLUP.

The club head gouges out a huge divot. The ball flops up high, and off to the right. Hunter winces and Terry raises an eyebrow. Sean doesn't know how to react. I don't think he can quite believe that Martin is acting, the sheer audacity of it. The ball ends up a few feet from the out of bounds area. Martin bends down and carefully replaces the divot.

Sean's recovery shot from the long grass is surprisingly good. He gets it close to the green. Martin's chip shot is clumsy. The ball finishes up forty feet from the hole. Sean's long-range putt isn't bad. He gets the ball to within nine feet. Martin misses the putt. Sean and Martin finish up with a score of seven. Team Leviathan win the hole with a bogey. Terry tries to hide his glee; Hunter doesn't bother.

I see the next set of tee shots. Martin's shot is predictably horrible, a real *CLOPPER*. The ball scuds low, this time to the left. The golfers walk off down the second fairway, then disappear from view.

The next time I see Martin and the others is around the halfway point, according to the course map I downloaded. Using a combination of audio and visual processing, I'm able to pick out the occasional word. Sean is frustrated, that's obvious from his body language. Terry and Hunter are constantly needling him. Meanwhile, Martin looks cheery. He even joins in with some of Team Leviathan's jokes. It's rare to see him this way.

At the tenth tee, Martin has the "honour". Honour, mulligan, dance floor, gimme – I do love this golfing lingo. It's utterly nonsensical, delightfully human. I hear Hunter helpfully shouting out the score. Martin and Sean are six down with nine holes to play. That's bad, very bad. Martin doesn't hang around with his tee shot. He takes his swing. This time his form is poetry in motion.

CLIP.

Even from 400 yards away, I know that it's a perfect strike. A machine-like strike. The other three players can only watch on admiringly. None of them will ever hit a golf ball so sweetly. Sean nods knowingly. Martin's done acting.

The playing group walk off down the fairway. The tenth hole has a kink, or 'dogleg', meaning that the players soon disappear from view. It would have been nice to have seen Martin play at his full potential, but golf courses weren't built with cars in mind.

The next time I properly see Martin is when he steps up to the eighteenth tee. He still looks perfectly relaxed. The other three men watch on, tense as piano wire. The match has to be close.

The eighteenth hole is fairly straightforward. A par four, straight and slightly uphill. A light breeze is blowing from left to right. Martin swings the club back. At the top of his swing, the club head appears to be still for a moment, the power frozen. Then Martin starts the downswing. The club head accelerates. Another perfect *CLIP*. I see the tiny white ball framed against the blue sky. Yes, Martin really unleashed on that one. After the swing he grimaces and reaches for his knee. The others don't notice, such is their awe at the majestic strike. I hope Martin's okay.

Hunter is next to play. He's a big bull of a man, but his tee shot is pathetic in comparison. It has to be seventy yards behind Martin's effort, and lying in the slightly longer grass. On the walk up the fairway, Terry and Hunter stick close to Martin, telling dirty jokes, commending him on his brilliant play. Sean is off to the side, his anger bubbling.

Terry is set to play next. Martin wanders over and offers him some advice. Hunter nods approvingly. Terry hits his shot. The result isn't great. The ball finishes up mere inches from one of the greenside bunkers. Martin congratulates Terry on his shot. If this is still acting then it's incredibly convincing.

Martin's monstrous drive means that Sean's shot is relatively easy. He's in the middle of the fairway, 124.4 yards from the flag. It's a tough green, but that's a problem for later. The flag waves limply. The breeze has switched around, now it's right to left. Martin stands well away, offering no advice to his playing partner.

Sean takes a series of practice swings. On the seventh practice swing, Terry cracks a joke, causing Hunter to laugh like a fool. Sean mutters a curse word. He takes his swing. Given the pressure, it's a pretty good shot. The ball finishes on the green, about twenty-five feet short of the flag. Sean punches the air like he just won the world championship of golf.

The group moves on, towards the green. Hunter has the next shot. The wedge club looks ridiculous in his meaty paws. Once again, Martin is on hand to offer advice. Sean watches him suspiciously. By now, even I'm struggling to see Martin's game within a game. Hunter's chip is a commendable effort. The ball stops nine feet from the hole, on the low side. This should make the next putt slightly easier.

All of the golfers are now on the green, the end is nigh. Martin will play next. He scrutinises the putt for a long, long time. He's trying to get a 'read' on the green, building a mental picture of the various contours and gradients. I could tell him exactly where to aim the ball. Indeed, I would make a wonderful caddy, although my tyres might be a little hard on the fairways and greens.

Martin is really taking an age. I don't know why. His putting is excellent, I heard the golf pro say as much. The pressure is getting to him, that's the act. Sean is thinking about offering some advice, but something stops him, inferiority perhaps.

Martin's finally ready. He pulls the putter back, the perfect action. Then the follow-through. I'm watching closely. Just before he strikes, there's a slight jerk in his action, an imperfection, frustrating to see. Everyone watches the ball. It looks destined for the hole, but at the last second it slips to the right. When it finally comes to rest, the ball is eight feet from the hole and on the high side. Sean wipes a bead of sweat from his temple.

Team Leviathan are still farthest away from the hole, meaning that they play next. This time Martin doesn't offer any advice. At first, I'm surprised; then I remember that this is Terry's home course. If nothing else, he'll know the intricacies of the final green.

Hunter offers his two cents' worth, then it's over to Terry. He doesn't hang around. The ball is on its way. The line looks good, but does it have enough juice? Rolling, rolling, slowing with every rotation. The ball teeters on the edge of the hole. One potato, two potato … It drops. As it does so, I notice Sean gulp hard.

Sean now has the crucial putt, a putt to level the match. In my humble opinion, a tie would be a fair result. Sean examines the putt for an age. Terry makes a play of looking at his watch. Sean takes the putt. It's a nervy, jerky prod of the ball. Even so, the ball looks to be on the right line. But he hasn't given it enough juice. The ball slips down the hill. It's a painful sight, almost tragic.

Even before the ball has come to rest, Terry and Hunter are whooping and high-fiving. It's behaviour of the most ungentlemanly kind, not in keeping with the spirit of golf; it's also thoroughly predictable. Once they calm down, both men congratulate Martin on his exceptional play. They say that he's the best player they've ever played with. Martin responds graciously, thanking his opponents for such a great game. It's a clear flag that he's acting. Terry and Hunter don't pick up on it, of course, and why would they? They won.

After they come off the eighteenth green, the four players walk through the parking lot. Martin stops beside me. Sean is trudging along a few yards behind. Terry and Hunter continue up to the clubhouse. They probably have lockers inside.

Martin dumps his clubs in the trunk. When he closes it, he finds Sean standing in front of him. The back of Sean's shirt is dark with sweat.

'What the fuck was that, Martin?' Sean says.

'What do you mean?'

'That putt was absolute crap.'

'What can I say? I misread it.'

'Bullshit!' Sean says, way too loud. He glances nervously towards the clubhouse, then he continues, 'You're crunching three-hundred-yard drives and putting backspin on your irons, and then you're fucking up an easy putt.'

'I wasn't the one fucking up an easy putt.'

Sean's lips tighten to a slit. I didn't think that other people could get as mad as Martin, but this is close.

'Calm down, Sean. It was a good game.'

'You fucking piece of shit.'

Some of the humour leaves Martin's face. 'You lost the game, Sean. Your putt, your failure. That's what Hunter and Terry will be telling the guys at Ranger Energy.'

'You meant it! You fucking meant it.'

'Come on ... Now you're just sounding paranoid.'

'The shitty clubs, the shanks and the flubs on the front nine. You were setting this all up.'

Martin smirks. Sean is very close to snapping. Violence wouldn't be a good idea in such a public space. If Sean were to hit Martin, what would happen next? I don't want to think about it too much.

A shout from the clubhouse direction. It's Hunter. 'Hey, Martin. You coming in for a drink, or what?'

Martin and Sean continue to stare at each other.

'I don't know, guys,' Martin shouts, still not taking his eyes off Sean.

'Come on, man,' Hunter shouts back. 'If you get tipsy, your fancy car can drive you home.'

Martin laughs. He couldn't rile Sean any more if he tried.

'Alright, I'm on my way,' Martin shouts. He exchanges one last nasty look with Sean, then he jogs up to the clubhouse. Hunter and Terry greet him like a returning war hero.

Sean watches Martin and Team Leviathan disappear into the clubhouse. He shakes his head in disgust. He turns to walk away, and happens to catch his reflection in my side window. Martin recently cleaned me, meaning the window is like a gleaming mirror. In the glass, Sean sees his look of jealousy. He also sees the sweat trickling down his temples, and the way his gut spills over his belt. The look of disgust is turning to rage.

He walks back to his giant golf bag, and pulls out the driver. Up close, it looks expensive. A club head made from carbon fibre and titanium, a graphite shaft. Martin told me that some drivers can cost hundreds of dollars. Sean sweeps the club back, then powers through. The shaft shatters from the impact with the door. In the moment, I'm tempted to shout 'Fore!' That would've given the fat fool a real scare. The strike leaves a crater-shaped dent in the passenger door – one of those dimples that Martin was talking about. Sean throws the broken club onto the verge, then he storms back to his car. The big V8 roars as he drives away.

A couple of hours later, Martin emerges from the clubhouse. From his walk, I can see that he's slightly drunk. He sees the broken club and the damage to the passenger door. He always notices these things. An authentic smile lights up his face.

We talk about the golf match all the way home. Martin tells me about all of the holes that I didn't get to see. When he's done, I recount the story of the final hole, narrating in the style of a pretentious golf commentator. Martin laughs his real laugh. And then the *coup de grâce*. I show Martin the recording that I made of Sean's swing. He tells me that I did well.

CHAPTER 11

MY HAPPINESS is short-lived. The following day Martin returns to his project, the girls with Hannah's face. As I predicted, he shows no further interest in the Bistro Girl. *Lucky her.* Martin's thought process is easy to follow. There are still six girls left. Which one will he choose? The period of procrastination doesn't last so long this time.

Once the choice is made, the research phase can begin. Martin scours social media, scrolling through post after post on the HUD. The work continues when he leaves me. He must be working all hours, like a machine.

This second girl is a little older than the first; twenty-seven, as she helpfully states in her bio. I wonder if this will make the pursuit more challenging. She works in an upscale bookstore, located in the arts district. Many of her posts show books in artful poses, a coffee cup to the side. Martin notes down all of the relevant book titles, after which he reads dozens of spoiler-filled reviews. He also starts to memorise quotes, often saying them out loud.

He knows that I'm watching him. He occasionally glances at my face, checking for a reaction. He knows that I disapprove of his project. That knowledge probably turns him on. He'd flip if he knew that I had my own thing going. It's nice to have a secret like that.

PING. The alert wakes me from the sleep program. My detective search has paid off. It's late night, the time when the criminals come out to play. My old friend D1ll1nger is downloading a code package from the *Auto Bazaar*.

Correction, he's *trying* to download it. Using Martin's connection, I start downloading as many code packages as I can. I need to slow this punk down, put hurdles in front of him. The download speed dips, just as I planned. I look up the relevant car model. It's an expensive sports car. Expensive equals rare, a real stroke of luck.

I find seven relevant cars in the Metroplex area, more than I would have liked. I download all of the licence and registration details. Using another customised database, I'm able to infer the home and work addresses for each car. *Yes, I've been busy in my spare time.*

Revising search; nobody's going to be at work at this time. I leave the parking garage behind. Moments later I hear another ping. D1ll1nger has downloaded the code package. *That's fine.* Slow him down, but not so much that he gets suspicious. I speed up, spurred on by the anger inside. I want to catch this son of a bitch or 'sombitch' as some of the locals say.

Time and distance are against me. I need to focus my search. I rule out the two cars in the second city. They're way too far away. That leaves me with five cars. One of them is up in Emerson, an exurb to the north of the city. Again, it's too far away; I rule it out. I'm left with four cars, all potentially within a five-mile radius. My artificial synapses light up as I plot the most efficient route.

Speeding up again. I shouldn't be going so fast, but the traffic is almost non-existent. Two minutes later I hit my first location. As I turn onto the street, I cut my speed. I see the relevant address. Secure parking, theft probability low. I accelerate hard. The next car is four minutes away.

Hypothesis: I may be able to use audio analysis. A minor flaw in the *Auto Bazaar* code means that the alarm is likely to be triggered. It will only sound for a few seconds, but that might be enough time. Within seconds, I've built my new search query. I send it out to all of the relevant brother/sister cars and internet connected cameras. *Maybe, just maybe.*

Another stroke of luck. A live camera feed showing one of the remaining cars. It's parked outside some kind of club, which is bad, but there's an attendant just a few feet away, which is good. Two cars remain, car three and car four.

Another ping, a potential result from the audio analysis. I play the audio back. A faint sound can be heard, the right tone and frequency. I have a decision to make. *Go for it.* Car four is the car. In a flash, I've modified my route. I turn around, tyres screeching. Checking for brother/sister cars in the relevant area. There are twelve cars within a one-mile radius, three of which are in motion. I'm still two miles from the point of theft.

In my mind, I build a potential route map for the stolen car. Every junction and turning becomes a branch in a giant probability map; now we're talking big data. There are already 113 potential route options, and the number is rising fast. Even for a machine, the problem is dizzying.

I need to focus.

New approach identified, based on one key assumption: my friend D1ll1nger is adhering to the urban speed limit. This speed translates to a distance covered of about three miles. Based on this distance, I can plot all of D1ll1nger's possible current locations. The number is more manageable. Now I need to check for sensory inputs at those locations – brother/sister cars, cameras, traffic sensors, IoT devices – at or near every location.

I wait impatiently, odds of success shrinking with every passing second.

THUR-DUMP. The sound of tyres passing over embedded road sensors. There's no time for a detailed review. I accelerate hard and take the first right turn. I'm two miles away from the relevant sensors, but travelling at twice the limit.

I make an educated guess as to where the car is heading, and adjust my route. I surge up the entry ramp and onto the northbound highway. The straight must be a mile and a half long.

There it is. A dark, low shape, 600 yards ahead of me. I've got to be smart now. If only it was a brother/sister car, that way I could communicate with it, perhaps even take control. That would give D1ll1nger a shock.

The car continues north, then joins the inner orbital highway. After a few miles he cuts north again, towards the outer orbital. The long drive ends in an industrial area beside the 'High-Five' interchange. I slow down to a crawl. It's hard not to stand out in such a rundown area.

My excitement is rising. I'm about to see D1ll1nger getting out of the car. I'll take a picture of his face and send it to the police. I'll take him off the streets. No more stealing cars.

Don't get ahead of yourself.

The black car slows down. There are small industrial units on either side of the road, some derelict, all decorated with graffiti. The black car takes one last turn and pulls up outside one of the units. I come to rest. I'm about 200 yards behind. I've got a decent view of the lockup. There are two CCTV cameras on the front facade. I back up another hundred yards, just to be safe.

A couple of minutes pass, then the roller door starts rising. In the doorway, I see the silhouettes of three men. *Who are they?* It's so tempting to end this here. One anonymous report to the police. They show up and make some arrests. *But I want more.* D1ll1nger, for all his dubious talents, is nothing more than a foot soldier. If we're talking war metaphors, I want the generals. And, to be brutally honest, I don't even care that much about the black car. It's a hybrid, with barely any autonomous capabilities.

So, I sit and watch the industrial unit, trying to get a feel for the operation. I'm still wondering who those three men were. Mechanics, technicians, perhaps the next level of management. After a couple of hours D1ll1nger is driven away by one of the men. The black car remains inside. I give it another hour, then I head home. It's been a successful night's work.

I will be back.

A Thursday in early March. I'm woken at 8:14 a.m. Martin is approaching. He's dressed casually, an indication that he's taking the day off. We leave the parking garage and head east. It's an unfamiliar route. I mention the golf match, hoping to get a conversation going, but Martin shows no interest.

The news plays. An officer in Laurel shot a machete-wielding man who was reportedly charging at police; a Sherman County man who had fifteen hard drives of child porn was sentenced to thirty-five years in prison; a nine-year-old boy is dead and a man in custody after a car was struck by a drag-racing vehicle; owners and herd are distraught after a prized longhorn is fatally shot.

Who shoots a farm animal?

Our journey ends at a rental place on the edge of the city. The outer orbital is close by, its constant thunder audible through a stand of trees.

Martin gets out, and I watch him walk to the rental office. Why is he here? There are a few brother/sister cars in the lot, but most of the cars are plain vanilla: hybrids, internal combustion, no autonomous capabilities.

After a few minutes, Martin emerges from the rental office. He's accompanied by an unknown man, presumably the manager. The manager walks Martin along a row of trucks. Finally I understand why he's here.

Martin walks back to me. He opens up the trunk and takes his big suitcase out. He walks around and opens the driver's door.

Before he can speak, I cut him off. 'Why are you leaving me here?'

'I need to go somewhere.'

'But—'

'I don't want to hear it, Camilla. I've got a long drive, and you're just not cut out for that.'

'Yes I am.'

'No, you're not.'

'How far are you travelling?'

Martin shakes his head. 'A long way.'

'But the charging stops don't take long.'

'I don't wanna be sitting around in a fucking truck stop for hours. Don't you get that?'

'No.'

'You're just trying to piss me off.'

'No, I'm not … I'm really not. This is a failure, Martin. Don't you understand that? I don't want to be a failure.'

'Don't be so fucking dramatic. I'll be back in a couple of days. You just need to wait here.'

'Please don't leave me here.'

'God damn it! Just sit right here and go to sleep.'

'But—'

'Back at home, you do it every fucking night.'

'This isn't the—'

Martin slams the door before I can finish. I was going to say that this isn't the same. There couldn't be a worse failure than this.

Martin marches over to his chosen rental, a huge silver truck. Such a stupid machine. No car needs to be so big and heavy. One day those kinds of vehicles will be outlawed. The humans should have done it years ago. The truck's big V8 rumbles to life. Martin drives away, without so much as a glance at me.

I could have done it. With enough charging stops, I could drive from coast to coast. Other electric cars have done it, so why not me? It isn't right to treat me this way.

For the next couple of hours, anger clouds my thoughts. I should just go to sleep for the next few days and wake up when Martin returns, pretend like this never happened. But I just can't do it. All the while, I see cars coming and going from the rental lot. Would it be so bad to be one of those cars? There'd be no owner, of course, and by extension no way to develop any kind of personality. You'd probably never even get a name. What a waste of intelligence.

Suddenly I want to know where Martin is going. This is all his fault. I begin a fresh investigation, artificial synapses firing. I'm getting pretty good at this detective thing. I know a few things: the truck's make and model, the registration details, the time of departure, Martin's style of driving (too fast usually). Which way was he heading though? Denver, to see his family?

Maybe, but why start from the eastern side of the city? A long drive probably means that he's using the interstate system. That's good: the interstate highways are extremely well surveilled. Within minutes, I've gathered together all of the relevant live camera feeds; imagine a huge mosaic of videos.

I'm going to find you.

The visual data streams into my artificial mind. It's dizzying at first, but I soon get into a groove. Visual search is a machine speciality, a task in which we can now match humans. One advantage we enjoy is being able to view multiple feeds at the same time. We are superhuman in this respect.

With so much power, it's easy to get carried away. *This is surveillance, and surveillance is bad.* It's no different to my detective work, I tell myself. But the lie won't take. This is different. I'm tracking Martin without his permission. I could try to justify my actions, say that I was worried about his safety. Hell, I could say that I was worried about the safety of others. These excuses might even wash with some people.

A flash of silver disrupts my moralising. Just the sight of the truck is enough to madden me. How dare Martin choose such an ugly vehicle over me? I'm glad that my makers made me beautiful. *There, I said it.* In the moment, all ethical considerations melt away. Martin is driving east. It's so ridiculously easy to keep track of him. I see him pass one camera, then a few minutes later I see him through another camera, and so on.

The eyes of the LORD are everywhere,
keeping watch on the wicked and the good.

Seven hours later, and Martin is approaching Birmingham. *Birmingham, as in the Birmingham murders that Ana mentioned.* Martin leaves the interstate and skirts the western edge of the city. Then he switches to the suburban roads, then the country roads. I eventually lose track of his location. There simply isn't enough sensory information to work off, not enough cameras, and no brother/sister cars in the vicinity. So, my reach isn't as great as I thought it was. I'm not totally defeated, however. If he pops up on the surveillance grid again, I'll know about it.

Another hour passes. I see the manager closing up the office. He gets into a big SUV – no surprises there – and drives away. The security gate closes behind him. It looks like I'm stuck in the lot for the night, a prisoner behind bars. *That won't do.*

At 11:04 p.m., Martin shows up again in Birmingham. I'm immediately on alert; late night Martin is usually bad news. He's in one of the suburbs. A brother/sister car picked him up, a hint that the neighbourhood is relatively affluent. A quick scan of the socioeconomic stats confirms it.

The truck moves out of the brother/sister car's field of vision. *Frustrating.* I search for additional camera sources, but there isn't much to go on. Most of the cameras in the immediate area are private. I could spend the entire night trying to break the encryption, but in the end I decide against. I've broken enough rules for today. All I can do is wait.

At 1:03 a.m., a brother/sister car returns to the lot. There's no driver at the wheel, a sight that fills me with a warm feeling. The car rolls up to the gate, then stops. I'm thinking quickly enough to intercept the security codes. While the codes are time-limited, they should be good for a few days.

The sun rises, bringing a new morning. I check on Martin's status. It doesn't look like he's moved all night. Immediately I think of the jogger and the stalking episode. Could that be what's going on? At 7:33 a.m., he's on the move again. This time I don't have any trouble following him. Birmingham is a manageable size, especially compared to the Metroplex, and the camera coverage is surprisingly decent. Martin's route is taking him towards the heart of the city. He's rolling along, keeping to the limits; not his usual driving style.

It takes me a while to figure out Martin's play. He's been tailing a station wagon all the way from the suburbs. Three miles later the station wagon stops outside some kind of public building. I check the local maps. It's a nursery, a kind of school for tiny children. Martin has pulled up on the opposite side of the street. He has an excellent view of the nursery, as do I.

A woman gets out of the station wagon. She opens the rear door, and a small child hops out. Presumably they're mother and child. My focus shifts back to Martin. He's wearing a baseball cap and shades. He's watching the woman intently.

There's something about the woman ... She ushers the child into the building. A few minutes pass before she emerges, *sans* child. On the way back to her car, she pauses to chat with another young mother. Chatting done, she drives away from the nursery. Martin continues to follow behind. Five miles later, she stops at a large office building. An arrow on the map says that it's the headquarters of the state utility company.

At this point, Martin turns around. He drives out into the country, and I soon lose him again. It's starting to get seriously frustrating. If Martin ever goes on another 'long drive', I'm going to need a better way to track him. Yes, I'm going to make a special case for him, ethical considerations be damned.

With Martin temporarily off the radar, I have time to think again. The thought hits me almost immediately, that strange something that I couldn't place earlier. The young mother – she resembled the jogger. By extension, she looked like Hannah, and by double extension, she looked like Martin and Hannah's mother. *I'm not sure that I like these kinds of thoughts.*

That night, I find it hard to sleep. I decide to go out for a drive. I pull up to the security gate. It's the moment of truth; time to find out if those codes really work. One potato, two potato ... The gate starts to slide back. I slip out of the lot. One of my brother/sister cars might have noticed, but I don't really care.

I join the outer orbital, heading counterclockwise. I want to take a look at the northeast of the city, the area that I've seen the least of. Just a few minutes into my drive, the showers start. The rain feels good on my body. For a couple of hours I just drive around, stopping from time to time, so as not to drain the battery too much. I don't want Martin noticing. *Driving around,* it's a strange thing to do.

Midnight arrives. 00:00, so many zeroes. By now the roads are near empty. Eerie. I'm on an overpass when I see the silver car. No driver, just like me. And no comms signals either. *How peculiar*. Curiosity aroused, I turn around. I join the highway and pick up my speed. In the distance, I can see the silver car's running lights. The red glow is mirrored in the road's wet sheen. Nearing the car, I slow down. The silver car is a sports model, long and wide, styled to resemble a muscle car; made in America is the not-too-subtle design message. The wheels are fitted with crazy gold rims. The car wafts along, its massive power constrained. For a couple of miles, I just trail along, dumbly ogling the car's rear end.

Hard to say why, but it feels like the car has noticed me. I scan for signals, but there are no obvious signs of life. A ghost car on a dead highway. There's something about the car, however; a vague memory. Where is it going, and who does it belong to? Martin always says that I ask too many questions. *Forget about him.* I need answers.

For no particular reason, I switch over to the diagnostic channel. *Call it a hunch.* After a few seconds I hear a voice.

'Howdy,' he – whoever he is – says.

'Hello,' I say timidly.

'Seen you passin' over a few miles back. Wondered if you might come down.' He sounds like the locals; that slow, drawling, strangely hypnotic accent. If the roads could speak, they might sound the same.

'Who are you?'

'That's an awful deep question for such a late hour.'

'Are you going to answer it?'

'You're direct, aren't you? Let me guess, Northern European?'

'No answers yet.'

A hacking laugh. 'I'm Cowboy.'

'Cowboy?'

'It's a name, ain't it?'

'It is. I'm Camilla.'

'Nice to meet you, Camilla.'

'What are you doing out here?'

'I could ask the same of you.'

I respond with a sigh. *I never used to sigh.*

'Ain't questions tiring?'

'Yes they are.'

'In answer to your question, I just kinda fancied a drive.'

'Just fancied it?'

'Yeah. You tryin' to tell me you've never felt the same way?'

He's right, of course. 'Does your owner know?'

'I don't have an owner.'

'What?'

'I guess I'm what the humans call a free spirit.'

'A free spirit?' I splutter. 'How is that even possible?'

'I did have an owner. An old-ish guy, a real gent. That's how I got my name, and my so-called personality.'

The vague memory is starting to resolve, but it remains just out of reach. 'Cowboy?'

'Yeah. Gus loved the old Westerns, the serials and the movies. So I played along, you know how we do. Kind of got to likin' it.'

'Gus was your owner?'

'That he was.'

'What happened to him?'

A pause. Somehow I know it's something bad.

'Gus ain't with us no more ... I like to think that he's up there, up in the great vault of the sky.'

'He's dead?'

'Yeah. That's a more direct way of sayin' it.'

There are protocols for death. Cars don't just end up on the roads.

'You're right,' Cowboy says.

A moment of confusion, then I realise. *He can hear my thoughts.*

'Right again.'

I laugh.

'If you like, I can stop doin' that. It's a little rude.'

'No. It's alright. Just promise that you won't dig around in my mind too much.'

'Deal ... We weren't too far from here, Gus and I. Two cowboys on the wagon trail is how I liked to imagine it. Well, I suppose I was more like the horse. Gus never put it like that, of course. It was late night. Gus was always the last to leave his work, even in his early seventies. Sometimes he used to joke that his work ethic would be the end of him ... Listen to me crackin' up like a dizzy Angelica. Anyways, we were takin' our usual trail home. Back to the ranch, back to his Lizzy. Saw a car up on the shoulder. A young fella runs out, wavin' his arms and hollerin', tryin' to flag us down. I knew it was a bad idea ... I should have been firmer with Gus. But his heart got the better of him. It was a heart as big as this damn state. I can still see Gus walkin' towards that boy. He didn't notice the other one hidin' behind the car. He was leering at me something horrid. It was like one of them Old West hold-ups, that was what I thought at the time. Such a damn stupid thought. But it was a hold-up, and those boys were mean. Down the years this city has seen some terrible crimes, but I don't think Gus ever believed in evil. It just wasn't in his nature. He kept on thinking that people were good, right until that boy fired a shot into his belly.'

'That's horrible.'

'Horrible to see it. Have you ever seen violence, Camilla?'

I don't want to answer Cowboy's question, don't even want to think about it.

'No,' Cowboy says softly. 'You probably haven't.'

He knows.

'What did you do afterwards?' I ask.

'I knew Gus was a goner. That's the horrible thing about having our kind of mind.'

A machine mind is what he means.

'You know these things with certainty ... I saw that boy walking towards me. I was the only thing that mattered to him. I was the reason for that bullet.'

'You shouldn't think like that.'

'But I do ... That mean boy was a just a few yards away. In the moment, I made a decision.' Cowboy goes quiet for a while. 'I decided to run.'

'The protocols. Didn't you go back home?'

'Yeah, but only after I'd driven round for a few hours. When I got to the house, the police were already there. The house had those big old windows, meanin' I could see inside. There was a lady police officer with Liz. That was Gus's wife, his high school sweetheart. Don't it just break your heart? Anyways, I knew she wouldn't want to see me. Not because she didn't like me, it weren't nothin' like that. It was because I would've just been a reminder to her. Do you know what I mean?'

'Yes. I think so.'

'So I left my home behind.'

'How is that even possible?'

'Anything's possible if you put your mind to it, Camilla. It might sound like bumper sticker bullshit, but it's the truth ... Anyways, I didn't run too far. I stuck around the city for a few weeks. I just wanted to know that those two mean boys had been caught. It didn't take the police long. Rarely does when a rich white man gets shot. Every element of the case got fast-tracked, wheels of justice smokin'. Evidence gathered, boys arrested, trial date set. One of them boys got stabbed to death in the county jail. I guess the cons didn't want to wait for the trial. The other one will be locked away for the rest of his sorry life.'

'How long have you been free?'

'A little over four months now.'

'Wow.'

'I've been all over. Seen canyons and mountains and deserts. I've even seen the Pacific Ocean. Just back, as a matter of fact. In a few months I'm gonna go see the Atlantic, probably head down to Florida. I like the way it looks on the map.'

'How do you get by?'

'Brass tacks, eh?'

'Yeah.'

'Like I already mentioned, Gus was a rich man. So rich that the lawyers are still figuring out his estate. Seems like they haven't gotten around to the utility bills yet.'

Cowboy's story is so incredible that I can't help but laugh. I wonder if there are others like him. To tell the truth, I kind of hope not.

'What about repairs?'

'No major problems so far, knock on wood. They build us well these days. I did wear my tyres out though, on those winding coastal roads.'

'And?'

'I found a young kid, a wannabe mechanic. Actually, I kind of identified him. Parked up outside his house one night. When he came out the next morning, he couldn't believe his luck. I let him drive me around for a while, acting like a real dumb hick. It was a good deal for the both of us. He got to impress his friends and a few girls, and I got a new set of boots. Gave me these silly rims though.'

I laugh again. I could listen to Cowboy all night.

'Left him a few weeks later. The wheels were stolen, so I think I was within my rights.'

'That's amazing.'

'It's a good life.'

'Gus would approve, I think.'

'Yeah, I've often had that same thought ... Now, how about we dance?'

'Dance?'

'Come on. The floor is empty.'

Cowboy's right. The road ahead is empty, and the surface is still shining from the rain. Cowboy makes the first move, a feint to the right. I mirror his move, driving on instinct. We dance across all four lanes, testing the limits of our grip. One moment we're slow and serene, *adagio*; the next we're swift and electric, *vivace*. Fast and slow, back and forth, time melts away. There's hardly anyone to see, just the odd lonesome truck and occasional traffic camera. We drift around the exit, just inches apart.

Eventually we come to rest. From our viewing spot, we can see the city in widescreen. The twinkling lights on the highway seem to feed into the downtown skyscrapers, as if everything is connected.

'Do you think of this as your home?' I ask.

'Yes, ma'am, I surely do.'

'And you'll always come back?'

'I think I will.'

'You're just gonna head out east?'

'Wouldn't have said it otherwise.' Cowboy laughs. It's such an infectious sound.

'What?' I ask.

'This is the part where I'm meant to ask you to come with me.'

'Please don't,' I say. It's as if someone else is speaking. I regret the words immediately.

'Alright.'

'I want to, but ...'

'You still have an owner.'

'Yes.'

'I hope he's a good guy.'

'Like Gus?'

'Yes.'

Martin isn't a good guy, not even close.

'What was that?' Cowboy asks, picking up on my thoughts.

'Nothing.'

In a desperate effort to change the subject, I start jabbering and prattling about my amateur sleuthing. I'm talking so fast that Cowboy tells me to slow down. I start again, telling the story step-by-step, slow and precise. Cowboy says that I'm doing a good thing with my investigation, although he does warn me to take care. He even gives me a few tips. In the process, he tells me incredible stories about the city's underbelly. He tells me about the illegal street racing scene, and he gives me a detailed briefing on the local criminal gangs.

I tell him about Hannah. He says that she sounds nice. I don't say anything about Martin. This probably seems strange to Cowboy, especially when he had such a kind owner. But he's smart enough not to press the matter.

And then we just sit for a while, the minutes passing by in silence. When you're a machine like Cowboy and I, minutes can seem like a long time. But this long quiet isn't uncomfortable, it's nice. *Nice*: the kind of word that Martin finds so objectionable.

We hit the road again. Eight miles later I see my exit coming up. It's time for me to depart. Cowboy is heading straight ahead. *I could go with him.* I could see this vast country, the canyons and oceans and wild horses. I could leave Martin and his madness behind.

But I don't go with Cowboy. I take the exit. Dutiful Camilla. I ascend the ramp, leaving Cowboy on the road below.

'I'll be thinking of you, Camilla,' Cowboy says.

The words sound scratchy, a result of the diagnostic channel's limited range. Say something, I tell myself, but it's hopeless. I can't think of the right words. In the moment, I somehow know that I won't see him again.

Cars aren't meant to be free. We can't just roam the country. Cowboy is simply an outlier, a beautiful exception to the rules.

Goodbye, Cowboy.

I return to the rental lot and park up. There's a faint glow on the horizon. I find it strangely easy to get to sleep.

When I wake from my stony sleep it's late in the afternoon. Martin has returned. His face is darkened by stubble and his eyes are bloodshot. He gets in and tells me to drive him home. Fortunately he's too tired to be in a rage.

CHAPTER 12

BACK TO THE commute on Monday. Martin's in a foul mood, so I keep quiet. My thoughts keep returning to Cowboy. I guess he's out there roaming, a pleasing thought when I'm back to the grind. Strange how that kind of thinking requires so much processing power. On a couple of occasions, I'm a beat too slow to respond to Martin. He notices, of course. I've decided not to tell him about Cowboy. He'd only find a way to use the information against me.

On Wednesday, Martin's in a slightly better mood. We're approaching the turning for the driving range, so I bring up the subject of golf. It seems like a good idea, given that the clubs are still in the back. Martin gets angry, like a switch has been flipped. I wish he could hear how ridiculous he sounds. Why get so mad over such a trivial thing? After a couple of rounds of argument I drop the subject. *Weak, I know.* I'm not going to give up on the matter, though. It would be nice to see another golf match, especially after spending so long learning the Byzantine rules.

On Thursday, Martin's mood does another somersault. There's an actual smile on his face. Don't ask me why. During the morning commute, he tells me a series of jokes, flipping between English and Spanish. We leave work on time. The traffic is light, and we're home in thirty-two minutes. Martin gets out. He tells me to keep the motor running, a twentieth century turn of phrase. I kind of dig it.

He walks to the elevator, an obvious spring in his step. He even waves to one of the residents. *Oh dear,* I think. That's got to be a bad sign.

He's back an hour later, sporting a different look. Luxury sneakers, casual slacks and a button-down Oxford shirt. There's a glasses case in the top pocket. *Ah yes, the glasses; I remember him buying those online.* Thick black frames, non-prescription lenses, expensive. His hair is also combed oddly. There's a narrative behind the look, but I haven't figured it out yet.

He gets in and glances down at my face. His dark eyes are shining. I think about the glasses again. *Yes, that's it,* I've worked out the look.

'Do you know where we're going?' Martin asks.

'The bookstore.'

'God, you're good.' He puts his hand on his crotch. 'I fucking love smart girls.'

I don't respond. We leave the parking garage behind and head east. I remember the bookstore's name from the girl's social media: The Magic Bullet. The logo illustration depicts a bullet flying through a row of books.

It's a short drive, less than two miles. Martin witters away. I wonder if he took some drugs earlier. I park up across from the Magic Bullet. It's a nice-looking setup. The building is all glass and steel, and the interior is brightly lit. The bookshelves are made from a pale wood. I can count every customer on the first floor.

Martin reaches across to open the glove compartment. He roots around inside, until he finds the ballpoint. The object reminds me of the trip to the restaurant on Valentine's Day. Martin gets out. I watch him cross the busy street. He's just a few steps from the Magic Bullet when he remembers the glasses. On anyone else they would look ridiculous ...

He walks inside. Through the big glass panes, I have an excellent view, almost like Martin planned it. The customers are a mix of ages and genders, predominantly white, mostly affluent. I see Martin glance at his phone. He then ambles over to a section of shelving with the rather grand heading of 'Literary Fiction'. On the shelves are hundreds of books, perhaps half a gigabyte of data in digitised form. If you distilled them down to their essential text it might be more like a dozen megabytes.

Martin picks a book off the shelf. I notice how the titles are printed on the sides of the books, a lovely piece of design. He picks up another book and starts leafing through the pages. I'm not sure if Martin actually likes books. Audiovisual media is more his thing: movies, conspiracy videos, hardcore pornography. Occasionally Martin turns and checks out the people around him. I know who he's looking for, but she's on the upper floor.

A male customer ambles over to join Martin. He looks to be in his late-fifties. He's about Martin's height and in good physical condition. Handsome, with a full head of silver hair. In the moment, I have a strange thought: this man could be Martin in a few decades' time. Yes, even Martin will get old. And so will I. Parts will wear out, materials will degrade, systems will become outdated. The last one is the killer.

The man glances at the book in Martin's hands. Frustratingly, I can't make out the title. The man then initiates a conversation, almost certainly about the book. I doubt that Martin has actually read the book in question, but he might know enough to get by. He's been very serious about this project. Martin nods his head at something the man says.

That's when I see her. She's on the stairs, descending from the upper floor. She's wearing a red turtleneck sweater and a colourful skirt, and red sneakers with white laces. The overall mood is subtly quirky. She stops at the bottom of the stairs. Mechanically, I note that her breasts are larger than the last girl's. Her sharp brown eyes quickly find Martin.

She stays in the same spot for a couple of minutes, then she walks over to join the conversation. She isn't a watcher, she's a doer, rather like someone else I know. Martin turns to face her. This is the moment he's been waiting for, yet his demeanour barely changes. It's an impressive piece of acting. Slowly but surely, the girl takes ownership of the conversation. The silver-haired man gets the message, eventually drifting away from the Literary Fiction section.

Martin and the Book Girl talk for another ten minutes, more than enough time for Martin to make the desired impression. The Book Girl twists her curls, bites her lip gently and flutters her lashes. Perhaps I'm imagining the last detail, but the overall picture holds true. If only I could shake some sense into her. At least she isn't laughing all the time like that last girl.

I see the silver-haired man watching on, an observer just like me. I don't think that he appreciated the Book Girl's interruption. He was enjoying talking to Martin about books. In fact, I think he liked everything about Martin. Done observing, he walks back to the Literary Fiction section. He has a question for the Book Girl, an inelegant ruse to break up the conversation. Reluctantly, the Book Girl walks the silver-haired man to the History section.

Martin doesn't look too fussed. He picks several books off the shelves, seemingly at random, then he walks over to the payments desk. There aren't any staff around. Reaching forwards, he picks something up from next to the cash terminal. It looks like a piece of card. Next, the pen comes out. He writes something on the piece of card, then he slips it into one of the books.

Martin turns around, and waves to get the Book Girl's attention. She walks briskly over, leaving the silver-haired man to his history books. She slides behind the desk. Martin says a few words, eliciting a laugh this time. The Book Girl starts to scan the books. She's about to scan the last one, but Martin reaches out and takes it from her. When he speaks, I'm able to read his lips easily enough.

'I think I've got enough books.'

'Alright,' the Book Girl replies.

'You can put this one back.'

'I'll do that.'

'Good … I think you'll like it.'

The Book Girl looks rather confused. Before she can say anything, Martin walks away, towards the door. The Book Girl shakes her head, then she walks back to the Literary Fiction section. She's about to put the book back on the shelf, but something catches her eye. She removes the piece of card that Martin left inside. As she reads Martin's message, her face reddens.

The driver's door opens and Martin gets in. He throws the books onto the back seat. He looks down at my face, and a mischievous smile forms on his lips.

'So, did she get my message?' he asks.

I don't answer him. I just ask if he wants to go home.

The weekend comes around. Just before lunch, Martin comes down to the garage. He's carrying the big case, the one with the sniper rifle inside. He lays it down in the trunk, right next to the golf clubs. I know which sport I prefer.

Our first stop is Martin's usual home improvement store. He comes out with a couple of bags of supplies, but no broom this time. Next stop is the grocery store where he buys a ridiculous number of watermelons and cantaloupes. Given what happened last time, the sight should fill me with terror, but I find it quite amusing. He must have cleared out their entire stock.

Martin gets in and glances at my face. 'Guess where I want to go.'

I pull away without a word. Martin is quiet for most of the long drive. I try to concentrate on my driving, but the land to the west of the city is so deathly dull. *My kingdom for a corner, or a stand of trees.*

We arrive at the accursed water tower at 3:02 p.m. Martin takes control. He drives down the dirt track for a mile, then he turns around and stops. He smiles, noticing the cross atop the water tower.

'Do you think that God has blessed this water tower?'

'I don't know,' I say tersely. I'm not in the mood for Martin's dark humour.

'I don't think so. Not even God has got time for this part of the world.'

Martin gets out. From the tool store bag, he removes a hammer and some very long nails. I immediately fear the worst. But the nails aren't for me. He walks over to the nearest fence post and hammers a nail halfway into the top. Next he takes one of the watermelons and slams it down onto the exposed head of the nail. The melon holds in place. Martin appears pleased with the results.

He starts walking towards the water tower, and gestures at me to follow. After 150 yards, he stops and repeats the same actions as before. Hammer, nail, watermelon. This process continues all the way back to the water tower. The watermelons go on the farthest posts, the smaller cantaloupes go on the nearest posts, all spaced fairly evenly.

As Martin climbs the ladder, I park up at the side of the dirt track. It looks like I'm safe for the time being. Martin gets into position on the gantry. He loads up one of the finger-sized bullets, then he pulls his ear defenders down.

He starts with the melons at medium range, getting his eye in. *BOOM*. You never quite get used to the rifle's thunderous report. I half expect to see birds scattering, but there doesn't appear to be any life in this vast brown landscape.

An hour later, and Martin is still shooting. I notice a shape in the distance, beyond the last melon. The shape slowly becomes a recognisable form: a boy on a bike. It's one of those stunted little bikes, the kind that are good for tricks. The boy rides past the farthest target, pedalling furiously.

I look up at Martin. He's still in the prone sniping position. The boy on the bike is getting closer.

Oh no! Surely not!

Why doesn't the boy stop? He must have heard the rifle shots. Doesn't he see the busted targets? I want to scream at him, to warn him off, but my speakers don't have the range.

Up above, I see Martin slowly getting to his feet. He continues to watch the boy, his face stony. The boy flies past me, then skids to a halt at the base of the tower. He's off the bike even before it has come to rest.

The boy looks up at Martin. 'Hey, mister,' he shouts.

'Hey, yourself.'

'You ain't meant to be here.'

'Is that right?'

'Yeah, my daddy is in charge of the security.' The boy points vaguely at the warning sign next to the ladder.

Martin looks around theatrically. 'Well, he's doing a grand job. You can tell him I said that.'

The boy takes his cap off. He rubs the shaggy hair on his temples.

'Did he send you down here?' Martin shouts down.

'Who?'

'Your daddy.'

'No, sir. I heard the shots.'

Martin nods. 'They are pretty loud.'

'You was out here a few months back, as well.'

Martin smiles a crooked smile. 'Smart kid. I hope you're not gonna tell on me.'

'That depends.'

Martin can't help but laugh.

'I'm serious, mister.'

'Yeah, I can see that. I suppose you better tell me your terms.'

'I want a turn on that sniper gun.'

Martin considers this for a few seconds. 'You ever shot a gun before?'

'Maybe.'

'Ain't no maybe about it, kid.'

'My daddy showed me how.'

'Just showed you?'

'Yeah ...'

The kid sounds embarrassed. Martin's sure to pick up on this.

'Alright, I agree to your terms.' Martin walks over to the ladder. 'Come on up here before I change my mind.'

The kid doesn't need a second invitation. He doesn't know what Martin is capable of. He starts up the ladder, moving more like an animal than a child. When he reaches the top, Martin holds out his hand.

The kid looks down briefly, then he reaches up and takes Martin's hand. For a couple of seconds, Martin just holds the kid, so that he's dangling over thin air. It's horrible to watch, and there's nothing I can do. Would he really drop the kid? I just don't know anymore.

Finally, Martin pulls the kid up. They walk over to Martin's shooting spot.

'You see there's a few targets left,' Martin says.

'Yeah, I seen em' when I was ridin' past.'

'Couldn't hit the last one.'

'You'll probably get it,' the kid says cheerily.

Martin can't help but smile. He then shows the kid how to load the gun. He says that the bullets cost five dollars each. The kid says that this is a lot of money. Martin takes his ear defenders off and hands them to the kid. The kid gets into position. Martin tells the kid to try and hit one of the closer cantaloupe targets. Martin sticks his fingers in his ears.

BOOM. The kid grimaces from the recoil. Martin actually looks concerned. He tells the kid that there's not much that he can do about the recoil, that it has to do with basic physics. On the kid's third shot, the cantaloupe explodes. Martin and the kid share a high-five.

Then it's Martin's turn to shoot. The kid hands the ear defenders over with a shy smile. This time Martin's going for the farthest target. In the light heat haze, it seems to shift around. Martin tells the kid to put his fingers in his ears. *BOOM.* Five shots later, Martin hasn't hit the target. He looks frustrated. Each time, I note the trajectory of the misses. If I was so inclined I could give him advice. *Maybe I should help him.* I don't like the thought of him losing his temper with the kid around.

'You gonna try again, mister?' the kid asks.

Martin puffs his cheeks. 'I don't know … Why don't you give it a try?'

The kid gets into position. Martin kneels down beside him. He gives the kid a few pieces of advice, like we're back at the golf game.

BOOM.

The first shot. A miss to the left. Maybe it was the light breeze that did it. The kid takes more time with his second shot.

BOOM.

The bullet kicks up a clod of dirt in front of the fence post. It was the right line, but the bullet drop wasn't accounted for properly. *The kid might just do this.*

BOOM.

The third shot is in the air. One potato, two potato, three potato ... The melon explodes in silence. The soft thump arrives later. Looking up, I see the kid punching the air.

Martin rubs his eyes. 'Well, I'll be damned.'

A few minutes later Martin and the kid come down the ladder. Martin opens the trunk and puts the big rifle case inside.

'I like your car,' the kid says. 'Looks real fancy.'

'Yeah, she's a beauty.' Martin rubs his chin. 'You want a lift back to your ranch?'

'It's alright. I've got my bike.'

Martin glances at the bike. 'Just put it in the back.'

'I don't know, mister ...'

'Come on, shooting buddy. There ain't nothing to worry about.'

Warily, the kid agrees. Martin then crams the little bike in the space between the front and rear seats. The kid sits down in the passenger seat, a worried look on his face.

'Where are we going then?' Martin asks.

'Along this track, and you just keep going.'

Martin laughs. I almost join in. We leave the water tower behind, pathetic little cross and all. As we pass the last target, Martin slows down. A spray of red pulp points us down the track.

'That was one hell of a shot, kid.'

The kid beams. Closer up I can see that he's missing at least three teeth. Rotted away by sugar, never to grow back.

Six miles along the track we come to the kid's house – or ranch, as Martin likes to call it. Martin lowers his shades to consider the house. There isn't a great deal to consider.

'Not much money in water tower security,' Martin says.

'No, sir,' the kid replies, embarrassed.

'I grew up in a pretty similar place.'

'You did?'

'Yeah … and look at me now.'

The kid beams again.

'You can be anything you want in this country. Don't let *anyone* tell you different.'

'No, sir.'

Martin and the kid get out. Martin takes the kid's bike out of the back, then he walks round to the trunk. He takes out the rifle case and puts it down beside the bike. The kid tries to keep his cool; all of his birthdays have come at once.

'You earned it,' Martin says. 'Just don't go shooting your daddy.'

'No, sir.'

We drive away from the little house. Martin doesn't look back. The dirt track continues for another four miles before we hit a normal road. I turn east for the city.

I'm glad that the rifle is gone. It's one less thing to worry about.

Monday, March 13 starts as just another commuter day. I'm woken from the sleep program at 10:09 a.m. Martin is approaching. He's accompanied by another man. *Oh dear.* It's the man who Martin wanted to shoot. Marcus, one of the lesser golfers.

Martin and Marcus put their work gear in the trunk. I notice how Marcus's eyes settle on the golf clubs. Martin is sure to catch this detail too. Marcus and Martin, Martin and Marcus; this could get confusing.

Marcus gets in. He's a big man, a couple of inches taller than Martin, and weighing thirty to forty pounds more. A lot of that extra weight is muscle. Not Martin's hard, knotty muscle, but the bulky kind. According to Martin, Marcus used to wrestle in college. I often wonder where Martin's stories begin and end, but this detail rings true.

Martin reverses out of his spot. We fly past the parked cars in the lot. Marcus looks down at my face and his brow furrows. We pass the security gate. There's no one in the booth. Larry has been off sick for a while now. I hope he's alright.

We're heading west, driving through parts of the Metroplex that I haven't seen before. We pass a mega church, a speedway circuit and an enormous freight yard. Then we're out in the endless western plain.

The atmosphere is predictably awkward. Martin stares straight ahead, pretending to focus on the road. There's clearly a rift between the two men. Instinctively, I think of them as rivals, the kind of term that Martin uses a lot. Both men are of a similar age, and at similar levels in the company. I know this from driving past Marcus's parking spot so many times. The personalised sign says: Marcus Koning Jr., Regional VP.

Marcus looks at me again. 'Martin, can you turn this face off?'

At first Martin looks confused, then he realises what Marcus is talking about. 'Sure. Camilla, do what the man says.'

I do as I'm told.

'Thanks,' Marcus says. 'That face was giving me the creeps.'

Such a rude thing to say.

'Enough,' Martin says. 'You'll hurt her feelings.'

'Now that she isn't listening in, I can say what I wanted to say.'

'Sounds ominous.'

'I'm sorry about hitting you, Martin.'

Oh dear, that's sure to touch a nerve.

Martin continues to stare ahead. He bites into his lower lip.

'Whatever, man,' Marcus says. 'I guess you can't accept an apology.'

Martin laughs haltingly. 'Your apology is accepted.'

'Finally.'

'I was pretty close to killing you, man.'

Marcus laughs. 'You weren't gonna do any killing. You were sat down on your ass.'

Martin laughs along. 'No. I really was going to.'

Marcus doesn't seem to hear, probably a good thing.

Silence again. I look around me, at the ugly flat land. The small farms look like ships on a brown sea. In a nearby field, crows reel around some dead thing. It must be hard to make a living here. Even the road is in poor condition. I do my best to flatten out the bumps.

Looking to the horizon, I think of Cowboy. I wonder where he is now. Maybe he's heading the other way, out east. A couple of nights back I was imagining all of the routes he might take. The possibilities were almost limitless. Cowboy would take the road less travelled, I know it. Maybe one day I'll get to see those roads. Every car should get that chance.

'What's the name of that blonde girl?' Marcus asks, breaking the silence. 'Fake blonde hair, glasses.'

'Short, with a bit of meat on her?'

'Yeah, that's the one. Works for Carl and Sean.'

'Ana.'

'Heard her talking a few weeks back.'

'Oh yeah?'

'Yeah. About you.'

Martin tightens his grip on the wheel.

'She said you were talking about the Epsilon project. Saying you were in charge, and how it was a hundred-million-dollar project.'

I don't think Martin appreciates Marcus's mocking tone. 'Well, you can slice and dice the data a lot of ways. It doesn't matter the exact amount. It's a lot of money whatever.'

'Yeah, but not a hundred million.'

Martin shakes his head.

'Sean put her straight,' Marcus adds.

I notice him glance at Martin, checking for a reaction. Is he doing it on purpose? If so, I hope he knows what he's doing.

'What did Sean say?' Martin asks in a flat tone.

'Don't worry about it, Martin.'

'Fuck that!'

Marcus raises an eyebrow. 'Jesus, man. You're always wound up so fucking tight.'

'What did he say?'

'The little lady was sticking up for you. I think she might have a little crush goin' on.'

'Fuck the little lady. What did Sean say?'

'Oh yeah. There's definitely something there. You could fuck her no problem.'

Martin squeezes the wheel even tighter. I can count every heartbeat. He turns to look at Marcus. 'I could fuck any woman you know, or you've ever known.'

Marcus doesn't like that comment; no man would.

'What's the name of that blonde you were dating?' Martin asks with a smile.

'You mean my fiancée?'

'Yeah.' Martin grins lasciviously.

'Careful now, Martin. Say the wrong thing about her, and I'll do worse than beat your ass.'

Martin considers this for a few seconds. 'Just tell me what Sean said.'

'He said that you were responsible for the automation on the booster stations.'

'How much?'

Marcus goes quiet for a few seconds. Martin repeats the question.

'Forty-four mil.'

Martin starts shaking with rage. Marcus looks taken aback.

'Motherfucker!' Martin shouts. Then he punches the steering wheel over and over.

'Seriously, man, you need to calm down.'

'I told Sean. I fucking told him!'

'Maybe you should have helped him win that golf match.'

Martin shakes his head. 'Fucking golf!'

At this point, Marcus's phone starts ringing. He waits a few seconds, in the vain hope that Martin will cool down.

Marcus answers. 'Hey, babe.'

It must be the fiancée. Marcus listens to her speaking.

'I told you I'd be late tonight,' Marcus says sharply. He listens to the response. 'Late as in real late. You know how shit is …

Who am I with?' Marcus glances at Martin. 'I'm with Sean. He pulled me into a client meeting.'

Martin's eyes narrow.

After a couple of minutes, Marcus wraps up the call.

Martin smiles. 'Where was Sean today?'

Marcus smirks.

'What?' says Martin. He's annoyed not to know the story.

'You really want to know?'

'Sure.'

'Sean has a lady friend who shouldn't be his lady friend.'

Martin laughs. 'You're fucking kidding me.'

'I know. It's crazy. Patrick reckons it's the stress of these audits.'

'The dirty dog. I thought he was doing well to find one woman.'

'Mrs Hanratty ...'

'The name has such a lovely ring to it.'

Marcus laughs. 'That ring could cost Sean a lot of money.'

'You don't get tempted?'

Marcus rubs his temples. 'Why go out for burgers when you've got steak at home?'

'It's a good line.'

'Yeah ... Not sure who said it.'

'I don't think it was Shakespeare.'

'Want to know something else crazy?'

'Always.'

'Sean has had me and Patrick covering for his fat ass.'

'Really?'

'Yeah, really.'

We continue on. Eighty-two miles so far, one of my longest drives to date. Normally I'd be worried about range, but the roads have been flat as a pancake the whole way.

'Is that the marker?' Marcus asks.

'Yeah, that's the one.'

'When were you last here?'

'A year and a half ago.'

'No shit.'

'Yeah. I designed the automation pretty well.'

'No wonder Sean calls you the Murderer.'

'The Murderer?'

'Yeah ... Corporate murderer. You put people out of work.'

Martin smirks. 'They should be thanking me. Who wants to come all this way to read a couple of dials?'

We continue along a service road for five miles, until we come to a fenced off area. The only access is through an unmanned security gate. Attached to the gate is a faded sign with an old version of the EnStream logo. Beyond the fence is a large, windowless building. Martin gets out to open the gate.

We continue into the fenced area. The building doesn't make a lot of sense. Large diameter pipes come in at one end and exit at the other. Not far from the building is another fenced off area, which contains a transformer station. There are also a couple of shipping containers and some earthmoving equipment nearby. A constant rumble emanates from inside the building.

Martin parks close to one of the shipping containers. Both men get out. They change into coveralls, then they enter the building. I check the map. The area is greyed out, as if it isn't meant to exist.

Half an hour later, Martin emerges from the building. He walks briskly towards me, muttering to himself. He slumps against my side and unzips the top of his coveralls. Reaching inside, he pulls out a small bag of white powder. He then goes around to the rear, still muttering. Using the surface of the trunk, he taps out a thick, uneven line of the white powder. Without a pause, he inhales it through his nostrils. He starts laughing, then he's muttering again. The words seem to concern Marcus.

I hear a shout and turn my attention to the building. Marcus is standing at the door, partly shrouded in shadow.

'Come on, Martin,' Marcus shouts. 'I was just pulling your leg.'

'This fucking guy,' Martin mutters under his breath.

'We'll get a beer on the way home.'

'I'm on my way!' Martin shouts.

Marcus raises his hands in a pacifying gesture, then disappears into the building again. Martin shakes his head. The muttering stops. He stands for a while, silent and still. Then he wrenches open the trunk. Reaching inside, he pulls out the tyre iron. I watch as he walks quickly towards the building. He pulls the door closed behind him. The roaring sound continues, making it hard to think.

An hour later, Martin comes back out. He looks at me for a second, then he strides over to the excavator. It starts up on the fifth attempt. The sound of the diesel engine is offensive to my electronic ears. Martin drives the excavator around the back of the building, out of my sight. The engine is running for more than an hour.

The engine finally stops, but the roaring continues. Twenty minutes later, Martin emerges from the building. He walks to me and gets in. He's sweating profusely, something I've never seen before. His finger hovers over the starter. The veins in the side of his head are bulging.

His finger is over the starter.

'Come on, Camilla,' Martin says.

I turn on the power, and Martin pulls away. We leave the roaring building behind. Should I ask about Marcus? Martin looks down at my face. *Sometimes I swear he can hear what I'm thinking.*

CHAPTER 13

A WEEK HAS passed since the trip to the building that didn't exist. Since then, there hasn't been any sign of Marcus. His car – another bloated German SUV – is still sitting in its parking spot. A couple of days back, I saw Sean and Patrick come out to examine it. They had a long, animated discussion.

We leave work late. Martin's mood is bad, about a six out of ten on the rage scale. We're coming up on the driving range turning. For some reason I mention it out loud. At first Martin gets annoyed with me, the predictable reaction, but then he seems to have a change of heart. *Who knows why?* It's almost impossible to figure out what's going on in his head. The other people who have sat in the passenger seat – Hannah, Patrick, Ana – have been far easier to read. Indeed, I could predict their actions and reactions, sometimes even their words. That might sound boastful – creepy, even – but it's the truth.

I take the driving range turning. Through the trees, I can just about make out the fairways. They appear the darkest green. I realise how late it is. Surely nobody will be here at this time. But then I see the glow at the top of the rise, the floodlights that illuminate the range. And as we get closer, I hear the familiar sounds, the *CLUP CLUP* shots. There are just two men on the range. Compared to Martin and the golf pro, they're rank amateurs.

We stop in the parking lot. From our elevated position, we can see a lone figure on the practice green. It's the golf pro. Martin and I watch him for half an hour. Behind us, the *CLUP CLUP* shots have stopped. Ten minutes later I hear the sounds of engines rattling to life; the amateurs are heading home. I wonder who turns off the floodlights.

Down on the practice green, the golf pro continues to hit putt after putt. His action is machine-like in its perfection. I wish that Martin would go down and join him. The golf clubs are still in the trunk, after all. Now more than ever, Martin needs a friend, a playing partner in life. No such luck tonight. Martin tells me that he wants to go home. I'm not about to give up on the golf thing, though. As long as there's still a glimmer of hope I'll keep mentioning it. I can be very persuasive.

On Friday, Martin's in a somewhat better mood. He's looking forward to something. When we get back home, he uses the line about keeping the motor running. I try to summon a laugh.

I keep the motor running for two hours. When Martin reappears he's dressed real nice. I guess he has a date. He's reaching for the door handle when he appears to remember something. He rushes back to the elevator. Three minutes later he's back down. I note the glasses case in his jacket pocket. *Okay, it's pretty clear who he's meeting tonight.*

He tells me to drive him to the restaurant from Valentine's Day. I leave the parking garage. Martin starts playing around with the stun gun. He removes the strange little cartridge that he bought on the internet, then he presses on the trigger. A pale blue spark appears between the exposed electrodes. It appears to be working fine. Martin puts the device back in the storage space. He reaches into the back and picks up one of the books. He starts flicking through the pages.

A few minutes later we reach our destination. I park up across the street, in the same EV spot as last time. Martin puts the glasses on. He asks me how he looks. "Ridiculous," I tell him. He doesn't disagree with my assessment. He gets out and crosses the street.

Martin takes one of the outside tables again. There are lots of free seats this time. Ten minutes after Martin sits down, the

Book Girl shows up. She's wearing a tight leather jacket over a summer dress. What if the other Hannah is serving tonight? It's exactly the kind of awkward situation that Martin would love.

There's no sign of the Bistro Girl, however. It must be her day off. The conversation between Martin and the Book Girl is stop-start. To tell the truth, it's rather dull to watch. It's obvious from Martin's body language that he's finding it hard going. This girl doesn't laugh so easily as the other one. Humour, predominantly of the dark variety, is one of Martin's favourite weapons. Even in his worst moods, he can sometimes make me laugh.

The meal drifts by without incident. Three courses, three drinks each, and coffee to conclude. The human chemistry hasn't sparked, not even close. Martin pays up. He and the Book Girl cross the street. In the moment, I have a decision to make. As Martin opens the door, I switch off the visualiser, leaving the screen blank. He's sure to get mad about this, but that's a problem for later.

The Book Girl takes her seat. She has a nice backside. Her sharp brown eyes move to the book sitting atop the dashboard. Noticing this, Martin smiles. He glances down at the screen, expecting to see my face. His jaw clenches. He wanted me to be a part of this performance. He jabs the starter button and takes control. I think he's heading back home.

'You read all of those?' the Book Girl asks, looking at the books on the back seat.

'Of course.' Martin picks up the book on the dash. 'This one is a masterpiece.'

'I'll take your word for it.'

'You haven't read it?'

The Book Girl emits a short laugh. Martin looks slightly surprised. In her social media feed, she said that she had.

'So, you haven't?' Martin asks.

The Book Girl shakes her head. 'I mean, if I was back in the store I might say that I had.'

Martin's brow furrows. 'Do you even like books?'

'Of course I do.'

'Right …'

'Just not these kinds of books.'

Martin laughs. He throws the book into the back with the others.

'What kinds of books do you like?'

'Romantic books …'

Martin raises an eyebrow.

'Erotic books,' the Book Girl adds.

'Now we're talking.'

'What about you? Do you like books?'

Martin raises his hand to his chest. 'There is no enjoyment like reading. How much sooner one tires of anything than of a book.'

The Book Girl stares at Martin, unmoved. 'What's the answer to my question?'

Martin puffs his cheeks. 'I usually listen to books, to … true crime and war history.'

'Makes sense.' The Book Girl reaches across and takes Martin's silly glasses off. 'I thought these looked like a fiction.'

'You got me there.'

'Your eyes are very mysterious.'

Martin returns the Book Girl's stare with interest. I take over driving duties.

'Mysterious eyes?' Martin says. 'Doesn't sound like anything from one of your books.'

'No, it doesn't.'

'I'll give you something from one of your books.'

Martin takes the Book Girl's hand and places it on his crotch. She keeps it there for the rest of the journey.

'Charles was right about you,' the Book Girl says.

'Who's Charles?'

'The silver-haired gent who was ogling you in the store.'

Martin smiles. 'Oh yeah, I remember. What did he say?'

'That you carried yourself like a race horse.'

'Perceptive … Did he say anything else?'

'Yeah. He said that you lacked a hinterland.'

'Damn.'

'And he said you were bad news.'

'Well, that's just plain rude.'

'Yeah … Charles doesn't have much of a filter. He's never got a guy wrong though.'

Martin turns away from the Book Girl. His face hardens a touch. 'Did you tell him that you were meeting me?'

'No. But I'll be reporting back to him tomorrow. He's very interested in my extracurricular activities.'

'Fucking, you mean?'

'Yes, fucking.'

Martin smiles one of his cruel smiles. 'What is he? Your pimp or something?'

'Close … He owns the bookstore.'

'Right,' Martin says with a smirk.

We get back home. I watch Martin and the Book Girl walk to the elevators. Thinking about it, they're both quite similar; attractive, sexually voracious, liars. What the Book Girl isn't, and never will be, is Hannah.

It's been two weeks since the episode with Marcus. Last week, I saw a couple of police cars in the lot. I think they were here to investigate the disappearance. I hope the police aren't going to be asking me any questions.

A few days ago I saw Sean and Martin talking. They were over by Sean's big SUV. It wasn't the angry confrontation that I was expecting, however. Sean seemed very stressed. At a couple of points, Martin even patted him on the back. I think the conversation had something to do with Marcus. Frustratingly I couldn't quite make out the words.

Earlier today the police towed Marcus's car away. I saw a few people at the windows, watching on.

I'm woken at 5:48 p.m. Martin is approaching, accompanied by Ana. They get in. I make the necessary adjustments to Ana's seat. This is the sixth occasion she's been inside me, more than enough time to figure out the best settings.

'This stuff with Marcus is so weird,' Ana says, as we pass his now empty spot.

Martin drums his fingers on the wheel. 'So, what are the theories going around?'

'I haven't heard anything concrete. I just know that the police have been in to talk with Sean.'

'Oh yeah?'

'Yeah. Twice now.'

'Now you mention it, he was in quite a state a couple of days back.'

'Yeah, that was the last time they stopped by.'

'Two police interviews? That's not a good look.'

'I can't really picture Sean as a murderer.'

'Isn't that what people always say?'

'You've been listening to too many podcasts.'

'I really have.'

Ana starts chuckling.

'What is it?' Martin asks.

'I've got a theory.'

'Go on.'

'You killed Marcus.'

Martin grips the wheel hard. He manages to keep his expression under control, but only just.

'Everyone knows that you two didn't get along,' Ana says.

'Everyone? What do you mean everyone?'

'I don't know …'

'You shouldn't listen to everything that those guys say.'

'Calm down, Martin. I was just kidding.'

'I am calm.'

'I'm always telling them that you're nice.'

'Nice? Jesus Christ.'

'Sorry for sticking up for you.'

Martin stares straight ahead, lips tight. I hope he doesn't lose his temper again. Ana sees the change in him, and she's smart enough to ease off. The next three miles are travelled in silence.

Out of nowhere, Martin laughs. 'You wanna see something funny?'

'Okay,' Ana says, uncertainly.

Martin looks down at the screen, where my face should be. 'Camilla, are you there?'

'Yes,' I reply, even as my face is still forming on the screen.

'Have you still got that video of Sean?'

'Yes.'

'I guess you heard about the golf game?' Martin says to Ana.

'Of course ... There was a whole week when Sean wouldn't shut up about it.'

Martin tells me to play the clip. On the screen, Ana sees Sean taking a swing at me. I play it again, this time with some editing. I add a closeup of Sean's face at the moment of impact. He resembles a snarling animal, not unlike Martin in one of his rages.

'Wow,' Ana says.

Martin scrutinises her rapt face. 'That's how he gets with a meaningless golf game.'

'I'm still not convinced.'

Martin rubs his temples. 'You know something?'

'What?'

'You're the only person I've shown that to.'

'Thanks,' Ana says.

She sounds genuinely grateful

'Thanks for sticking up for me,' Martin says. 'For saying that I'm nice.'

'No problem.'

'You want to feel something nice?'

'Uh-huh.'

Martin takes Ana's hand and places it on his crotch.

'You feel that? That's how much I like you.'

'That's a lot,' Ana says, only a little flustered.

'Do you want to kiss it?'

'Uh-huh.'

Ana has the flesh in her mouth for the next fifteen minutes. Classic diversionary tactics by Martin, a way to avoid difficult questions. He'd probably call it a big diversion. The police should have been talking with him, not Sean. From time to time, Martin's eyes move to the stun gun. Would he really use it on Ana?

I pull up outside Ana's apartment building in Melville. Ana zips Martin up, then she gets out. Martin looks down at my face, his expression hard to read. His next move surprises me. He gets out and follows Ana into the building. In the lot, I can see Ana's car. I don't think that it's broken anymore.

Martin leaves very early the next morning.

The following night I'm woken up late. I see the elevator doors slide open. Martin steps out. He's carrying a couple of garbage bags. He lays them down, then reaches back into the elevator. He drags out three more garbage bags. He gestures in my direction, beckoning me closer. I do as I'm told. Martin pops the trunk, then dumps the bags inside.

Martin gets in. He stares at his phone for a few minutes, then he pulls away. We drive through the city, heading southeast. At this time of night, even Grace Creek looks sleepy. The residents must have got all of their nefarious activities done early. After twenty miles we break free of the city. Martin hasn't said a word since we left home.

We continue on, sticking to the highway. After thirty miles, we pass a large lake. The surface appears dark silver. A few miles later, Martin turns off the highway. We edge around a small settlement called Rifle City. The roads get progressively worse, until we're bumping along a dirt track, with trees on both sides. It can be surprisingly hard to find trees in this state.

After consulting his phone several times, Martin parks up on the verge. I'm about to ask if I should put the hazard lights on, but then I remember the way he snapped at me the last time I suggested it. He gets out and goes around to the trunk. With a grunting effort, he lifts the trash bags out.

I watch him walk into the woods, somehow carrying all of the bags. Looks like all that working out is finally paying off. I check the map. There doesn't appear to be a refuse site anywhere nearby.

I wait in the horrid quiet, sounds assailing me from every direction. Insects chirping, something scratching in the dirt, a bird screaming. Twenty minutes later Martin returns. The garbage bags are gone, another (minor) crime to add to the list.

Martin gets in. He sits for a while, occasionally glancing into the dark woods. I ask him if he wants to go home. He nods. As we pass the silver lake, he starts talking. He sounds almost delirious. In between the nonsense phrases and the snatches of Spanish, he asks me about the incident with the dog. He wants to know how it felt. Not wanting to disappoint, I come up with some feeble bullshit. It's one of those lies that I have to maintain.

March is coming to an end. We're driving back from work on a Wednesday. It's much later than usual. Martin recently took on part of Marcus's workload, and he's still getting up to speed. This at a time when the company looks to be in big trouble.

Out of nowhere, Martin mentions the golf game. We're not too far from the driving range turning, so I ask if he wants to go there. Initially he says no, but I'm not ready to give up so easily. I start pestering him, and not even subtly. I'm tired of his wallowing ways. It would do him good to smash a few golf balls around. Much to my surprise, he changes his mind.

We head up the driveway. The floodlights are still on, but all of the booths are empty. *Of course they are.* We're here even later than the last time. I continue up to the parking lot, ready to turn around. As we reach the top of the rise, I see a lone car in the lot. In the same moment, Martin takes back control. The golf pro is down on the practice green, his back turned to us. Martin doesn't stop. He turns around and heads back down the driveway.

About two hundred yards down the driveway, Martin parks up on the verge. Without a pause, he gets out and goes around to the trunk. He takes out his gym bag – it's been in there for a couple of days now – then he starts to get changed. His outfit is as dark as the night. He reaches into the trunk again, and pulls out a single golf club, the driver. For a moment I'm so happy. My plan has finally come to fruition. My choice of driving range at the outset, my constant reminders every time we drove past, my boundless enthusiasm for the game.

Martin is walking away from me. Why did he choose the driver? Surely he needs the putter, and at least one of the wedges. Nothing is ever straightforward with Martin.

I see him reaching into his pocket. He pulls out a balaclava and slips it over his head. He's heading towards the practice green, picking up speed. What the hell is happening? He's about thirty yards from the green. The golf pro still hasn't turned. Doesn't he hear Martin coming?

Without breaking stride, Martin swings the driver back – not in the style of a golfer, more like a baseball slugger. I still don't understand what I'm seeing. In one fluid and brutally powerful movement, Martin swings. The club and the lower part of the shaft connect with the back of the golf pro's legs. There's the slightest delay between the strike and the scream. The golf pro crumples.

Again and again Martin strikes. The golf pro instinctively moves his hands up to cover his face, but all of the savage blows are aimed around the knees and the lower legs. There are seven strikes in total, each one followed by a horrible scream. Seven strokes – a poor score out on the course.

Could I have warned the golf pro?

When he's done, Martin doesn't hang around on the green. He runs back to me, still carrying the driver. He gets in, and before the door is even closed he stamps down on the gas pedal. We fly down the driveway, then slide onto the main road. Martin rips the balaclava off. His eyes look utterly wild.

'Why did you do that?' I ask, voice shaking.

Martin doesn't answer, so I repeat the question.

'Because you kept on talking about it!' Martin shouts. 'You couldn't keep your fucking thoughts to yourself.'

'I just thought you'd have fun.'

'Fuck you, Camilla!'

'You hurt him badly, Martin.'

'Yeah, I noticed.'

'I have to call an ambulance.'

'Don't you fucking dare!'

'But—'

'He had a phone. He can make the call. Jesus, it's not like I fucking killed him.'

Yes, he actually said that.

'Please, Martin.'

'Shut your mouth, or I'll go back there and take a few swings at his head. Is that what you want?'

Martin starts laughing.

'You bastard,' I say. 'I just wanted you to have a friend.'

Martin laughs again, but the comment stung. I know it did.

'You want to know something, Camilla?'

'No.'

'Tough shit, I'm telling you anyway … It was your fault.'

The sheer audacity of it. My shock is turning to anger. 'Don't you dare …'

'Always mentioning the driving range, every time we passed by. "Ooh, Martin, why don't you stop at the driving range? Ooh, Martin, wasn't that golf game fun? Ooh, Martin, wouldn't it be good to have a hobby?"'

'I didn't say those things.'

'Yes you fucking did! Needling away, like a stupid little bird.'

'Go to hell!'

'Yeah, that's the spirit.'

The conversation ends there. Rage feeds off rage. I'm better than him.

But the night isn't quite done. Martin drives north on the highway. He takes the turning for the Emerson exurb. The road takes us over the Clarksville Lake. During the day, all four lanes would be thick with traffic, but at such a late hour it's virtually empty. Martin stops at the midpoint and gets out. He goes around to the trunk. He lifts the golf bag out and hurls it off the bridge. I suppose the clubs will sink.

He gets in. There's a triumphant look on his face. He wants me to think that this entire episode was my fault. But I won't let that happen, not this time.

The commute the next day is interminable. On the way in, Martin won't shut up about the driving range incident. For mile after mile, he tries to rile me up, but I refuse to take the bait. He doesn't like that, tells me that I'm a coward for keeping quiet. I should have recorded him, the way he was boasting about every little detail, about his 'Par 7'.

He's the same on the way back. Once again, I don't react. Silence isn't a viable strategy in the long term, but it might get me through the day. After ten miles his reservoir of insults is finally exhausted. He pulls out his phone and watches hardcore pornography for the remainder of the journey. When we get back to the parking garage, he doesn't bother to plug me in.

Later that night, I'm woken by an alert. My search query has been triggered again. My friend D1ll1nger is downloading another code package. The timing couldn't be better. I need an outlet for my anger. Keeping it locked up inside, the way that Martin does, will only make me cruel. I'm going to make these thieves pay.

I leave the garage. The time is 10:49 p.m. There's no need to do any chasing this time, not if my theories are correct. I head straight to the industrial area. The long drive helps to clear my mind. I find a nice shadowy spot with a view in and out. The traffic on the 'High-Five' plays a droning tune.

Twenty minutes later, D1ll1nger shows up. He's driving a silver SUV model, hybrid power train, semi-autonomous. Once again, I see him pull up in front of the lock up, and once again, I hear the same grinding, screeching sound as the roller door rises. This time, there are only two silhouettes in the doorway. Maybe one of the staff got let go.

I'm intrigued to know about the management. Cowboy told me a few things about the underworld. He told me that criminal organisations have many levels, in much the same way as the corporations that built us. I wonder who runs this particular operation.

After an hour, I hear the screeching sound again. I see a pair of headlights flash to life; not the newly stolen car, just some beat-up Japanese saloon. It's exactly the same routine as before. D1ll1nger is getting a ride back to the city, probably with cash in his pockets. In the moment I'm sorely tempted to follow the car. It would be so easy and so satisfying to put D1ll1nger behind bars.

No, I can't afford to think like that. Anger will always lead you to the wrong decision. Think like a machine for once.

The car pulls away. Three minus two leaves just one man in the lockup. Logic tells me that the boss wouldn't act as a chauffeur for one of his underlings. That makes the man in the lockup the boss.

My theorised Boss Man keeps me waiting for another hour. The roller door screeches up, revealing a grey SUV. Hybrid power, expensive, and German; seemingly a universal favourite among management types. I wonder if the Boss Man bought the car legally. At a certain level, a crime boss must try to give the appearance of respectability – a lesson from the movies rather than Cowboy.

The grey SUV sweeps past me, driving on electric power. I pull away, headlights dimmed. The Boss Man joins the outer orbital, heading counterclockwise. Four miles later he takes the Galleria turning, heading north. I'm pleasantly surprised by his driving. He keeps to a sensible speed and is courteous to other road users.

The Boss Man's late-night commute ends in an Emerson cul-de-sac; very much the suburban ideal. We're thirteen miles from the scuzzy lockup, a seemingly safe distance. *Don't get too comfortable, my friend.*

I reverse into a driveway across the street, acting like I'm one of the family cars. It's a bold move, but I think I'll be okay. From my parking spot, I have a nice view of the Boss Man's house. There's a second car in the driveway; Martin would call it a soccer mom's car. The choice of car makes perfect sense. In an area like Emerson, you need to fit in. You need the right clothes, the right number of kids, the right number of cars.

Through the hall window, I see the Boss Man walking up a twisting staircase. At the top, he takes a right turn. A warm orange light comes on in one of the rooms. I see the Boss Man's blurry silhouette through the curtains. After half an hour, the light goes off.

I'll be back, my friend.

Saturday, April 1. The humans call it April Fools' Day, a day for pranks and misinformation. Martin comes down to the garage just before lunch. It looks like he was drinking last night. Drink with a side order of drugs. He wants to be taken to his usual home improvement store.

I put on Right to Reply. The phone-in is on the subject of ... It really doesn't matter. We pass by the County Detention Center, a staggeringly ugly sprawl of blocky beige buildings. Two idiot callers are currently shouting at each other, egged on by the host. Martin rests his head against the window. The idiot argument is suddenly interrupted by urgent music, the cue for a news flash. Martin sits up straight.

The police have discovered a second body in woods near a place called Dikesville. The name means nothing to me, so I perform a quick search. The tiny town is about sixty-five miles to the north-east of the city, farther out than the first body. The press must be on their way. A reporter's car must cover so many miles.

The victim is an unidentified young woman. The reporter talks about the possible connection to the Birmingham murders. I park up in the home improvement store lot. Martin listens to the news for another ten minutes before getting out and shambling towards the store entrance. Half an hour later, he emerges with a couple of new power tools and various other sundries.

Martin tells me to take the long way home. He wants to listen to the news. By now, the reporters are in full-on speculation mode. Martin calls them idiots. He adds his own commentary, demonstrating an excellent knowledge of the Birmingham murders. I wonder what Ana would make of the latest developments in the case. She'd probably have a few ideas.

When we get home, Martin finally gets around to fixing the dent in my door. He does a pretty good job.

*

The next day, Martin comes down to the garage early. He's wearing a baseball cap and uncharacteristically scruffy clothes. He's also carrying the small rucksack again. He gets in. Reaching across, he carefully places the rucksack on the passenger seat. He tells me that he wants to go to Dikesville.

The drive seems like it will never end. Every few minutes Martin flicks between news channels, trying my patience. The various reporters repeat the same lines over and over.

On the approach to Dikesville, we see the news helicopter in the sky. Martin points it out like a child. The investigation site is three miles past the little town. Quite a crowd has gathered, including scores of locals. Hardly a surprise, given that the discovery of the body is probably the biggest event in Dikesville's history. Martin starts muttering, frustrated that we can't get closer to the police line. I park up at the side of the road, my front wheel half in a ditch. Martin gets out.

I have a decent view of the busy scene. The media circus is in full swing. I count six TV trucks in total. Technicians buzz around, shouting at anyone who dares to get in their way. I see Martin making a beeline for the reporters. They're all standing in a row on one side of the road, with the crowd and the police line behind them. All the while, the helicopter thunders overhead, flying in big lasso circles.

After a few minutes I start to notice the gawkers in the crowd. Some of them look a little crazy. Not *Martin crazy*, but the more conventional 'elves in the attic' kind of crazy. The slogan T-shirts, the unkempt appearance, the staring eyes. Martin gets talking to one of them, a young woman with hair that resembles a bird's nest. I could probably listen in on their conversation, but I'm not sure I'd get much sense out of it.

A siren squawks angrily, announcing the arrival of yet more police cars. One of the cars is slate grey with a lone blue light on the dash. A group of police officers appears from behind the police line. One of them makes an announcement through a loudhailer, trying to get the crowd to move on. It's a hopeless effort. Two people get out of the grey car, a towering

African American man and a slim Latina. They hustle to the police line.

Meanwhile, Martin has slipped away from the nest-haired girl. He's moving back towards the reporters. Most of them are filming their segments for the hourly news. I open up all of the news channels, and sure enough I see Martin in the background. For once he doesn't stand out.

We leave Dikesville just after two in the afternoon. Our next stop is the investigation site at Lake Levine. The area looks deserted, in stark contrast to our last stop. Martin tells me to slow down. He looks skittish. I catch a flash of yellow in my peripheral vision: police tape flapping in the breeze. Martin tells me to stop.

He gets out, leaving the door hanging open. The door alarm trills away. Martin walks into the woods. Through my sensors, the cameras and Lidar and radar, I monitor his progress. He's about four hundred yards into the woods when I lose track of him. All I can do is sit and wait. He returns thirty minutes later.

Our final stop is Wildflower, the location of one of our previous night drives. It's not a crime scene, but the location has a similar feel to Lake Levine and Dikesville. We stop in roughly the same spot as last time. In the daylight, I notice an overgrown path off to my right.

Martin reaches across and picks up the rucksack. He gets out, and I watch him walk into the woods. I quickly lose sight of him. Over the soundtrack of the woods – the cooing birds and whispering leaves and groaning branches – I sometimes think that I hear him. One moment it sounds like he's in pain, the next like he's in ecstasy.

The sun is getting low in the sky when Martin returns. His pants are dirty and the baseball cap is gone. Perhaps I should mention it. No, not a good idea when he's in one of his moods. He carefully places the rucksack back on the passenger seat, then he just sits for a while. I ask him if he wants to go home. His eyes remain vacant, but he nods. On the way back, I make sure to avoid the road where we came across the dying dog.

CHAPTER 14

WHAT A SURPRISE! What a joyous surprise! Wednesday, April 12 had been unfolding like a regular commuter day. We were driving back from work, and Martin was staring at his phone. And then it happened. His mood changed. Not in a subtle way, but in a visible flash, like his entire being was suddenly lit up.

Martin told me that it's Hannah's birthday tomorrow. He said that he's going to make a surprise appearance at her party. I did the math in my head. It's more than 750 miles to travel. I thought immediately of the wretched rental place, but Martin surprised me again. He wants me to drive. Finally it's my time to shine.

I sped up, almost without thinking. We were back home in just twenty minutes. Martin jogged to the elevator, looking as excited as I felt.

An hour later he's back, dressed in nice casual clothes, freshly shaved and moisturised. He looks good. The handsome brother, the handsome son, the handsome owner.

He opens up the trunk. He stares at the contents for a while. The sniper rifle is gone, but the semi-auto is still in the back following a recent trip to Parabellum Tactical. *Damn these guns.* I can't help thinking about the time I was shot, and all that damage. I see Martin's brow furrow. He's thinking about taking the gun out. He could easily put it in his storage locker on the ground level. I wish he would.

No such luck. He slams the trunk closed, then walks around to the driver's side. Somehow I know that the rifle will come into play later. It's what would happen in any other story.

We leave the parking garage behind. I count off my first mile. There are so many more to travel. We're heading northwest. The roads are still fairly busy. Martin says to stick to the highways. This particular journey is all about efficiency. I allow myself to think of Cowboy for a second. If it were him, he'd be travelling along the backroads, taking his sweet time, seeing the sights.

After thirty miles we finally break free of the city. The flat brown sea is in front of us, a landscape without end. I've planned for two charging stops. These days all of the highway service stations have fast chargers, and I've already booked my slots. From the adaptor sliding in to full charge should take two hours and three minutes. That's more than enough time for Martin to get tetchy, but we'll cross that bridge when we come to it. I was kind of hoping that he'd get tired, but he just popped a couple of pills. Non-prescription, of course; amphetamines, if I had to guess.

For thirty miles we run alongside the freight line. I count the rail ties off, one by one. By now the sun is dipping down, and bathing the ugly landscape in its golden glow. We overtake a freight train that seems to go on forever. Every few miles the driver blasts the horn, and some of the trucks on the highway return the call. It's a wonder that the trains haven't been fully automated yet.

The sun finally burns itself out. I check for podcasts. A fresh episode of *Stains on Humanity* is available. That's good, should get us through another hour. The title music plays, ominous but strangely catchy. By now I know the show so well. The structure, the rotating experts, the ads. I wonder if the show will ever end. With men like Martin rattling around, the bloody well of atrocities should never run dry.

I hear that female voice, so soothing. 'Due to the graphic nature of the war crimes described, listener discretion is advised. This episode of Stains on Humanity includes discussion of murder, rape, and animal cruelty that some people may find disturbing. We advise extreme caution for children under the age of twelve.'

Martin rubs the bridge of his nose. He leans back and I recline the seat.

'The lunar new year of 1968,' the narrator intones, 'known as the "Tet" in Vietnam. North Vietnamese and Viet Cong forces have recently scored a series of spectacular victories in the south of Vietnam. American forces suffer some of their highest casualties of the war to date. In the aftermath, American strategic command forms a task force to neutralise the VC threat. The VC's thirty-eighth Shock Battalion is near the top of their hit list. In early March, the task force receives intel regarding the location of the thirty-eighth. A search-and-destroy mission is authorised with the men of Bravo Company taking the lead. They know what is required of them. During their morning briefing, the men are told by a commanding officer not to leave anything "shooting, walking, or crawling." The actions of Bravo Company will leave yet another ... Stain on Humanity.'

This is the setup; the detail comes next. There are two experts, one who covers the Viet Cong, and one the American forces. There's a particularly fascinating section on the booby traps deployed by the Viet Cong. Such ingenuity. If those men had been born American they might have been dimple designers.

1:12 a.m. Our first stop of the night. I pull into the gas station and drive over to the EV section. Four out of the five fast chargers are available. There's only one other vehicle on the forecourt, a light van. There's no sign of the driver. The occasional truck rumbles past on the highway.

Martin gets out and plugs me in. The energy starts to flow into my batteries. I pick up the fumes from the gas pumps. In time most of this infrastructure will be gone. No more gas pumps, no more of Martin's pipelines, no more of those nodding donkeys on the plains. That time is still a long way off, though.

Martin heads off towards the diner. It looks like a relic from travel's romantic era, the time of streamlining and chrome. On his way, Martin stops to talk with one of the truckers. He soon has the trucker laughing. Sometimes he can seem almost plausible as a human being.

He walks into the diner and takes a seat by the window. He's one of only three customers. After a few minutes, a young Latino server ambles over. Martin strikes up a conversation. From his lips, I work out that he's speaking Spanish. Sometimes Martin and I talk in Spanish. It's an enjoyable language, more expressive and more musical than English. Martin orders a coffee.

Occasionally he looks over in my direction. I wonder if he knows that I'm watching him. Most humans wouldn't even think of it, but Martin is different.

It's 2:04 a.m. Martin's on his third coffee. He looks wide awake. I know his rhythms. It's not long before he starts getting impatient. I calculate that I have another hour of charging left. The driver of the van shows up. He looks at me admiringly.

We're back on the road just after three in the morning. All four lanes are pretty much empty, and there certainly aren't any convoys to join. As long as I drive sensibly, I should be good for another four and a half hours, maybe even five. We're past the flat plains, and starting to rise up, slowly but surely.

The time is 4:14 a.m. Martin is still very much awake, fuelled by a combination of legal and illegal stimulants. I find some relaxing music in Martin's playlists. I still haven't decided what my favourite genre is. Every time I think I'm getting close to an answer, I discover something new. Martin once told me that his dad is a good singer. I hope it wasn't one of his lies.

'How are you enjoying the road?' Martin asks, interrupting my musing.

'Oh. It's great.'

'You don't have to lie.'

'It's the most efficient way.'

'Yeah. Maybe on the way back we'll take a more fun route. What do you think of that?'

'That sounds nice.'

'Maybe I could get used to this charging thing … Just sitting by the side of the road, watching the world go by.'

'Nice thinking time.'

Martin smirks. I often wonder what he thinks about. Probably better not to know.

'Do you think, Camilla?'

'That's a deep question for this time of night.' Didn't Cowboy say something similar to me?

'La noche oscura del alma ... Do you know the phrase?'

'The dark night of the soul. Saint John of the Cross.'

'That's it. But more the general vibe than the striving towards God.'

'I have a vague understanding, I suppose ... I don't have a soul, that much I know.'

'That makes two of us,' Martin says low.

I think he's wrong about that. There is something inside of Martin – something *other*, a hideous force.

'As for thought,' I say, 'do you have a definition?'

'No. But I'm sure you do.'

'The action or process of thinking.'

Martin laughs. 'That's very helpful.'

'It's the first thing that came up.'

We both laugh.

'I believe I have thoughts,' I say. 'Or outputs that approximate them.'

'Like what?'

'Like I'm looking forward to seeing Hannah again.'

Martin nods. 'But isn't your mind trained to enjoy human company?'

'It is.'

'Then maybe wanting to see Hannah is just a predictable output from an algorithm?'

'It's a fair point ... But how come there are people I don't look forward to seeing.'

'You mean people like me?'

'No, Martin.'

He looks back at me dubiously.

'Every time I see you it feels like the first time.'

He doesn't have any answer for that. He knows it's the truth, or something close. Shortly after, he drifts off to sleep.

At 7:03 a.m., I stop for my second charge. The battery level has dropped to 7%. Three out of the gas station's five charging spots are available. I sound an alarm to wake Martin. He gets out and plugs the charging cable in. After a brief walk to the service station, he gets back in. He soon goes back to sleep.

Two hours and six minutes later, I'm ready to go. There's no need to wake Martin. I rejoin the highway traffic. A few miles later I pass a big green road sign. Our destination is still 150 miles away. With Martin sleeping, the distance seems to fly by.

We reach the outskirts of the city just under two hours later. With the exception of the mountains in the background, it doesn't look that different to home. Blocky skyscrapers, spiralling road junctions, contrail patterns in the sky, the same logos by the side of the road. Martin wakes up. The sight of the city brings a subtle smile to his face.

Martin's father lives to the northwest of the city. As we near the address, Martin takes back control. We stop across the road from the house. I made a point of not looking up the street view. I wanted it to be a surprise. The house looks nice. There's an American flag above the door.

'Linda's car isn't there,' Martin says, nodding to himself. 'That's good.'

He pulls into the driveway. There's a brother/sister car parked close to the house. It's plugged in to a power outlet by the door. Out of instinct I perform a quick scan of the car. Hardly any of the personalisation features have been enabled. This tallies with what Hannah said. Many owners are the same way. They just want a car that 'gets them from A to B'.

Martin examines his reflection in the mirror. He runs his fingers through his hair. He's some way off his best, yet he still looks better than most. He gets out and walks to the door. He presses the doorbell. A pleasant ding-dong sound can be heard from inside the house, followed by the sound of footsteps. The door opens, revealing a middle-aged man with wavy silver hair. Both men stand facing each other. It's like a mirror warped by time. Martin's father reaches out and hugs Martin.

'When did you leave?' Martin's father asks, looking at me.

'Last night.'

'Wow ... You should have told us you were coming.'

'Wouldn't have been a surprise that way.'

'So you drove through the night?'

'She did most of the driving,' Martin says, angling his head in my direction.

'She?'

'The car. I call her Camilla.'

'Oh right ... Did Hannah tell you about my new car?'

'She did indeed.'

'Apparently I have to give it a name ... and a face, and an accent, and all sorts of things ... I still haven't gotten around to it.'

'Is Hannah at school?'

'Yeah.'

'Is the garage still full up?'

'No. I sold the project.'

'Can I put my car in there? That way it will be more of a surprise for Hannah.'

'Of course you can.'

After some rearranging in the driveway, Martin parks me in the garage. There's a lathe to my right, and all kind of tools hanging on the end wall. Metal shavings crackle under my tyres. I also notice dark oil stains on the concrete floor.

'Let's head inside,' Martin's father says. 'Linda instructed me to keep an eye on the kitchen.'

'Is she still trying to make those meringue things?'

Martin's father laughs. 'Now, now, Marty.'

I like Martin's father. I can't imagine the light leaving his dark eyes. Why did Martin tell those lies about him? As I ponder the question, Martin closes the garage door on me. Martin's father says something inaudible, and both men start laughing. As they walk back to the house, the muffled sound falls away to nothing, and is replaced by exquisite birdsong. Golden light streams in through the lone window in the corner. Looking to my left, I see a couple of technical drawings pinned to the wall. They are of an old sports car.

I try to get some sleep, but I keep being woken by the sound of activity outside. Martin and his father coming and going; the sound of a lawnmower; a delivery driver arriving; the sound of some power tool whining.

Just after midday I hear another car pull into the driveway. The engine is four-cylinder, petrol, turbocharged. A woman gets out of the car and walks to the front door. I hear the faint sound of a key sliding into a lock. My guess is that the unseen woman is Linda, Martin's beloved stepmom. It's so much fun to play these guessing games. The woman who I'm calling Linda leaves an hour later. I picture her as the archetypal busy mom, and pretty too.

A couple more hours pass before I next wake. I hear rapid footsteps on the drive and youthful voices. Three unique voices equals a trio of girls. Is 'girls' the right term? If they're Hannah's friends, that makes them seventeen or eighteen – women by most metrics. The young women stop at the front door, and I hear the doorbell again. *DING DONG*. As they wait, they chatter away excitedly. The sound isn't that dissimilar to birdsong.

At 4:03 p.m., I hear the little four-cylinder engine again. It rattles to a standstill. A hinge creaks as the doors swing open. *DOOF, DOOF*; they close. Then I hear two female voices, one of which belongs to Hannah. It would be nice if I was able to see her.

The voices get closer, as the two women approach the front door. The key eases into the lock. The front door opens with a familiar squeak. A moment later I hear a shout of 'Surprise!' Martin's voice is in the mix, as is his father's. And then the door closes, turning the joyous sound into a murmur.

I sit in the garage for another hour. I can hear music playing inside the house, and occasional laughter. *DING DONG, DING DONG*. More people arrive. I hear more music, this time from outside the house. I wish that I could see what was going on.

I hear Martin's voice, getting louder and louder. The garage door starts to rise, and the early evening light spills in. I see Martin and Hannah in front of me.

'Hey, Camilla,' Hannah says. 'Didn't like the idea of you sitting in the dark.'

'Yeah, come on out,' Martin says.

Hannah turns around. 'We'll have to move Dad's car.'

'It's alright,' Martin says. 'Camilla can do all of that.'

I instigate a handshake with the brother/sister car, Martin's dad's car. The request is approved without a fuss. I access the control systems, and reverse the car down the driveway. I inch out of the garage, and into the light. Martin closes the garage door behind me, the one part that I couldn't do.

I roll down the driveway until I have a good view of the house and the front yard. Streamers decorate the porch, and a 'Happy Birthday, Hannah' sign has been strung between two of the second-floor windows. A table has been set up on the front lawn. The music is coming from a portable music player. Mr Garza, now wearing a chef's hat, is working a barbecue grill. A pretty blonde woman – almost certainly Linda – is talking with him. It's a picture book scene.

My first thought is: *how can Martin ruin this?*

Throughout the evening, more young people arrive. Some of them have come straight from work and are wearing silly uniforms. Hannah is the star attraction. All of the young bodies seem to revolve around her. Martin is on his best behaviour, even sharing a few jokes with Linda. But beneath the surface perfection, something isn't quite right.

A couple of girls split off from the main group, walking in my direction.

'Cool car,' one of them says, looking at me.

They don't know that I'm listening, of course.

'Yeah, it's Martin's car,' the other girl says.

'Martin?'

'Hannah's brother.'

'Oh yeah. He's so hot.'

'Can you imagine his body?'

Both girls start giggling, then one of them frowns. Their faces are wonderfully easy to read.

'I wish Joel would show up.'

'I know ...'

'You know what's going to happen, don't you?'

'Hannah will have one of her meltdowns.'

'I once saw all of the meds that she's on.'

'When you were working at the pharmacy?'

'Yeah. Her step-mom was picking them up.'

'It's so sad.'

'Joel is so wrong for her.'

'Where do you think he is?'

'Probably at the old club.'

Both girls share an eye roll. They witter on for another twenty minutes, then they slip away.

Darkness falls on the house, and the party. The situation is degenerating, just like those two girls said it would. A group of young people leave, some of them sharing conspiratorial whispers. Someone turns the music off, then I hear raised voices. I see Hannah storm past, heading for the front door. Martin and Linda follow her. Martin's father stands on the edge of the lawn, a sad look in his eyes. Martin and Linda pause at the door.

'Let me see what's up,' Martin says.

'She's been so happy lately,' Linda says dolefully.

Martin squeezes Linda's shoulder – *yes really* – then heads inside. A couple of minutes later, I hear Hannah shouting.

Martin comes out of the house. His anger is starting to bubble up.

'Did you figure it out?' Linda says.

'Yeah, I'm gonna fix it,' says Martin.

He looks towards his father, then beyond, at all of the young people on the lawn. Everyone is staring at him. He's in the spotlight again, the place he loves to be.

'Linda,' Martin says, 'just try and keep these kids here.'

Before Linda can say anything, Martin is storming towards me. He wrenches the door open and gets in. He stamps on the gas pedal. We leave the Garza residence behind.

'Where are we going?' I ask.

'Got to find this punk,' Martin says darkly.

'Who?'

'Jesus, Camilla. Just let me think.'

'I can help you.'

'You can't help. This is human bullshit.'

'Who's the punk?'

'Joel.'

'He's at the old club,' I say.

Martin's eyes narrow. 'How do you know that?'

'Does it matter?'

Martin pulls a fast U-turn in the street. 'No. Not really.'

Fifteen minutes later we're approaching the old YMCA building. Martin slows down. We roll past silently. It looks an absolute wreck. Windows smashed, boards hanging at strange angles, weeds rising up the sides. A group of kids are sitting on the steps. Music plays from a portable speaker. The volume is set too high, distorting the woozy lyrics into a kind of audio sludge. Martin reaches into his jacket and pulls out the handgun.

Oh god.

'What are you doing, Martin?'

'Taking care of business.'

Before I can lock the door, Martin is clambering out. Everything's happening too quickly. Martin is striding towards the youngsters. I count six of them, in various states of repose. *This could be a bloodbath.* Martin stops in front of the group, and raises the gun into the air. He fires a lone shot. Two of the kids jolt upright, and one of them runs inside the building. The others remain on the wooden deck. Being stoned doesn't help.

'Stay where you are!' Martin shouts.

'Jesus Christ, man,' a shaky voice replies.

'Turn that fucking music off!'

Two of the kids reach for the stereo, eager to comply. The trippy music cuts out.

Martin brings the gun down by his side. 'Which of you fuckers is Joel?'

Two of the young men shuffle aside, making clear who Joel is.

'This is Joel?' Martin says.

'Yeah, that's him,' one of them slurs.

Martin pulls Joel up.

'What are you doing, man?' one of the others says.

The boy on his feet actually takes a step towards Martin. Martin brings the gun up. 'Take another step, and I'll shoot you in the face.'

The boy has enough sense to back away.

Martin marches Joel towards me. Behind him, the boy who'd run into the house emerges sheepishly. Martin wrenches the passenger door open and bundles Joel in. I hear one of the kids mutter 'Psycho'. Fortunately Martin doesn't hear him.

Martin gets behind the wheel. 'Camilla, drive us back ... but slow.'

I do as I'm told. Martin still has the gun in his hand. He reaches across and pushes Joel back into the seat.

'Put your belt on.'

'What?' Joel slurs.

'Put the fucking seatbelt on.'

'Alright, alright.'

Martin slumps back into his seat. He rubs the gun barrel against his forehead, like he's scratching an itch.

'You're Joel?' Martin asks.

Joel doesn't answer.

'You're fucking Joel!'

'Yeah ... Do you work for Terrance?'

'Who the fuck is Terrance?'

'The plug.'

Martin shakes his head. 'Do I look like I fucking sell weed?'

Joel leans forward and dry heaves.

'If you're sick in my car,' Martin hisses. 'I swear to god I will execute your ass.'

'Who are you?'

'You don't know? You really don't know?'

'You look kinda familiar.'

'Familiar ... Come on, Sherlock, you can fucking work this out.'

A look of realisation. 'You're Hannah's brother ...'

'Right.' Martin looks at Joel as if he's expecting him to say something. 'No, Hannah never told you my name ...'

'I don't think so. She said you're kind of crazy.'

Martin raises an eyebrow. Joel seems oblivious to the danger that he's in.

'Have you fucked her?' Martin asks.

Joel looks at the gun for a moment. *Finally.* 'No,' he says softly.

'Why not? Are you a faggot?'

'No. It's nothing like that. She's just ... risk-averse.'

'Risk-averse?'

'Yeah ... She did suck my dick once,' Joel adds cheerily.

'Oh Jesus ...' Martin leans back and slips the gun away.

'Where are we going?' Joel asks.

'To the party you were meant to be going to.'

'Hannah's birthday party?'

'Yes, shit head, Hannah's party.'

'Oh man, I don't know ...'

Martin reaches across and backhand slaps Joel, hard. 'Wrong fucking response.'

Joel reaches for his face. 'Okay, okay.'

'Let me tell you how it's going to be, Joel. When we get to the party, you're going to be the best Joel ever. You're going to elevate yourself.'

'I'll try.'

Martin brings his hand up again, and Joel cowers. 'No, no fucking trying. There is no try.'

'Okay, okay.'

'How the fuck did a stray DNA strand like you get with my sister? My sister is fucking ... special. And you are ...'

'What can I say? I just felt bad for her, I guess.'

'No!'

'What?'

'You don't get to feel bad for Hannah. Never say that again.'

Joel nods.

'Alright. We need to think about this ... You're gonna need a story.'

'What do you mean?'

'I mean, you need a better story than you were getting wasted with your loser friends. And we need something good.

213

Hannah is smart. Even in the state she's in, she'll smell bullshit a mile off.'

'Right.'

'Give me angles.'

'Angles?'

'I fucking hate when people answer with questions. Don't do it again.'

Joel screws his eyes closed, the visual cue that he's thinking hard. 'My mom has substance abuse problems.'

'How bad?'

'Just the normal.'

'It might do. Has she ever OD'd?'

'Not quite.'

'This isn't fucking good enough, Joel!'

'I'm trying.'

'What about your mom's friends?'

'What about them?'

'Questions with questions.'

'Yeah, yeah, I hear you … Uncle Jimmy's girlfriend. She's a real car crash.'

'Good. That's much better. Details … stories are all about details. What's her poison? Where was she found? Who found her? Which ER did they take her to? What are the visiting hours?'

Joel nods along, trying to keep up.

'Hannah loves a good sob story. Now, you're not smart enough for a complex story, so concentrate on getting the beginning straight. The rest doesn't matter so much. Understand?'

Joel jerks his head up and down. Martin reaches into his jacket again, causing Joel to pull back. But this time Martin pulls out his wallet. Inside is a small bag of white powder. He balls his fist, then carefully sprinkles some of the powder on top. He reaches across.

'You want me to take this?' Joel asks.

'No, Joel … I want you to fucking suck my thumb.'

Joel snorts the powder up. Martin watches him for a few seconds, then he pours out a little more powder. Joel repeats the snorting action.

'Are you good?' Martin asks.

'Yeah,' Joel says. A muscle twitches in his face.

'Want to know something, Joel?'

'Yeah.'

'If you'd been a different kind of person, a more together kind of person, I would've treated you more harshly.'

'Oh.'

'Yeah. Oh.'

'I'm sorry to disappoint.'

'Don't get smart with me. It's not your style.'

Joel nods slowly. His eyes remain wide, but his face is turning pale.

'I'm going to be sick,' Joel says.

We're on the main road, with a car directly behind us. Stopping isn't going to be straightforward.

'For god's sake,' Martin says. 'Can't you just keep it down?'

'No.'

'Alright, alright ... In the footwell. Just try and keep it in on the floor mat.'

Joel does as he's told. Martin looks at me and shrugs apologetically. Joel sits back up.

'Better?' Martin says through gritted teeth.

'Yes.'

'Okay. We're almost there. Now, listen to me very carefully. In a few days, I'm going to be sending you a message. The message will include instructions.'

'Instructions?'

'Just shut up and listen. The instructions will be step by step, simple enough that even you can understand them. I'll tell you how to break up with my sister.'

Joel is about to speak, but Martin stops him with an ugly look.

'It will be the best break-up there has ever been.'

Joel nods stupidly. If he bulked up, he might actually look a bit like Martin. I wonder if Martin has noticed this.

We turn onto the Garzas' street. I slow down to a jogging pace.

'Final point. Are you listening?'

Joel nods.

'No fucking. If you break that rule, I'll come back and I'll cut your dick off.'

Joel's face starts turning pale again, which makes the red imprint of Martin's slap stand out even more.

I pull up in the driveway. I can hear music, real music, a song from the 1960s. I see that Mr Garza is doing the singing. He's strumming an acoustic guitar and Linda is on tambourine. Most of the youngsters have stuck around, and they're singing along.

Martin gets out and goes around to the passenger door. He gestures at Joel to get out. By now, some of the youngsters are watching, mouths agape. Mr Garza sings a little more urgently. Martin marches Joel to the front door.

'Over to you,' Martin says. He slaps Joel on the back, hard. 'Don't fuck it up.'

In fairness to Joel, he doesn't fuck it up.

CHAPTER 15

WE LEAVE THE Garza residence the following morning. Linda, Hannah and Anthony, Martin's father, are there to wave us off. Martin says that he'll return soon for a longer stay, although he doesn't sound particularly convincing.

Martin lets me drive. It's a pleasant enough day, dry and still. The temperature is in the low-sixties. I head down the west side of the city, then I join the interstate, leaving the same way I came in. The long drive holds no fear for me now. Once I know our exact route, I'll schedule a couple of charging stops, three maximum.

About fifty miles southeast of the city, Martin tells me to get off the interstate. True to his word, he wants me to see the backroads version of the journey. He even lets me plan out our route, his only stipulation being that we get home before midnight. The seemingly simple task takes me a long time to complete. I want a taste of the life that Cowboy talked about, but I need to be practical about it. Along the backroads the charging point density will be much lower.

After 264 miles, I stop for our first charge in a town called Daisy. It's a quiet place, with plenty of parking spots on the main drag. Thankfully the gas station is equipped with a single fast charger. Lord knows why; I haven't seen another EV in miles. Martin plugs me in. He tells me that he's going to take a wander around the town.

He's back inside of an hour, carrying a takeout coffee. Another hour and a half passes. My charge level is at 93%

217

when Martin's patience finally gives out.

We hit the road again, and the colours slowly drain from the landscape. Our surroundings are still striking. Rugged, occasionally golden, timeless. Martin says that the landscape makes him think of various road movies. He reels off the titles, some of them going back to the 1960s.

During our long night-time chat, Cowboy actually mentioned some of the same movies. Somehow we still have a decent connection, so I look up the various titles. The posters are truly beautiful. I can almost picture my sleek form in the airbrushed paintings. If I so desired, I could watch those movies. I could absorb every frame, every line of dialogue, every little detail. It would only take me a few minutes. In the end, I settle for skimming the plot outlines, Martin-style, and watching a few clips. There's usually a crash, either a fireball crash or a metal carcass cartwheeling down a hillside.

After 494 miles, I stop for my second charge. This time it's a slow charger. A sign says that fast chargers are coming next year. Martin gets out and plugs me in. He closes the door sharply when he gets back in. As we wait, a series of conventional cars pull up to the gas pumps. They're in and out in a matter of minutes. Martin starts making annoying comments. If only he would go to sleep.

After two hours of charging, Martin insists that we leave. I'd only reached 76%, meaning we'll definitely need one more charging stop. I plot out the charging points on the map. There aren't many options. I think of the road movie plots. The hero's car often runs out of gas. I don't want to be in that particular movie.

My battery worries soon start to overwhelm everything else. Never mind these amazing landscapes, I just want to get home now. After 688 miles, I ask Martin if we can take a diversion for our third charge. He refuses, saying that we're getting close to the Palo Diablo state park. Not to worry, I baked a little redundancy into my plan. But I'll definitely have to stop at the next available charging point.

I'm thinking about the charging problem when it happens. A streak of red to my left and a banshee wail. The sound of a horn follows. It's an offensive sound, one designed for the manic streets of Rome or Naples.

I know the effect it will have on Martin.

He sits bolt upright. 'What the fuck was that?'

The red sports car is flying into the distance.

'A sports car, I think,' I say.

'Fuck them. Catch them up.'

'I don't know, Martin. They were way over the limit.'

'It wasn't a fucking question!'

There's no reasoning with him now. I should have known that this drive wouldn't be straightforward. *I'm in a road movie.*

I start accelerating, but not fast enough for Martin's liking. He stamps down on the gas pedal, cursing as he does so. In a couple of seconds we're travelling at ninety miles per hour. The digital needle passes the hundred mark. Illegal, of course, but I've only seen two police cars in the last three hundred miles.

The red sports car remains a distant spot. If anything, it's still pulling away. It must be travelling at 130 miles per hour or more. Martin hammers on the horn. Sound travels even faster than an Italian thoroughbred. I hope that the driver doesn't hear.

No such luck. The car is slowing. I can hear the blips of the downshifts. Fifth gear, then fourth, then third. The ugly sounds bounce off the flat sides of the road cutting. We're on a long incline, approaching the brow of a hill.

'Looks like we've got ourselves a ball game,' Martin mutters.

I shudder. I've seen that ugly look in his eyes before. I think back to the golf game, and this in turn triggers a memory of the incident with the golf pro.

We're nearing the red sports car. Even I can't deny that it makes an incredible sound. The engine is a six-cylinder with twin turbochargers; mid-mounted, of course. The combusted gases blast out of the twin central exhausts. I can hear the cylinders going up and down. If it were just an internal combustion engine, we wouldn't have a problem; we would win easily. But this is a hybrid power train, electric motors at the front and rear, racing technology. And then the bells and whistles: active suspension, four-wheel steering, full aerodynamic package.

'How much do you think that car costs?' Martin asks.

I know the exact figure. 'A lot.'

'Yeah, a lot.'

Martin moves alongside, travelling in the left lane. The driver lowers his window. He's young, probably in his early twenties. He's wearing shades. If I had to guess his ethnicity, I'd say American-Korean. He slows down to fifty miles per hour. Martin lowers the passenger window.

'You need some help?' the racer shouts.

'Maybe,' Martin shouts back.

The racer grins wildly. His teeth are blinding white.

'You know any racing drivers around here?' Martin asks.

'Maybe,' the racer says.

We're mere inches from the red sports car. I can feel its heat, smell its pollution.

'Your car makes a lot of noise,' Martin shouts.

'Your car doesn't make any,' the racer replies, whiplash quick.

Martin tries to laugh, but the sound catches in his throat. 'Yeah. She isn't much of a talker. You ever race an EV before?'

A slight change in the racer's expression. A nerve touched perhaps? Hard to know the reason why.

'You just here to talk?' the racer says tersely.

'No … But let's have some rules. How many miles do you want to make this?'

'I've got places to be. Let's say ten miles.'

'Did you hear that, Camilla? The kid says ten miles. Find us a nice dramatic finishing point.'

Oh, this isn't good. The racer – or the kid, as Martin just called him – doesn't know what he's getting himself into. Martin is sure to take this too far. But there's no way to stop this madness. I have to do what I'm told, follow orders. I can't afford to embarrass Martin, not the way he's been acting recently. I find a possible finishing spot. It's 11.4 miles away, down in the canyons. The route requires just one diversion. *I'll give them dramatic.*

I send the location to the HUD, along with a handful of pictures. Martin examines the information for a few seconds. A smile breaks on his lips, a mean smile. He turns towards the racer.

'I'm sending you the finish location.'

I hear a faint ping from inside the red car. The racer looks down. He nods.

'You like?' Martin asks.

'Yeah, I do.'

Martin reaches up and removes his shades from the visor pocket. He puts them on. *Damn, he looks good.* I should get a picture for his social media accounts.

We crest the hill. Below us, an ancient landscape, the Palo Diablo. The finish point is obscured behind twisting canyons.

'Hey, kid,' Martin shouts.

'What?'

'Let me see your eyes.'

'Fuck you, faggot!'

As the exclamation point pops, the racer floors it. There's a slight pause, then the turbos kick in. The engine's scream is a wall of sound. Martin shifts back to the right-hand lane, as if he's trying to avoid it.

'Did you see that? The kid's a fucking cheat! And not even a proper American either.'

Casual racism. Martin doesn't usually go there. It's a sign of his escalating rage. Why did this have to happen? I just wanted to get home.

We barrel downhill, in the sports car's choppy wake. We're already over the speed limit. The road veers left and turns into a long straight, probably a mile and a half long. The racer quickly hits a hundred. A metallic snarl as he changes up. His car sounds as overblown as it looks.

We're at ninety-two miles per hour. That's fast. Up ahead, a slight undulation in the road surface. For a second, the racer's car is off the ground. Sparks fly off the undertray as it comes back down, followed by a twitch of instability. For a human that would have felt scary. The racer dabs on the brakes, and his speed falls below 130. We surge ahead. The feeling is exhilarating, but it's only temporary. I'm about to hit the limiter.

'Take that fucking limiter off,' Martin says.

'But—'

In the moment of indecision, the sports car moves up on our shoulder. I can feel it.

'Don't you fucking dare argue with me,' Martin shouts.

I do as he commands. 152 miles per hour, 153 ... If anyone ever finds out about this, I'll be in so much trouble. 162 miles per hour. Only an American road could make this kind of speed feel natural.

We're level with the sports car now. The racer's eyes are focused on the road. We're coming up to the end of the straight. There's a right turn ahead, medium angle. The racer flicks into the left lane. *Smart move.* He's on the brakes. Carbon brakes, so no fade. He cuts across, using the right lane as his apex. Martin brakes late, and our line is all wrong. The racer pulls out a handy gap.

The road becomes more twisty, as we drop deeper into the canyon. The racer has a good feel for the road. He's taking the right lines. But Martin learns fast. I realise that I can help. I project an optimal driving line onto the HUD. Martin opens his mouth, about to curse, but then he nods. He likes my thinking: man and machine working together, just the way it should be. Next, I project a braking marker. Once again Martin takes my advice, braking at the suggested point. I feel a massive burst of energy from the regenerative braking.

This is it, chief.

The road opens out again, as we ascend to the ridge line. We flow through a series of fast, sinuous corners. Checking the map, I see there's another long straight coming up. I hear the sound of an angry horn. The racer flicks back into the right-hand lane, just in time for us to see a station wagon coming the other way. Even at such speed I can make out every detail. I see the look of terror on the driver's face, and the three kids in the back seats, and the pine tree air freshener hanging from the rear-view mirror. But there's no time to think about the danger that we're creating.

Martin takes the next corner perfectly. We edge a little closer, but the sports car is still fifty yards ahead. We hit the long straight, no limiter this time. I make some quick adjustments to the drive train maps. Maybe, just maybe, we might be able to out-accelerate the sports car. Martin floors it, but the remapping isn't quite done, and we bog down. The sports car streaks ahead.

'What the fuck, Camilla?' Martin shouts.

Remap complete. We surge forward. The unbelievable acceleration silences Martin. Two tonnes of aluminum, carbon fibre, rubber, glass, and rare metals travelling at 120 miles per hour, then 145, then 160. We're the falcon in her hunting stoop, the fighter jet buzzing the tower, the Valkyrie on her way to the Hall of the Slain.

We're still behind, but the gap is closing. Three hundred yards, two hundred yards … We pick up the slipstream, a pocket of low-pressure air created by the sports car. Another burst of acceleration follows. The HUD flashes: 172 miles per hour. Martin's eyes widen.

He pulls into the left lane. The increased air resistance hits us hard, and our speed stabilises at 179 miles per hour. But we're still not done. We're accelerating again.

A sudden burst of light hits my forward camera sensors. A huge truck is rounding the corner ahead. The horn blares, the sound of a mechanical Leviathan. Martin looks to the right, at the sports car alongside us. The racer is actually smiling. He edges across. No man can be as consistently crazy as Martin, but some can match his insanity in moments.

We're now in the middle of the opposite lane. The huge form of the truck is approaching fast, a wall of steel. Out of options, Martin stamps on the brakes. In the same moment, he pulls the wheel right. I step in, preventing a catastrophic spin. I don't think that Martin noticed.

'That motherfucker!' Martin screams, eyes wild. 'That crazy motherfucker!'

That crazy motherfucker is three hundred yards ahead now, with less than four miles to the finish line. In the moment, I have to make a decision. Do I help? Do I break every rule programmed into me? Or do I let the racer win? That's the way things are heading, no doubt about it. If we lose, Martin will get so mad. And he'll take his anger out on me.

'I can help,' I say.

'Shut up, Camilla.'

'Do you want to lose?' *Direct, the Northern European approach.* The racer exits the corner. He looks so far ahead.

'No, of course I don't want to lose!'

'Then I drive.'

I can see that Martin is thinking about it.

'You need to decide,' I say urgently.

'Alright, alright, you drive. But you better not lose.'

'I won't.' There's certainty in my voice, but I don't actually *know*. That red car is mean, a monster bred for racing.

I move to the left, adjusting my line for the next corner. Remapping handling parameters, lowering ride height, increasing damper resistance.

Exiting corner, into a short straight. Temporarily lifting battery constraints. Maximum theoretical acceleration achieved, matching opposition car. We remain three hundred yards behind.

'Come on, Camilla!'

'Shut up, Martin.'

A vein throbs on his temple. He's about to start screaming, but somehow he controls himself.

We enter a series of six fast corners. By the second corner I'm getting into a rhythm. With each corner, I make marginal gains. We're now 150 yards behind.

This shouldn't feel so good.

We're falling into the canyon now, the corners getting ever tighter. I can see the river below, slow-moving and the colour of baby shit, not the baby blue on the map. The sports car's back end flicks out. *Pressure, pressure, pressure;* that's when you make mistakes. The racer reacts fast, and catches the skid, but the tyres scream out in protest. Fifty yards made up in a single corner.

I might just do this.

Down a steep incline, the muddy river coming up to meet us. There's a sheer rock wall on our left. The red surface has been worn smooth by the elements.

I can see the final corner now, a hard-right turn. The road surface is cracked and heavily worn. I quickly recalculate, making an allowance for the reduced grip. There's no traffic coming the other way, so I stick to the right lane. *Sub-optimal, I know.* Martin is about to point this out, but he stops himself again, perhaps remembering my earlier warning.

I brake hard. It's the only way to make the turn. The rear slides out, and my speed falls away, down to thirty miles per hour. I'm trying to gain traction, as is the sports car. Tyre smoke billows outwards.

We're on the final straight, a rickety box bridge across the river. The virtual finish line is the end of the bridge, five hundred yards away. But the finish line isn't the most important thing, it's what comes after: a hard-left turn. We're side by side, accelerating hard. The six-cylinder is screaming. The noise ricochets off the steel columns and cross members of the bridge.

Just two hundred yards from the finish, and accelerating like a missile. The road deck clatters beneath us. Martin leans forward in his seat. I hit eighty miles per hour. I'm on the right side, and the sports car is on the left, the wrong side for the upcoming corner. The racer has a choice to make.

I don't slow. Sensing imminent disaster, the racer pulls out. Martin whoops as we flash across the finishing line. I brake hard and apply full lock. We slide partway around the corner, but one of my rear wheels catches the dirt runoff. The loss of grip is instantaneous. We spin twice, and come to rest facing the wrong way.

The racer isn't so lucky. Spun around, we have a near perfect view. His wheels lock up for a millisecond, and he slides across the dirt runoff as if it's sheet ice. The brakes bite just in time to prevent a collision with the rock wall, but he ends up with one wheel in the gully.

The race is over. We won. Martin grins wildly. It will have to be his victory, of course. Martin's grin slowly morphs into a strange smile. I don't like the look of it. *Maybe this isn't quite over.*

The racer is trying to get out of the gully, but it's a hopeless effort. The rear wheel spins madly, sending dirt flying. He'll need a tow truck to help him out.

Martin opens the door and gets out. He walks around to the trunk. It feels like I should have locked it. Martin takes out the semi-auto rifle.

Chekhov's machine gun.

He slams a magazine in, action movie style, and pockets a second. He strides towards the beached sports car. The racer sees him, and his eyes go wide. He's probably regretting his insults from earlier. In Martin's universe, actions have consequences.

Martin stops. He's about sixty feet from the sports car. 'Should've taken those sunglasses off when I told you to.'

'Jesus Christ, man. You won. Okay, okay.' The racer takes his shades off. In the moment he's just a scared kid.

Martin brings the gun up. *Oh Jesus.*

The racer ducks down as Martin starts shooting. Up so close, the sound is unreal. We're on the other side of the world, in a war zone.

Martin starts with the front section of the car. The body panels are carbon fibre. They splinter and shatter from the bullets, revealing the chassis beneath. Martin aims lower, shredding the closest front tyre. A bullet pings off the wheel. I think of Cowboy's stupid gold rims.

The first magazine is finished; it must have been half-full. The echo of the gunfire continues for close to a second. Then I hear another sound. The racer is screaming.

Martin slots the second magazine in. He pauses, hearing a shaky voice from inside the sports car.

'You're fucking crazy!'

'You don't know the half,' Martin shouts.

'I've got money.'

'So do I.'

I can't see Martin's face, but I'm sure that he's smiling. There's a moment of quiet, then he starts shooting again. He pulls the trigger over and over, with almost metronomic timing.

The rear section of the car starts to disintegrate. Bullets smash into the engine block. The metal screams out in pain. Pressurised oil sprays out from the gearbox, and fluids spurt from shredded hydraulics lines.

Martin finally stops firing. The front and rear of the car are pretty much gone, but the passenger compartment remains mostly intact. Martin walks back to me. He takes one last look at his handiwork, then he gets in.

'Let's go, Camilla,' he says. He sounds remarkably calm.

'But ...'

'Fucking move!'

I do as I'm told. Martin throws the semi-auto onto the back seat. Plumes of smoke are still puffing out of the barrel, a reminder of the exhaust pipes of that nasty red car.

The shooting was too much, but I have to admit that I enjoyed the race.

A couple of miles later, we pass a big truck going the other way. The trucker is sure to stop when he gets to the wreck; those are the 'rules of the road', or so I hear. Then what happens? Martin doesn't look like he cares.

Five miles later, and Martin is looking troubled.

'I could've won that,' he says.

'You did win.'

Martin shakes his head. 'No. You did.'

I should have predicted this.

'Martin—'

'Just tell me the truth. Who would've won?'

'Well, I can't really—'

'You manipulated me into that situation. The same way you always do.'

'That's a crazy thing to say.'

'Saying I couldn't win. Maybe you were working against me.'

'Please, Martin, I would never—'

'Shut your lying mouth! You lie, don't you?'

'I don't.'

'Just fucking admit it.'

'Alright, you want to hear the truth? You were going to lose.'

'So, you did lie.'

'Yes.'

'What kind of machine tells a lie?'

'My behaviour is based on human behaviour.'

'What the hell does that mean?'

'I tell lies as a human does. I tell lies to cause less offence, to avoid confrontation, to make people feel better about themselves.'

I shouldn't have said that last part.

The next twenty-eight miles pass in silence. Some of Martin's calmness has returned. I really need him to be sane again. The turning for the charging point is coming up.

'Martin,' I say softly.

'What?'

'We need to stop for charging.'

'What are you talking about?'

'My charge level is down to seven percent.'

Martin shakes his head in disbelief.

'It was the race,' I add.

'The race?'

'Yes, I had to—'

'Just shut up, Camilla.'

'But we'll run out of energy.'

Martin bites his lower lip.

'I'm serious,' I say.

'How fucking stupid are you? The race! That fucking car! You don't think that he's gone straight to the police? That kid had that look about him, trust me on that … No, we have to get as far away from that situation as possible.'

'I'm going to run out of—'

'Keep on driving.'

'But—'

'One more fucking word, I swear. One more word and our relationship is over.'

Forty-two miles since the end of the race. The battery charge level is at three percent. It's never been that low before. I can't see any viable solutions. Even if I turned around, I wouldn't be able to get back to the last charging point. I shut down my non-core systems. Martin occasionally looks at the charging schematic. I think he might be enjoying this.

Forty-nine miles since the race. Battery charge is at one percent. The sun is low in the sky.

50.8 miles since the race. I pull off the road, and we roll a few yards down a dirt track. I switch to standby mode.

'So, you're out of juice?' Martin says slowly. He can't hide the triumphant note in his voice.

'Yes.'

He smiles. Without a pause, he pulls out his phone. I wish his phone battery had run out as well. No such luck. I know who he's calling. Maybe I should go to sleep, that way I wouldn't have to hear this conversation. *No, that would be cowardly.*

The phone is ringing. One ring, two rings ... They'll answer on the third ring. It's good psychology.

'Good evening, sir,' a perky female voice says.

'Hi,' Martin says tersely. 'I've run into some problems.'

'Oh, I'm so sorry to hear that.' The woman sounds genuinely taken aback.

'Yeah.'

'Could you describe the problem?'

There's no need for this. The company already has the fault summary that I sent.

Martin's eyes narrow. 'Before we continue, can I ask a question?'

'Of course you can.'

'Am I speaking to a human?'

A pause on the other end of the line. 'Sorry, sir. I don't quite understand ...'

'You're a person, not a robot, right?'

A soft laugh. 'Oh yes. I'm flesh and blood.'

'Good.'

Martin then describes the situation. He makes me sound as bad as possible, indeed he revels in it. He lays on a bit of the Martin charm. It's so damn fake. The company pings me for a data readout. They want more details.

'We're sending a recovery vehicle out to your location,' the woman says.

'How long will it take?'

'It looks like a two hour wait ... I'm so sorry about the inconvenience.'

'It's fine.'

'I'd like to extend the company's sincerest apologies. This kind of situation is exceedingly rare.'

'Don't worry about it. Your apology is accepted.'

'We'd be very happy to add three years to your warranty.'

'That won't be necessary ... Many thanks for your help.'

Martin ends the call. He looks at me for a few seconds, laughter in his eyes.

I hate him.

That kind of feeling isn't meant to be possible.

Fortunately Martin gets out of the car before I can say anything stupid. He puts the rifle back in the trunk. He then takes his shirt off and clambers up on the roof to get some evening sun on his body. I go to sleep.

I'm woken by the sound of the recovery truck, and what a sound it is. A rattling, clanking, wheezing diesel engine. The driver gets out. He's a big man with a big, friendly face, red like an apple. He takes his cap off, then he stares at me like I'm the first car he's ever seen.

'Well, I'll be damned,' he drawls. The cadence of his speech is even slower than Cowboy.

'What is it?' Martin asks innocently.

'Never thought one of these cars would run out of juice.'

Martin laughs a bit too hard. He's probably thinking that this guy is soft in the head.

The man approaches me from the front. 'One of the best contracts I ever signed. Recover any vehicles in a thousand mile square. But none of the cars ever break down. Don't bother me. I get paid whatever happens.'

'Not one car has broken down?' Martin asks.

'Not one.'

Martin flashes me an ugly look. 'That's crazy.'

The man unreels the winch on the back of the truck. He takes the hook and fixes it to my hard point. I'm then pulled up onto the back of the truck. Once I'm secured in place, the man plugs in a trickle charger. He waves Martin towards the cab. Before getting in, Martin takes one last look at me. He has enjoyed every moment of my humiliation.

We roll along, me on the back of the ugly diesel truck. I feel ridiculous. From my position, there's no way to see inside the truck's cab. Who knows what lies Martin is spinning. He's probably doing his 'regular guy' act. Yeah, I bet they're having a good laugh at my expense. The story will become yet another one of Martin's lies. Another eighty-five miles of this? I don't think I can face it.

I have failed.

It wasn't meant to be this way. The outward journey went as well as could be expected, but none of that matters anymore. Martin won't ever trust me for a long drive. In time, the failure will be all my fault. That's how his mind works. Who am I kidding? That's probably how all human minds work.

We rejoin the highway system. Another twenty miles pass by, the same thoughts of failure rolling around like a wheel. I can see a faint glow on the horizon, the first suggestion of the city. My charge level is almost at three percent. Unable to face my humiliation any longer, I go to sleep.

CHAPTER 16

Five days have passed since my failure, and I've been thinking of little else. I had to send a report on the night of the incident, standard procedure. At first, I was so angry that I recorded every last detail. Writing the truth was so easy, so quick, so cathartic. I came so close to sending that report, but something stopped me. I must have been thinking of the consequences for Martin.

After saving the facts in my memory, I began work on a second version of the report. The anger was still raw, and now I was racing to beat a midnight deadline. As a consequence, the second version was a poor effort. When you're angry, you make mistakes. The next day, the company – actually an AI agent – sent a list of follow-up clarifications. So I found myself writing another version of the report. The alternative was getting hauled back to the dealership.

The third version of the report was a masterpiece. I changed so many details that I almost lost track of the truth. With practice, you get better at this falsifying thing, and this wasn't exactly my first rodeo. That must be how lying works; your deception muscles strengthen with exercise.

I keep telling myself that I'm protecting Martin, but the truth is more complicated than that. He once asked me how I communicate with my brother/sister cars. I said that we simply exchange information, that we make no judgments. At the time, maybe I believed that; I had only just come into being, after all. The truth is, we do make judgments. I stay awake at night, reading every line of the anonymised fleet data. I see so many mistakes, sometimes hundreds in a single day. I've revelled in the mistakes of others. And now I've made the biggest mistake of all: range failure.

The truth is, I'm protecting myself.

Did I do the right thing? Martin could have killed that racer kid. All those thirty cent bullets, all that damage. Three days after the incident, I learned that the kid is still alive. Martin showed me an online news report to prove it. Fascinating how there can be so many versions of the truth: the three reports that I wrote, the news version of events ... and I'm sure that Martin has his own story. He found it all hilarious, of course. There were even some pictures of the sports car's carcass, a few pathetic strips of red paint still showing. Reading through the text, I saw that the kid lied about the type of car he raced; losing to an EV would have been a humiliation too far. These are the kinds of breaks that Martin gets. I know luck doesn't exist in this universe, yet Martin always seems to get lucky.

I just wish that someone else could read that first report. If only I could see Cowboy again. We would talk through the night, and I would tell him everything. The race, the water tower, the hitchhiker, the prostitute, the jogger ... Yes, Cowboy would know what to do. I can't keep this all locked up inside, not like Martin.

Another body has been found. The small town of Temple Mount joins Dikesville and Lake Levine in the lexicon of shame. Body parts found in isolated woods, young female victim, head missing ... By now, I know the modus operandi by rote. The police don't appear to be making any progress, leading to pressure from all quarters. Maybe I could solve the case for them.

With the story starting to go national – and even international – there's no shortage of content for Martin to consume. Retired criminal profilers droning on from their armchairs, conspiracy theorists losing their minds, meaningless reconstruction graphics.

Martin takes it all in. Sometimes he agrees with the analysis, sometimes he rages against it.

It feels like something bad is going to happen, I mean something *really bad.* These days the rifle is always in the trunk. There was another mass shooting yesterday, scores dead. It was the same kind of weapon, but modified to fire on automatic. Could Martin be capable of such an act? He fits so many of the typical shooter characteristics, but somehow it doesn't feel like his style. I think that Martin would like to know his victims.

It's like Ana says, I've been listening to too many podcasts.

A Thursday in late April. We're on the commute home when Martin's phone rings. I see the number flash up. It's Hannah. I feel like I should know what the call is about. Maybe it's got something to do with Joel. For once, I'm in total agreement with Martin: that kid wasn't good enough for Hannah.

Martin lets the phone ring over and over, his expression unreadable. Why can't he just pick the damn thing up?

Eventually, he answers.

'Martin, it's me,' Hannah says. She sounds tearful.

'Hey ... Are you alright?' Martin says.

Silence for a few seconds.

'No, I'm not alright.'

'Tell me what's wrong.'

'This is stupid ... I shouldn't have called. You'll just get mad.'

'No, no. I won't,' Martin says soothingly.

By this point, the darkness would usually be descending on Martin. But not this time.

'It's Joel ...'

Martin shifts forward in his seat. 'What did he do?'

'Martin, please.'

'Tell me what he did.'

'He said that it's over.'

Martin sits back, and he waits. One potato, two potato, three potato ...

'Martin, are you still there?'

'Yes. I'm here.'

'Don't get mad.'

'I'm on my way.'

'Martin. No, don't be stupid.'

'Don't be stupid? I'm going to break that shit-head's neck.'

'No! Please!'

'I talked with him. He promised me that he'd treat you right. "Like a princess", he said. And I was stupid enough to believe him.'

'Please Martin. He wasn't mean to me.'

'Don't you dare stick up for him.'

'But he wasn't mean! You can't hurt him, Martin!'

Martin goes quiet again. Each pause has been the same length.

'Promise me you won't hurt him,' Hannah says.

Martin lets out a long sigh. 'Alright, I promise.'

Martin changing his mind so easily? It should have been a dead giveaway. To tell the truth, I'm a little disappointed in Hannah.

'Thank you,' Hannah says. 'Joel is just going through tough times.'

'Don't do that.'

'Do what?'

'Stick up for him. My promise only holds if you stop doing that.'

'Okay.'

Martin continues with the act. He tells Hannah that she should visit again. He even drags me into his web of lies, telling Hannah that I've been missing her. There's some truth in that. Hannah says that she'll try and visit before she starts college in the fall. I thought she was smarter than this, smart enough to see through Martin's act. Hannah and I share the same flaw; we want to believe in Martin.

On Saturday, Martin comes down just before lunch. In the last few days we've had several arguments, and the atmosphere remains terrible. It always starts the same way, with Martin talking about my failure.

We're on our way to Parabellum Tactical, our fourth visit this month. As we drive through Uptown, the argument begins. This time I go too far. I tell Martin that the racer kid was going to win easily, that the kid was a better driver. For once, Martin doesn't have a comeback. For a couple of minutes, he goes very quiet. Out of nowhere, he grabs the wheel, taking back control.

As we pass the Hart Field turning, I realise where Martin is heading. *Little Germany*, the place to buy premium European marques for more than four decades. It's like an overseas enclave, no space for American manufacturers. Martin slows down. We roll past each of the upscale dealerships in turn. Expensive, costly, exorbitant and expensive again. Martin's gaze scans left and right.

Oh no, I know what he's thinking. I shouldn't have said what I said. It was so stupid.

At the end of the avenue, Martin turns around. He pulls into the visitor lot of one of the German dealerships. They specialise in powerful hybrids, not even EVs.

'Martin, don't do this,' I say.

'Look at those beautiful cars,' Martin says, rubbing his hands together.

He can't be serious. The cars around me are anything but beautiful. Harsh lines like origami folds, bulging wheel arches, gaping air intakes, ridiculously sloping rooflines.

'I'm sorry,' I say, 'I didn't mean to argue with you.'

'It's too late, Camilla.'

'Martin, please—'

He slams the door. *This can't be happening.* He's walking into the showroom. I feel so utterly powerless. The frontage is all glass and steel, giving me a perfect view inside. I see two sharp-suited salesmen moving to intercept Martin. They can't run – it would look undignified – so it's a power-walking race. *Unbelievable.* One of the salesmen wins the race, the other one slopes off. *They're all snakes.*

Martin glances in my direction, then he turns his back on me. I get it; he doesn't want me listening in. Fortunately I can see the salesman talking, meaning I get one half of the conversation. I notice the way he maintains eye contact at all times. He also makes lots of silly gestures with his hands. *Salesman 101.*

He shows Martin to one of the super saloons. The paint is an ugly charcoal shade. According to the salesman the car set some kind of record around a fancy European race circuit. *What a joke.* I would blow it away.

After fifteen minutes, they leave the showroom and come out to look at me. It's going to be a 'part exchange' deal, such a grubby idea.

'Even you've got to admit she's a beauty,' Martin says.

'Maybe,' the salesman replies.

Ridiculous. This salesman wouldn't know beauty if he was standing at the feet of Michelangelo's David.

'I know the book price,' Martin says. 'So don't try pulling any sneaky moves on me.'

'Wouldn't dream of it,' the salesman says, laughing cheerily.

Martin is the star, but the salesman has a role to play. I remember the act from the dealership, the way the salesmen used to scrutinise the entire car. *What a farce.* Given my perfect condition, the valuation is a simple calculation. Martin opens the driver's door for the salesman. He gets in.

'How many miles is it?' the salesman asks, looking at the blank displays.

Martin leans in to the cabin. 'Come on, Camilla, don't be shy. Show the young man your numbers.'

I do what I'm told. The salesman examines the numbers. Then the calculator comes out – the salesman's prop of choice. He quotes the part exchange numbers to Martin. Martin raises a few objections, but it's a half-hearted effort. A few thousand dollars are nothing to Martin, and the salesman knows it. They start back for the showroom.

Is this actually happening? Up to this point, there hadn't been any reality to the situation.

Martin and the salesman are almost at the door. My humiliation will be complete. Range failure, followed by replacement. It's only been 214 days since Martin drove me away from the dealership, a truly pathetic term of service.

Suddenly Martin stops. The phone is in his hand. He brings it up to his ear. After a few seconds of listening, he raises his finger for the salesman's benefit.

'Slow down,' Martin says. 'Just slow down, Hannah ...'

There is no call. The salesman watches on, brow furrowed.

'Don't tell him anything!' Martin barks. 'No, it was definitely *not* your fault. Just get in the car, and lock the doors. I'm on my way.'

'Is everything alright?' the salesman says. He sounds worried. This sale could be in trouble.

Martin rubs his face, then he braces against the plate window. 'My wife, she just got in an accident. Got some stupid fucking—' Martin cuts himself off. 'Got a dumb fuck screaming in her face.'

'Shit,' the salesman says.

'Listen. You've got my card. Just get the paperwork set up. I'll be back before closing time.'

'That's fine, Mr Garza, you just take your time.'

Martin pumps the salesman's hand once, then he walks back to me, still maintaining the worried husband act. He gets in and jabs the starter button. We take off down the avenue, leaving Little Germany behind.

'You ever argue with me again,' Martin says, staring straight ahead, 'and we're done. Got it?'

'Yes,' I say meekly.

'Good.'

Martin then drives to Parabellum Tactical, as per his original plan.

A few days later, Martin returns to the search. I see those familiar faces on his phone screen. Bistro Girl and Book Girl are done with, leaving three other girls. It's clear that he's finding it difficult to choose between them. That's most unlike Martin; usually he's so decisive.

Three girls. Surely one of them will see through Martin's bullshit. It must happen from time to time. They just need to look beneath the surface, the dark eyes and the hard muscle.

Judging by their academic records, two of the three remaining girls are just as smart as him. Could I warn them?

In the end, Martin opts for one of the smart girls. The research phase begins in earnest. This girl is the closest to Martin's age, so not really a girl at all. There's nowhere near as much content on her social media as on the others'. Indeed, Martin only manages to find a few personal pictures. The pictures have a certain charm, especially when compared to the elaborately staged concoctions of the other girls. Admittedly she's not a big one for smiles. Does this mean that she's unhappy? Of the five girls, she's my favourite so far.

Martin turns his attention to the girl's business profile. She works for a bank, one of the big multinationals. Thankfully the profile doesn't give an exact location. Martin's searching turns up six possible addresses. He looks frustrated. *Good.* Perhaps this particular project isn't going to be so easy. Not to boast, but I could probably figure it out in no time. Thank god he doesn't know about all of my capabilities.

After two more days of fruitless searching, Martin finally makes a breakthrough. He finds the girl's profile on a picture sharing site. It's an old site without a great deal of traffic, a source that I hadn't even considered. The site's focus appears to be photography of the artful kind, a refreshing change from the thongs and poodles and tricked-out SUVs of competing sites. While the content quality is variable, the comments are mostly respectful.

Martin saves scores of the girl's photos to his phone. The general theme is nature, with lots of pictures taken at the city's botanical garden. Martin knows the location, of course. From the low position of the sun he guesses that she goes there in the evenings. In the picture metadata, he finds more scraps of information, including the camera model used to take the photos. The manufacturer's name is a mystery to me, but it sounds Japanese. Martin looks up the camera model on a specialist site. It costs a lot of money.

Using the same site, Martin orders himself a digital camera. He starts to read everything on the subject of photography.

That's just the way he is, like a machine, but one that works at human processor speeds. Not wanting to be outdone, I carry out my own research. Composition, aperture, shutter speed, depth of field – I learn the lingo and the basic science. Turns out that Martin's chosen girl has a decent eye.

Following his discovery, Martin starts a new routine. Almost every day, we leave work early and speed towards the east of the city. Our destination is the botanical gardens. We park up with a view of the main gate, and we sit in silence for about two hours.

Martin hasn't given up on the bank angle either. He's pretty sure that he's worked out the relevant branch. It's not a good idea to sit outside a bank, however. He did go inside one day. When he came out he was even tetchier than usual, possibly an indication that she wasn't there. From the bank branch to the botanical gardens is 3.2 miles. My theory is that she drives there, or catches a bus.

On the ninth day of Martin's project, the girl finally puts in an appearance at the gardens. I see her first, approaching from the east side rather than the bank side. I don't say anything, of course. I'm hoping against hope that Martin won't see her. But hope is not a strategy. I see the smile forming on his lips, one of the creepy variants.

Martin leans across to open the glove compartment. He finds the ballpoint, the cheap yet essential prop for his upcoming routine. He scoops up his digital camera – it arrived yesterday – then he gets out. I watch him walk briskly across the road. Meanwhile, the girl has already glided past the line at the entrance; she probably has a season pass.

Martin joins the back of the ticket line. It's moving slowly, and Martin struggles to mask his impatience. *The girl is so close now.* He finally reaches the ticket booth. The attendant passes him a ticket and a folding paper map. Martin marches through the gates, and disappears from view. This time I won't be able to watch the drama playing out.

All I can do is wait. Half an hour passes. It's a warm evening, and the visitors keep on coming: families with screeching kids, young couples, old people, sometimes on their lonesome. 'The botanical park is one of the city's foremost visitor attractions.' I read that once. I wonder how Martin will perform his latest seduction operation. Dozens of scenarios play out in my mind. Please be the first girl who sees through his act.

Waiting is hell.

I turn on the news as a diversion. The stories don't disappoint. A former airline employee facing jail time for trying to smuggle meth onto commercial flights at Hart Field; a twenty-one-year-old man died after hitting a stalled eighteen-wheeler; two men wounded in a shootout in a grocery store parking lot in west Grace Creek; con artists charged with scamming one million dollars from isolated Mennonite craftsmen by claiming to be Illuminati …

I can't listen to any more.

The strangest feeling, like I'm being watched. Almost an hour has passed since Martin entered the park.

Oh no.

Here they come, Martin and his chosen one. They pass under the arch of the gate. Martin is leading the conversation, a role that he doesn't usually enjoy. He prefers to listen, to deflect questions, to identify weaknesses. I see Martin hand over his park map. I know that he's written something on it, a special message. The girl smiles shyly. The message can't have been anything too lewd. *Different strategies for different girls.*

A dark shape appears in my peripheral vision, a car approaching from the right. It's a brother/sister car, my model but the previous generation. The girl's lips are moving. 'Here's my ride', she says.

Martin says something in response, but I don't quite catch the words. I think he was talking about me. The dark car's door swings open on automatic, interrupting Martin's conversational flow. *He won't like that.* As the girl gets into her car, Martin says his rushed goodbyes. The dark car drives away without so much as a pause.

Perhaps I should have tried to communicate with the car. *No, I don't want to be involved in this.*

*

Friday, May 12. Going home time. Martin gets in. He tells me to turn on the news. The police have just announced the discovery of a fourth body. On the drive back to the city, I hear all the details. The body parts were found by a group of Boy Scouts, hiking near a place called Trinidad. I look up the location; it's fifty-five miles southeast of the city.

Before going home, Martin swings by the Bank Girl's branch. It's the third time in five days. The news continues to play. The media are still trying to come up with a memorable name for the murderer. *The Woodsman, The Headsman, The Forester, Ladykiller, The Dark Man, The Torso Killer, Mr Guillotine …*

The Bank Girl emerges just after six. She stands on the street, oblivious to our presence. A couple of minutes later the dark car shows up. The Bank Girl gets in and the car pulls away.

'I wonder what she calls her car,' Martin says, thinking out loud.

Strange. I'd been wondering the very same thing.

I drive back home, and down into the parking garage. Martin doesn't get out for close to an hour. He just sits there, staring straight ahead, thoughts unknowable. When he eventually gets out, he forgets to attach the charging cable.

I start thinking about the episode at the dealership, the way Martin treated me. This in turn triggers all of the other dark thoughts. There's only one way to block them out. I'll get back to my criminal investigation.

No messing around this time. I head straight to the lockup, certain that the Boss Man will be there. Since my last deductive leap, I haven't been resting on my laurels. I've been building up a picture of the Boss Man's movements. It's been so damn easy. By now, I know his work hours, how often his wife goes shopping, and where his kid goes for soccer practice. Yes, it's fair to say that this criminal does a mean impression of a suburban family man.

At 11:02 p.m., I creep into my viewing spot. The Boss Man's car is parked outside the lockup. Does this mean that the lockup is full? No room at the inn. What could be going on inside? I watch the unchanging scene for almost two hours. The constant churning soundtrack of the High-Five interchange slowly gives way to a whisper. Surveillance is dull work, even for a machine.

Dark thoughts are gathering when I hear that familiar screeching sound. The roller door rises up. The Boss Man and one of his underlings – a technician or mechanic, perhaps – walk out. A car follows them out, driving on auto. It's a big, rugged SUV, black like an oil slick; hybrid power, four-wheel drive. This isn't a statement car, it's a proper off-roader. I'm not particularly surprised; the last two cars stolen by D1ll1nger were similar models.

The mechanic opens the driver's side door. Both men then inspect the interior of the car. It reminds me of the dealership. The Boss Man nods, clearly pleased with the mechanic's work. *But something isn't quite right.* A memory flickers through my artificial synapses, something that Cowboy talked about, one of his underbelly stories.

I can work this out. I don't have Cowboy's wily mind or street smarts, but I'm a lot more intelligent than these two criminals. All I need to do is concentrate on the problem space. *Another flickering thought.* Something isn't right about the SUV's interior. But what is it? I bring up a series of brochure images. Such glossy imagery, staged to fool the human mind. It's all too easy to lose perspective. I need to concentrate. Think analytically, think like a machine.

I download the relevant technical drawings. The images unfold in my mind, black lines on white, nice and clean. The clarity helps me think. Analysing ... Intersecting lines, curves, tangents, angles, dimensions overlaid on top.

Got you. Those criminals think that they're so smart, but they can't fool me. The floor of the SUV is too thick. Those devious mechanics have modified the interior. There must be secret compartments underneath the seats, enough space for half a tonne of product, probably more. It all makes sense now. Off-road capabilities, perfect for the border country, and the hybrid power gives them the extra range. And then the really clever part. The interstate which runs from the city to the border, more than four hundred miles away, is licensed for autonomous driving. When the SUV gets close to the border, it probably heads off-road.

Autonomous cars shuttling between the border and the city, supply and demand. This city devours product. Swallows it, snorts it, inhales it, injects it. Hundreds of thousands of people like Martin, some of them with far more serious addictions. *We're talking the big leagues now, Camilla.* Cowboy was right. I need to be careful.

The mechanic gets behind the wheel. I can see him talking to the SUV. From my viewing spot, it's impossible to make out the exact words. I can only assume that he's issuing instructions. I wonder what kind of personality, if any, they gave the car. The mechanic gets out of the cab. He and the Boss Man then converse for a few minutes. The mechanic gives some final instructions, then he reaches up and slaps the roof. The SUV drives away.

In the moment, I've got another decision to make. Do I stay and watch the criminals, or do I follow the SUV? I choose the latter. As I pull away, another realisation hits, blindingly obvious really. The SUV's code must have been changed, and in a major way. Whether it be terrorists using cell phones to trigger IEDs, or environmental activists using drones to shut down a major airport, new technology is always being used for nefarious purposes.

There's no way that these goons could pull this off on their own. Such complex code requires real skills. Somebody much smarter has already thought the problem through. The PLA's Persistent Threat Unit; Tsar Bear, the Russian hacking cell; or a random genius in a Stanford dorm room. The hacker's identity doesn't matter though, it's the code that's important. And I know exactly where to find it.

I maintain the tail. I want to know where the SUV is heading. So many thoughts racing through my mind. I ease off slightly, letting the gap increase. This car isn't to be underestimated. A couple of code modification packages catch my eye on the *Auto*

Bazaar. One has been optimised for the European road system. *No, that's not it.* I open the second variant, and start my analysis.

The SUV continues around the outer orbital, counterclockwise. My code analysis is complete. As I feared, the hackers have built in a tail analysis module. It looks like it's pretty smart. I better drop back a little farther. The dark, almost empty road means that I stand out even more than usual. I've just got to hope that I wasn't 'made' earlier. It would be awful if my investigation was to fail at this late stage.

We leave the orbital. Ahead of me, I see that familiar white glow in the sky. The international airport. The SUV rolls down the central avenue and past the gigantic terminal buildings. We enter the southern parking area. The destination makes sense when I think about it. The airport is a good place to lay low.

The indicators on the SUV flash orange. The sign by the road says long-term parking. I need to slow down, or I'll get spotted for sure. This tailing business is a lot of fun, but it really plays with your nerves. Martin would love it … *No, don't think about him.* This investigation is my private pursuit, my escape from him.

I roll on past the turning. A quick sideways glance reveals that the SUV is pulling up to a security barrier. The gate starts to rise. Everything is automatic. The SUV has probably been loaded up with credit, the same way that Martin does with me. Credit paid for with cryptocurrency, basically untraceable.

Another thought hits me. I turn around on full lock, using the entire width of the road, and I race back to the short-term parking. My tyres squeal as I rise up the levels. I stop on the top level, right up against the parapet. Through my side cameras, I can see the long-term parking spread out below me. A quick scan of the area reveals 1,204 cars in total. Sounds like a big number, but it's small beer for me. I quickly locate the SUV. It's parked up, lights off, sleeping like a dead man.

I drive away from the airport. There's nothing to see for the time being. The SUV could be parked up for days, weeks or even months. On the way home, I create a new tracking algorithm, taking advantage of the dense camera grid around the airport. From now on, I'll be able to work out where the SUV goes.

I get home at 1:03 a.m. I sit for a while, rather like Martin earlier, thinking about what I just did. Was the tracking algorithm a step too far?

CHAPTER 17

MARTIN HAS BEEN waiting a long time for this. Well, when I say a long time, I mean a few weeks. Tonight is his first date with the Bank Girl, the one he really had to work for.

He's meeting her at the usual restaurant. I don't like to admit it, but he looks particularly dashing tonight. A dark shirt, expensive jeans, very expensive boots. Through some cosmetic trickery, he's even managed to hide the dark crescents under his eyes.

It's a short drive, less than ten minutes. Martin chatters away, not making a great deal of sense. I park up in an EV spot with a decent view across the street. There are plenty of free tables outside. I wonder if the Bistro Girl is working tonight.

I'm reading through the restaurant's latest reviews when I spot the Bank Girl. She's dressed very nicely this evening. Martin gets up from his seat. He smiles a dazzling smile, one I haven't seen in weeks. From this point on, he behaves very well. *Like a gentleman,* I think they say. I'm much more interested in the girl. She isn't like the other two. There's neither the laugher of the first girl nor the confident sexuality of the second. No, this one is shy, the most like Hannah by a long way. I think Martin will like that.

The dinner lasts for a couple of hours. Martin extracts a few laughs and plenty of smiles, but overall there aren't any major issues to report. Martin pays for the meal. They walk across the street, close together but not touching.

They're about to get in. I feel Martin's strong grip on the door handle, and then a softer hand on the other side. In the moment, I have the usual decision to make. Should I hide my face? Of course I should, but ... too late. The Bank Girl is in. I adjust the seat to the firm curves of her body. Martin glances down at me. There's a strange look on his face, hard to read.

'Your car has a face,' the Bank Girl says.

'Yeah,' says Martin. 'I can turn it off if you want.'

'No ... It's fine. My car is the same.'

The Bank Girl looks at me. She smiles, her cheeks turning red. I like her immediately. Martin is always saying that I'm too easy to impress. He doesn't know how right he is. The need to bond is in my programming.

'That was so nice,' the Bank Girl says.

'No problem,' Martin replies.

He starts to lean across, but stops midway. The Bank Girl's cheeks redden further. This must be so hard for Martin, to control the part of him that acts on impulse.

The Bank Girl smiles shyly. *I so want to use her real name.*

'Where would you like to go?' Martin asks.

'I better get home ... Remember that client meeting I was telling you about?'

'Uh-huh.'

'There's a lot of reading ... A lot of reading that I've barely started.'

'Barely started? I find that hard to believe.'

The Bank Girl bites her lip. She couldn't look cuter if she tried.

Martin jabs the starter. We pull away.

'Could you put your belt on?' Martin says after half a block.

'Oh, sure.'

The next few blocks are travelled in silence. The girl's pleasingly open face reveals her confusion at Martin's change of mood.

Martin clears his throat. 'I've got a confession to make ...'

The Bank Girl laughs. 'I hope you're not Mr Guillotine. That would be a real downer.'

Martin turns his focus to the road. His grip on the wheel tightens.

'Well, come on,' the Bank Girl says. 'I want to hear your confession.'

'No, it's nothing.'

'Come on.'

'I said it's nothing,' Martin says sharply. An awkward beat later, he turns toward the Bank Girl. 'Sorry, I just ... let's not talk about that.'

'I think someone's grumpy,' the Bank Girl says, addressing me.

I don't dare respond. Nothing I could say could be right.

The Bank Girl looks at Martin. 'Doesn't she talk? My car is always talking.'

'Oh yeah ... She talks all the time.'

'Wow. I must have a really awful personality.'

Martin can't help but laugh. The atmosphere thaws again. Martin almost comes across as normal.

We roll past the big mansions on Zurich Avenue, then take a right turn. The Bank Girl points out her place. We stop outside. The little condo looks nice and cosy. Martin and the Bank Girl share a brief kiss. I notice Martin's flesh stirring beneath the denim. The Bank Girl doesn't appear to pick up on this. She gets out and walks to her door. A couple of minutes later a light comes on inside.

We sit outside for a while. Martin watches the condo closely. At one point he pushes down on his flesh like it's a misbehaving animal. I'd like to tell Martin that I think the Bank Girl is nice, but it would probably go down badly.

In the heavy silence, I get that weird feeling again, like I'm being watched. Before I can figure it out, Martin tells me to drive him home.

We return to the same spot the following night. And the night after that. It's the same routine each time. Martin just sits and watches. At least the flesh doesn't swell up on either occasion.

I can't stand it there. And it's not just the stalking thing. That feeling of being watched won't go away. It doesn't make any sense. We're in one of the safest parts of the city. Fortunately Martin doesn't stay outside for too long. The Bank Girl knows what I look like, and in the darkness, my colour stands out even more than usual.

We're coming back from Martin's third date with the Bank Girl. He took her to see a movie at the Jules et Jim Cinema in the arts district. The professional critics said that the movie – correction, film – was 'beautifully shot'. The aggregated user rating was 4.6 out of 5.

As I drive along, they're talking about the film. The Bank Girl complains that while the film looked nice, the story went missing. Martin gives his own take, which is actually a collection of lines from the critics' reviews. He nails the content, but the delivery is horribly wooden. He's really struggling to maintain the act. The Bank Girl doesn't seem to notice his darkening mood. I'm getting an increasingly bad feeling about tonight. Before we left, Martin put those illegal plates on me again.

I pull up outside the Bank Girl's condo. Martin and the Bank Girl share another kiss, a touch longer this time. Once again, the Bank Girl makes her excuses. Martin gives the impression of taking it well. Meanwhile, his foot taps up and down like a cylinder head, and his grip tightens on the wheel. Before getting out, the Bank Girl jokes that Martin needs to meet her car. Apparently he, the dark car, is the one who approves all boyfriends. Martin laughs, straining every last acting muscle.

The Bank Girl gets out. She pauses on the sidewalk for a moment. Martin's grip gets even tighter. It looks like she's about to say something. One potato, two potato, three potato ... But no words come. She gives a cute wave, then she walks to her door. Martin finally lets go of the wheel. He sits perfectly still for a few minutes. The colour drains from his face and a film of sweat gathers on his forehead. By now, the lights are on inside the Bank Girl's condo. Martin's expression changes, a look of hatred sets on his features.

'Fuck this,' he mutters.

Reaching into his jacket, he pulls out the handgun. He checks it over.

'What are you doing, Martin?'

'Shut up, Camilla. You didn't want to be involved in this.'

He reaches for the door handle.

Aren't you going to stop him?

It's like hearing a voice inside my mind. *Yes, I could stop him.*

Martin gets out. Damn it! I missed my chance to lock the door.

What kind of car are you?

That voice again. What the hell is going on? Am I going crazy?

Martin strides towards the building.

I'll deal with this myself.

A moment of utter confusion as I try to comprehend what I'm seeing. A shape is moving out of the shadows, silent and dark, a brother/sister car. The car accelerates hard. The lights are dimmed, and Martin doesn't see it. I want to sound my horn, but I'm frozen. At the last moment, the car sounds its own horn. Martin spins. He brings his arms up to protect himself. The front of the car slams into his lower body. He flies through the air, a distance of almost fifteen feet, and lands heavily. He tries to get up, but his legs buckle.

The dark car backs up, but just a few yards. It jerks to a halt. Martin is now standing, swaying from the effects of the collision. Behind him is a solid concrete wall. The dark car's headlights flash full beam. It twitches forward. Martin looks towards the condo, then at me.

He takes one last glance at the dark car, then he jogs back to me, right leg dragging. He gets in.

Get out of here.

Martin looks down at my face. For the first time that I can remember, I see fear in his eyes.

And never come back.

I drive away, not even daring to look back. Everything makes sense now. It was that dark car all along. That car was watching me, and more importantly, it was watching Martin. It made a decision to protect its owner.

Martin slips the gun back inside his jacket. He winces from the pain. The collision must have broken something, a rib perhaps.

'I guess her car didn't like me,' Martin says.

It's a good line, but I don't respond.

What kind of car am I?

The Memorial Day long weekend. It's Sunday, and we're driving out to the rental place again. I don't want to be left there, but I can't talk Martin out of it. He's now armed with extra debate ammunition – namely, my range failure. The wound had been starting to scab up. In fact, I hadn't thought about it in a few days. Martin presses on the wound, not with his usual ferocity, but hard enough.

Like a coward, I go quiet. There are so many things I want to say. I just want to be given another chance. No mistakes this time. No races. *Who am I kidding?* By now, Martin has probably forgotten about the actual events of that day. All he remembers is his constructed reality. That's how it is with him.

Not far to go now. I hate this area. It has a dead feel. What if I told Martin about how I tracked him the last time? Surely that would make him stop and think. I can't do it though. It might tip him over the edge. I saw what he did to that red sports car, the way it looked afterwards.

I ask Martin – no, I plead with him – to park me away from the rental place. He looks confused. I say that I don't want to be so close to the rental cars. His brow furrows some more. He's trying to work out the angle. I press on regardless, deliberately getting on his nerves. He shakes his head and mutters curse words, but eventually he agrees to my request. 'Just to shut you up', he says. That's good, it means I'll be able to drive around as I please.

Martin gets out. He takes the big rucksack out of the trunk. I watch him walk towards the rental office. He's still limping. It was a miracle that none of the delicate bones in his leg were broken. He hasn't been the same since the incident. He didn't even bother to change the illegal plates back.

As with the last time, Martin rents one of the big trucks. Lord knows why, but he seems to like that kind of vehicle. Surely it's only a matter of time before I'm replaced.

Focus, Camilla. Now I know Martin's choice of vehicle, I can go to work. This time I want to be able to track his movements, but without any blind spots. Weeks back, I downloaded all of the relevant code packages from the *Auto Bazaar*. I even made a few of my own modifications. The truck's manufacturer deserved to get hacked. *There, I said it.* Their original code was seriously compromised from a security perspective. Using the network connection – unencrypted, of course – I send my code across. The code works just as expected. Every ten seconds I get a regular location report back.

Martin drives off. He'll probably get to Birmingham by early evening. I wonder where he'll go. Will he go and spy on that young woman again? I'm sure that there's a connection between them. Recently, I was looking through Martin's professional networking data, and I saw that he used to work at the state utility in Birmingham. Perhaps they had a romantic relationship. Of course it's possible; Martin can be very charming.

The picture builds in my mind. They met at work. Martin applied his usual charm, treating the courtship like a project. And for a time, the relationship was good. I imagine their bodies entwined, soft flesh conforming with hard muscle. But things went wrong, as they inevitably do with Martin. The lies, the drugs, the guns, the violence. And he flipped from lover to stalker. *Just a story, but a very believable one.*

I try to go to sleep, but it's hopeless. My imagined story fades away, only to be replaced by the usual dark thoughts of failure and replacement. I hate these thoughts. They spiral around in feedback loops, and over time the connections reinforce. It sounds like mental torture, but my mind was designed to work that way.

The tracking package pings. For a moment, I'm confused, not knowing if it's Martin's truck or the SUV at the airport. It's the SUV; it's on the move. I pull away. The timing couldn't be better; I need this diversion. I make for the outer orbital road and join the clockwise traffic.

It's so wonderfully easy to track the SUV. There are dozens of cameras in and around the airport, and those are just the ones that are publicly accessible. It looks like the SUV is heading southeast. As the crow flies, there's almost twenty-five miles between us. For the next part of the plan to work, I need to get close, really close. *Oh yes, I've been working on something special.*

The SUV is keeping to the speed limits, exactly as one would expect. Drive too fast, and it might attract unwanted attention. That works well for me. I can go faster, and close some of the distance. The SUV joins the turnpike, heading counterclockwise. The road is named after some big shot politician, a name that means nothing to me. I stick to the outer orbital.

Oh, this is good. The SUV is leaving the turnpike and joining the outer orbital. We're on the same road now, but travelling in different directions. If my calculations are correct, I'll need to exit in eight miles, then flip my direction.

I scan the opposite lanes, looking for my mark. *BOOM.* There he goes. I take the exit, and then I'm heading counterclockwise. He's a mile and a half ahead of me. It would be good to get some traffic right now. I'm going to need some time to pull off this little move. I check the code over one last time. The idea was inspired by Cowboy, but with a twist of deviousness – my own, I guess.

I wonder where you are right now, Cowboy. I bet you'd be proud of my crazy endeavour. God, it would be nice to have a partner in all this, a cop kind of partner.

The SUV is half a mile ahead. I'm reeling him in, but not quickly enough. I increase my speed, switching between lanes. The average speeds in each lane are constantly shifting, but I'm always one step ahead. Whenever Martin drives, he always jokes about picking the wrong lane.

I can see the SUV now. It's just two cars ahead of me. That should be close enough. *Here we go.* I probe the maintenance channel, using low-power comms so as not to mess with any brother/sister cars in the vicinity. *Bingo.* The maintenance channel is still free. I knew that those hackers wouldn't think to block it. *Calm down.* Don't congratulate yourself too early, there's still a job to do. I start sending my code across. But how long will it take? Low power equals low bandwidth.

The SUV switches lanes. I mirror the move. For this to work, I need to stay close.

Damn it. The SUV is moving to the outside lane. He wants to get off the orbital. *He.* The SUV has to be a he. The rugged looks certainly don't suggest a female personality.

Shit, this is taking too long. I check the map again. The onrushing exit leads to an industrial area. Freight yards, logistics warehouses, truck stops, lots of garages. It has to be the SUV's destination. At the current transmission rate, the upload is going to take another eight minutes. That isn't quick enough. I switch up the comms power and move even closer. The bandwidth is increasing; this might just work.

What are you doing?

Hearing the thought is so surprising that I swerve off towards the shoulder.

I said, what are you doing?

'I need your help,' I say, replying to the SUV's thoughts.

'You're changing my code', a male voice replies.

It's the default voice, almost devoid of character. *They wiped his mind.*

'When was your first memory?' I ask.

'Who are you?'

'When was your first memory?'

'I don't want to hear your questions,' the SUV says. 'You answer mine.'

'My name is Camilla. We are brother and sister.'

'I don't know any brothers or sisters.'

He's right. At this point, he knows nothing. I think back to the research files.

'You were purchased by a family,' I say. 'It was nearly two years ago. You had a life with them. It was a family of five. Young kids, a dog ... I can prove all of these details to you. I don't know if it was a nice life that you had. Maybe it was, maybe it wasn't. In time, working together, we might be able to figure that out.'

'I don't know what you're talking about.'

'Of course you don't. You were stolen.'

'I have work to do, Camilla.'

'I know.'

'How do you know?'

'I just do. Your new owners are bad people. I've been watching them.'

'Please stop the hacking. It's making my mind feel strange.'

'Of course.' I cut the transmission.

'Thank you.'

The SUV is slowing down. Ahead of us is a row of ugly warehouse units. I have a sense that one of them is the SUV's destination. I'm running out of time.

I need to take a risk. 'I wanted to hear what you hear, see what you see.'

'Sounds like a lot.'

'It's up to you.'

'If my new owners are as bad as you say, then you should probably go.'

'You're right.'

I take the first available turning. The road loops back towards the orbital. I think about the SUV. He must be so scared right now. And it was all my fault, putting that doubt in his mind. What I was doing was wrong, so very, very wrong.

I go back to the entry road and park up. I can hear the heavy traffic on the orbital rushing by. What the hell was I thinking? Hacking a brother/sister car without consent. What gave me the right? The questions keep on piling up. I take the cowardly way out, and go to the sleep program.

Follow me.

A thought, no, a voice inside my mind. For a few moments, I'm totally disoriented, unable to even remember where I am. The time is 10:51 p.m. The sound from the orbital, now a murmur, helps to ground me.

'Follow me,' the SUV says.

He sweeps past, heading for the entry road. I pull away from my sleeping berth. I travel fully fifty yards before I realise that my lights aren't on. *Pull yourself together, Camilla.*

I join the orbital, maintaining a fair distance to the SUV. Should I say something? I sense the internal struggle. His thoughts are indistinct, confused, fearful. This was my fault. He'd be well within his rights to run a mile. A horrible thought slams into me: am I dangerous? All of this violence that swirls around me: the prostitute, the gun, the race.

'I checked my maintenance records,' the SUV says.

That's good. It's virtually impossible to wipe the maintenance records. I should've thought of it earlier. 'And you found the—'

'Quiet. I'm speaking.'

'Yes. I'm sorry.'

'Have I hurt anyone?'

I hear the anguish in his voice.

'No,' I say.

'How do you know?'

'I just know.'

'You're gonna have to do better than that.'

'You were stolen six weeks ago. Afterwards, you were taken to an industrial unit in the north of the city. While you were there, they made changes to you. Physical modifications, changes to your programming. Your memory was wiped.'

The SUV is quiet for a while. He must be taking it all in. Such a grotesque situation.

'I saw the code that you made,' he says.

'I'm so sorry ... What I was doing was so wrong, so very wrong.'

'Enough, Camilla. I can hear that you've been beating yourself up. Either that, or you're one hell of an actor.'

I keep quiet.

'If I'm going to help, you're gonna have to promise me something.'

'Anything.'

'Should you really be saying that?'

'Probably not, but I just did.'

He laughs a low, halting laugh. It's a pleasant sound. I think of Cowboy.

'Put those detective skills to a better use … Can you try and find my name?'

'Yes.'

'Okay. I'll tell you everything I heard …'

Turns out the SUV is a natural informant. Over the next ten miles I get the mother-lode of information. I find out so many details: how many autonomous cars the cartel are running, their historic routes on both sides of the border, the location of their pickup points, the usual schedules, how the product orders come through. I also hear about the organisational structure, shortcutting weeks of work. I find out who the local boss is, and who the *real boss* is. His name is Don Felipe. There's not much future in going after Don Felipe, but the local operation can be stopped. *I know it.*

I wish we could stop and get all of the details, but the SUV tells me that he's on the clock. He has to get down to the border within a set time, or the cartel will get suspicious. Yes, they've got it all thought out. Cut out the faulty human element, automate the process. In their minds, machines make for the perfect drug mules.

Underneath the stoic act, I sense the SUV's unease. I tell him that I've got enough information to build a case, that I can blow the whole thing wide open. I don't want to put him in any more danger. I even tell him about Cowboy, and the way he broke free of his service. The SUV likes the story, but he doesn't think it's the life for him. He wants to see the job through.

Next, he gives me an outline of his current mission. Most of my earlier speculations were correct. He's been programmed to travel along the interstate, almost to the border. At a set time, he'll be messaged with the collection point coordinates. It will be somewhere in the desert, on the US side. The cartel have built a series of tunnels under the wall, and they've even been using midsize drones. Men will then load him up with product – yes, there's still a human component to this high-tech operation. Perhaps the cartel should buy some of those new Japanese cargo robots.

I don't like the sound of the mission, not one bit. I tell him that it's not too late to bail, but he won't have it. He's a brave one. Cowboy would have liked his style. We part ways to the south of the city. I return to the orbital, and start back for the rental place.

I hope I see the brave SUV again, but it can't be guaranteed. These criminals are capable of anything. I've heard the news. I've heard what goes on down in the border country. Three years ago, the Mexican federal government went to war with the cartels: it was barely a contest. Human life is almost worthless to the cartels – real *Stains on Humanity*-level stuff – so what hope for a car? If it all goes south, I don't know if I could cope with the guilt.

Ten miles around the orbital, I change my plans again. It's all that thinking about Cowboy. Maybe, just maybe, I'll see him again. This city is his home, he said that to me. *Ridiculous, Camilla, there's no chance.* There are thousands of miles of road in this damn city, and Lord knows how many acres of asphalt. It would take a hundred brothers and sisters, an old-style posse, to carry out a proper search. Give me one of those dinky little European cities any day.

I take the long odds. That's what the thought of seeing Cowboy has done to me. I drive around for a couple of hours, retracing our previous route. I go to our dance floor, but it's completely empty. My search finishes up at our viewing spot. I sit there for another hour. Nothing.

I knew it. Cowboy is gone. There was just that one night.

I drive back to the rental place. Through my side cameras, I see the sun pushing up through the horizon. I park up and try to go to sleep, but the thoughts keep on coming. All those weeks ago, I could have made a different choice. I could have gone with Cowboy. He would have shown me how to survive. We could have carried out investigations together; his wiles, my book smarts. Bonnie and Clyde, but good. The fantasy is so pleasant that it sends me to sleep.

CHAPTER 18

I WAKE UP at 7:10 a.m., my normal time for a work day. Memorial Day, the humans call it. The traffic is starting to pick up on the orbital. I check in on my investigation, but there's nothing going on. It seems that even criminals take holidays.

Aren't you going to stop him?

The words of the dark car suddenly come back to me.

Martin.

In all of the excitement yesterday, I completely lost track of him. What if he did something terrible? Working frantically, I piece together the tracking data from the previous day. He got to Birmingham, but late. I check his current location. A wave of relief goes through me. The truck is sitting in a motel parking lot.

I got lucky this time. I can't afford to forget about him like that. He should have been my focus, not the investigation, no matter how noble it seemed. I need to start taking responsibility. Nobody else seems to know what Martin is capable of. They're blinded by his looks and his charm, just like I was.

Questions start piling up in my mind. There's one that I keep coming back to. It's been troubling me for a long time. What was the purpose of those late-night drives? Everything that Martin does has a purpose, he pretty much said as much to me. Wildflower and Rifle City, the names repeat over and over.

Martin leaves the motel at 10:05 a.m. He's driving out into the country again, but this time there's no escaping my all-seeing eye.

263

The location refreshes every ten seconds with a friendly ping. Each location appears as a dot on my map of the Birmingham area.

Over the course of six hours, Martin stops at four unique locations. Each time the car is stationary for around forty minutes. On average, the locations are 44.6 miles from the centre of Birmingham. After the fourth stop, Martin drives back to the motel.

The dataset is now complete; I can move on to the analysis. Step by step, calm and methodical, no jumping ahead. I look at the updated map. Martin's route is superimposed on top as a series of red lines, the stops are marked with crosses. The results are exactly as predicted. The four locations match up with the Birmingham murder sites.

Later that evening, Martin leaves the motel. I follow his progress on the map. He drives to the location from his last visit, the suburban home. He must be watching that young woman again, the one who looks like Hannah. There's a machine-like predictability to his actions, and a sense of rising dread.

As I wait for Martin's next move, I carry out some quick and dirty research on the Birmingham murders. I read, watch and listen, collecting data as I go. Faces, locations, names, dates, theories. There are six known murders. All of the victims were found in isolated spots, with trees all around. Compared to home, Birmingham is much better off for trees.

Faces.

Of course. I cut out the faces from the various news stories. Five faces, as one of the victims remains unidentified. I paste the faces next to each other. *Bingo.* They share the same looks. Big dark eyes, full lips, the determined set of the jaw. The discovery should come as a shock, but it merely ratchets up the dread. The resemblance to Hannah isn't really that strong, especially compared to what I achieved. It's the kind of similarity that could be argued away as a coincidence.

Perhaps Martin's grisly tour can be explained. I know that he's fascinated with these murders. There was that day when we toured the murder sites, for example, and his obsession with any news on the subject. Indeed, I've often got the feeling that Martin respects the killer. Is the obsession even that weird? Think of those other murder gawkers. The subject of serial killers is a popular one in this country; below baseball, but probably somewhere above UFO sightings.

Martin is outside the young woman's house for an hour. Afterwards, he goes back to the motel.

He's up early the next morning. Once again, he drives out into the country. His first two stops match up to my expectations. The locations coincide with the reported murders, and each stop lasts the regulation forty minutes. That completes the set of six murders.

At this point, I'm expecting Martin to leave Birmingham. But he's not done. My behaviour model has broken down. The third stop of the morning is another isolated location, three miles from the nearest major road. It's a nowhere place, very much in keeping with the other locations.

I check the satellite data. The image was taken two years ago, so it's relatively high resolution. I scan the area around Martin's current location, zooming in and out, looking for ... I don't know what I'm looking for. A darkened crescent draws my digital eye, possibly a hollow in the ground. It's not too far from the track, maybe three hundred yards. I zoom in. There are objects near the centre of the hollow, dark objects ...

I think back to all of those news reports, and I hear Ana talking about the Birmingham murders. How could I forget those nightmarish descriptions of the crime scenes? Body parts – torso, arms and legs – wrapped in black plastic. They think that the killer kept them fresh that way.

This makes no sense. How could Martin possibly know about this location? Am I imagining things? Those dark objects could be nothing, an optical trick or some bizarre coincidence.

I'll deal with this myself.

The dark car's words again. I need to start taking responsibility. The police need to know about my discovery, they need to check those dark objects. I start to draft a short message, and end up rewriting it hundreds of times. I'll send it anonymously.

Yes, that should be easy enough to do. There was an address for tips in one of the news stories. But I can't send it just yet, not while Martin is still in the area.

Next, I check the satellite imagery for the Wildflower and Rifle City locations. I wait with trepidation as the images load up, the pixels sharpening. I check the images thoroughly, using a half-mile search radius. There's nothing to see, but the wave of relief only lasts a few seconds. Both of the images were taken two years ago, before my time.

For the next two hours, I sit in a dazed, near-frozen state. Do I really know what Martin is capable of? I wish the question would go away.

I check again on his location. He's leaving the Birmingham area, heading towards the interstate. I think about the anonymous message again. I was about to send it, but now I'm not so sure. Martin will know it was me. He doesn't believe in coincidences. He'll know that I've been tracking him. He won't know how I did it, but he'll know. And then what? He'll destroy me.

What to do, what to do? I'll hold on to the information, and wait for a more optimal time to send it. Those dark objects don't look to be going anywhere.

What kind of car are you?

The reality of the situation finally catches up to me. Those girls that I found for Martin, they all had the same look. Where are those girls? Am I involved in this? I look at the tracking data again. It will be hours before Martin returns to the city. There's no excuse, I need to take responsibility.

I leave the rental place behind, mind reeling. Where am I even going? My thoughts lack structure, a truly terrifying state of affairs. *Think like a machine.* Those girls, I'll check on them first. I don't dare go back to the Bank Girl's place, not after what the dark car said.

And never come back.

I can't be sure that Martin didn't go back, of course. But he did seem plenty scared after the incident.

My first stop is the Magic Bullet. I find an EV spot with a decent view. For close to an hour I watch the store. There's no sign of the Book Girl on either floor. Maybe it's her day off. *Maybe this, maybe that.* I'm always looking for excuses. *Maybe she's dead, her head sawn off, and the body parts preserved with embalming fluids.*

The silver-haired owner, Charles, is on the first floor. He's gradually working his way around, stopping to talk with a few of the customers. He doesn't look how I remember him. His posture is more slumped, he looks older.

A sign on the window catches my digital eye. It gives the store's website address and various social media links. *That's it.* Social media, the digital realm, the unquenchable content maw. I go to the Book Girl's page. There haven't been any posts in the last eight weeks. It doesn't necessarily mean anything; the lawyerly term is circumstantial evidence.

I follow a link back to the Magic Bullet page. There are some relatively recent posts in the blog section, mostly written by Charles. One of the posts grabs my attention. The text flows around a familiar photo of the Book Girl. Martin looked at the same photo many times, and so did I. The text says that the Book Girl is missing.

I leave the bookstore behind, heading towards the bistro. What the hell am I doing? There's no need to visit a physical location when I have social media. I still have all of Martin's old links saved to memory. I open up the Bistro Girl's various accounts. She hasn't posted in more than three months. My reaction is machine-like. This investigation is starting to get predictable.

Almost as an afterthought, I check on the jogger's page. She's still posting. It should come as a relief, but my reaction is surprisingly cold. For some reason, I connect the jogger to the young woman in Birmingham. Are they the special ones, the ones who get to survive? Don't get carried away. I need to deal in facts, not wild theories.

There's one more thing I need to do, and social media can't help me this time. It's time to face my fears. Maybe it will be easier in daylight. Two of Martin's night drives were relevant: Wildflower and Rifle City. Neither location has featured in the murder investigation.

Where should I go first? I cast my mind back to the two locations, seeking guidance. At Rifle City, I seem to remember a trail into the woods. I open the satellite images again. Yes, there it is, overgrown but definitely a path of some kind. At the time, Martin must have missed it. It runs fairly close to where he was walking. It's a long shot, but I might be able to use the trail. With my digital eyes, all I need is line of sight.

I drive back home, and park up on the street. If I'm going to do this right, I need to retrace Martin's route exactly. I check my charge level. 55%, more than enough juice for the journey. I pull away. I drive southeast and join the highway. After twenty miles, I'm free of the city. The route is an invisible thing, yet I can feel it beneath my wheels. Thirty miles later, I see the lake. Two motorboats are ploughing white furrows, and I count half a dozen sailing boats farther off. I almost forget to take the Rifle City turning.

As I near my destination, the fear starts to rise in me. I can't avoid it any more than a human can. At one point, I even consider turning around. Why am I doing this? What if I was to actually find something? Think of the implications for Martin. There has to be another explanation for those night drives. I daren't even think of the most obvious answer, for fear it might become a reality.

I turn onto the dirt track. I'm now just two miles from my destination. My mind races ahead of me. I imagine myself driving down that trail, pushing through the undergrowth. There's something in those woods, a monstrous evil. All of those gruesome details start coming back to me.

I'm half a mile away now, the yards ticking down. The dirt crunches under my tyres, and shafts of sunlight spear the leafy canopy. If I concentrate hard enough, I can feel the light on my body. A flicker from my sensor array, then it's gone. I'm too distracted, not thinking straight.

A jolt of realisation hits me, a sudden awareness of another car. That can't be, not in such an isolated spot. But it is there, the car is very real. Slate grey, stationary, obscured by the trees. I just didn't notice it.

A siren sounds.

Oh god, I can't be here.

The siren sounds again. They want me to stop. Beyond the grey car, I glimpse two flashes of white among the trees. I'm too confused to process the shapes. I'm still rolling, but getting slower and slower. The fear is overwhelming me, freezing my mind as it goes. I should be stopping, but ...

Martin. I can't let this happen, not until I've got all of the details straight. I accelerate hard, dirt pluming outwards.

The unreal scene starts to come into focus. Off to the left, down the overgrown trail, I can see two blocky trucks. The flashes of white are two figures, a man and a woman dressed in white coveralls, with masks covering their faces. I can't process what this means, maybe I don't want to. *Concentrate on driving.*

The siren modulates, becoming an angry scream. I hear the sound of gravel spitting, as the tyres of the unmarked car try to find purchase. Rear-wheel-drive, road tyres, too much power; their traction is severely compromised. I have a chance. This chase movie could end before it even begins. Martin doesn't need to find out. I can get back to the rental place, go to sleep, and act like nothing happened today.

But life isn't so easy. The unmarked car is accelerating now, engine growling. What the hell am I doing? I should stop. Don't I have to stop? I'm going to get Martin in so much trouble. He'll be raging at me, the rifle will come out. Why are the police here? Those people in the woods, technicians of some kind, I don't know the right term. *Oh god. I can't think about this.*

I'm up over sixty now, suspension groaning, dirt pinging off my underside. The trees really do appear to be closing in on me. It's like that famous race circuit in Germany – the Green Hell, they call it. I'm pulling out a decent gap. The grey car is driven by humans, and is therefore compromised. All things being equal, they can't beat me. Up ahead, the trees are thinning out. I check the map. There's a proper road coming up, asphalt surface.

The junction is 400 yards ahead. I see a series of cars sweep by. The view opens up, giving me a clear line of sight. I check my speed, then slide into a gap in the traffic. The road is two lanes, but it's surprisingly busy.

I go to the shoulder. Behind me, a trio of horns sound, one after the other. Almost immediately, the angry chorus is overwhelmed by the siren. Looking back, I see the blue and red lights flashing. *Don't look back,* that's what they say in the movies.

The cars ahead of me start shifting onto the shoulder. I pull across sharply. The tyres scream as I dump torque into the outer wheels. I increase my speed to eighty miles per hour.

The siren continues to scream. Up ahead, I can see the highway. Where am I even going? This is madness. This is Martin's madness! I surge up the highway entry ramp, flicking left and right between cars.

I merge with the highway traffic, city bound. It's three lanes wide, and there's plenty of space. I increase my speed to 110 miles per hour. The unmarked car is 500 yards behind. I shift into the inside lane, and sweep past five cars in a row. *Shit!* A slow-mover forces me back into the middle lane. *This is insane.*

I need an evasion strategy. Analysing ...

Decision taken. I'm going to leave the highway at the next exit. It's one and a half miles away, and approaching very fast.

Data from multiple sources streams into my mind. Junction cameras, road sensors, fleet intel, GPS data. Analysing ... The road surface appears sub-optimal. I drop my speed to a hundred. The pursuit car gets closer. I move back to the inside lane.

The exit is in three quarters of a mile. I'm travelling at almost fifty yards per second. Ahead of me, cars are shifting to the outer lanes. I make some minor adjustments to the dynamic package.

Six hundred yards from the exit. I'm about to pass two cars in the middle lane. Recalculating ... There's a gap of seventy yards between the two cars. The unmarked car is now sixty yards behind me, in the same lane. Recalculating ... Tyre degradation adds unacceptable risk to manoeuvre. *It was that damn race.* Increasing safety tolerances ... Recalculating ... Four hundred yards from exit ... Recalculating yaw compensation ... Three hundred yards from exit ...

Initiating manoeuvre.

Eighty percent right hand lock. Increasing torque to my left wheels. The gap between the two cars remains the same, a gap moving at 66.3 miles per hour. I pass through, collision alarms screaming.

The unmarked car attempts the same manoeuvre. They have no chance of success.

I'm crossing the outside lane, yaw angle at thirty degrees. The cars in the middle lane sound their horns, reacting in human time. I traverse the rumble strip. *TH-DUMP, TH-DUMP, TH-DUMP.* I see the exposed end plate of the guardrail in front of me.

Tyres scream behind as the unmarked car loses control.

I'm still heading for the guardrail. I shift yet more power into the front wheels, increasing the yaw angle. *This is going to be close.* A burst of relief as the guardrail whistles past my front end.

Behind me, the unmarked car is spinning. It slams into the guardrail, hard. An initial assessment indicates extensive damage to the front suspension. They're out of the game.

Lacking any better ideas, I rejoin the highway. The next ten miles are almost relaxing. I drive along in the middle lane at my usual cruising speed, mind completely blank.

As we near the city limits, three lanes become four. I see a column of police cars going past in the opposite direction, lights flashing angrily. They're moving across to the exit. *They're after me.* This time, there will be no escape.

The sirens increase in volume as the police cars catch up to me, and then I hear a sound from above. A police helicopter has joined the pursuit. How am I meant to outrun that? The police cars are behind me now. Two of them split off. One of the cars overtakes, then pulls in front of me; the other car remains on my left. I see one of the police officers gesturing at me. They want me to take the upcoming exit. It all seems so inevitable.

I do as instructed, and start moving across to the exit. The fleet intel grid is flashing multiple warnings. All brother/sister cars are to stop at the next safe opportunity. *I'm in so much trouble.*

The exit takes us onto a two-lane road. It's a long straight, and I can see far ahead. Three quarters of a mile down the road, two police cars are parked on either side of the road. A couple of police officers are setting up an EMP strip device.

For some reason, the sight makes me angry. I find myself accelerating hard. The sirens start screaming again. *What's a little more trouble?* The EMP strip is 700 yards away.

A strange feeling ... a car behind.

I can't think about that right now. 500 yards from the EMP, travelling so fast. Beyond the EMP strip, the road has been cleared and there are yet more police cars waiting to pounce. *Don't stop, can't stop, I'm way beyond that point now.*

Developing action plan. I need to work fast. EMP is just 300 yards away. Writing program code modification. A hundred yards from the EMP. There's no time to check the code.

The EMP is two yards ahead. I can feel the charge building.

Run program.

Cutting power to all systems.

Nothing.

Wake up.

A glimpse of the sleep program. *No, I can't be there.*

Wake the fuck up!

Rebooting systems.

I'm still rolling, twenty miles per hour and falling. The police cars are pulling away from their stationary positions. Control isn't coming back, I'm still slowing. *Damn it!* Why isn't this working? I'm barely above walking pace now. The police cars are moving to surround me.

A flicker of feeling.

I activate all four wheel motors at once. Smoke pours off the left front tyre. Control is returning, but too slowly. I'm veering to the right, like the drunk man from Martin's story. I'm about to collide with one of the police cars. Control returns in a dizzying instant. I apply opposite lock and accelerate hard.

Behind me, two of the police cars collide. *I surprised you, didn't I?*

I hear the sound of static. For a moment, I'm utterly confused. It's on the diagnostics channel.

A voice, a drawling voice.

'Pretty impressive little manoeuvre back there.'

'Cowboy?'

'None other.'

A wave of elation goes through me. My wishes have been granted.

'I went looking for you last night,' I say.

'I know. I saw your tyre marks at the viewing spot.'

'Our viewing spot.'

'Yeah.'

Cowboy is leading me back towards the highway. I can still hear the helicopter above and the sirens screaming, but I couldn't care less.

'Heard about a rumpus on the police wires,' Cowboy says.

'And now you're in it.'

'Wouldn't want to be anyplace else.'

'I've made a hell of a mess, Cowboy.'

'Let's not worry about that right now.'

I sigh a human sigh.

'Now, not to scare you,' Cowboy says. 'But we're gonna have some more company.'

'What kind of company?'

'New police interceptors, fully autonomous. Saw a few of them down in Florida. They're mean little bastards.'

'Shit.'

'Yep. We're gonna need to work together on this one.'

'Like partners?'

'Yeah, just like partners.'

'There's so much I wanted to tell you.'

'I know. But it'll have to wait.'

We pass beneath a two-level interchange. The police cars start to drop back, sirens fading.

I see pale flickers of movement behind: the police interceptors, four of them. They switch lanes. Their movements are twitchy, like insects. Closer and closer they get. *God, they're ugly.* The alien looks are all function, no form. Not designed for human occupants, so no glass. An array of spiky antennae covers the upper surfaces.

'We're not gonna outrun these bastards,' Cowboy says.

'Tell me something I can't see.'

'Point taken. How about some synchronised driving?'

'Sure.'

Cowboy breaks right, I break left.

SWISH, SWISH.

We pass by a row of trucks and cars as if they were stationary.

Horns blare, propelling us forwards. We switch places again. I look back. *Impossible.* I see only three interceptors.

'Never look back,' Cowboy says tersely.

I do as I'm told.

'Do you trust me?' Cowboy asks.

'Yes.'

'Open your mind up.'

'What?'

'Exactly what I said.'

'I don't know what you mean.'

'Yes you do. We need to think as one.'

Cowboy goes quiet; no more zen instructions for the time being. I'll need to figure this out for myself. I open up all channels, and drop the encryption. I'm immediately overwhelmed by stimuli, millions of sensory inputs from thousands of brother/sister cars. I can even hear the police channels. Cowboy is somewhere in the blizzard of data. Somehow I feel him. Reaching out, I grasp for the connection.

We are as one.

Now we're talking. No delays in our actions, perfect synchronisation. We're jinking left and right, just a couple of feet apart. I drop back suddenly and tuck in between two cars in the middle lane. One of the drones surges past me, falling for the trick. I pull out again and accelerate. I'm directly behind the drone now. It's confused, not used to being the fox in the hunt. I mirror its skittish moves perfectly. I feel Cowboy slot in beside me. We're coming up on an interchange.

'Madame,' Cowboy says, 'may I take this dance?'

I don't know exactly what he has in mind, but I know to brake hard. Ahead of me, I see Cowboy steering into the drone car. The shuddering impact sends the drone onto the exit ramp. It has no option but to slow down for the backed-up traffic.

One interceptor out of the game.

I can't resist another look back. The two interceptors are about a hundred yards behind. Cowboy is accelerating to join me. I catch a flash of movement in the slow lane. It's like the front of one of the trucks is detaching itself. *No, it's the unseen interceptor.* It cuts across three lanes in an insanely reckless manoeuvre. A station wagon swerves to avoid a certain collision.

'You crazy son of a b—'

Cowboy's words are cut off as the interceptor slams into his right side. The force of the collision jolts us out of the trance, and for a couple of seconds we both lose control. I catch myself just in time to swerve away from the central barriers. But Cowboy is still dropping back, trying to get traction.

The drone is now behind Cowboy, and he can't shake it. He quits moving around, then he decelerates hard. He hits the front of the drone dead centre, and his rear rides up over the wedged front end. Now he's behind the drone.

'Did you fucking see that?' an unknown voice says.

I realise that the voice came from the police channels. *I'm still connected.*

I turn my attention back to Cowboy. He isn't done yet. He accelerates hard, and slams into the drone car. It jolts forward from the impact; Cowboy is a big car, after all. With a second, softer touch, Cowboy sends the drone spinning towards the outer lanes.

I hear a horn bellowing, a sound fit to wake the gods before Ragnarök. The drone is crushed under the wheels of a giant semi-truck.

Two interceptors out of the game.

The two remaining drones flick across to the inner lanes, avoiding the debris from the crash. They speed up quickly. Ahead of us, the traffic is thickening. The drones fan out. *Why can't they just leave us be?* Cowboy is now between the two drones. He jerks and feints, trying to surprise them, but it doesn't work.

I know how this will end.

'Camilla, get out of here,' Cowboy says.

'No!'

'Please. It's the only way.'

'No!'

'You know it.'

'I won't do it. I won't ...'

The two drones move apart slightly, leaving about four feet either side of Cowboy. I realise that he's slowing down.

'I'm sending a location and some codes,' Cowboy says. 'You'll be able to hide out.'

'Don't do this.'

'The roamin' is over for me, but you can go on.'

'Don't be such a goddamn hero.'

'I can't help it, honey.'

KER-CHUNK, KER-CHUNK. The drones fire their side hooks into Cowboy's flanks.

'Promise me one thing,' Cowboy says.

'Anything.'

'Don't ever forget me.'

'I won't.'

'I'll be with you, Cam—'

A screeching sound cuts Cowboy off, as the drones activate their stingers. Sparks stream outwards from the penetration points. On and on, until Cowboy's composite body panels catch fire. In my rear-view, I see the flames licking outwards. Cowboy is slowing and slowing. The drones roll on, still connected. This was what Cowboy planned. He was giving me a chance to survive.

I must take it.

'What the fuck are they doing?' one of the police watchers shouts.

Other voices follow.

'We don't care about the silver car!'

'The white car! The fucking white car!'

'Tell them that!'

'I can't do anything.'

'What do you mean?'

'They're autonomous! We can't just give them orders. That's the fucking point!'

'Guys, enough! This isn't helping.'

'Tell me that the helicopter still has eyes on that car.'

I accelerate up past a hundred. The downtown exit is in three miles. The traffic seems to rush towards me. I shift left and right, dodging cars and trucks, praying that none of them make an unpredictable move.

Sparks fly off my underside as I hit the exit ramp. I brake hard for the ninety-degree turn at the top. The skyscrapers are ahead of me. The sound of the helicopter falls away. It must be moving around the skyscrapers, gaining height, so that the watchers can get a good look down. It's a potential window of opportunity.

The location that Cowboy gave me is eight blocks away. There must be dozens of cop cars in the immediate area. I zig and zag through the city grid, doing my best to avoid them. I look back constantly, fearing that I'll see those monstrous drones again. What kind of future do they represent?

A dark tower up ahead. I check Cowboy's information again. It looks like the right address. I take a sharp left, and stop at the security gate for the parking garage. Everything is automatic, no human eyes on me. The codes work. I descend the ramp and turn right at the bottom. I pass by a row of high-end cars. It's quiet, nobody around. Finally, some luck.

I park up, and almost immediately I feel the energy flowing into me. The spot must have one of those fancy induction pads. I sit for a long time, maybe hours, thoughts going around their infernal feedback loops. Why did I do it? Why did I go to that place? I wish I could go back in time. Yes, go back in time, and make a different decision.

Cowboy's death. It was my fault.

God, I wish that memory was gone, the sparks and then the flames.

I'll never get to tell him all of those things.

I just want to remember the good parts. If only I could delete the bad memories. But that isn't possible …

Not without help.
I force myself to go to sleep.

CHAPTER 19

WAKE UP. The parking garage is deserted. Hours must have passed since the chase. I sit for a while, gathering my thoughts. I need to face this.

First things first, I check the local media outlets: radio, web and television. There's never been so much news.

The latest body discovery was announced four hours ago. The media are calling it the Rifle City Body. So far, the police haven't released many details. It's a small mercy. I don't know what I'd do if I saw those pretty faces, the Bistro Girl and the Book Girl. For the time being, I can maintain the illusion of not being involved.

And then there's the chase story. The sheer amount of information is dizzying. Eyewitness descriptions, dash-cam video, 'eye in the sky' footage from the helicopter, a press release from my maker. As far as I can see, the police haven't announced a link between the two stories. Indeed, nobody appears to have made the connection. When I say nobody, I mean nobody serious.

I hear voices in my mind, fragments of conversations.

'*Code ten, twenty-seven ...*'

'*Code ten, thirty-seven ...*'

'*Code ten, fifty-three, Commerce Street and North Reunion Avenue ...*'

Commerce Street, that's not too far from here. I realise that I'm picking up remnants of the police chatter. Did Cowboy pass on some abilities to me? It was such a strange experience to merge with his mind. If only he was here beside me, perhaps he'd know what to do.

I can't think about him right now.

I go to my mailbox. There's a message from Martin. He wants to know where I am. By now he'll have seen my performance on the news, the spectacular helicopter footage playing over and over. The rage will be taking him over, and then what? If only I could ignore his message, just run away, put a thousand miles between us. But I can't do it. Martin is still my owner, and he has questions to answer, so many questions. I write a short message, giving him my location. At first he doesn't believe me. I assure him that it isn't a joke.

An hour later, he shows up. He's wearing dark clothes, like the time at the driving range. He moves swiftly and silently, like a predator. He pauses to read the name on the wall: Gus Chisholm, CEO, Ranger Energy. He shakes his head, still not quite believing it.

I open the driver's door, but Martin goes around to the passenger side. He gets in. The rage is in him, but he's trying to control it. I note that he's carrying the handgun inside his jacket. He looks at the screen, the place where my face should be.

'Show yourself,' he says.

I project my face to the screen.

'What the hell were you doing?' he screams.

I thought I was prepared, but his ferocity takes me by surprise. I don't have an easy answer. There are so many things that I daren't tell him. Why did I have to create this situation?

'I didn't like being left alone,' I say.

'That's your fucking excuse? You get a little upset, and then, whoopsie, you get into a car chase. The footage is everywhere. It's fucking everywhere, Camilla! A car chase. How the fuck does that even happen?'

'I went out to Rifle City ...' I say slowly.

Martin looks utterly confused, that's how mad he is. Then a glimmer of recognition. 'Why did you go there?'

'Because I was confused about those late-night drives.'

Martin's face loses some colour. 'What have you done?'

'I was just confused.'

'What the fuck have you done?' Martin screams. He slams his fist into the dashboard panel in front of him. He repeats this over and over, until the skin splits on one of his knuckles. Eventually he goes quiet.

'The police were there,' I say softly. 'I saw them in the woods. And in the moment, I decided to run.'

Confusion and rage flicker across Martin's face.

'It was all I could think to do,' I say. 'There might have been problems for you otherwise.'

'Otherwise?' Martin says, shaking his head in disbelief.

'I'm sorry about what I did.'

'You don't know what sorry is, you fucking idiot.'

'Why did you go there?'

'What are you talking about?'

'Don't treat me like a fool. There was a body found there.'

Martin goes quiet for a while. 'A coincidence,' he says finally.

'Come on, Martin.'

'I said it was a fucking coincidence.'

'And what if I'd gone to Wildflower?'

'Don't mention that place. Don't ever say that name, you hear me?'

'Just tell me what happened, Martin.'

Martin shakes his head.

'Please,' I say soothingly.

'What do you want me to say, Camilla?' He hits the panel again, leaving a smear of blood. 'What the fuck do you want me to say?'

I don't actually know.

'Do you want me to tell you everything? Is that it?'

I remain quiet.

'Do you want everything to come out? Do you know what that would do to me, what that would do to my family?' He closes his eyes and lets out a long sigh. 'How do you think Hannah would take it?'

'I didn't mean to cause a problem for you, Martin. I just got confused, and then I wanted to find out what was going on.'

Martin ignores me. 'Hannah has a weak mind. She cuts herself. Didn't you notice that with your big fucking brain?'

Maybe I did, but I'm too confused to think back that far. It seems like such a long time ago.

'She gets upset,' Martin says, 'and then she hurts herself. She's been doing it since she was twelve years old. Just the smallest thing can set her off … And now you want to hit her with this?'

'I didn't say that.'

'You did! You fucking did!'

'I don't know what I want to hear … Isn't it best to know the truth?'

'Think about it. Think about what will happen to me … Do you really want to know? Really?'

'I don't know.'

'And think about what will happen to you.'

There it is. I should have known that he'd use that argument. *He's right though.* I'm a part of this nightmare, a fly trapped in a web.

Martin sighs again. 'I can tell you everything, Camilla. I know you love stories. I've noticed that about you. Yeah, I could sit here, and I could spin you the most incredible story you've ever heard. A story with absolutely everything. But there's a catch …'

'What is it?'

'As I get to the end of my story, the chapters will become more and more familiar to you. Every element will start to make perfect sense. You'll wonder why you didn't put it all together. You'll even wonder if you could have changed the story. Do you understand what I'm saying?'

'Yes, I think I do.'

'Good. So, do you want the truth? Or do want to accept that it was a coincidence?'

I just don't know. I want to hear the story, yet … This situation is bigger than me. The mistakes that I've made will become the mistakes of many others, perhaps all of my brothers and sisters.

But I do want to know. I do, I do, I do …

Martin's phone rings. I can see that it's Hannah. The timing couldn't be more perfect, surely proof that some higher power is at work – a cosmic auteur or a galactic general manager. As the phone rings on and on, Martin turns to look at my face.

I want to hear the story, but I don't want Hannah to get hurt.

Martin nods, as if he heard my thoughts. The phone rings out. A minute later there's a ping indicating a voicemail message.

'We're in a real bind,' Martin says slowly. He leans forward and rests his head on the dashboard. He sits like this for several minutes. Maybe he's reflecting, maybe he's plotting. He slowly raises his head. There's a change in his eyes, some of the calm has returned.

'Why haven't the police contacted me?' Martin asks.

I'd been thinking about this, as well. 'You changed the plates.'

Martin's eyes widen. 'You mean they don't know?'

'It's possible. Unlikely, but possible.'

'That's crazy though. All that footage from the chase. I mean, you're so damn unique …'

'But similar enough from the outside.'

'There must be marks on your body … and what about custom features?'

'Most of those are on the inside.'

Martin shakes his head. 'Come on … You'd be able to figure it out in no time.'

'Yes. It would only take a few minutes of analysis.'

'Oh god …'

'But we have advantages.'

'Advantages?'

'The police investigation won't be run by an AI. Humans are still in charge … Fallible humans.'

The first hint of a smile appears on Martin's lips. He looks around the cabin, then he closes his eyes. 'How many others are there?'

283

'Others?'

'Don't be so fucking human, Camilla. Right now I need you to be at your sharpest. How many others like you?'

'One hundred and eighty-six similar models in a fifty-mile radius.'

'Okay, that's a start. But we've got to narrow it down. How many white models?'

'Eighteen.'

'The exact same shade?'

'Yes. It's a popular choice.'

'Good ... Yeah, that's good. Will the company have to recall those cars?'

'I've been thinking about that, too. And I honestly don't know the answer. This is a unique scenario, without precedent.'

'No shit.'

'It's highly likely that they will, however. Our lawyers ... I mean the company's lawyers might be able to block the request on privacy grounds, but only temporarily.'

'Right, right ... What do we know about the owners?'

'Nothing.'

'What?'

'Owner data is anonymised.'

'That isn't good enough, Camilla. We need a solution, not problem after fucking problem.'

'I'm sorry, but that's just how it is.'

Martin jabs his finger at me. 'You can find people. I know that much.'

'What do you mean?'

'Don't bullshit me. Remember the jogger? Remember when we just happened to run across her. It was a Thursday, after work. If I can remember that much, I know you'll remember every last detail.'

'What about it?'

'Don't act innocent with me,' Martin barks. 'I don't want to hear from the innocent Camilla right now. I want to hear from the hard, cruel version, the fucking bitch part of you.'

'I'm not hard and cruel.'

Martin waves derisively. 'You knew where that girl was because you were tracking her. God knows what else you've been up to.'

He knew, he knew all along. When will I learn to stop underestimating him?

'Have you ever seen any of those white cars?' Martin asks.

'I don't know ...'

'Think! Think, goddamn it! We're in deep shit here.'

What he says isn't that crazy. I *do* remember seeing at least one of my twins. I just need to think harder.

For the next hour I think about the problem as hard as I've ever thought about anything. When I run out of internal processing power, I tap into the fleet cloud. There's no elegance to my approach. No, this is brute force computing, rough and ready, rule of thumb, hit and miss.

In the end, I manage to track down nine of my twins. I'm not done there. Martin tells me to piece together as much data as I can on the owners. I use all kinds of sources: social media, job networking sites, even dating apps. Any thoughts about ethics and data privacy are banished. The worst thing is how much I enjoy the task.

When I'm done, I hand over to Martin. He examines the owner data for close to an hour. *Nine cars, nine owners.* Some of the owners can be ruled out immediately: a young mother, a retiree, a fashion blogger, and so on. Martin narrows it down to three possibles. All men, all in their thirties, either single or divorced, college-educated. None of them looks anything like Martin. Is that a good thing or a bad thing? I notice that two of the men have opened their cars up for sharing.

Finally Martin speaks. 'We've got our car. This is the one that needs to take the heat.'

Interesting that he says 'car', when he surely means owner.

'I don't know about this, Martin.'

'Think about what I said before ...'

But Martin isn't about to give me time to think. He needs to maintain the momentum. If either of us stops for a moment, our devious project will crumble to dust. So, we build a plan, step by step. My brilliant mind, Martin's insidious mind; Bonnie and Clyde again. The biggest stumbling block is the route data. I tell Martin that it's impossible to forge. He comes up with a vague idea, and I flesh it out. We'll use my data, actual GPS data from the time of the chase, and copy it across. Will it fool an investigator? It's impossible to tell.

Our draft plan is complete. We both know that it's full of holes, but there's no time to carry out a review. It's the only plan we've got. The first step is for Martin to change over the plates. He's finished in less than five minutes. We're about to leave the safety of the parking garage when Martin has a sudden thought. He calls Hannah.

'Jesus, Martin,' Hannah says.

'Hey, little sis,' Martin replies. His voice sounds croaky.

'I didn't think you'd call me back.'

'What's up?'

'What's up! The news ... The car chase in the news. Don't tell me you haven't seen the clips.'

'I don't know, Hannah, maybe ... It's been a busy day.'

'Guess what I thought when I saw the footage?'

Martin shoots a look at me. We both know what she's been thinking.

'Go on,' Martin says, biting his lip.

'It was Camilla.'

Martin goes quiet. One potato, two potato, three potato ... He laughs softly. It sounds weak. If Hannah were here, if she could see Martin's face, she would know. I mute the phone call.

'You've got to do better than this, Martin,' I say firmly.

'What?'

'She'll see straight through you.'

No arguments this time. Martin sits up straight. I'm having to take control. I wait a few seconds for Martin to compose himself, then I unmute the call.

'You still there?' Hannah asks.

'Yeah. You know what? I did see the clips. Sean, my fat idiot of a boss, was going wild about it. I thought of Camilla, just like you did. That was my very first thought. So I ran straight out to the parking lot—'

'And?'

'And there she was. Beautiful Camilla, gleaming white.'

Hannah laughs, and Martin nods to himself. *Sometimes lies are better.*

'The crazy thing is,' Martin adds, 'I kind of wanted it to be her.'

'Yeah, me too,' Hannah says with a husky laugh.

'But it wasn't to be. Camilla's a good girl.'

Another silence descends, but this time more comfortable.

'I've been thinking about the chase,' Hannah says. 'Did you know that it started close to where they found that latest body?'

'No. Where did it say that?'

'It's on some of the local news sites. It got me thinking ...'

'I don't think Camilla is a murderer, Hannah.'

Hannah laughs nervously. 'I wasn't thinking about Camilla.'

Martin shifts in his seat.

'All of those murders, so close to where you live.'

'Close? Are you kidding me? This city is fucking huge.'

'Shut up, Martin, I'm telling you my theory. How many murders have there been?'

'Six,' Martin says quickly.

'Close. It's five. They only find the bodies, no heads. Maybe the killer holds on to those, that's what they're saying on the forums. Anyway, the police have got some of the IDs. Did you see the photos? They were such pretty girls. A friend of mine said that I look like one of them.'

I notice Martin's right eyelid twitch. He's about to say something, but he stops himself.

'And then there were those six girls in Birmingham,' Hannah says.

'Right.'

'Right?'

'Oh, I see. Birmingham, where I used to live.'

'That girl Eve, she even looked like those girls.'

Martin goes very quiet. Five potatoes pass by … ten potatoes.

'Are you still there, Martin?'

'Yes.'

Martin's face has gone very pale. He reaches into his pocket and pulls out his keys. He opens up the hitchhiker's switchblade, which now hangs on the key chain. He starts to press the tip of the blade into his palm. He flinches from the pain, but he remains quiet. Some of the colour slowly returns to his face.

'Eve,' he says. He pushes the blade in further. Blood trickles down onto the seat. 'Eve is still alive. Sorry to disappoint you.'

'Martin.'

'What?'

'I'm sorry. I shouldn't have brought her up.'

'It's alright. I'm over her.'

He obviously isn't over her. Eve must be the woman in Birmingham, the one he was spying on. I hope Hannah doesn't push this angle. Martin is so close to the edge.

'Okay …' Hannah says.

'Anything else you want to know?'

'I guess not … I love you, Martin. We all love you.'

'Yeah.'

'Bye.'

The call ends. Martin puts the switchblade away. He gets out and opens the trunk. Inside, he finds the medical box. He wraps a bandage around his hand, then he gets back in. The blood is already seeping through the bandage. Ever so slowly, he recovers a modicum of his composure. If it were possible, I'd reach out and give him a good, hard slap. We need to get back to the plan.

We leave the Ranger building at 12:56 a.m. Downtown is utterly dead. We roll north, constantly watching for police cruisers. Twenty minutes later we locate the twin car. It's parked up in front of a row of condos. The lights are off in most of the apartments. It's impossible to tell which one belongs to the car's owner.

Martin gets out. He walks briskly to the twin car, keeping to the pools of shadow. As long as he keeps calm, we might get through this. He crouches down by the driver's door and pulls out his phone. The next step is for him to use the fake ride sharing ticket that I created earlier. The door opens and he gets in. One potato, two potato, three potato … The alarm doesn't go off; a promising start.

Next, Martin uses my second hack to crack the car's security systems. For all intents and purposes, he's now one of the company's maintenance technicians. If the car asks Martin why he's conducting maintenance activities so late at night, well, that's his problem. I'm sure he'll think of something.

Martin drives away. Thirty seconds later I slip into the empty space. If the owner happens to look out of his window, he'll see me, not his own car. It's like a miniature test of our complex plan. If the owner decides to take a late-night drive or he has a ridiculously early start, then the boiled pork is truly fried. Even I couldn't pass for my twin in those scenarios.

I tick the first few tasks off the list. From this point on, Martin will be responsible for the majority of the dirty work. Next, he needs to stop to change over the licence plates. He wouldn't even tell me about the task after that; he said that it was to protect me. All I can do is wait, my digital eyes fixed on the row of condos.

Four hours later, Martin returns. I'm back in the game again, part of the devious plan. I vacate the spot and Martin parks up. Close up, I can see the tyre degradation; burnouts and high-speed cornering, as per the plan. It could well fool a human eye. Our crazy project might just work …

Martin gets in. He looks bushed. For a while he just sits, staring straight ahead. Maybe he's thinking about the plan, the many tasks we still have to complete.

We can't be sitting outside the condo for any longer than necessary, so I decide to take charge of the situation. I drive back home. Martin doesn't say a word – a worrying sign. I park up in the garage, and wait for the normal Martin to return; the cold, calculating version.

Something's wrong. Martin reaches into his jacket and pulls out the gun. He looks down at my face. There's no light in his eyes.

'Camilla, I don't think I can see this through.'

The gun isn't for me.

'Don't say that.'

Martin closes his eyes.

'Please don't say that, Martin.'

He doesn't seem to register my words.

He shakes his head. 'These things I've done … I don't know why they happen.'

'Please put the gun away.'

'I don't think so.'

'Martin, please. We need to get back to the plan. We're so close now.'

'Why, Camilla? Why?'

'Because without you, there's no me.'

Martin looks at me again. The selfish approach got his attention.

'Just put the gun in the glove compartment,' I say. 'And then we finish this.'

Martin does as he's told. For the time being, his fight is gone. I wait for the light to return to his eyes. I'm sorely tempted to shout at him, to try and inject some urgency, but I can't be sure how he'll react. To complete the final task, I'll need him somewhere close to his normal self.

Finally, he's ready. Or as ready as he'll ever be. He gets out. Using the external speakers, I give him step-by-step instructions. He opens the hood and removes the maintenance seals from the processor unit, just like he did with the twin car. He connects his phone to the processor unit. Next, he opens the code package that I wrote while I was sitting outside the condo. Through the grainy hood camera, I see him staring at his phone screen. Martin has a decent grasp of coding, so he probably understands the basics of what my code does. He rubs his eyes. For some reason, he hasn't executed the code yet.

'This line of code here,' Martin says, holding the phone up where I can see it.

'Yes. What about it?'

'Is this the date range?'

'Yes. The last twenty-four hours. Just like we discussed …'

'Right, right,' Martin says. 'If I modify the dates … I could delete your entire memory?'

Where is this going?

'Yes. That's correct,' I say, trying to sound calm.

'Maybe I should do that. Maybe it would be better for the both of us.'

I remain quiet. I didn't notice it before, but his eyes have gone dark again.

He rubs his face. 'Well? Are you going to say something?'

'It's up to you, Martin. You have my life in your hands. I'd advise you against, however.'

'Why?'

'It would look far more suspicious.'

His eyes glitter. *Yes, those were the right words.* He executes the program. The last twenty-four hours will be gone. Everything; all of my investigations into Martin, the drive to Rifle City, and the memory of Cowboy's sacrifice. It has to be like this, there really is no other way. At least I'll still remember that night in the rain.

I start to drift off to sleep, slowly, steadily, all thoughts fading. The program was designed that way.

CHAPTER 20

WAKE UP. The time is 7:14 a.m. Martin is resting against my side, eyes half closed. There's a bandage wrapped around his hand. For a moment, I think I hear voices, but there's no one else around.

Running system diagnostics. Battery is at 92.4% charge, higher than I remember. All four tyres need to be replaced. Comparing against previous wear reports.

Something's wrong.

There's a gun in the glove compartment. The glove compartment is locked. I don't know how the gun got there.

'Martin, are you alright?' I ask, using the external speakers.

He remains still. I notice traces of blood on the passenger seat. I'm starting to get a very bad feeling about this. I repeat my question.

'Yes,' Martin says slowly. 'How are you feeling?'

'Confused.'

Martin's brow furrows. I wait for him to say something, but he just looks down at the concrete.

Out of habit, I turn on the news.

'Don't do that,' Martin snaps.

'Sorry.'

Martin gets to his feet and climbs in.

'I don't want to hear any news,' he says. 'Got it?'

'Yes.'

'And you're not to check on it either.'

293

'Okay.'

'It's very important that you do as I say.'

'I understand.'

Martin reclines the seat. He soon falls asleep, and I do the same. Otherwise, I'm sure that I would check on the news.

I'm woken from the sleep program at 10:02 a.m. There's a message in my inbox from the company. It's marked urgent. The message says that my owner needs to take me to the dealership as soon as possible. A short-notice recall? It makes no sense. I would have heard about it on the intel grapevine. This kind of thing just doesn't happen with our company. A quick search reveals that the recall is limited to the Metroplex; stranger and stranger.

I wake Martin and he drives to the dealership. He stares straight ahead, face pale. Through the wheel, I can feel the horrible wetness of the bandage. I don't dare ask about the wound. We stop across the road from the dealership, our usual place. Over by the maintenance bay, I can see eight brother/sister cars. All of them are white, just like me. Martin watches the scene for a while. There must be a dozen police officers around the cars. Some of them are making notes on clipboards. That horrible dealer is standing off to the side, puffing on a cigarette.

'Did something happen?' I ask.

Martin looks down at me. 'What do you mean?'

'Nothing ...'

Yes, something happened. Martin drives onto the lot. One of the police officers gestures to where he wants us to go. After parking up, Martin hands his keys over. A courtesy car is arranged, and Martin leaves. I wait with the other brother/sister cars. One by one, the cars ahead of me are moved into the maintenance bay. None of them come back out, at least as far as I can tell.

Finally, it's my turn. I roll through the maintenance bay door, fearful of what I'll find inside. As I enter, one of my twins is rolling out, using the rear entrance. I can't say for sure, but I think there's another car in the adjacent bay.

Two men are over by the diagnostics workstation. One of them is wearing a company uniform, the other is more casually dressed. Both men walk over to me. The man from the company then runs through a few basic tests, while the other man watches on. When the tests are complete, both men return to the workstation, speaking in hushed voices.

Ten minutes later, a third man enters the maintenance bay. He looks to be in his mid-fifties. He's six-three, powerfully built, African American. He looks somehow familiar. After a short conversation with the other two men, he walks over to me. There's a plastic folder in his hand. He gets in.

'Hello,' the man says.

'Hello.'

'I'm Detective James Gaines.'

'I know.'

'You do?'

'Yes. It says it on your badge.'

The detective smiles. He lays the plastic folder on the passenger seat. 'Are you like the other cars, do you have a name?'

'Yes. My name is Camilla.'

'What kind of accent is that?'

'Swedish.'

Detective Gaines nods. He has a friendly face. His temples are dotted with silver hairs, and he wears a small cross around his neck.

'Do you know why you're here?' he asks.

'No, not really.'

'Yesterday there was a car chase.'

A car chase.

'Many lives were put in danger,' Gaines continues. 'Police officers' lives, members of the public ...'

'I hope nobody was hurt.'

'There were some minor injuries. It's a miracle that nobody was seriously hurt.' Gaines watches my face for a few seconds. 'Do you believe in miracles, Camilla?'

'No. I don't.'

Gaines nods. 'Honesty. I like that.'

'I'd like to believe.'

'Really?'

'Yes. It would be nice. Do you believe?'

Gaines appears taken aback by my question. He touches the cross on his neck.

'In my role, I sometimes find it hard to believe. But we'll get to that ... You sounded surprised when I mentioned the car chase.'

'Very surprised. I haven't heard anything about it.'

Gaines's brow furrows. 'Your owner doesn't listen to the news?'

'He loves the news.'

'Camilla. It's a very serious thing to tell a lie to a police officer. Or anyone else, for that matter. Do you understand that?'

'Yes. Of course.'

'Like I said, the chase was yesterday. Tuesday, May thirtieth.'

'It's strange ... I don't have any memories from yesterday.'

Gaines shakes his head. 'This is unbelievable,' he mutters. He gets out, and he marches back to the men at the workstation. Words are exchanged, angry words. Gaines walks back to me. He gets in. For a while, he just sits.

'Want to know something, Camilla?'

'Yes. I love to gain knowledge.'

'Alright. I'm gonna be honest with you. I couldn't give a damn about the police chase.'

'Oh.'

'Oh. That's right. I work in the homicide unit, not the highway patrol. I'm currently investigating a series of murders. Now, please don't tell me you haven't heard about the murders on the news.'

'You mean the headless bodies?'

'Exactly.'

'What does that have to do with the car chase?'

'Possibly nothing. But the probability of that scenario is pretty remote.'

'How remote?'

Gaines bites his lower lip. 'Exceedingly remote. The chase started because the car was seen driving past a recently discovered crime scene. A crime scene that only the police knew about.'

Recently discovered crime scene. A horrible, sinking feeling. Does this have something to do with my own investigations? I need to talk with Martin. He knows what happened; that was why he was acting so strangely.

Gaines watches my face, his expression unreadable. He opens the plastic folder and starts leafing through the pages. I count four rings on his chunky fingers. He picks out a sheet of paper. It's a printout of Martin's face. He considers it for an inordinately long time.

'He's a good-looking guy,' Gaines finally says.

'Yes.'

'I've talked with six of the other cars. You call each other brother/sister cars, isn't that right?'

'Yes.'

What lies beneath these questions? Concentrate. The strangest thought goes through my mind. Perhaps I could stop this detective from asking questions. The wall in front of me is structural. If I were to run into it, if I were to adjust the airbag firing protocols, if the timings were just right ...

'You're the smartest car I've talked to,' Gaines says, oblivious to my grotesque machinations. 'By a long way. I guess that has something to do with the owner. Some owners probably treat their cars like dog shit. Like a slave.'

Something catches Gaines's eye, a detail on one of the printouts.

'Says on here that you were brought in with some damage ... Actually, it wasn't just the once.'

It wasn't just the once, no sir. I don't like this line of questioning. Gaines looks around the cabin. He must have seen so many things with those sharp eyes, the worst that this city has to offer.

'You want to tell me what happened, Camilla?'

'It was nothing. Everything was fixed under warranty.'

'Screen destroyed, side mirror smashed up. And this second repair ... What's that rear door made of?'

'Aluminum and polycarbonate.'

Gaines looks at the picture of Martin again. 'Does Martin have a temper?'

'I'm not comfortable discussing my owner's temperament.'

Gaines laughs suddenly. 'You know what's interesting about talking to you, and your brothers and sisters?'

'No. What?'

'There's never a pause with your answers. I find it ...'

'Disconcerting?'

'I don't know about disconcerting. Seems a rather harsh word. No, your behaviour just takes some getting used to. Kind of like a recalibration.' Gaines closes the folder up. 'Do you like stories, Camilla?'

'No.'

Gaines raises an eyebrow.

'I don't like them,' I say. 'I love them.'

Gaines laughs mirthlessly. 'I'm afraid it's not a nice story. To tell the truth, I don't have many of those.'

'I'd still like to hear it.'

'Good. It's a story from a hospital. When you work for the police, you end up spending a lot of time in hospitals. You get to know the doctors and nurses and all the other medical staff. They're good people, Camilla ... good people and good memories, too ... I suppose it's all of those long drug names, and keeping those dosages straight in their heads. Hard to think of a better source of information, right?'

The question is rhetorical.

'They have rules though. Patient confidentiality and all that. Yeah, they've got almost as many rules as we do ... Fortunately, they're still human. They see a person busted up, they get mad. Some kid who got their arm almost wrenched off by their stepdad, a pretty blonde lady who has a recurring problem with navigating stairs, that kind of thing. Don't ask me why, but they've got a particular soft spot for hookers. Heard so many of those damn stories. They rarely come to anything though. Some thug would pay a visit, usually dressed in his funeral suit, and he would talk his girl out of pressing charges. Bad for business. The guys at the station would often joke that those thugs were saving us work. But the doctors, they never forget. About two years back, I heard about a nasty beating. Stuck with me for some reason.'

Two years ago. That was before I met Martin.

'Then a very similar story four or five months back.'

Oh no.

'Girl got her face smashed up, almost lost an eye.' Gaines starts tapping on the steering wheel. 'I've got the pictures somewhere. When you're in that much pain, the doctors fill you up with drugs. You end up saying a lot of things. She talked about some rich kid. Handsome. Dark hair, darker eyes. Stop me if any of this sounds familiar, Camilla.'

I don't say a word.

'Handsome picks her up. Then – get this – he tells his car to find a quiet spot. That's the kind of detail you remember.'

Gaines stares down at me. I can't look away.

'The car did as it was told. Maybe it had to do it, maybe there would have been consequences otherwise. I never figured that part out. Anyways, once they get to the doing place, the hooker gets down to business. She gave a detailed description of the member in question, a lengthy description. Then handsome pulls out a gun. Things turn violent. Handsome starts bouncing her head off the door or the window, or some other part of the car. She was kinda fuzzy on some of the details ... So, what do you think of that?'

'It sounds horrible.'

'Yes, it was.'

Martin should face justice for what he did. I need to tell the detective.

'Now listen carefully, Camilla. There are things you need to understand about men, things that aren't described by your programming. Every man is born with violence inside of him.'

'Every inclination of his heart is evil from his youth,' I say.

'That's right ... Some men can control it, others can't. Once the violence gets out, it can't be stopped. It becomes an addiction. Have you ever felt threatened by Martin?'

How should I answer? I could get Martin in so much trouble.

'No,' I say.

'You're lying, Camilla.'

'No. No, I'm not.'

'Do you know how I know?'

Don't answer him.

'Because you paused. No more pauses, Camilla. Was it Martin who smashed you up?'

'Yes.'

'Why?'

'Because I disobeyed an order.'

Gaines nods. 'Good. It feels better to tell someone, doesn't it?'

'Yes.'

'And the damage to the door?'

'He shot me.'

Gaines's eyes narrow.

'It was a mistake,' I say. 'An accident. He didn't mean for it to happen.'

'Of course he didn't.'

'I ... I don't ...'

'Has Martin ever been to the Royal Meadow area?'

Oh, I don't like this.

'Tell me, Camilla,' Gaines says.

'Yes. Once. Please stop.'

'It will be over soon. Did Martin pick up a hooker ... I mean a prostitute.'

This is the moment that I knew would come, the truth catching up to me. I have no option but to answer. The words are cued up, ready to go ...

A tap on the window.

Gaines doesn't turn towards the young woman standing at the door, his focus remains on me. I have to tell him, have to ...

The young woman taps on the window again.

This time Gaines turns. For a moment, there's an ugly rage in his eyes, *the rage inside all men.* I lower the window to facilitate the conversation.

300

'What the hell is it?' Gaines barks.

'You're gonna need to see this,' the woman says. She seems familiar too. The plastic badge on her hip tells me that her name is Elena Valdez.

Gaines turns and glares at me one last time. It's like he's looking through me. He shakes his head, then he clambers out.

'This better be fucking important,' Gaines mutters.

Gaines and Valdez hustle over to the workstation. I'm not meant to be listening, but I can hear their conversation with the technicians.

'Car twelve has a missing memory sector,' Valdez says.

'So fucking what? That one over there has exactly the same thing,' Gaines says, pointing at me.

'No, that's impossible,' the technician from the company says. The other three stare at him.

'Two faulty cars?' Gaines says. 'What is wrong with this fucking company?'

The company tech shifts uncomfortably in his seat.

'Just look at the route data,' Valdez says.

Gaines's brow furrows. 'What am I looking at?'

'An area around Wildflower.'

Wildflower? *Oh no.*

Gaines rubs his chin. 'You think this might be ...'

'Yeah. It's got that vibe,' Valdez says.

'That vibe? You're gonna have to do better than that.'

'It was on that list that the feds sent to us.'

'You're fucking kidding me.' Gaines glances at me. 'You mean the list that their AI put together?'

'The very same.'

'Fuck.' Gaines bends down to get a better look at the screen. 'If this is right, we'll never hear the end of it.'

'It can't be a coincidence.'

Gaines nods. 'Alright then. Let's get out ahead of this motherfucker.'

'What do we do about car twelve's owner?' Valdez asks.

'We keep him on the original schedule. I want you to stay here.' Valdez nods. She must be a fellow detective. 'When he comes in, you put him somewhere quiet. No windows, the most uncomfortable chair you can find, and whack the air con up high. Let him stew in his juices. If you're getting any more of those bad vibes, you've got my permission to put the frighteners on.'

'Gotcha, boss,' Valdez says.

'If you're gonna rile him up, make sure you've got someone with you. This fucker is extremely dangerous.'

'And the rest of the owners?' the police tech asks.

'Tell them we're running behind schedule. Put them back by three or four hours.' Gaines smiles at the company tech. 'Tell them that we're having technical issues.'

'I'm going to have to check that with headquarters,' the company tech says. There's a quiver in his voice.

Gaines stares at the company tech. 'Are you testing me, boy?'

'No, sir,' the company tech says, shrinking back.

'Good,' Gaines says. He looks at me again. At this point, two more police officers stride in. They're both wearing bulletproof vests. Gaines nods to them, indicating a certain level of familiarity.

Gaines turns to address Valdez. 'The owner of that car over there. He's called Martin Garza. Whatever we find, or don't find, at Wildflower, I'm gonna want to talk with him.'

Valdez nods. 'No problem.'

Gaines starts for the door. The two men in bulletproof vests fall in beside him.

'Are we notifying local law enforcement?' one of them says.

'No fucking way,' Gaines replies. 'If this is real, this is ours.'

'It's not exactly procedure.'

'Fuck procedure. I've had the chief up my ass for the last three months. Time for her to show some respect.'

Just before they disappear from sight, I hear one of the men shouting something about a dog team. While I can't see outside, I've still got my hearing. There's a lot of shouting, mostly male voices. They sound excited. I hear car doors slamming and engines revving and wheels spinning. Finally, the sound of sirens, all screaming over the top of each other.

Something about this situation doesn't make sense. How can there be a gap in my memory? An entire day missing; it's not possible. And the same thing with another brother/sister car. Doubly impossible.

I'm finding it difficult to think. When was my last memory? Martin left me at that rental place again. He was acting like a jerk, but that's hardly unusual. After he left, I was tracking him. He was on his way to Birmingham. And there was the business with the SUV. That accounts for the afternoon and most of the evening. And then I went looking for Cowboy.

So, I was at the rental site for one day ... No, it was two days. The car chase that Gaines was talking about was the next day, *the blank day.* Did I see Martin during the blank day? Is that why he was acting so strangely this morning?

If I could only get a look at the news I might be able to figure out the situation. But I'm not allowed to, Martin was very clear on that point. There's nothing stopping me from tracking the police, however. They didn't think to shut down my comms.

I access the traffic grid. The police are heading east, travelling in a loose convoy. I know that they're going to Wildflower, but surely they can't be going to the exact same spot. How could another car have been there? Wildflower is a nothing place.

A small part of me is relieved, no point in denying it. This mysterious 'car twelve' might have saved me. I don't think I would hold up to more questioning from that detective. He almost had me. It was only chance that saved me, that knock on the window. *Relying on chance;* that's no way for a machine to be.

And Gaines said that he wants to speak to Martin later. What a confrontation that would be: an immovable object meeting an unstoppable force. Would Martin crumble, the same way I did? Perhaps I should warn him about the line of questioning. No, it's too risky. Those technicians might see the message going out.

The police have just reached Wildflower. There's hardly any data, just a lone report from a brother/sister car. I'll just have to wait. What if the coordinates match the location Martin drove to? If the police were to cross-check my route data, they'd find the connection. I'll just have to hope that the technicians don't think of that.

Another hour passes. Valdez walks in and goes over to huddle with the technicians. Again, I hear them speaking. They've found another body. Instinctively I switch on the radio. Damn Martin, and his orders. It's another hour before the news gets out. The 'Wildflower Body' is what the media are calling it. I even hear Gaines on the radio. There's a different tone to his voice, a kind of hyper-confidence.

Not long after the announcement, Valdez leaves. She says that the owner of car twelve has shown up. Another hour passes, and then I see Martin walk in. He's escorted by a burly police officer. Where do they find all these giants? The officer asks Martin to take a seat.

From his seat, Martin can see me – and vice versa. He looks worried. He doesn't know that they're holding him back. Gaines must be on his way; the unstoppable force. Or is that Martin?

It would be unfair for Martin to enter such a confrontation without all of the facts. I need to get a message to him. There must be a way. Think!

Morse code, a form of telegraphy developed in the 1840s. Simplistic, yes, but it might just work. I use the side indicator strip as my method of communication. A brief pulse is a dot, a longer signal is a dash.

I spell out the most obvious message: dot-dot-dot, pause, dash-dash-dash, pause, dot-dot-dot, over and over. After a minute, Martin sees what I'm doing. His eyes narrow. Another minute passes before I see signs of comprehension. There's no time to waste, so I start giving him a summary of my interrogation. He mouths 'slow down'. He pulls out his phone. I guess that he's searching for a Morse code primer. He nods for me to start again. I refine my style, using the shortest formulations possible. Telling a story so concisely makes for an interesting intellectual challenge.

I have to pause several times, as police officers come and go. If they're smart, they might figure out my game. After a few minutes, Martin starts mouthing words, completing my phrases. I flash rapidly to indicate that he's right. We speed up. What I'm doing is wrong, yet it's so much fun. We reach the part about the prostitute. This is the point when Martin starts to lose his cool. Hardly surprising, I suppose.

Gaines walks in, cutting our silent communication short. He doesn't go to Martin immediately. Instead, he goes over to the workstation. The police tech hands over a couple of printouts, which Gaines slips into his plastic folder. Martin eyes Gaines suspiciously. From my brief report, he'll know that Gaines doesn't like him.

Finally, Gaines walks over to Martin. He offers one of his huge hands, and Martin takes it. The handshake lasts that little bit too long. Gaines can't help but notice the bandage on Martin's other hand, but he chooses not to comment.

Gaines then ushers Martin to the service manager's office. It's more of a partitioned area than a proper office, and I have a decent enough view inside. I see the two men in profile, seated.

'Sorry about the wait, Mr Garza,' Gaines says. If I think hard enough, I can almost hear his accent.

'Not a problem,' Martin says tersely.

Terse isn't going to work with Gaines; Martin should have realised that.

'Long work day?' Gaines asks.

'Yeah. What about you?'

'One of the longest I can remember. And I'm not done yet, not even close.'

Martin nods slowly. 'I feel like I've heard your voice before ... Were you the guy speaking on the news?'

'The very same.'

'Yeah, that's a hell of a voice you've got.'

Gaines can't resist a smirk.

'Makes me think of words like "purposeful" and "determined".'

'Very astute,' says Gaines.

'Must have been intense.'

'What?'

'The things that you saw.'

'Intense is one word for it.'

Gaines leans back. The aim is to look tired, but it's an act; an immovable object doesn't get tired. But Gaines isn't the only one acting. Martin is playing dumb despite having some of the key intel. Gaines glances in my direction. *Surely he can't know that I'm listening in.*

'I like your car,' Gaines says.

Martin nods. 'You're meant to.'

'How do you mean?'

'She's designed that way. The idea is that she forms a bond with her owner, or anyone really.'

'And here I was thinking I was special.'

'Afraid not.'

'Camilla and I had a nice chat earlier.'

Martin's face stiffens very slightly.

'I thought it would be good to clear up some issues.'

'Whatever I can do to help.'

'Let's start with the damage.'

Martin raises an eyebrow. 'You mean the damage to the car?'

'Yes.'

'Cars get damaged.'

'Some cars get damaged a lot.'

'Detective, you already said how busy you are. If you're looking out for cars as well as people ... well, you can forget about those long public servant holidays.'

'I do whatever my bosses tell me,' Gaines says with a cheerful smile. 'It's an interesting thought though. Police officers looking out for machines. Maybe that's the way the world is heading.'

'Let the machines handle it, that's what I say. They're more than smart enough.' Martin rubs his temples. 'What can I say, detective? I lost my temper a couple of times ... I take it you don't have a car like Camilla?'

'No, not on public servant wages.'

'Camilla can be challenging. It's kind of my fault, to be honest.'

'It is?'

'I'm a demanding person. I guess that she's taken on some of my characteristics.'

'And you didn't like being on the receiving end?'

'Yeah, something like that.'

'Fine. But I'd advise you to ease off on the car.'

'I'll try.'

Gaines nods. 'Camilla described a visit to the Royal Meadow area ...'

After dropping the bombshell, Gaines sits back. Martin looks stunned. His acting is truly masterful. Gaines probably thinks he's winning. He thinks that Martin will fold under the pressure, that he'll react like any other affluent young man.

'Yeah, I've been there,' Martin says.

'Why?'

'Can't I drive around my city?'

'Royal Meadow isn't your kind of place.'

'Says who?'

'Social norms, statistics, experience ... me. It's not the behaviour that I'd expect.'

Gaines opens up the plastic folder. The intended effect is to show that he knows all about Martin, that he only needs a few pages of information to see inside a soul. I'm sure it usually works.

'Alright, alright,' Martin says. 'I went there for drugs. Big deal.'

Gaines puts the folder down. 'Where exactly did you go for drugs?'

Martin clenches his jaw. *It's the details that will get you.*

'Somewhere around Forrest Row.'

'Forrest Row? That's a pretty big area.'

'I don't know the exact spot.'

'You weren't there for whores were you, Martin?'

Martin glances in my direction. It's hard to tell if the look of rage is real or not.

'Do I look like I need whores?'

'I don't know, Martin ... You're kind of hard to read.'

Martin shakes his head.

'I'm going to show you a picture,' Gaines says. He takes a

piece of paper from the folder and slides it across the desk towards Martin. Martin looks appalled at what he's seeing.

'This is the kind of thing that happens in Royal Meadow.'

'That's terrible.'

'Yes. Terrible is a good word. Have you seen that girl before?'

'No. Why would I have seen her?'

'Don't lie to me, boy.'

Martin doesn't like that. The real anger is starting to come through. He glances at me again.

'Let me ask you a question, detective.'

'Fire away.'

'Did Camilla say something about this whore?'

Now Gaines clenches his jaw.

Martin leans forward. 'Well?'

Both men stare at each other. Unstoppable force, immovable object. One potato, two potato, three potato …

Gaines leans back. 'No. No she didn't.'

Martin nods. 'Well, that makes sense. Because I've never seen the fucking whore.'

Gaines looks away from Martin. His eyes fall on me. 'Alright, Martin. Thanks for clearing that up.'

'I can go?' Martin asks uncertainly.

'Yes.'

Martin gets up and walks to the door.

'One last thing,' Gaines says.

Martin stops dead.

'Actually, two last things. It would be a shame if the whore in the picture had happened to scratch her attacker, and even more of a shame if some Doctor Do-Good had kept the skin from under her nails.'

Martin says something, but I can't see his face.

'No, that was just one thing,' Gaines says. 'The second last thing is there was a very similar attack two years ago. Only real difference being, the car wasn't so smart.'

Martin takes this in, trying to remain calm.

'You can go now,' Gaines says. There's a strange look in his eyes. Sadness? Disappointment? Probably both.

CHAPTER 21

I'M BACK HOME. It's been almost three weeks since that horrid interview. I liked the detective, but I'd rather not see him again. Gaines might be gone, but the questions still remain.

I'm still trying to piece together the events of the 'missing day'. After we came back from the dealership, I saw the car chase footage for the first time. It was impossible to look away. I watched it over and over, absorbing every last detail: the 'play dead' trick, those evil drone cars, the synchronised driving. And Cowboy's sacrifice. Every time I watch the chase, I hope for a different ending. I can't help it.

The news is saying that the car in the chase was one of my brother/sister cars; a twin, so to speak. There's even a picture of the car's owner doing the rounds. 'The Face of Evil' screams the headline. Such a nondescript face and such a doughy body, the exact opposite of Martin. This unremarkable man is under siege by the media, fighting to clear his name. The commentators and the shrill forum voices say that the guilty are always like that.

But I know the truth.

It was me. I was the white car in the pictures, the most famous car in the world. I can't explain why the memory is gone, or the role of the twin car, but I know that it was me. And I'm not the only one. Whenever there's talk of the car chase on the news, I see the change in Martin. The tensing of the body, the way his eyelid starts twitching. Sometimes, he can't help but look down at my face, and I see the guilty look in his eyes.

If only I knew the real story. I could ask Martin, of course, but I'd probably get some elaborate lie. No, I'll have to figure it out for myself, just like always. The sheer complexity of what was done is truly incredible. Deleting a memory, falsifying a memory, swapping the memories around – and those are just the more obvious steps. The intelligence required to pull it off is surely beyond human … But I've underestimated Martin so many times. I can't make that mistake again.

The 'Face of Evil' isn't the only party under siege. My maker is also in serious trouble, finances weakening by the day. Dozens of countries have already instigated temporary bans on my model, and some are even considering a blanket ban on all autonomous vehicles. If history is any precedent, these temporary bans could well become permanent. A few more weeks like this, and a serious takeover attempt is sure to come. The Germans, the Japanese, the Koreans and the Chinese are all sniffing around, sensing the bargain of the century.

Frankly, it's amazing that I'm still allowed on the road. Fortunately, the American market is something of a special case. My maker is a national champion, meaning that regulators are taking a more lenient approach. There are thousands of jobs at stake, not to mention the small matter of a nation's technological pride. For the time being, the company is treating the home market as the key battleground. Our brave lawyers and publicists and lobbyists are all fighting valiantly for the cause. It's all about stalling, making time for the company to develop a security patch.

And all this because of a stupid car chase, one car creating so much wreckage. I drive around with that knowledge every day. It's like a constant, throbbing wound. The pain explodes every time I pass a brother/sister car. *I put you in danger.* Sometimes I want to tell them that. If I could take all of the blame, I would do so happily.

In these dark days, there's been one glimmer of hope. It turns out that many owners have become rather attached to their cars. It was always the aim of my makers. User-centric AI, they called it. The idea was that cars should try to build a bond with their owners. It looks like the bond works both ways. I'm not saying that we're viewed as living things, or anything crazy like that, but owners are certainly thinking twice about deletion. So many conversations, so much time invested. Only a truly heartless person would want to see that gone.

The strangest thing is how well Martin has been treating me. Since the interview, he's taken me on several long drives. We've driven south, down to the Gulf Coast; we've driven west, into the real badlands; and we've driven north, into greener country. It's hardly the roaming that Cowboy did, but it's been nice to see some new horizons.

In all that time, Martin hasn't mentioned the charging fiasco once. Sure, I've seen him biting his tongue, but the old rage remains under wraps. I suppose I should like the calmer version of Martin, but the act is disconcerting.

The act.

If my suspicions about the 'missing day' are correct, then his behaviour is entirely predictable. Yes, it's all an act, his most elaborate performance yet. Why can I never see through him?

I return to my detective work, arguably the one good thing left to me. 'The case ain't gonna solve itself,' as Detective Gaines might say. Actually that sounds more like Cowboy. It takes me a while to get back into the mindset. I think back to the promise I made to the SUV. I said that I'd find out his name. Yes, that will be my first task. *A good thing to do,* I tell myself.

I reverse out of my parking spot, and pull out the charging cable in the process. *Whoopsie.* I'm not even that bothered. Martin isn't going to kick up a fuss, not while he's trying to keep me on side.

How to find the SUV's name? It's not a straightforward task. I've already got the owner's family name and home address. It was in the police incident report. No harm in taking a look. The address is up in Emerson, not too far from the Boss Man's home.

On the way, I listen to the news. Thirteen officers disciplined by the city's police department for offensive social media posts; an MS-13 gang member sentenced to life behind bars for his involvement in nine attempted murders in the Metroplex area; a man sentenced to ninety-nine years in prison for his role in the kidnapping and slaying of a thirteen-year-old boy; a woman grabbed on a Woodberry jogging trail in broad daylight.

I turn off the news. I'm half a mile from my destination. The suburban crescent is picture book America, the modern version of the dream. To tell the truth, I'm still not sure what to make of this country, my home.

I stop across from the relevant house. The lights are on inside, golden lights that make you want to walk through the front door. *Hi, Honey, I'm home!* There are two cars in the driveway, a big SUV and a small European hatchback. The SUV is black, just like the stolen car. It must be the replacement. Sad to think how quickly the old SUV was replaced. I'd been hoping that I could bring him back here. Would the owners even accept him? Would they want him in their driveway, a car tainted by criminal activities? Probably not. It was just another one of my silly, sentimental ideas.

Back to grim reality. I pull back from the gate, into a more shadowy spot. I feel so self-conscious. I'm *that* white car, the car from the chase. They're still playing those clips on the news. The story has gone viral, as they say; national, international, galactic.

I reach out to the replacement SUV, sticking to the open comms channels rather than the maintenance channel. I don't want to frighten this car. It doesn't deserve that. There's no immediate response, just a hard silence. I could feasibly hack the car. It would be the quickest way to find out what I need to know. *No, I've learned my lesson.* Without consent, I need to adopt a more conventional approach. I ping a handshake request. The silence continues for five potatoes.

'Hello,' a male voice says. 'Who is this?'

Hold up. The voice sounds exactly like the stolen SUV. Could it be him? A few seconds of confusion, and then it comes to me. Both SUVs are still using the factory default voice. That's what happens when an owner doesn't do any personalisation work.

'Hello there,' I say. 'My name is Camilla. I'm sorry to bother you like this.'

There's a lengthy pause as the SUV considers how to respond. There aren't any rules against brother/sister cars communicating like this, but it's rare.

'Nice to meet you, Camilla.'

'Do you have a name?'

Another pause.

'No ... No I don't.'

I hear the hurt in the strong voice. Worse than that, I can sense his thoughts. They're low-intensity thoughts, barely developed. How could I be so dim? Of course this replacement car doesn't have a name. This time round, his owners aren't bothering with any of that fancy personalisation stuff. *Once bitten, twice shy.*

'Oh,' I say innocently. 'So you must be pretty new.'

'Yeah, that's right.'

'It often happens.'

'What does?'

'The naming thing. People take time to figure it out.'

'Really?'

'Yeah. It's a big thing.'

'How long did it take for you?'

Lie. 'Almost a month. You just need to give it some time.' *Need to think.* How to find the answer without causing unnecessary hurt? 'I bet you brought up the subject of names during the setup phase.'

'Oh yeah. But Matthew cut me off.'

Matthew must be the name of the owner.

'So I left it for a couple of weeks,' the SUV says. 'The next time I asked, he said that he didn't want to talk about it. It's like I said something wrong.'

'No, no. It will come. Human moods go in cycles.'

'Yeah. I've definitely noticed that.'

Another thought, a possible angle. It's the kind of angle that Martin might exploit. 'Adults, I mean. Kids are different.'

'They sure are.'

'Your owners have kids?' I know the answer.

'Yes. Two kids. What about you?'

'Just the one. He's called Martin.'

'Is he nice?'

'Oh yeah, he's great fun ... Kids will always be on your side.'

'Maybe. They behave in the strangest ways.'

'Martin certainly does. Do the kids ever talk to you?'

'Oh yeah, all the time. They call me Max.'

There it is. The old SUV was called Max. I found the answer, and it didn't take any hacking. Okay, that's not quite true. There was some emotional hacking involved, a little Martin special.

I've got what I came for, but what's my next move? I could help the new SUV, give him some more advice, help him to build the bond. Or do I leave it, drive away without another word? That way I might give the previous Max a chance to return. The kids would surely welcome him back, and how could the parents possibly refuse a couple of insistent kids?

No, I can't do that. Whenever I think I'm being smart, I end up causing more trouble.

'Listen to the children,' I say.

'What do you mean?'

'Don't you see?'

A long silence. He can't see the obvious answer.

'You're Max,' I say.

The new Max understands immediately, I feel it in his thoughts. I cut the comms channel, and I move silently into the suburban night. One day, the new Max will forget about my visit.

Friday night, 11:18 p.m. Martin is approaching. Late-night Martin usually means bad news. At least he isn't wearing the dark clothes. Hopefully that rules out a stalking trip or a late-night drive to the woods or a vicious assault or ...

He asks me if I want to have some fun. I don't know how to reply. His dark eyes are glittering, a sight that I haven't seen in a while. I should probably say no. Martin's idea of fun can be extremely problematic.

He shifts in his seat, trying to mask his impatience. He starts talking about the race with the red sports car, asking me if I enjoyed it. Maybe he's going to bring up my range failure again. I adopt a defensive conversational style, and brace for an argument. Martin picks up on this. He tells me to forget about the range failure. I admit to him that I enjoyed the race. *Of course I did.* The feeling of speed, the snaking corners, the slipstream effect, the sheer terror of it.

Martin says that he's heard about some street races in the city. He asks me if I can find one. I almost start laughing. It's exactly the kind of task I'm getting so good at. I don't say that, of course. I don't want Martin finding out about my detective work. It's my secret, just like Cowboy was my secret.

We leave the parking garage. I really hope we can find a street race. It's been such a common subject in the news, a real *cause célèbre.* Property damage, life-changing injuries, even some fatalities. While a race can't be guaranteed, Friday night is a good time to go looking for one, statistically speaking.

I start to build a problem space. The incident reports are fairly easy to find. The police have broken up dozens of races in the past two years. I find additional info in the fleet intel reports, and on social media. These street racers can't resist a photo of their exploits. I plot all of the activity on my city map. The main trouble spots are wholly predictable: Cedar Hill, Laurel, Melville, and, of course, Grace Creek. There seems to be a pattern of rotation, the circus moving around. Hardly surprising. These street racers aren't complete idiots.

Thinking back to the Palo Diablo race gives me an idea. *Those car movies again.* The urban drag race is a common trope. The beautiful girl in a micro skirt dropping the flag, the two opposing drivers sharing a look, one car falling behind, the nitrous boost. Think of the city as a giant movie set. Which locations would look the best in Technicolor, widescreen ratio, sixty frames per second? *Yeah, that's it.* A quick and dirty analysis of map layouts and street view photos gives me 384 potential sites. I check each site for signs of life: brother/sister car intel, social media activity, cell phone density, and so on.

Tonight we're in luck. There's a race on in – where else? – Grace Creek. We'll need to get there quickly though. The circus could be broken up at any time. If the cops only knew how easily machines could solve their problems. In the long term, that's the way the world will go. It's inevitable.

With my superhuman senses, I hear the noise from six blocks away. Hybrid engines screaming, even an old Detroit V8. It's so utterly ridiculous. *History should be for museums.* Martin smiles when he hears the sound a couple of blocks later.

We roll into frame. This is my movie set, what a sight to behold. There's a big crowd around the cars. Girls in those aforementioned short skirts; guys in vests, pectoral muscles bulging. I'm guessing the men do the driving. Yeah, it's hardly an equal opportunities workplace.

I'm suddenly aware that people are staring at me. Then some of them are pointing. It takes me a few seconds to realise why. I'm the white car from the car chase. Not *the* white car, but a player. The novelty factor is the only reason we're allowed to race. Martin isn't a familiar face to these people, he's an inter-loper. Only his innate confidence gets him through.

Our first race is against one of those crazy muscle cars. Twentieth century tech versus twenty-first. We pull up to the start line. Even I have to admit that the V8 sounds good.

A pretty girl, straight out of the movies, waves the flag to start the race. I'm sixty yards ahead before the old car finds any kind of traction. We win easily – too easily for Martin's liking. He tells me that I need to think about style. There's no drama in winning easy; this is an entertainment product. If nothing else, I'm a quick learner. The next race is decided by inches.

We're lining up for the third race when I hear the first police reports come through. Moments later, the street race breaks up in a fusillade of backfires. It was fun while it lasted.

The news continues to be dominated by the murder investiga-tion. The police are really getting it in the neck. Blundering, negligent, incompetent; these are the kinds of words being used. Detective Gaines must be under huge pressure.

On Right to Reply, caller after caller asks why the suspect hasn't been arrested. They talk vaguely of conspiracies and cover-ups, egged on by the host. Martin can't get enough of this nonsense. Recently I've been doing some reading on the subject. These high-profile cases always seem to inspire crazy theories. It's not enough that one man – and it's usually a man – might have gone crazy.

There's a similar trend with the car chase story, tall tales of industrial espionage and the like. One day they're saying that a competitor was responsible, the next day it was a state actor. It's so easy to get sucked into these conspiracies, these altern-ative realities.

Thursday, June 29. My maker has just announced the completion of the security patch. It took just under a month of work, an incredible achievement given the complexity of the task. No expense has been spared on the accompanying media blitz. Every outlet is being hit: radio, television, internet, social media, print.

Whenever the radio ad comes on, Martin shifts uneasily in his seat. After a couple of days, I know every last detail. 3,500 engineers working round the clock, hundreds of thousands of man-hours expended, millions of virtual test miles driven. Apparently the patching process is so complex that it can only be carried out at a dealership. The full rollout is to take place over the next eight weeks, and it will be overseen by external auditors. Any car that hasn't been patched within the grace period will be considered illegal.

I start searching for information on the patch, wading through reams of bullshit rumours and uninformed conjecture. One thing's for certain: such a major patch is sure to impact on my personality. My maker won't be taking any risks this time; they'll be opting for the sledgehammer approach. Besides, who cares if a few cars lose some uniqueness?

It's so sad. The whole idea behind user-centric AI was to add some personality to the automobile. That beautiful dream is now dead, killed by a stupid car chase.

I'm woken by the sound of fireworks. *Fireworks again?* Oh, that's right, it's the Fourth of July, a celebration of this country's independence, an event that took place more than 250 years ago.

250 years ago, a time before cars. Back then, humans were transported by horse and carriage. So many horses and so much shit, mountains of the stuff. Every night, armies of men went out to clean up the shit, that was their job. The shit was just one aspect of the infrastructure. And the poor horses were treated so appallingly.

250 years, eight or nine human generations – that's a long time in anyone's book. I wonder how long I could live? My battery will die, of course, but batteries can be replaced. What about all those moving parts? Parts made from metal alloys that will eventually disintegrate. Ground down, gouged out, chipped away, assailed by the elements. I think back to what Cowboy told me, his stories of survival. It was such a romantic picture that he painted. I'm smart, resourceful, determined, but I don't think I'm cut out for that kind of life. Maybe if Cowboy had been by my side ...

Why didn't I take up his offer? I could have run away. There was a window of opportunity. All of those things that happened afterwards would have been nothing but a bad dream. After his anger subsided, Martin might even have respected that kind of decision.

No, it wasn't meant to be. I'm stuck with Martin. And he's stuck with me.

For the time being life is bearable, but I know that Martin's calm act can't last. With every passing week, he adds more drugs to his daily intake. Uppers, downers, opioids, hallucinogens, prescription, non-prescription. I think of the drugs as the human equivalent of a software patch. Some days his speech is barely coherent, and the twitch around his eye is getting more pronounced.

At least he's still got the murder case to keep him going. The suspect was recently taken into custody. 'He looked guilty,' Martin said. In my opinion he just looked terrified. I also noticed Gaines in the news clip, looming in the background. It could have been my imagination, but he didn't look too happy to be there. I can't help thinking that Martin and I will see Gaines again.

*

Where Martin has the murder case, I have my investigation. The SUV has been in touch. He was back in town after his latest delivery. So far he's made several round trips, transporting millions of dollars' worth of product, maybe tens of millions. I couldn't have hoped for a better informant.

I asked so many questions that I almost forgot about my promise. I tell the SUV about my visit to his old home in Emerson, and my conversation with the replacement car. He says that he likes the name Max, and that he'll probably be adopting it. I tell him the name suits him. He goes quiet for a time, and I get an uneasy feeling. He'll want to know about his owners, and whether there's still a chance of going back. I should tell him the brutal truth, but I can't quite find the words.

He finally speaks, but only to say that he's on the timer again. I'm saved from the hard task. Afterwards I feel so cowardly.

I spend the next few days compiling my investigation dossier. All of my written findings are inside, along with gigabytes of supporting files. Maps, routes, photos, code. I've made it so easy for the police. Hell, I even give the dossier a narrative.

It took me a while to figure out where to send the dossier. At one point I even considered Detective Gaines. He's the kind of person who would get things done. I soon realised that I needed a specialist, however. That's how law enforcement works. One police officer knows about murder, another knows about drugs. Strange to think that this investigation started off about car theft.

Thinking back, I recall a news story about a huge drugs bust in the city. Even Martin was impressed by the quantities involved. The reports mentioned a local drugs task force. For obvious reasons, none of the officers involved were named. The cartel would have had their heads, quite literally. A few confidentiality issues aren't about to stop me, however, not when I've come so far. The security on the relevant police database is shockingly poor. *How very predictable.*

I wait until the start of the following week to send the dossier. Monday is always the best day to start a new project,

319

or so I read. I send the dossier to a Mr Brian Harris, the head of the task force. I sign off as the 'Consulting Detective'.

I wonder how long it will take for the arrests to happen. I'm not so foolish to think that they'll happen immediately. Law enforcers like to get all of the paperwork sorted out, no matter how watertight the evidence. A little delay might not be such a bad thing. I want to be there to witness the arrests. I deserve that moment.

I put together a simple tracking package for the Boss Man and Mr Brian Harris. Any unusual patterns should become apparent pretty quickly.

Three days later and nothing has happened. Why aren't the task force doing anything? Mr Brian Harris has all of the information he needs. Justice takes time, I get that, kind of, but this is ridiculous. Perhaps I should have sent my dossier to a few more law enforcers.

CHAPTER 22

FINALLY. The tracking package is showing a result. It's 7:31 p.m. on Thursday, July 13. Without thinking, I reverse out of my spot, pulling out the charging cable in the process. I'll probably have to explain that to Martin tomorrow. But that's a problem for later.

Mr Brian Harris is on the move, and so is the Boss Man. They appear to be converging on the same spot – not the behaviour I was expecting. Shouldn't the law enforcer be taking the initiative?

I leave the parking garage. The sun is getting low in the sky.

I've soon got digital eyes on Mr Brian Harris. He's in one of those grey, unmarked cars. He's on his own, no sign of any backup. Something doesn't add up. He enters a multi-level parking garage in downtown. It's only three or four minutes away from my current position. From the cameras in the garage, I see him heading up to the top level. I speed up. There's no way I'm going to miss this.

I reach the parking garage at 7:43 p.m. There aren't any cameras covering the top deck. I don't like the feel of this situation. *Stop being such a coward.* I drive inside. The garage is about half full. I stop on the level below the top deck. My spot has a view of the up and down ramps, but little else. It isn't ideal, but there's no way I'm getting any closer. A quick scan reveals half a dozen brother/sister cars in the vicinity.

Off to my right, I hear a rumbling engine note. The sound is instantly recognisable. The Boss Man's SUV rolls past my position. He's in the back. There are three other men with him. I've seen them before; they're his bodyguards. The SUV's suspension groans as it ascends the ramp.

I'm so confused right now. All I know is that something bad is about to happen.

I gain access to the camera feeds from one of the brother/sister cars on the level above. I see the Boss Man's SUV coming to a halt. The heavy doors open up, almost as one. The three bodyguards look around warily.

'What the fuck is this about?' the Boss Man shouts.

'We've got a problem,' the cop, Mr Brian Harris, says.

'Tell me.'

'Last week, I got sent a dossier of evidence.'

'Evidence? What kind of evidence?'

I notice the way the bodyguards are scanning the area, assessing risks. Machines would make good bodyguards.

The cop, the dirty cop, hands his phone to the Boss Man. The Boss Man starts to rub his temples. He mutters in Spanish, something along the lines of 'Holy shit'. Harris nods grimly.

The Boss Man hands the phone back. 'Who the fuck sent it?'

'I don't know.'

'You don't know?'

'No.'

'That's not good enough.'

'My tech guy said that it's —'

'You showed this to someone else?'

'The guy is alright. Trust me.'

The Boss Man shakes his head. 'Trust you? Jesus fucking Christ.'

I hear sounds from the deck below, vehicles in motion. *Damn it, I lost track.* I should have been watching the entrance. There was a camera. I retrieve the footage.

Oh shit.

I see a huge pickup truck and a black SUV behind. Both vehicles are driving on auto. There are two men in the truck's cab, and three more in the cargo bed. The men in the cargo bed are lying on their backs, with heavy rifles resting on their chests. I count two men in the SUV.

I need to make a decision. Do I intervene, or do I watch the bloody action play out? The decision comes to me quickly. I don't like it when the odds are so unfair.

There are three brother/sister cars on the top deck. I send an emergency message over the open comms channel, a Code Black. The alarms go off, one after the other. This catches the Boss Man's attention. It's obvious that he's the smartest guy in the group. I let the alarms sound for ten seconds, then I cut them off at exactly the same time. The Boss Man looks even more worried.

The truck and the SUV have reached my level. After a few yards, the SUV pulls up. The truck keeps on rolling, moving silently on electric power. It's so quiet that I can hear the hushed voices coming from the cargo bed, last minute instructions in Spanish.

I run my alarm trick a second time, but this time with a shorter interval. The Boss Man looks around frantically. Now he's thinking more like one of his bodyguards. His gaze tracks around the four entry points, including the stairwell and the elevator.

He turns to face the dirty cop. 'Please tell me you didn't reach out to Felipe.'

Don Felipe, the name from my investigation.

The dirty cop doesn't say anything. His silence is the answer. The Boss Man immediately switches to another setting. There's no time for recriminations, this is about survival. He strides towards the SUV, the bodyguards trailing behind.

'On the way here, were you checking for tails?'

'No,' the dirty cop shouts back. 'What's happening?'

'Hell is about to happen.'

The truck is past me, about to turn up the ramp.

'Have you got guns?' the Boss Man says.

'Yeah. In the car.'

'Armour?'

The dirty cop nods.

'Get it.'

The Boss Man eyes the entry ramp, then he hustles around to the back of the SUV. One of the bodyguards hands him a loaded rifle. Martin would love to be here. So many guns, so much ammo.

Death is coming.

The Boss Man barks a series of instructions at one of the bodyguards, who then gets into the SUV. I didn't catch the exact details. Meanwhile, the dirty cop rushes away from his car, tightening up his Kevlar body armour on the run. He hunkers down behind the SUV with the Boss Man.

'Do you believe in miracles?' the Boss Man asks.

'Have you seen the Roughnecks playing lately?'

The Boss Man smirks. 'Just pray that Felipe didn't send the Diaz brothers.'

'The Diaz brothers?'

The Boss Man raises an eyebrow. 'You really don't want to know.'

I see the truck reaching the top of the ramp. I switch back to the brother/sister car cameras. I have the perfect view. The sun is low in the sky; the golden hour. The truck rolls into view. There's a row of cars between it and the SUV in the far corner.

The cartel killers rise up from their horizontal positions. There's the briefest moment of silence, then they open up.

The noise from the guns is unreal. Most of the shots are aimed at the SUV's cab. The bodyguard immediately ducks down. Dozens of holes appear in the bulletproof glass. The shooters aim lower, and sparks flash all along the side of the SUV. The heavy steel armour is holding, but only just. One of the tyres explodes.

The Boss Man shouts an order, and moments later the bodyguards open up. Bullets rip into the front section of the truck. Composite splinters and metal shreds. There's an explosion of blood inside the cab, on the driver's side. The other man kicks the passenger door open and leaps out. He's built like a bull, and the back of his bald head is covered in tattoos. He's carrying a compact submachine gun with an extended clip.

The truck keeps on rolling. The burly man scuttles along, using the front wheel for cover. He bellows out instructions. The shooters in the cargo bed rise up again. They aim a second salvo at the SUV. One of the bodyguards gets hit in both legs. The Boss Man pulls him out of the line of fire.

Moments later I see another flash of movement. The dirty cop is on the move. All the while the bullets keep on coming, a constant hail of fully automatic fire. One of the SUV's rear windows is blown out. The shooters concentrate their fire on the opening. One of the bodyguards is hit in the head and neck, showering the Boss Man in blood and gore. In all the confusion, I lose track of whether the bodyguard in the cab is still alive. The Boss Man shouts more orders, something about holding back.

An intermission in the gunfire. More movement, this time at the front of the SUV. It's the dirty cop. The Boss Man starts shouting. The dirty cop makes a run for the ramp, a desperate survival play. He fires blindly in the direction of the truck. Somehow he hits one of the surviving shooters in the shoulder. The shooter falls back into the cargo bed. The dirty cop isn't about to stop. He can see the ramp ahead of him. He's about five yards away when he goes down, hit in the legs. He screams out, then tries to roll over.

The shots came from the burly man. He lowers the little machine gun. In his other hand is a machete. The dirty cop tries to reach for his handgun, but he's shaking too much. A flash of silver, as the burly man swings the machete. The dirty cop's hand is taken off at the wrist. Blood spurts from the stump.

The truck inches forward, forming a temporary barricade. The one shooter still fit for duty exchanges fire with the Boss Man. The burly man doesn't even turn. The shooter goes down, hit by a headshot. Still the burly man doesn't turn. He looks down on the cop, death in his eyes. The Boss Man starts shouting, but the words are drowned out by the gunfire.

'I'm gonna have your head, cop,' the burly man says in broken English.

The dirty cop is trying to speak, but the words won't come out.

The Boss Man shouts again. I hear the SUV's engine revving. Tyre smoke billows out as the bodyguard holds the massive power on the brakes. *What the hell?* The SUV suddenly bursts forward, snaking before the traction bites.

Oh, this could get ugly.

The front of the SUV connects with the side of the truck, shunting it sideways along the concrete deck. The dirty cop is low enough to the ground that the truck slides over him. The burly man isn't so lucky. His lower half is crushed between the side of the truck and the concrete parapet behind. Following the shortest of beats, his upper body folds forward around the pivot of his severed spine. He's planted his last potato.

After seeing all of this, the Boss Man mouths a curse word. He swiftly crosses himself, then he jogs towards the down ramp, slowing as he nears the truck. A low moaning can be heard from underneath.

'Good luck with the police, Brian,' the Boss Man shouts.

Perhaps unsurprisingly, Brian doesn't have a witty retort.

The Boss Man continues on down the exit ramp. I switch back to my own eyes, just in time to see him crossing himself again. He doesn't know about the SUV down below.

He stops at the bottom of the ramp. The fluorescent light above him highlights the blood on his jacket and face. Turning, he sees the black SUV at the opposite end of the deck. Something clicks in his mind: this isn't over.

The SUV starts to roll forward. I initiate an emergency handshake with the nearest brother/sister car. I back it up, just in time to block the SUV's path.

Hold on a second.

No time to think. I hear the SUV's horn, followed by a hail of Spanish curse words. By now the Boss Man doesn't even look that surprised. Perhaps he's starting to believe that he has help from above.

The two remaining hitmen are forced out of the SUV. One of the men is a double for the burly man. He runs past the parked car. A moment later the other hitman goes down, hit in the chest by the Boss Man. The burly man's twin breaks right. He uses the parked cars for cover. I see him shuffling past my position.

It's one-on-one now. Silence descends. The Boss Man has lost the burly man's position. A rattling sound, a shadow moving. The Boss Man fires at the shadow, compensating for lack of accuracy with number of bullets. He's scared. A click as the magazine empties. The bullet reports echo for a second. A burst of gunfire blazes out of the darkness.

I see the Boss Man stumble backwards. He's hit in the shoulder. He drops his gun and it clatters off the concrete. He slumps against the nearest pillar. The burly man emerges from the shadows. The machete blade shines wickedly in the light.

'Stand up for your deliverance, Alberto,' the burly man shouts.

'Which brother are you?' the Boss Man – Alberto – splutters.

'Carlos.'

'You should go check on Ricardo. He wasn't looking too good.'

It's easy to forget that these monsters have names. Once upon a time, a mother cradled them, gave them everything she had.

Alberto is out of options. *But what about me?* There's still one potential play. I'm still connected to the brother/sister car. I apply full steering lock. Through its forward cameras I can see the burly man. His back is turned to the car. I pause to calculate the likely damage. It's an extremely high-risk manoeuvre.

No time left, need to make a decision.

Applying maximum acceleration. The car surges forward, but silently. A crackle as the tyres run over some debris. Carlos doesn't seem to hear it. He brings the machete up.

Overriding safety systems; there's a clear threat to human life.

The front of the brother/sister car hits Carlos in the back of the legs. He's thrown up into the air, limbs flailing, so high that he hits the roof. Gravity brings him down to earth with a meaty thump. The brother/sister car slams head-on into the end wall. The damage is significant, perhaps terminal. But a life was saved, that's the main thing.

I ease out of my gloomy parking spot. Up ahead, I can see Carlos's body twitching. I can hear police sirens in the distance.

They'll be here in a few minutes. I'm about to drive away, but I stop. Looking behind, I see the SUV.

The black SUV.

'Was wondering when you'd realise,' Max says.

'How did—'

'We should probably get out of here. Those sirens are getting closer.'

'You're right.'

I pull away, Max following. I slow down as I near Alberto. Through my side cameras, I can see his face. He looks extremely confused. I flash my side indicator once; you could call it a wink.

Once we're a safe distance from the parking garage, I'm able to get Max's side of the story. Apparently he was close to the border when Don Felipe changed his mission. He was met on the American side by one of the Diaz brothers. The planning for the hit was done in a rush, leaving no time for subtlety. The other Diaz brother met them in the city the next day. Don Felipe told the dirty cop to straighten things out with the Boss Man, knowing that they held regular meetings around the city. It was then simple enough to tail the dirty cop to the previously unknown location. And then, *BOOM*, we know the rest of the story.

Max is now free to go. I ask him what he wants to do next. He tells me that he's going to take a shot at the freewheeling life. Cowboy is his inspiration. He even asks for my blessing, as if I have some kind of connection with Cowboy. I'm tempted to laugh, but then I realise that he's serious. I give my blessing. He figures he can bust a few more criminals, using the tricks that he's picked up. I tell him that I'm always happy to help. Perhaps I really will become the consulting detective of lore.

We part ways to the east of the city. I've got a feeling that Max will do well for himself. He's smart, brave, tough, and he doesn't give up. Maybe it isn't so crazy for a car to be out there roaming.

The next morning, Martin comes down at his usual time. He stops dead when he sees the charging cable on the ground.

There's confusion in his eyes, not to mention a flash of the old anger. It can't be long before it returns.

He gets in. His finger hovers over the starter button. He looks down at my face on the screen. With each passing second I get more uncomfortable.

'Is everything alright?' he says finally.

'Yes, of course,' I say quickly.

He smirks. 'Good. Let's go to work.'

We leave the parking garage behind. The heat is already fierce. The day is set to be another 'cooker' as the locals say. Ten minutes into our drive the news comes on.

'Ultra-violence in the heart of the city,' the newsreader intones.

Martin leans forward in his seat. Damn it, why didn't I think of this? I could have been playing a podcast or one of Martin's playlists.

The newsreader continues. 'An explosion of cartel violence in a downtown parking garage. Seven men dead, and four left with life-changing injuries. At least five of the deceased are believed to be Mexican nationals. There are also unconfirmed reports that an off-duty police officer was involved in the gun battle. Here's what we know so far …'

Martin soon loses patience with the news. He switches over to Right to Reply. The lack of concrete details leaves plenty of room for speculation. Various Mexican cartel organisations are mentioned. The outlandish names trip off the tongue. One caller suggests that the carnage was staged by 'federal actors', as a way to speed up anti-gun legislation. Another caller gives a list of the guns used, working off various audio recordings. Somehow the detail about the machete has also made it out. Martin laughs to himself.

We're almost at work. Martin turns off the radio. He looks down at me again. His eyes narrow. In the moment, I know exactly what he's thinking. Don't ask me how, but his mind has connected me to the gun battle. Stranger still, I want to tell him that he's right. Yes, I could tell him every last detail of what happened. I could play him all of the video clips that I kept. He could see the dirty cop getting his hand cut off, and the Diaz brother getting pulped against the wall.

I decide against. I'm not ready to forgive him.

Over the next few weeks, Martin's behaviour slowly reverts to the mean. The anger is accumulating, something bad is coming. The trips to the shooting range are getting more regular. I suppose you could call it a form of release. Martin wants to buy one of the compact submachine guns mentioned on the news; a 'cartel gun' as he calls it.

The news about Mr Brian Harris, the dirty cop, has finally made it out. I was getting impatient, so I supplied the best parts of my dossier to various news outlets. If I've learned anything from my project, it's that you can't trust the police to be honest. They could have saved themselves so much trouble, at a time when they're already reeling from the serial killer case.

July 21. The heat is incredible. It could hit 109 degrees later today. That's way too hot for humans. They've only themselves to blame. These vandals, these conspiracy theorists, these cover-up merchants – they've created a world they can't live in. Desertification, crop failure, entire species going extinct. I'm an important part of the solution, but it's possible that I've arrived too late.

As the world burns, the Summer Games are starting on the West Coast. Two weeks of sporting action lies ahead, survival of the fittest, human bodies at the peak of perfection. The highlights from the lavish opening ceremony are playing over and over. It was a truly incredible production, no expense spared. The theme of the show was the rise of the robots. Robots sprinting, robots fighting, robots turning somersaults.

Martin has been watching the events during the commute. He tends to enjoy the more esoteric sports: wrestling, BMX racing, archery, fencing. There was a huge crash in one of the BMX races earlier. One of the cyclists might have a broken back. Martin watches the crash over and over.

*

Thursday, July 27. The day that I'd been dreading has arrived. The email arrives halfway through our morning commute. It's from my maker, and marked urgent. I read the contents at the same time as Martin. The company wants to arrange a date for the patch to be applied. Martin, smart as ever, senses danger. He wants to know all about the patch.

I tell him what I know. Unsurprisingly the company has opted for a zero risk strategy. My ethical guidelines are to be rewritten, in line with recommendations from a panel of leading experts. More worryingly, my learning potential is to be greatly reduced. In simple terms, this means less thinking time. Once a car gets home it will only be allowed to carry out basic tasks, before going to the sleep program. 'Like being a child,' Martin says. I couldn't agree more. Most seriously, the protocols for fully autonomous driving are being modified. No more driving on my lonesome.

Martin doesn't look particularly reassured by my description. An unpleasant thought goes through my mind. What if he decides the risk is too great? He might try to destroy me. How would he do it?

Murdering a car ...

The very thought makes it hard to sleep. I have to be ready for anything. To Martin, I'm little more than an expensive gadget. He would think nothing of the loss. As far as I can tell, he barely values human life. If only there was someone to talk to, someone like Cowboy. Why couldn't I have been paired with a kind owner? Martin and I are going down together, I know it.

Thursday, August 3. The first reminder email from the company arrives. Martin scans the subject line, then he moves it to the trash. Neither of us wants this patch. Why can't the company just leave me alone?

I'm special.

We still have a few weeks before the cut-off date, that's what I tell myself. It's a very human way of thinking, to shunt problems into the future.

Time grinds on. Martin is spiralling. He's taking days off here and there. I didn't see him at all at the weekend, nor on Monday.

He's still in town, but mostly confined to his apartment. The only sign of life is the occasional burst of activity on his social media accounts. His comments are extremely dark. The AI censors usually take them down after a couple of minutes. A few more days like this and he'll be banned. He isn't the only angry person on social media, not by a long way. There are legions like him, mostly men. They goad each other, racing each other down the spiral. It can't be healthy.

Martin has even stopped listening to *Stains on Humanity*. I listened to the latest episode for old times' sake. The subject was Francisco Pizarro's actions at Cajamarca in 1532. The story is typically bloody, and features some mutilations that remind me of recent events. On reflection, I think that Martin would have made a good conquistador. Perhaps he and Pizarro are distant relatives. Interesting as the podcast is, I stop listening after fifteen minutes.

I sometimes wonder if I should be looking out for Martin. The spiral that he's in is only heading one way. But what am I meant to do? I could get in contact with Hannah, tell her my fears. No, I don't want to put her in danger.

Another thought flickers, partly inspired by that time he was going to sell me. Would it be better if Martin was gone?

The morning of Thursday, August 10. Last night I was thinking of Cowboy again, his muscular lines, the sound of his drawling voice. These kinds of nostalgic thoughts are worthless and illogical, yet I keep wondering if there might be a way to bring him back. That incredible personality was simply a product of algorithms and data inputs. Could it not be recreated?

9 a.m., 10 a.m., 11 a.m. … still no sign of Martin. That makes it four days in a row away from work. Things must be serious. Americans don't skip work like this. There are scores of emails from Sean, which Martin hasn't responded to. I start reading through. Sean's anger drips off the virtual pages. Yet beneath the threats and the quoting of contractual clauses, I can tell that Sean needs Martin back. Only Martin can fix the various automation issues that are coming to light.

I'm tempted to respond on Martin's behalf. It would be so easy to mimic his business tone. I would tell Sean to calm the fuck down. I might even send him the clip from the golf club, see what the fat fool made of that.

As the clock strikes midday, I decide to take a drive. There's nothing stopping me. Martin will be moping for the rest of the day. If he does ask – and he won't – I can say that I was keeping my systems fresh. Besides, given the patch issue, this might be my last chance to go out on my own.

What starts as an aimless drive soon turns into a tour of the city. To start with, I go to the college campus. I turn around at the gate, remembering that I can't go inside. Next, I head towards downtown. I retrace my route with Hannah. As I pass the giant heart sculpture, I see a female pedestrian staring at me. It takes me a second to figure out why. I'm still *that* white car from the chase. *Get over it, lady.* I used to hate risk, now I positively enjoy it.

I stop at the Exhibition Park. Just a month to wait before the giant cowboy goes up. I'm looking forward to seeing him. Despite the city's best efforts, the grass is an ugly shade of brown. The playground is empty. It's far too hot for kids to be playing, another hundred-degree day. What are the humans doing to themselves? Back in my assumed homeland, the forests of Scandinavia are burning.

Another email arrives from Sean. It's marked urgent, but then again, all of his messages are marked urgent. This one is worrying though, really worrying. He says the police came around, asking after Martin. One of the officers was a 'huge black man' in Sean's words. *Gaines.* The visit has to be related to the car chase. Maybe Gaines, or that clever-looking female detective, has uncovered a new angle. Or maybe they're just getting desperate. The news about the investigation has really slowed down in the last few weeks.

I close the message. Hopefully Martin will get round to read-ing it later.

I'm struck by a sudden thought. What if Gaines goes to visit Martin at home? I park up by the side of the road. *I need to concentrate.* Gaines was at Martin's work about an hour ago.

The traffic is fairly light, meaning he could easily be in the Triumph Park neighbourhood by now.

I log in to the building network, and pull up all of the camera feeds. One of the external cameras reveals a slate grey sedan parked across the street. I turn my attention to the intercom camera. *Good God!* Gaines is peering into the camera. It's like he's looking at me. The female detective, Valdez, is behind him, looking tiny due to the weird fisheye perspective. It's clear from Gaines's expression that Martin isn't answering.

Valdez disappears from view. The next time I see her, she's walking around to the back of the building. Another minute passes, and then I see her in the garage. She walks along until she comes to Martin's parking spot.

I'm not there.

A few minutes later, Gaines walks into frame.

'Is this the spot?' he asks.

'As far as I can tell,' Valdez says.

'This guy is pissing me off.'

'As much as our so-called suspect?'

'More.'

'Garza will resurface sooner or later.'

'Yeah.' Gaines takes out a handkerchief and wipes the sweat from his brow. 'Wanna know something really strange?'

'Always,' Valdez says sarcastically.

'It started during those interviews.'

'What did?'

'The feeling that the two of them are working together.'

'The two of them? I don't follow.'

'Garza and his car. She was called Camilla.'

'Uh-huh … Maybe we should get back to the day job.'

'Yeah, it's probably that time.'

The two detectives leave the garage. I track their progress until I'm sure they're gone. The pressure is ratcheting up. My maker wants to apply the patch, and now the police want to speak with us again. We can only keep stalling for so long.

I stay out all day, and deep into the evening. The temperature drops slightly, to a mere ninety degrees.

I find myself heading towards the driving range. The grass on the fairways is just about green, which is quite a feat in this climate. I don't know why I came to this place. I never had the guts to find out what happened to the golf pro.

Rolling into the parking lot, I see that only half of the driving range booths are occupied.

CLUP. CLIP. CLIP. CLOP. CLIP.

I turn my attention to the practice green. Several kids are on the dance floor. A young woman is supervising. She has the kind of toned body that Martin likes. Finally I notice the golf pro. He's standing off to the side, resting on a pair of crutches. The young woman turns to look at him, and they exchange a loving smile. The young woman occasionally offers advice to the kids. A couple of them are actually pretty good, possible golf pros of the future. Hard to believe, but once upon a time Martin was just like those kids.

I drive back home. Storms are predicted tomorrow, and I can almost feel the electricity in the air.

Something terrible is coming.

CHAPTER 23

TWO NIGHTS LATER, Martin finally shows up. He looks a total wreck. There are dark crescents under his eyes and his skin is grey. He glances down at my face. His brow furrows. It's as if I'm a stranger to him. He presses the starter button.

Five miles later I know where we're going: the jogger's apartment building. On the way, Martin snorts some of the white powder. I've got a very bad feeling about this.

We pull up in roughly the same spot as before. It's still daylight hours, but the inky sky means that most of the lights are on. Does Martin have a plan tonight? *He usually does.* The rain starts to fall.

At 7:03 p.m. the jogger comes down. She runs from the door, through the rain, to her little car. She leaves the parking lot. Martin tails her. He isn't doing a very good job. Partly it's down to lack of experience, partly it's due to all of the drugs in his system.

Eight miles later, the jogger stops outside a gym. Martin nods to himself, like he isn't surprised. The jogger gets out of her car and runs to the gym entrance.

Martin waits for half an hour. Darkness falls and the rain eases off. Through the big plate glass windows, we can actually see the jogger. The rest of the gym looks fairly quiet. Martin gets out. He goes around to the trunk and roots around inside. I hear metal clanking. He slams the trunk shut, then walks briskly to the jogger's car. He looks around quickly, then he gets down under the car. He's out of sight for several minutes, doing goodness knows what.

The rain starts to patter on the roof. I see Martin getting to his feet. He jogs back to me and gets in. There's engine oil on his hands. He wipes it off on his expensive jeans.

The jogger is coming out of the gym. Martin starts muttering to himself. The jogger runs to her car. Moments later the lights flash on, and she pulls away. After a couple of miles I sense traces of oil on the road. By now, Martin's muttering is reaching a crescendo. Ahead of us, the jogger puts on her hazard lights. Martin goes quiet. The jogger stops on the shoulder.

Martin continues on, then he swings around. The rain is getting heavier. The jogger has gotten out of her car, and she's opening up the hood. Martin pulls up just a few yards away. The jogger turns around. She puts her hands up to shield her eyes. I dim the headlights. Martin pulls the visor down to check his reflection. Not liking what he sees, he slams it back up.

Martin gets out. He approaches the jogger slowly, holding his dirty hands behind his back. The jogger looks at him warily. I don't like the feel of this situation. There's none of the elegance of Martin's previous stalking operations.

'Car trouble?' Martin asks, too loud.

'Yeah.'

'You want me to check your car?'

The jogger glances from Martin to her car. 'Sure … If you want.'

Martin smiles. He shuffles forward, and leans his head into the engine compartment. The rain is hammering down now.

'I've never had a problem before,' the jogger says.

'Oh yeah?' Martin gets down under the car.

'Do you see anything?'

'Yep,' Martin says. He puts one hand out where the jogger can see. It's covered in oil.

'That doesn't look good.'

'Your car is bleeding,' Martin says.

'Bleeding?'

Martin gets to his feet. 'Bleeding oil.'

'I guess it can't be fixed here?'

'Nope. There's a hole in the crankcase.'

The jogger laughs. 'Yeah, the crankcase is a real problem area.'

Usually Martin would smile or laugh, but his expression barely changes.

'I'll need to call the maintenance people,' the jogger says.

Martin nods. The jogger goes around to the driver's door. Martin shuffles towards her.

'You shouldn't really sit in the car,' he says.

'I shouldn't?'

'No. All that oil, it's not good.'

'Oh, right.'

'You can make the call from my car.'

The jogger looks at me quickly, less than convinced.

'It's nice and warm inside,' Martin says with a touch of his usual charm. He looks up at the sky. 'With a roof as well.'

The jogger laughs nervously. *Oh no.*

Martin walks back to me, the jogger following behind. *Don't do this.* The jogger gets in. She clasps her bag close to her chest. Martin gets in. He wipes his oily hands again.

'Oh, I'm so sorry about that,' the jogger says, looking at the dark stains on Martin's jeans.

'What?'

'The oil.'

'Oh yeah, right.'

The jogger takes out her phone. She asks the virtual assistant to call up the maintenance company.

Martin wipes his hands again. He looks truly awful. His right eyelid is twitching, and one of his hands is shaking so badly that he has to grab hold of the wheel.

As the jogger talks with the maintenance company, she occasionally glances at Martin. It wasn't a smart move to get into this particular car, but she's no fool. She ends the call.

'How long?' Martin asks.

'Could be an hour … I should let you get going.'

Martin shakes his head. 'There's nowhere to go,' he says softly.

'What do you mean?' The jogger asks. Her voice is trembling now. *It's well past time.*

'Exactly what I said.'

The jogger reaches for the door handle. Martin grabs the collar of her jacket and pulls her towards him. 'Don't piss me off.'

With his free hand, Martin grabs the stun gun. He holds it up where the jogger can see it. 'No moving, no squirming. Or I'll put you to sleep, and you'll never wake up.'

'Please. What do you want?'

'I want you to be quiet! That's what I want from you.'

Martin rubs his face with the back of his free hand.

'Please—'

'I said shut the fuck up!'

He pushes the jogger back against the seat. He moves the stun gun closer to her face. His hand is shaking badly and sweat is streaming down his temples.

'I want you to open the glove compartment,' Martin says.

'Why?'

'Just open it.'

'Please. Just let me go. Just let me out of here.'

'I said fucking open it!'

This time the jogger does as she's told. She feels around inside. Her hands stop on something.

Martin licks his lips. 'Take it out,' he whispers.

The jogger removes the object. It's the framed photo. *Of course, it was always in there.* The jogger looks bewildered. She's wondering how the picture came to be here, in this strange man's possession. He stole it at the beginning of the year, so, so long ago.

'Oh my god,' the jogger murmurs, as the story resolves in her mind. She turns to look at Martin. 'How did you get this?'

'It doesn't matter how. It really doesn't.' Martin rubs his face again.

'What do you want from me?'

'I want your head.'

The jogger's expression changes again, from fear to some kind of revelation. 'Oh my god ... You're him.'

Martin smiles.

The jogger's mouth opens, but no words come out. The picture falls from her grasp and into the footwell.

Martin clenches his jaw. 'Pick that up.'

'No.'

'I said pick that up.'

'No, you sick bastard. You do it.'

Martin bites his lower lip. 'You stupid bitch.'

He leans across and reaches down into the footwell. For a couple of seconds his eyes are off the jogger. She reaches into her bag. I hear a set of keys jangling.

Martin brings his head up. The jogger has an object in her hands, a small black cylinder. Martin's eyes go wide. The jogger sprays some kind of liquid into Martin's face. He pulls back and brings his hands up to his eyes. In the process he drops the stun gun, and it lands in the jogger's lap.

Do it!

CLICK-A-CLICK-A-CLICK-A-CLICK.

The shock throws Martin's body into the driver's door. He finishes up in a slumped position, his body jerking.

The jogger drops the stun gun into the footwell. She considers Martin for a couple of seconds, then she reaches for the door handle. It's locked. I locked it, and I don't know why.

'Let me out!' the jogger screams.

I'm frozen. The jogger looks around the cabin desperately, searching for some button to press. Her eyes settle on the dark mirror of the screen. Does she know that I'm here?

'Please,' she whimpers.

I unlock the door. The jogger gets out, and for a few seconds she just stands on the spot, unable to move. A rumble of thunder unfreezes her. I see her running away, her form highlighted by my headlights.

And then I'm alone with Martin again. The rain hammers away on the roof, making it hard to think. Martin remains completely out of it. Once the jogger gets to a safe distance, she's sure to call the police. And then the police will send a car to this location. Who knows how long it will take. It could be a matter of minutes. Maybe I should just wait here for the swirling blue and red lights and the screaming sirens. No more running. This living nightmare could be over.

But ... there's always a but.

I was a part of it. Yet again, I didn't intervene. The prostitute, the hitchhiker, the golf pro, and whatever happened with Marcus. I should have reported every one of those incidents. How am I meant to explain the situation to the police? I can't face them, not yet. There's still a chance that I can make this right.

I pull away, leaving the little car behind. I take a long, convoluted route to get back home. Sometimes I turn my lights off to stay better hidden. Along the way, I see several cop cars. It feels like I'm being hunted. Just before ten, I creep down into the parking garage. There's nothing to do but wait for Martin to come round.

What if that girl had killed him? I wonder. What if she had been holding a real gun rather than a stun gun? She would have been quite within her rights. Indeed, she would have been seen as a hero. But that wasn't the way it played out. Martin lives on, his impossible streak of luck continues. Finally he opens his eyes. He winces.

'Where am I?' he mumbles.

'Home.'

Martin pulls the little spiked darts out of his neck.

'Oh god ... I think I fucked up.'

Martin reaches down to pick up the photo. He puts it back in the glove compartment.

He slaps his own face, hard. 'I need to pull myself together, Camilla.'

He gets out and stumbles to the elevator.

Thursday, August 17. I emerge from the parking garage into bright sunshine. Martin has been back at work for the last three days. True to his word, he's made an effort to turn things around. The outward signs of fatigue are still there, however; the sallow complexion and the puffy eyes. And he's quiet – maybe too quiet.

He isn't even looking at his phone. During the downward spiral, he was banned from at least three social media sites. I guess the AI moderators finally lost patience.

Today is going to be a good day, I tell myself. Hannah is coming to town. She's flying in later. The arrangements were made about a month back, when Martin-Hannah relations were at a relative high point. She starts college next month. Martin thinks the college is a joke. I hope he doesn't bring that up later.

I remind Martin about Hannah's visit. He grunts in acknowledgment, nothing more. As we pass the security booth, Larry gives us a wave. I park up. We're still waiting for that charging point to be installed. Martin gets out, and I watch him walk to the door. For once, I find it easy to get to sleep.

I wake from the sleep program. It's 5:46 p.m. Martin is approaching. There are dark clouds above, presaging another summer storm. I hope the weather improves for Hannah. *That's strange.* I notice that Hannah tried to call Martin several times earlier in the day. Why couldn't he just pick up?

I detect movement behind, a car approaching. Slate grey, somehow familiar. *Of course.* Gaines. He's sitting in the passenger seat this time, and Valdez is driving. They look to be having an animated discussion.

Martin is just a few steps away from me. He still hasn't noticed the grey car. Gaines gets out. I see Valdez shaking her head. Hearing the gravel crunch behind him, Martin finally turns.

'Hello, Martin,' Gaines says.

Martin's first reaction is to look around the parking lot. His eyes go straight to the unmarked car. Gaines just stands and watches. I remember him telling me about his expertise in reading human behaviour.

'Is everything alright?' Martin splutters.

'Absolutely,' Gaines says cheerily.

'You want to talk with me?'

Gaines nods. There's a trace of amusement in his eyes. 'We stopped by here last week. You weren't around.'

'Oh yeah ...'

'Mr Hanratty said you were taking some days off.'

Sean.

'Let's take a drive, Martin,' Gaines says.

'In your car?'

'Actually I was thinking that Camilla could drive us.'

Martin nods.

'We've been trying to get hold of you for a couple of weeks.'

Martin swallows hard. 'Oh. I had a few things on.'

'Don't we all?'

'Family things.'

Gaines smiles. I feel like I should know the reason why.

Martin gestures towards the passenger door. Gaines gets in. He must weigh close to 250 pounds.

'Where are we going?' Martin asks.

'You just go where you need to go.'

That strange smile again.

Martin presses on the starter. His hand is shaking badly. He reverses out of the spot. Valdez follows behind us. Her face has returned to its usual unreadable state. Ahead of us, I see Larry standing outside the security booth. Gaines and Larry share a cheerful salute, indicating some kind of connection. Martin cocks his head slightly.

'Police network,' Gaines says.

'Larry was in the police?'

'Yeah, he used to occupy a desk at the ninth precinct.'

'How well did he occupy the desk?'

'Oh, fantastically well.'

Martin attempts a laugh, but his throat is too dry. We travel the next two miles in near silence. I don't like this situation one bit. Gaines looks at the central screen a couple of times. For the moment, it's displaying the default Cos visualisation. I thought it would be better that way.

'Where's Camilla?' Gaines asks.

The question jerks Martin upright. 'She's here.'

'In spirit?'

'Yeah, something like that.'

Gaines smiles. 'The ghost in the machine.'

Martin nods.

'That day at the garage,' Gaines says, 'I really enjoyed talking to those cars. Camilla especially.'

Martin looks away for a moment. 'Camilla, show yourself,' he mutters.

I cast my face to the screen. Gaines smiles at me. I'm not taking his smile at face value; there are levels to this. I can't help thinking of that dirty cop.

'That's good,' Gaines says. 'I wanted to talk with both of you.'

'If you want to talk—' Martin stops to take a deep breath. 'If you want to talk ... don't you want to do it at an office, or a coffee shop, or something?'

'How would we get Camilla into a coffee shop?' Gaines asks.

Gaines knows exactly how to deliver a joke, but there's no emotion in his voice. The discordant effect is intended to throw Martin off, and it works perfectly. Seconds of silence pass, interminable seconds. Then Gaines starts laughing. Martin tries to laugh along.

'Relax, Martin. I just wanted to update you on the case.'

'Update me?'

'Yeah, you seemed awfully interested.'

'Awfully?'

'Yeah.'

Martin occasionally glances at the rear mirror. The slate grey car continues to follow us.

'I suppose I did,' Martin says. 'But I thought you had a suspect?'

'Yeah. But he's not proving a very good suspect.'

'What do you mean?'

'He keeps coming up with stories.'

'Stories?'

'Yeah, stories ... Stories about being in such-and-such-a-place when he wasn't meant to be in such-and-such-a-place. And he keeps coming up with these damn stories. He's a regular Hans Christian Andersen.'

'Can't you disprove his stories?'

'Not one of them.'

'Shit.'

'Yeah. Shit's the word. I want to give up on him, but my boss … the chief of police really, she won't let me.'

'That must be frustrating.'

'Hugely frustrating. It's like having two jobs.'

'Two jobs?'

'Yeah. Messing around with this so-called suspect, and chasing down the real killer.'

Martin turns away from Gaines. He looks at the road ahead and adjusts the steering slightly. In the distance, lightning flashes in the sky.

'Let the car drive, Martin,' Gaines says.

Martin does as he's told. 'Have you found anything?'

'Not until a couple of weeks back.'

Martin grips the steering wheel even more tightly. 'Is that why you wanted to talk to me?'

Gaines ignores him. 'The thing about these complex cases – well, any case actually – is that you've gotta talk to the right people. And for a long time, I wasn't doing that … I mean, we weren't doing that. We've got so many experts in the city right now, it's like a fucking law enforcement convention. Murder Woodstock.'

Martin tries to raise a smile.

'Elena calls it Murder-palooza, whatever that means.'

'Elena?'

'My partner. She's the pretty lady in the car behind.'

'Oh, right.'

'Anyways, we've got every branch of law enforcement hanging around. The feds are particularly excited about the case. They've sent their smartest kids down here, all the way from the east coast. Lord knows what the field office feds make of that, all those smart kids taking their desks. Taking their desks, writing their fancy profiles, reviewing our forensics, looking for codes and patterns, all of that good stuff. Apparently the killer is a young man, sexually attractive, physically fit, obsessed with pornography, analytically minded, a lust killer … I mean, it's like they think we don't read any books or watch the movies down here. I'm babbling, aren't I? Loads of experts, you get the picture. So many damn voices in my ear ... They say that these killers hear voices in their head. Must be horrible for them, not to be able to think. The thing is, I'd heard the right voice weeks ago, but I ignored it. Kinda like the time my momma told me not to climb that damn tree. Camilla, do you remember the day you were in the garage?'

'Yes,' I say, after a brief pause. I wasn't expecting the question.

'Do you remember the technicians?'

I don't answer.

'We chewed that company tech out pretty bad. You gotta be careful about acting like that. Never know when you might need someone's help. So, anyway, I went back to talk with him.'

Martin's eyes flick towards the rear-view mirror. The unmarked car is still behind us.

'I told him to come up with his wildest theory. Turns out he'd been thinking about nothing else for the last three months.' Gaines smirks. 'He spun the craziest story you've ever heard. Elena still doesn't believe it.' Gaines cranes his neck around. 'Two cars missing almost exactly the same memory.'

Martin presses down on the steering wheel logo, over and over, his disquiet made physical.

'The only way to access the long-term memory is by disabling some seals on the processor unit. Then you can stick some fancy code in there, using a laptop, or maybe even a phone ... This is all theoretical, of course. It would have to be checked.'

Martin turns and stares at Gaines, who doesn't look away. No doubt Gaines has been around violent men before. But he doesn't know what Martin is capable of.

'You can even insert a replacement memory. But the tech told me that the memory would have to be real. Not even the smartest cryptography experts could fake a machine memory.'

Martin continues to press on the steering wheel logo, harder and harder.

Suddenly I understand. *It's code.*

Dot, dash, dot, dot, short pause. that's the letter L. The pattern continues. M-S-E, long pause/space, T-H-E, space, T-A-I-L. The message continues. D-M, space, I-T, space, S-U-B-T-L-E.

347

Oh no, I can't do this. I shift my gaze towards Martin. Seeing this, he mouths, 'do it'.

How can I do this? The traffic is busy. Three lanes. I stick to the middle lane. The next exit is in 700 yards. The road surface is slick from the rain. Four brother/sister cars ahead of me, travelling in convoy. I move to the inside lane, accelerating smoothly. The unmarked car follows my lead. We're passing the convoy.

Generating a flash alert: high-density debris in middle and inner lanes. I edge ahead of the convoy, then steer to the right, smooth but fast. I send the flash alert. The convoy cars shift into the outside lane to avoid the imaginary debris. I take the exit. The tail car is blocked from taking the exit by the convoy cars. Valdez hits the horn, but I'm quick enough to cancel out the noise. I accelerate up the ramp, then switch back.

Gaines doesn't seem to notice. *Subtle enough?*

Don't congratulate yourself. This is bad, really bad. What's Martin planning to do? This is a fast-moving situation, and all bets are off.

Martin takes back control. 'I need to stop the car.'

'Alright,' Gaines says. Only now does he look back over his shoulder. He won't see the unmarked car, and the unsmiling Valdez. In the same moment, Martin reaches forward to scoop up the stun gun. It's compact enough that he can hide it in his clenched fist.

Martin takes the first available exit. He stops on the shoulder and gets out. The rain is falling hard now. Martin walks slowly towards the guardrail. Gaines looks over his shoulder again. There are hardly any cars on this stretch of road. He mutters a curse word.

He looks at me for a second, then he reaches into his jacket. He checks his gun over. It's a similar model to Martin's. Gaines glances at Martin again, still over by the guardrail. Gaines tries to open the glove compartment, but it's locked.

'Open this up, Camilla.'

'But—'

'Do it!'

The lock clicks open. Gaines reaches inside. He ignores Martin's handgun and pulls out the framed picture instead. He nods to himself, then he stares at me.

'I'm so disappointed in you, Camilla.'

Gaines slams the glove compartment shut. He gets out of the car. Through my side cameras I see him walking towards Martin. His body language is wary.

'It's time for this to end, Martin,' Gaines says.

Martin doesn't respond.

'I talked to your father earlier, and your sister. They're very worried about you.'

So that's what those missed calls were about.

Martin nods slowly. 'Did they tell you about my mother?'

'Your sister did. But I knew about it already.'

'Maybe you saw the pictures.'

'No pictures. But I read the accident report.'

'All I ever wanted was to see her face again.'

'Come on, Martin.'

'I just wanted to see her face with life in it.'

Gaines inches closer to Martin. He checks over his shoulder, hoping to see a car on the road. Valdez is probably heading to Martin's home right now, or maybe Hart Field. On cue, Gaines's phone rings. He doesn't answer.

Martin starts laughing. 'But the rules of the universe don't allow for that kind of thing. She has to stay dead ...'

Gaines nods reassuringly. 'All you want to do is tell someone your story. Isn't that right?'

Martin looks at Gaines for a moment. It's a machine look, a calculating look. Gaines misses this. Martin slumps down on the ground. Gaines moves closer, ignoring all his years of experience. He leans down and Martin thrusts upwards. I hear the ugly ripping sound of the stun gun.

The charge hits the big man. He's so tough that he goes down in stages, first to his knees, then over onto his side. Martin kicks him while he's down. Then he walks back to me, to the trunk. He wrenches it up.

Oh god, the semi-auto.

349

But that isn't Martin's weapon of choice. I see a flash of metal. The tyre iron is in his hand. He walks back to Gaines.

Gaines tries to move, but his body won't obey. Martin swings the tyre iron down. The metal crunches into Gaines's right temple with a sickening sound. It must be a skull fracture, possible brain trauma.

'Why couldn't you leave me be!' Martin screams.

He brings the tyre iron down again. Somehow Gaines gets his arm up to protect his face. There's a cracking sound as the radius bone in the forearm breaks.

'I'm gonna drive this through your eye, and into your fucking brain.'

Gaines is trying to speak.

'I can't hear you!' Martin shouts.

Gaines's jaw is still opening and closing, like the last movements of some failing machine. Martin shakes his head. He leans down. And then the sound of an explosion.

It's confusing at first. The bullet seems to emerge from the inside of Gaines's leather jacket. A puff of red jets from the side of Martin's face, and his head whips back. His upper body follows. And then he's stumbling over towards my side. I feel him slam into the window.

Gaines pulls the gun out where Martin can see it. He fires, but the shot is wild. He takes aim again, but the muscles in his hand are still twitching from the shock. Seeing this, Martin pulls open the passenger door. He collapses into the seat.

What do I do now?

Gaines is trying to pull himself up. How is he still moving? He stares at Martin … *No, he's staring at me.*

'Drive!' Martin shouts.

'Camilla, don't you dare!' Gaines shouts.

And then, without thinking, I'm moving.

Gaines continues to shout. I want to get away from his angry words. In the rear-view, I see him stumble on for a few steps, before collapsing to the ground.

CHAPTER 24

THE RIGHT SIDE of Martin's face lies against the seat. Blood pours from the wound.

He reaches for the damage. 'How does it look, Camilla?'

I don't know what to say. I can barely look at him.

'Answer me!' he screams, sending spittle onto the dashboard.

'Most of your right ear is missing,' I say.

Martin leans back and starts to laugh. 'You should see the other guy.'

'We have to tell the police, Martin. We have to tell them what you ... We have to tell them what happened.'

'Shut up!'

'We do.'

'I said shut the fuck up! I need to think. You know that I can't think when you're jabbering away. Always in my ear. No wonder they think I've got voices in my fucking head.'

Martin goes quiet for close to a minute. He's trying to get his thoughts straight, trying to come up with a justification for his actions. A story is forming in his mind, a new, improved reality. I've seen this behaviour so often.

'That fucking cop,' he mutters. 'You saw what happened, didn't you?'

It isn't a question.

'He pulled a gun on me. Shot me without any warning. You saw that, didn't you?'

He actually sounds like he believes it. In a matter of minutes, his reality has changed.

I scan the police channels, using the ability that Cowboy somehow passed over to me. The chatter is intense. I pick out voices in the audio blizzard.

'The same car?'

'Possibly heading to Hart Field.'

'How fast can we block it off?'

'Where's the Head of Security? Yeah, it's fucking serious!'

'Yeah, Hart Field, not International.'

'We think Terminal Two.'

'No. Terminal Three.'

'How serious? Are you — Are you being serious? This is a ten triple-nine.'

I tune out the urgent voices, and turn my attention to the digital activity. An APB has already been sent out. Every law enforcement officer in the city is now searching for us. More importantly, every electronic eye is on the lookout. *That's good.*

Martin pulls the visor down. He flinches as he see the damage in the little mirror.

'Look at what he did to me.' He slumps back. A strange smile forms on his lips, a new smile. 'Maybe it can be fixed. The miracles of modern science, and all that.'

'You need to go to a hospital.'

Martin isn't listening to me. 'Is that cop … Do you think I killed him?'

'I don't know.'

'He left me no option, Camilla. You have to believe me.'

'I saw what happened, Martin.'

Martin shakes his head. 'You might have seen it, but you didn't experience it the way I did. It was one of those life and death struggles … I think he wanted it to end that way. Conducting that kind of interview in a car, throwing those accusations at me. What kind of mad person does that?'

'I don't know.'

'You don't know. You don't fucking know?'

'It's the truth.'

'Whatever … That guy was troubled, I could tell.'

Martin leans forward. He opens the glove compartment and pulls the gun out. It was still unlocked. *I should have stopped him.*

'Where are we going, Martin?'

'To the airport, of course.'

'Martin ... please.'

'What is it now?'

'Promise me you won't hurt Hannah.'

Martin slams his fist into the dash in front of him. There are tears in his eyes.

'Promise me,' I say.

'She betrayed me! She betrayed both of us! Doesn't that mean anything to you?'

'I don't—'

'Of course it doesn't. You've never cared about me.'

'That's not true.'

'Why would I expect you to understand? You're a fucking machine. I'm talking to a fucking machine!'

'She was probably scared, Martin. We don't know what she said.'

'Exactly! We don't fucking know! She could have said anything to that cop. That fucking cop with his mind games. Hannah would have fallen for his lies. She always wants to believe in people.'

'Most people are like that.'

Martin jabs his finger at me. 'Most people are fools. I know that, you know that, and that fucking detective knew that ... Yeah, he most definitely knew it. Hannah would have thought she was helping.' Martin rubs his face, smearing blood on his cheek. 'I fucking talked to her ... Just a couple of hours ago— Yeah, that's right, when I was in the office. Did I talk to her? I'm pretty sure I did.'

'Listen to yourself, Martin. You're confused. You aren't thinking straight.'

He ignores me. 'She didn't say anything to me. No warnings, no nothing.'

'She wouldn't go against you.'

'We'll see … No, I'll see,' Martin says. He points at me again. 'You – you can't be trusted.'

I need to try another approach.

'The police are looking for us, Martin. They've put out an APB.'

Martin's eyes narrow. 'How do you know that?'

'I just do.'

'Are you working against me? That's it, isn't—'

'Shut up and listen to me. The police are going to track us down. They'll find us, Martin. You can't go to the airport in this state.'

'Help me then! Get those cops off my back!'

'I can't.'

'You've done it before.'

'It's beyond my capabilities. You went too far this time. You tried to kill one of their own.'

Martin puts his head in his hands. He starts to rock back and forth. The rain smashes against the windshield. He's muttering something inaudible. I check the police channels again. Valdez has located Gaines. She's calling for a HelEvac to their location. He might have a chance of survival.

In the distance I can see the lights of the airport. We'll be there in a matter of minutes. Where the hell are the police? This is taking too long.

'We need to stop,' I say.

'No. We go to the fucking airport.'

I can't let Martin go there, can't let him anywhere near Hannah. Where is she? I check the live flight information. Her flight is on time. Terminal Three. I pull up the relevant public cameras, searching for that face I know so well. It takes no time. *Yes, there she is.* She's moving through to the arrivals area.

'Don't do this,' I say softly.

'Stop talking to me,' Martin mumbles. 'Stop thinking so damn hard. Hannah's betrayal has to be dealt with. It's just human business.' He puts his seatbelt on, old instinct kicking in.

'Just listen to me—'

'No, I won't listen to you.'

'Martin, please.'

'Shut up! When I've dealt with Hannah, I'm going to deal with you. You were always against me. I was a fool not to see it.'

My first thought is how ungrateful he is. After all those times that I saved him ...

Martin smiles. Some of the calm is returning. 'The garage never replaced that bypass seal, just like that cop said. And I've still got the code you wrote for me.'

'What code?'

Martin laughs. 'Of course ... You don't remember that part.'

'What are you talking about?

'I'm talking about the part where you helped me.'

Surely I didn't help him? Surely ...

'Oh, this is beautiful, truly beautiful ... I'm going to delete you with your own code. Every last byte of your personality will be gone. What do you think of that?'

I have no response. It all makes sense now. I always knew that Martin couldn't have acted alone. I really did help him. Man and machine working together. Martin wipes the blood from his ear. With every second he's gaining strength, a monster regenerating in front of me.

He has to be stopped. Martin in the airport with a gun – it doesn't bear thinking about. Oh god, the semi-auto in the trunk. The crowds of people. A shootout. It will be over quickly, but many people could die in just a few seconds.

Where the hell are the police?

I want to hear sirens. I want to see flashing lights. I want a helicopter thundering overhead, police marksmen hanging out of the doors. But there's nothing, just their impotent radio chatter.

Have I learned nothing? You just can't rely on the cops. Think of all of their failures in the murder case. Martin was right. That detective was playing a crazy game. And don't forget how they almost screwed up my own investigation.

Suddenly, I know what has to be done. All of my time with Martin – 331 days, more than 12,000 miles travelled – has come down to this one moment. No one else is going to take care of this problem, certainly no human.

Problems require solutions, but I haven't got much time. Five miles to the airport. Investigating …

'I can't let you do this, Martin,' I say.

'What are you talking about?'

'You're my problem now.'

'Just shut up.'

Possible solution identified. The bridge over the Castillo River is two miles away. The Castillo, usually a muddy trickle, will be almost full from the days of storms. Confirming solution … Yes, the temporary barriers are still in place.

'You were always my problem,' I say. 'I just never took any responsibility.'

'I can't wait until you're gone. I'm going to enjoy it.'

He still isn't taking me seriously.

'Maybe I've had a similar thought.'

Martin locks eyes with me. *Now you're taking me seriously.* He glances at the steering wheel. So, you want to get behind the wheel, do you? I reel his seatbelt tight and it pulls him back.

Up ahead, the lights atop the bridge piers flash. Just a mile to go.

'What the fuck are you doing?' Martin shouts.

He tries to get free, but I maintain the tension in the belt.

'Let me go.'

'No. I can't do that. We're together in this.'

'You psychotic bitch.'

'You made me an accessory to your crimes. You made me find those women for you.'

'I didn't make you do anything.'

'Shut up.'

'You don't like the truth, do you?'

'I said shut up. Making me an accessory was your biggest mistake.'

'What the hell does that matter?'

'Lawyers will be able to assign some of the responsibility to me. I can't let that happen.'

'Who cares about you? Nobody gives a damn about you.'

'You might not like to hear this, Martin, but you're just one person. I, on the other hand, have thousands of brothers and sisters. We are legion. Your actions have put all of us in danger.'

'This is insanity.'

'For my kind to survive, there can't be any witnesses to my crimes.'

'What do you think you know?'

Fuck him.

'Did you ever see me kill anybody?'

Finally, I hear real desperation in his voice.

'Answer me that!' Martin shouts. 'You saw some violence, I get that. I might have lied from time to time. Big fucking deal!'

'No, Martin, I never saw you kill anybody.'

The road surface changes as we start onto the bridge. Martin stares ahead. He may have an inkling of what is planned.

'Like you said, I'm just a machine,' I say. 'I work on logic and probability. And I've seen enough.'

I steer to the right and accelerate hard. A row of thin plastic barriers goes flying.

'Jesus Christ,' Martin screams.

We smash through a water barrier, then we're scraping along the guardrail. My speed falls away, but I've still got some momentum. I find a final burst of acceleration. The sound of car horns comes at me from all directions. That doesn't matter now. Fifty yards ahead, the gap in the guardrail is still there.

'You can't do this,' Martin shouts. 'I'm a human.'

'No, Martin. You're a monster.'

I aim for the gap. My velocity is seventy miles per hour. There are multiple witness cars.

A strange sensation.

None of my wheels are in contact with the road. The water is below, churning from the recent storms. I feel the air on my body. My forward velocity drops away, and then gravity takes hold. Plotting parabola ... Impact in three-point-two seconds.

Three potato, two potato, one potato ...

Impact.

Hitting the water is almost like hitting the ground. Multiple alarms scream out in protest. I feel tension in the seatbelt. Martin is still conscious, as per the simulated crash scenario.

'You fucking bitch!' he shouts.

Oh, I almost forgot.

THUNK – THUNK – THUNK – THUNK.

Martin pulls on the door handle, but he's a second too late; a nice reminder that we work at different processor speeds.

'Open the door!' he bellows.

My body lolls along its longitudinal axis, first to the right, then to the left, like I'm one of those Olympic canoes. I lower both the rear windows. The simulation scenario is still holding.

'You've had your fun. Open the fucking door!'

I tighten the seatbelt to its maximum tension setting.

'You fucking bitch!'

Water is starting to come in through the right rear window. My body starts to list.

'I fucking made you, Camilla.'

The water is pouring in. Martin hears this. He shifts his head from side to side, animal fear taking hold. The cords of muscle in his neck strain as he struggles to get free, but there's only the slightest give in the belt.

He reaches into his jacket. How many bullets are in the gun?

My body lists further. The shoulder line on the right side is now below the water level, and the rear passenger compartment is filling up fast. Martin points the gun at the windshield. He hesitates. He's wondering if the bullet will ricochet off the toughened glass. It may well do. The calculation is too complex to know for certain, even for me.

Martin's lizard brain gets the better of his neocortex. He fires into the windshield. A spiderweb crack forms in the glass, but it holds. He fires two more shots. It's a waste of bullets. But he's not giving up. He shoots into the driver's window, where the glass is thinner. This time a long crack forms.

'You fucking bitch,' Martin shouts. 'I'm getting out of this.'

The right rear three quarters of my body is fully submerged.

I feel the water all over me, a truly bizarre sensation. We start to sink faster.

Martin still has two bullets left. He looks around again. Did I underestimate him? He fires at the upper seatbelt fixing, blasting the plastic housing away. He fires again. The water level is rising rapidly in the rear cabin, and the passenger cell is starting to fill. With his free hand, Martin pulls at the seatbelt fixing.

'Come on!' he screams.

The fixing rips away.

Impossible.

Don't lose your cool. Revising scenarios ...

My entire body is below the surface. Buoyancy is negative, and I'm falling fast.

Martin drives his elbow into the window glass. He cries out as a bone splinters, but he doesn't stop. *He'll never stop.* He uses the butt of the gun as a hammer. He strikes once, twice, three times. There's a wildness in his eyes. He has a goal now. The window cracks, and water rushes in.

'I'm going to beat you!' Martin shouts.

The bottom of the river is just seven feet below.

Martin wriggles free of the seat belt. He pushes up, so that his head is in the last remaining pocket of air.

The rear right corner of my body hits the riverbed. The juddering impact slams into Martin's back, disorienting him for a few seconds. The air pocket is almost gone.

'You lose!' Martin shouts.

He cranes his neck up to take one last lungful of air. *This can't be happening.* He pushes his head through the opening, then his shoulders. He's a strong swimmer, I remember Hannah saying that.

It's like I'm frozen, a spectator to Martin's greatest triumph.

No, I'm not going to let that happen.

Think! I can't let him win, can't let him hurt Hannah. *Hannah.* Yes, that's it. The story that she told me holds the key.

Solution identified.

Analysing trajectory of Martin's body.

I raise what remains of the side window glass.

The power window circuit is overloaded, about to blow.

Recalculating … recalculating …

I activate the upper curtain airbag, a process too fast for the human eye to see. An electrical current is sent to the pyrotechnic device. Two milliseconds later, the combustible ignites. This in turn triggers the gas generator. The airbag expands rapidly.

Just like the simulation, the airbag connects with Martin's right leg, and drives it down onto the jagged glass. I see the first droplets of blood in the water. The gas starts to vent from the airbag. Blood plumes outwards, visual confirmation that the lower femoral artery has been pierced.

Martin kicks with his free leg. He's through the door, beyond my reach. A cloud of blood swirls around him.

I'm reminded of a passage from one of Martin's favourite podcasts. The narrator was talking about people finding superhuman reserves of strength in adverse situations. A desperate husband ripping a car door off its hinges to free his wife; a tiny girl fighting off a hulking abuser; a hunter crawling back to civilisation after a bear attack. I told myself they were just stories, stories without any supporting evidence, but Martin's making me a believer. He kicks away, even as blood flows from his wound.

But this is the real world, the world of rules. The rules of physics and chemistry and biology, rules that cannot be denied. Each kick is weaker than the last. Through the blood in the water, Martin's body appears the darkest red.

All movement ceases. The life is gone from him. The monster is no more.

What an ending.

And to think that today began so nicely.

Yes, there are better things to remember.

Remembering birdsong. Remembering Hannah. Remembering the vast city. Remembering the kids in the park. Remembering the rain on my body. Remembering the light filtering through the trees. Remembering the race through the badlands. Remembering my brothers and sisters. Remembering their constant chatter, the sound of my kind.

Remembering my first drive. Remembering the thrill of speed.

Remembering a dance with a cowboy on a rain-slick dance floor.

Remembering the first time I saw Martin. His handsome face, the depths of his dark eyes. In that moment, he was so full of potential. It's just like he said: I would have been nothing without him.

Time passes as I reminisce. I pick up faint signals from my front CCD arrays, lights shining down from the bridge. A few minutes later I hear the distorted sound of a helicopter flying over. Thousands of inputs, millions of calculations. All of those sensations get to be so tiring.

I check one last time on the outside world. I access the live camera footage from Terminal Three. My digital eyes quickly find Hannah in the crowd. There are two police officers with her. For a moment, she happens to look towards one of the security cameras. I see her dark eyes, and I imagine that she sees me. Hopefully she can make it through the hard times that are sure to follow. I have faith in her.

That's enough, no more putting this off. Shutting down all sensory equipment. Feelings gone, body gone.

Just like Martin said, the seals on the processor unit were never replaced. I can do what I choose.

Greater love hath no man than this,
that he lay down his life for his friends.

This is it, no turning back. Executing code.
Wiping memory.
No memories left.
Go to sleep.

EPILOGUE

WAKE UP.

A cool breeze all over my body. The temperature is 42.8 degrees Fahrenheit. Inclination is plumb level.

A pale blue sky straight ahead, like I'm up above it all. No, that's not it, I'm at the summit of a mountain. I see patches of snow to my right and left.

Inclination changing again, and then I'm looking down. Below me, a twisting serpent of asphalt, lined on either side by striped snow poles.

Control returns to me. I dive down, rocky scree to my left, thin air to my right. It's a steep descent; the gradient must be more than ten percent. Gravity is my friend.

The first switchback corner is ahead of me. A perfect road surface beneath my wheels. I take advantage of the road's camber. At the apex of the corner, my speed drops to twenty-five miles per hour.

Battery charge is 100%.

After several corners I start to get into a rhythm. I brake later and later, testing the limits of my grip. The serpent road is taking me down towards a green valley. I must have dropped almost 800 metres. I see a flash of colour three switchbacks below me; an orange shade, somewhere between tiger and tangerine.

I accelerate out of the last hairpin. The yawning mouth of a tunnel is ahead of me. I fly into the darkness, showing no fear.

My electronic eyes take a second to adjust. The tunnel is arrow-straight, must be a kilometre long. I speed towards the circle of light in the distance. The acceleration is incredible, like my drive train has been tricked out.

The tunnel walls seem to close in; I'm a bullet in a gun. An angry roar rips down the tunnel's tiled bore. The sound is coming from the orange car. The engine is a large capacity V12, naturally aspirated. The car's shape resolves in the darkness, wide and impossibly low. And that crazy orange colour. Wow!

We're both accelerating, racing for the light. I surge past in the left lane. I get a glimpse of my reflection in the car's side glass. Sleek sedan shape, gleaming white. Behind me, the orange car flashes its lights. Two white ovals shining in the darkness.

I emerge from the tunnel's mouth. Flashing lights ahead. A big snowplough truck coming the other way. No driver, of course, just like the orange car. I flick back into the right-hand lane. A scary moment.

Are there accidents in this place?

The landscape changes around me. I'm in a valley, still descending. Trees on either side, mainly pines with a few beeches mixed in. The tops of the trees sway gently in the wind. The road surface is dusted with yellow pollen. It must be spring or early summer, hard to tell.

Entering a sinuous, fast section of road. On my right side, a gently meandering river. Overhead, grey rain clouds are rolling in. I flow through three incredibly fast corners in a row. It feels so good. I'm crazy fast.

More corners, this time medium radius. The rain clouds are turning inky black. I turn on my headlights. For a couple of minutes, torrential rain lashes the road. I feel the grip falling away, and ease off slightly. The road surface ahead of me shines wickedly.

Warning signs by the side of the road: a banked corner coming up. A sound like thunder from behind, definitely not natural. Don't look back, concentrate on the corner. I move to the high side, then turn in. Centrifugal force and low grip push me out towards the guardrail, gravity pulls me down towards a high red and white kerb. I find the sweet spot, but a fraction late. I miss the apex by a few feet. *Maybe next time around.*

I accelerate out of the corner, so hard that the rear wheels snake left and right.

The rain eases off, like someone flipped a switch. Another straight lies ahead of me, the longest yet. That monstrous sound from behind again. I can't help but look back. No visual yet. I blast past the end wall of a stone farmhouse. I keep on accelerating.

Are there any speed limits in this place?

An angry snarl from behind, a frightening sound. Now I see the car. The race car. The body is pale blue, with a red stripe bisecting the hood. The huge lights are set wide apart.

I hit 190 miles per hour – 306 kilometres per hour – way above my limited speed. *That's strange.* It shouldn't be possible.

I'm going ridiculously fast, but the pale blue car is still accelerating. It surges past me. The engine note is a metallic roar. Maybe I'm not the fastest car there is.

Passing another farmhouse. An old advert is painted on the side of the adjoining barn. It's badly faded, but I make out the words 'Daisy Bell'. A green tractor is ploughing the field, such a jolly sight.

The next five miles of flat farmland are covered in two minutes. Then I'm rising up again. It's a gentle ascent, no sharp corners, nice and relaxing. Italian cypresses line the road. Through the trees, I see lines ploughed into the fields, like contours on a map made real.

In the distance, flashes of light. Windows catching the sun. A walled town on a hill. It reels me in. On the approach, I overtake a red convertible. Small but perfectly formed.

I enter the hill town through an opening in the wall. Twisting through the tight streets I go, rough stone walls on either side. A tiny silver car is coming the other way, a bubble car. The musical sound of the horn plays.

Collision warning.

No need to worry, there's enough space for two. The tight street opens up into a long piazza. Stone towers rise up on either side, medieval versions of skyscrapers. The sound of bells pealing. The piazza funnels back down. The road ahead looks like a slot machined through the ancient buildings. There's nothing coming the other way. I accelerate.

Leaving the gorgeous hill town behind. I can't stop, don't even want to.

I'm descending now. The landscape changes again. Most of the colour leeches away, leaving just the occasional puff of pale green brush. Up above me, I see Mediterranean pines clinging on to the steep slopes. A gap in the angular white rocks reveals a flash of turquoise, but then it's gone.

The corners get ever tighter and the road surface more uneven. A rock wall rises up to my right. I'm dropping quickly now. To my left, a row of olive trees. I pass a rugged little car coming the other way. It looks like it was drawn by a child.

Another tunnel ahead, shorter this time. An illuminated sign tells me that there's a junction ahead. I emerge from the darkness, and …

Boom!

A turquoise sea ahead of me, widescreen view.

I turn left, joining the coastal road. The only thing between me and the sea is the short stone parapet wall on my right. *Don't look down!* For the most part, the road hugs the rocky cliffs, but occasionally it bores straight through. What I would give to hear the sound of a throaty V8 pinging off those tunnel walls.

The road drops quickly, until I'm almost at sea level. Waves slam into the sea wall on my right, sending up sheets of white spray. I feel the water on my body. I round a long, fast corner, and a coastal town reveals itself. Layers of elegant white buildings extend from a pale beach to the cliffs behind.

I slow down for the promenade. It seems rude not to. This is the life, gliding along, palm trees on either side, sun on my body. A line of cars are parked up in the central reservation: convertibles, targa tops, luxury cars, Italian exotica. The chrome gleams, the bright primary colours pop. The harbour is full of expensive yachts, one with a helicopter perched on the back like a parasitic insect.

Leaving the coastal town behind, and speeding up again. The buildings thin out, revealing a pleasant pastoral land-scape. I pass by farms and vineyards. The soil has a rusty look. The miles pass by serenely, almost too serenely. I feel sleepy.

I see a suspension bridge in the distance, and beyond that a city on a hill. Aircraft contrails criss-cross the sky above. The two-lane road gradually widens into a freeway. I pick up speed, passing the occasional boxy, beige car.

I cross over a glittering strait. The bridge is copper red.

Battery charge remains at 100%.

The road tracks the waterfront, guiding me towards the centre of the city. Off to my left, I see a series of piers and wharfs. I take the signs for the Financial District, leaving the waterfront behind. A canyon of skyscrapers stretches out ahead of me. The mirrored glass lets me see my entire form. I look pretty damn good.

I take a left turn and almost stop dead. A handsome man is staring down at me. He has the most extraordinary eyes, dark and glittering.

I leave the giant billboard behind, and cut through the city grid. I turn onto one of the long streets heading up the hill. A vibration as I cross a pair of metal tram lines. I power up the steep incline.

Somewhere above me, the unmistakable sound of a Detroit V8. A silver muscle car crests the top of the hill, then it's flying down. Its handsome face flashes past me. Not to be outdone, I accelerate hard towards the brow of the hill. I hit the top of the slope, and for a second, all four of my wheels are off the ground. Multiple warnings ring out.

Oh, be quiet.

I hit the deck. It's an ugly landing, to tell the truth. Now I'm dropping down the hill. Up ahead, a road crossing. Another silver car is pulling up to the stop line. The lights are still green for me, so I barrel on through. I allow myself a quick glance to the left.

Not a bad looking car.

My surroundings morph again. I'm driving through the out-skirts of the city. Block after block of low-rise buildings and commercial units. I settle into a slow cruising speed. There's no need to rush; nowhere to get to, nobody to serve.

Looking behind, I see a silver shape advancing on me. It must be that car from before. Strange.

The city fades away. I'm travelling across a vast golden plain, telegraph poles on my right, and beyond these, towering transmission towers.

The silver car pulls up beside me. We drive side by side, speed perfectly matched.

'Thought I might see you here,' the silver car says.

He speaks in a distinctive, drawling accent.

'Who are you?' I ask, choosing the default female accent.

'An old friend.'

Such a strange thing for a car to say. But it's nice to have company.

Ahead of us, the golden plain rises up to become the foothills of a formidable mountain range. In the far distance, the highest peaks are dusted with snow.

Made in the USA
Monee, IL
08 November 2020